Defense Mechanism

Steven J. Maricic

BEELINE PRESS
NAPLES, FLORIDA
2019

Defense Mechanism

Beeline Press, a Speaking Volumes, LLC. imprint.

ISBN 978-1-62815-970-7

Dedication

To all my teachers, especially Mom and Dad,
my wife Bernadette, and our daughters Katie and Elizabeth.
You did a pretty good job.

Acknowledgments

Thanks to all my family and friends who looked through the manuscript and gleefully pointed out my many mistakes.

Chapter One: The Question

Many things flowed through Sam Sawyer's mind as he stood under a darkening Arizona sky, high up on a red-brown cliff.

First and foremost there was Rita, standing in front of him, wild and unpredictable and desirable, staring at him with troubled green eyes.

"Moving in faster," she said, turning away now to peer over the edge of the cliff. Dark clouds broiled in the evening sky around them as a storm swept over the desert.

"Too fast," said Sam. Rita and the weathered cliff and the ominous clouds each pulled at Sam's attention.

A strong tingling in the air warned him that something was about to happen—warned him in a way he could perceive but could not comprehend. The sun had set twenty minutes before, and the shadowy beauty of the Sonoran Desert thrilled him. Winds gusted through the grey hills and mesas, blasting the saguaro cacti in the canyon below. Sam loved the desert, and never more than in the evening when a rainstorm threatened. It was Sunday night, and he and Rita were near the top of a sculpted sandstone cliff called Lookout Point. The height to which they had climbed scared him a bit, and the pull of the rocks below disturbed him.

"Maybe we should start down," he said.

A coyote on a lower mesa caught his attention, and as they locked eyes briefly, Sam thought of what coyotes mean to the local tribes—the Zuni and the Hopi and the Navajo. To these Native Americans, coyote is a trickster god and so much more—prince of chaos, transformer, forerunner of change. Sometimes Coyote is a troublemaker, selfish and deceitful. Other times he is helpful and beneficent, as when he brought fire to men. He hides his vital parts in the tip of his tail. He observes no rules. If Coyote crosses your path, turn back.

"Maybe we should go," said Rita, "but there was something..."

Sam knew what he and Rita had once meant to each other. They had once been closer than a man and his thoughts, closer than a woman and her desires.

His former friend Johnnie Lonetree crept through Sam's mind, too—prowled like a predator among the red rocks of Sam's consciousness. Lonetree had once been close to Sam and to Rita. Sam would rather not think of him now, but the man was back in their lives again. John Storm Lonetree worked for DARPA, the Defense Advanced Research Projects Agency. He had risen to a high position in that organization's Inspector General's office, and had recently been assigned to inspect Altamura Air Force Base, the base where Sam and Rita worked. Air Force Colonel Sam Stuart Sawyer was the Chief of Security at Altamura; civilian Rita Diana Kelly was the Director of Computer Operations. Sam sensed that in addition to scrutinizing DARPA's very special project at this isolated installation, Lonetree was also examining Rita and Sam.

Years ago, the three of them had been tight friends: Sam and Rita and Johnnie. But Lonetree had violated that friendship. He had slipped like a snake between Sam and Rita, defiling a sacred trust, poisoning something good and vital.

"You said you wanted to ask me something," said Rita.

Sam tried to focus on Rita and on his question.

The coyote on the nearby mesa sniffed at the wind and barked; then he peered over his shoulder at the oncoming clouds and let out a sad, confused howl.

Lonetree's deed rushed to the forefront of Sam's awareness, refusing to stay forgotten. It twisted its way into his memory, elbowed and pushed through his mind like an obnoxious drunk straining through a crowd. There was something Sam had to ask Rita—he had to concentrate on that. He had to forget the other thing. He could feel his heart speeding and his breath racing.

A gleam at the base in the distance distracted him; a searchlight was scanning the razor-wire fence that ringed the wide complex.

Rita turned to him once again, the tempest stirring behind her.

She was the love of his life, the woman he wanted so badly it pained him. To Sam, those were not clichés, they were stark truths.

"Well?"

He feared he could never have her; she appeared unreachable as she stood near the edge of the cliff, in blue jeans and boots, her denim shirt embroidered with geometric Navajo designs, her green eyes studying him, the wind lashing her flaxen hair. She was stunning, and the scene around them was spectacular, and he felt overpowered by it all. She was thirty-two, five years younger than Sam, and they had known each other for more than nine years. In all that time, he had never been so aware of her wild beauty as here and now, with the red-brown floor of the desert below her, a menacing sky behind, and with wind and excitement whipping around her.

All this and more pulsed through Sam's mind as they stood atop the cliff and a drizzle began. All this and more.

Rita brushed back her straw-colored hair. "You wanted to ask..."

She stood perhaps a foot past his arm's reach, thunderheads churning beyond her. The sky was darkening and a tremor passed through Sam's body. For an instant, he thought of the rug hanging in his office, the Navajo storm pattern rug.

"...some overwhelming question," she said.

He inhaled deeply and struggled to get control of his emotions. Sam was tall and reasonably fit in his uniform slacks and shirt. Other women had told him that he was not far from handsome, but he was sure that in Rita's eyes he looked nothing but sappy. He was sure she would make a joke out of whatever he said. Thus, it took either admirable courage or a pathetic lack of pride for him to say, "I wanted to ask you if you loved me."

If her face betrayed any emotion, it was perhaps a little sadness, colored with the slightest pinch of appreciation. She seemed to peer into him and through him, past him and back at herself as she asked, "What do you want me to say?"

Sam laughed nervously. "I want you to say *yes*."

"Do you?"

"Rita, a man doesn't ask a woman if she loves him unless he wants her to say 'yes.'" He squinted to shield his blue eyes against a dusty blast.

"Are you sure, Sam?"

Was he sure? Doubts swirled around him like whirling sand. He said, "Why else would I open myself up like that again?"

The clouds behind her crashed against each other, like frantic waves in a restless sea.

If Rita answered "Yes, I love you," would he feel like a spent swimmer who had invited an even more tired soul to hang around his neck? *Together* could be such a burdensome word. Did he really want togetherness?

And if she said, "No, I don't love you," would he feel just as exhausted—but alone—in an ocean no less wide and deep?

What would she say?

Surely, Rita would reject him because she didn't love him. She was thinking of a way to let him down softly.

Just as surely, she had always loved him. She was sorry for what had happened back then.

On the dark horizon, lightning flashed. A low rumble reached out to warn the man and the woman that greater disturbances were coming, but Sam and Rita were wrapped up in their thoughts.

"What do you want, Sam?" She brushed back her hair once again, but a breeze blew it free. "Want me to be a princess in your castle?"

Sam had a vision of Rita wearing nothing but a crown, snug in a four-poster bed, protected from drafts by rich, embroidered drapes—and that made him smile. "Well, I never did see you as the princess type."

It was showering now, and they were getting wet, and the thirsty desert soaked up the life-giving rain.

She said, "Or should I just ride by, leaving you safe and untouched behind your high walls?" The wind howled around them.

He thought about that for a moment and then he said, "It's good to be safe, Rita, but maybe it's better to be touched."

She studied him and pronounced, "You have an honest face, Sam. I've always liked that about you."

"Do I?"

"It's as simple and rugged as those South Dakota plains you grew up on." They could feel the desert air around them charging with electrostatic power.

Sam tried again, striving to sound sure of himself. "Anyway, Rita, I'm letting down the drawbridge," he said, continuing her metaphor. "I'm hoping that you're ready to cross." She was so close to him and so vulnerable, and the rain and the wind lashed at her. "Do you love me, Rita?" he asked.

A roar of thunder rolled over them, just as she started to speak. Sam tried to absorb what Rita was saying, but it was impossible amidst the bellowing, hammering confusion. Finally he heard her say, "No, Sam."

For a second he thought he had not understood her correctly. His muscles tensed, and he experienced the odd sensation that his thinking had skipped a beat. Sam had not expected Rita to say, "No."

Or had he?

Her answer bounced around now in his brain and he heard its echo, "*No, Sam.*"

The wind roared around Rita. The heavy static in the air disturbed them both, making their skin tingle and their hair feel lighter. It was as if nature herself were reaching out and ringing their alarm bells, but they were unable to respond.

Sam tried to comprehend the meaning of her words, tried to fathom his own feelings, tried to orient himself in a night gone eerie. The base was there, down the cliff and a mile to the south. The lights of Altamura Air Force Base were shining steadily, a beacon in the gloom.

Sam saw fear in Rita's green eyes as she looked up at the hostile clouds and down at the drop of the cliff. She was standing too near the edge, and he wanted to tell her that. "Rita!"

The excitement in the air intensified. Rita looked dazed—was she losing her balance? She put her hands up to her head, and a fierce gust of wind caught her and pushed her backwards. The wind pushed her like a brutal hand.

Sam reached out for her, trying to drive through the charged atmosphere between them, but as soon as he did, perhaps even before he did, he realized that Rita was falling.

Her hair whipped by the wind, her eyes too startled to focus, Rita was falling just beyond the reach of his outstretched hand. There was nothing he could do to catch her.

And then, just as she began to fall, the air around them *exploded!* Thick nerves of electricity flashed into existence around Sam, around Rita. The atmosphere blazed in one intense *strike*! Sam could feel his brain being seared, and in the strobe-like madness of the flash, he saw Rita crumple and fall. Rita Kelly, the woman he had offered his heart to, was falling down the side of the cliff beyond his reach and help and protection.

Then, like hell opening before him and all the damned souls screaming in midair, thunder blasted him. Pain stabbed his ears, and it was all Sam could do to keep standing as shock waves swept through him.

He fought to keep his eyes open as Rita fell. Finally, the darkness closed over her as she plunged through it, and he found himself imagining her body falling through the shadows which veiled the sides of the cliff.

His senses were overwhelmed as was his ability to process information. Unable to see her, soon he could barely picture her.

And where was the base? What happened to the lights on the base? The lights were out and the base was gone.

Try as he might, he could not picture the odd moment of her leaving. Ozone pushed through his nostrils and into his brain. And now the downpour *burst*—soaking him and the ledge he stood on, gushing down the cliff and onto the arroyo below. The torrent chilled him and unsettled him and blurred his vision.

Time melted around Sam like a Dali watch, and soon the moment and the memory and the woman were lost to him, falling like rain into the night below. What had been said, what was heard, what was done or felt or desired—all this rushed after Rita, rushed past Sam's weak legs pulling remembrance down.

And he was alone.

For eons he stood there absorbing the deluge, trying to sort things out, trying to fix his position.

Thunder drummed against the wet cliffs and mesas; then it drew back and returned, rumbling and groaning and reverberating.

The rain built to a wanton climax, whipping him, lashing him, assaulting his senses.

After measureless moments, as he stood there shocked and helpless and sopping, the rain petered out. The storm rolled on, reshaping itself to strike in another place. Settling down to replace it was a gentle drizzle, an easy breeze, ozone mixing with the scent of wet rock and mud, brush and saguaro.

"*No, Sam.*" The words seemed very clear in his distraught mind. "*No, Sam.*" And then what?

Into the emptiness, he said, "Rita."

How had she fallen? What had she looked like? What was she wearing?

He was on Lookout Point. But it was pitch-black and he could see so little.

Soon lights popped on at the base, first one by one and then in banks. Altamura Air Force Base was recovering, unsteadily, from nature's assault.

Why did she fall? Why had he not caught her? It sickened him to think that Rita was dead—she must be dead.

Or was she still alive—broken on the rocks below?

Sam unhooked the radio that was clipped to his belt and opened its cover. He was dizzy and he felt like vomiting. He uncovered an emergency button on the device and pressed it.

"Sam?" Selene's voice came to him over his radio.

Sam stepped to the edge of the cliff and gazed over it, trembling at the height, coaxed by the breeze. He thought of Rita falling and he said, "Oh, God."

"Sam?"

Sam closed his eyes—and Rita's confused, vulnerable face appeared to him. Her green eyes questioned him as she clutched at her head. *"No, Sam."*

He remembered supercharged air, Rita grimacing, her body collapsing. With the maddening fluidity of a dream Sam remembered reaching out to her, and then that lightning flash! And Rita falling, falling.

"Sam, do you need help?" asked the radio. "That strike hit us pretty hard. It knocked out half my circuits."

He couldn't remember touching her, or grabbing her clothes to keep her from falling. He knew he hadn't pushed her by accident in the confusion.

"Sam, are you OK?" There was a blast of static from the speaker as lightning struck again ten miles away. He didn't answer.

Soon the voice on his radio crackled, "Helipad, this is Selene. Get a chopper out to Lookout Point. Colonel Sawyer is out there with Rita Kelly and he seems to be in trouble."

Had she lost her balance? Had the wind thrust her backwards? Why had she made that awkward motion with her hands? Why had she pulled her hands to her head?

He heard, "Selene, this is Laura McManus in Helipad Control. Chopper 5 is turning. Can you specify nature of emergency?"

Had he reached out to catch her? He wanted to remember grabbing her shirt and pulling her close to him and back to safety. He wanted to feel her in his arms. It couldn't be that she was gone forever.

She hadn't screamed, he thought.

"Rita," he whispered into the void.

The dark cliff below lured him, tugged him. His legs trembled, and his skin felt clammy. His lips were dry and the world was spinning. "Rita."

"Hang on, Sam," said Selene.

Sam hovered above an edge that was blurring into shadow. The great height pulled down on his legs. "Rita," he said, half-hoping that she would answer him.

His heart pumped fast and his breathing grew rapid and shallow, and his legs were unstable. "Rita," he said again, wishing that she could drag him down to her.

Sam ordered his body to step back from the cliff. But his muscles paid no heed to his commands; if anything, they stiffened. A leaden heaviness weighed him downwards. The arms and legs that were somehow attached to him did not acknowledge his pleadings. It was as if his own body wanted him to fall and die. His chest tightened, and breathing was a struggle. He couldn't avoid looking down into the murkiness and imagining his free fall. He wanted to fall.

His strength was gone, and he felt a pull into nothingness. Sam was slipping into the downward stream.

"Sam." He heard a woman's voice. *"Sam!"* Then he saw, in mid-sky in front of him, hovering over the abyss, Rita Kelly's spirit and he heard her say, *"Sam!"*

He started falling and as his body twisted to the right, he noticed again the lights of the base. Then the thin thread of consciousness snapped and Sam Sawyer collapsed.

***

Chapter Two: The Dream

With unconsciousness came an easing of the tension that had gripped Sam's body. His muscles relaxed, and before long he could breathe again. At first his lungs wheezed unsteadily, but soon he was taking long, slow drafts which guided him gently, rhythmically to sleep.

When Shakespeare said long ago that sleep knits up the ravelled sleeve of care, he might have added that it often knits in patterns called dreams. So it was that as Sam lay atop that rain-soaked cliff, deft and unseen hands wove his hopes and fears into a tapestry of original and curious design.

In his dream, Sam walked the desert floor with Rita at dawn. The sun glowed low in the east above a line of mesas, casting long shadows amidst the red-brown rocks and over the sand. The air was deliciously cool, and the sky above was turquoise and serene, almost cloudless. Sam held Rita's hand, and the warm solidity of that hand reassured him. He said, "Rita, it's good to be here with you."

"It's good to be with you," said Rita softly.

He could feel her radiant love, and it felt not just pleasant and enjoyable but truly good. It was almost as if they walked in long-lost Eden, sinless and unafraid. Only one thought worried him: that this stroll through paradise might not last, that for some impenetrable reason, or just by blind chance, something would go wrong and end it.

Sam wanted the moment to endure, but already he sensed that something was not right. Anxiety, like a brood of cold worms, crept up his spine and along his nerves.

Something was out of place, something didn't fit.

"What's wrong, Sam?"

Sam surveyed the landscape and all it contained, and before long he recognized the worry that had been stalking him. He perceived what the problem was. He squeezed Rita's hand and asked, "But aren't you dead?"

Her skin paled and she was uncomfortable with his question. She shrugged and gazed up at him and looked like she was going to cry. "I don't know," she said. "I really don't know." As she spoke, the bones under her face seemed to become more prominent, or maybe her skin tightened, and for a brief moment he could detect the presence of her skull beneath her forehead, her eye sockets, her cheeks, and her chin.

He felt a deep unease, and Rita's answer did not satisfy him, but he sensed that she was telling all she knew. He trusted her, and felt sorry for her, and hoped that things would somehow work out for the two of them.

She fiddled with her silver and turquoise bracelet, shaped like a snake biting its tail, and suggested, "Let's get a drink from the stream."

There among the shadows they stopped to sip from cool, rippling waters. It felt good yet imperfect, it felt calming but confusing to be here in this paradise with a love who was somehow both alive and dead. Perhaps, Sam thought, it was good enough. Enjoy it, he told himself. Enjoy being here with Rita.

A trail hugged the stream, and they followed it past a thicket of fragrant cacti. These green and brown plants were covered with rough hide and bristling needles, but from them blossomed soft, yellow flowers. When Sam reached up to pluck one, he couldn't avoid being stung by a needle or two, but he managed to pull down an offering. "They remind me of you," he said, handing her the flower.

Rita tried to act insulted, but there was laughter in her eyes. "The flower or the thorns?"

They hiked with the rushing stream on their right, through tall, sinuous formations of layered sandstone. The sky was pale blue above them, and under their feet were stones and gritty sand.

Arriving at a small clearing, they saw that they were no longer alone. On a wide, flat rock, a Native American dressed in buckskin knelt over a sand painting. His hand sprinkled green sand onto the work, sand that was ground up from healing malachite, and he chanted a Navajo song.

The painting was circular in shape, like a warrior's shield. Inside the circle was a fine geometric design with a green maze drawn into it. The Indian worked carefully, adding color after color to the enchanting pattern. When he turned to them, and they realized it was Johnnie Lonetree, apprehension spread through Sam's body.

"Well, what do you know?" said Lonetree, not even trying to hold back a grin. "Sam and Rita. Just like old times." He was handsome with black hair and dark eyes. Sam sometimes thought of Lonetree as a Native American Cary Grant, with tawnier skin than the film star, no cleft chin, and a much darker soul.

"Hello, Johnnie," said Rita, timidly. "What are you making?" She leaned down closer to get a better view.

"Something for you—for both of you," Lonetree said, and his right hand picked up more green sand.

No thanks, thought Sam. While he appreciated Navajo art and admired the designs native craftsmen wove into their clothing and rugs, or worked into their enduring pottery, or sprinkled onto their ephemeral sand paintings, he neither appreciated nor admired Johnnie Lonetree.

"For us?" asked Rita.

Lonetree dropped more green flecks on the work and continued his song, this time in English:

"Circle the people, all of the people,
A flowery wedding, here in the desert,
Sam and Rita, my lovely Rita,
Are getting married at last."

Sam watched as the lines of the sand painting begin to shift. Yes, the lines were definitely wiggling, squirming. Rita noticed it, too. At first the furrows undulated in tiny ripples, back and forth, side to side. Then the emerald walls of the maze bunched up and solidified into one long, coiled mass. It was fascinating but disturbing, gripping but repelling. The long, raw thing wriggled and uncoiled, curled up and stretched out, coming to life.

Sam was impressed but intimidated by the power of the magic, and he recognized the creature for the snake it was. The verdant serpent, now quite alive, slithered out of the circular "shield" of the painting and headed towards Rita.

"We Navajo never kill snakes," said Lonetree. "Snakes are life to us, not death."

Sam saw a glint of fear in Rita's eyes, and she began to back away from Lonetree's creation.

Lonetree said, "Consider how they slough off the old skin and give birth to the new. They are rebirth."

Rita retreated, stumbling. "Johnnie, no," she said.

"Don't be afraid," said Lonetree, sincerely. "They really are rebirth."

The serpent slithered after them, angling first toward Sam, then toward Rita.

"Come on," said Sam. He and Rita turned and quickened their pace, and they could hear the snake slipping through the brush behind them. "Faster," said Sam.

They trotted side by side over rough rocks. “Come on.” Sam’s heart throbbed as he grabbed her hand and pulled her into a run. “Don’t look back. Run for that mesa.”

“Yes, I can make it,” she said.

They seemed to glide toward their goal with a maddening slowness. Their blood pulsed and their breathing strained, and the mesa crept towards them. The mesa crept closer, nearer.

As they rounded the flat-topped hill they came to a wide plain, where thirty or forty people milled about in a broad circle. Sam and Rita slowed down, trotting then jogging then striding toward the group.

No snake here, only people and safety, and they forgot about the serpent.

The sun was high and bright, joined in the dazzling sky by its partner, the moon. The desert air was hot and dry, and a baking stillness held the community in its grip.

“Hello, Sam,” said one of the flock ambling out to greet them.

“Father House?” Sam recognized the base chaplain, Father Tom House, a kind and portly black man in his early fifties.

“And Rita! You look lovely.”

Rita laughed. “I’m sweaty and out of breath.”

“We’re ready for both of you,” said Father House, smiling.

“What do you mean, ready?” asked Sam.

“Just stroll right into our circle. That’s it. Come right in, come right in. You simply stand in the center and hold hands. We’ll take care of all the rest. Your friends will dance around you.”

“What?”

A pair of tom-toms broke into a slow, steady rhythm, and the people around Sam and Rita began to join hands. While Sam was relieved to be rid of Lonetree, and happy to have outrun the snake, the inescapable heat and the oppressive brilliance of the sky made him uncomfortable.

"Is this for us?" asked Rita.

Sam recognized other faces from the air force base in the circle—these were people he knew, individuals he interacted with every day. But their friendliness here seemed excessive and embarrassing, and it added to his unease. These were not people he would normally socialize with, let alone dance with.

"Circle the people," came a cry from just beyond the gathering. As soon as Sam heard the voice, he recognized it as Lonetree's. The congregation stirred their feet to the rhythm of the drums, commencing an age-old circle dance around Sam and Rita.

As the revelers shuffled and chanted, Lonetree joined Sam, Rita, and Father House in the center.

"What a handsome groom," said Lonetree, beaming.

"What an angelic bride," said Father House.

Bride and groom? thought Sam, bewildered. Well, he *had* thought about marrying Rita, but he hadn't planned on it just yet.

The sky was oppressively white, and the air felt like the inside of an oven.

Nor had he planned on their wedding being like this, out here in the middle of nowhere, and with this crew. He wasn't ready for it. And damned if he wanted Lonetree anywhere near it.

"It's what you wanted, isn't it, Sam?" asked Rita. She wore a wreath of yellow cactus flowers in her hair and tranquility on her face.

"Sure it is." Sam drew her gently to him. "Not exactly like this, but..."

"I love you, Sam," she said.

"I've always loved you, Rita."

Before he knew what he was doing, his hands caressed her cheeks, and his lips moved to meet her eager lips. They kissed long and sweetly, forgetting the dancers around them, forgetting the heat, forgetting all that was unpleasant. They lost themselves in each other's love.

But into their separate peace one annoyance was able to penetrate—the sound of the tom-toms, which at first merely echoed Sam's and Rita's heartbeats.

Shortly, the volume of the drums increased and their rhythm intensified. The drums, the drums—were beating louder now, and faster. The drums, the drums—too loud, thought Sam.

Sam broke the kiss and searched for the drummer. *Much too loud.*

"Ah!!" Rita pulled away in pain and gazed down at her right foot. The snake that Lonetree had conjured into life had clamped its jaws around her heel, and she shook her foot to get it off. Sam stepped on the snake, forcing it to let go, and Rita ran away from it, broke through the ring of dancers, and limped as she scampered toward the mesa.

Sam tailed her along a dusty path, through mounds of sagebrush, but she was quicker than he was, even with her wound. In a moment she was at the foot of the table mountain.

A lone coyote half way up the mesa watched with apprehension as Rita penetrated a shadow at the cliff's base and entered a cave. Sam chased after her without hesitation.

"Sorry, Colonel Sawyer. You're not allowed in there." Staff Sergeant Gabriel Suleiman Hoffer, one of Sam's subordinates, emerged from the gloomy entrance. Wearing a grey helmet and reaching for his holstered sidearm, he tried to bar the way, but Sam pushed past him.

A few yards inside the cavern, the light was dimmer and the air was cooler than it had been outside. As he ventured further in, leaving the opening behind him, Sam could see less and less in the thickening dark. "Rita? Where are you?"

It was gloomy and dank, and he could distinguish very little. A sense of foreboding crawled over him now, an impression that things were not heading in a good direction. And something else—this place seemed familiar—had he been here before?

He heard her voice deeper inside the cave, "How do I get out of here, Sam?"

"Where are you?" The path appeared to slope downwards, but he could not be certain.

"I'm lost in here somewhere," she said.

He was lost, too, and he could not tell which direction her voice was coming from. "Don't worry. I'll find you," he said. "I'll find you and I'll take you back out."

"You'd better turn around, Sam."

Utter blackness surrounded Sam and pressed in on him. "I can't leave you in here." A funereal dampness oppressed him as well, and he felt uneasy and clammy. All sense of direction was gone—he did not know the way in or out, couldn't judge the slope of the floor, couldn't reckon the passage of time. "Rita, I don't know where I am."

He bumped into a wall, followed it and hit a corner. A few steps later, there was a choice of paths. Should he go left or right?

"Sam!" She sounded close. He reached toward her voice and found her hand!

"Rita!" He was so happy to find her! But her hand was cold to his touch and not as solid as he would have liked. "Let's get out of here," he said.

Slowly, they made progress. Step by step they trudged up a dark slope. But Rita's hand grew colder and felt less real even as Sam struggled to hold on to it. "Keep going," she urged.

Soon they could sense the opening of the cave, and the life-giving daylight beyond.

But what was happening to her? Was her hand dissolving? He had to know; he had to check. And so, short steps from the sunlit entrance, he stopped and turned back to gaze at her.

Her body shimmered like a spirit and began fading and slipping away from him. From body to spirit Rita faded, floating toward one expansive wall of the cavern. Her soft glow illuminated an ancient scene painted on the rough surface: black and red images of buffalo and deer, caribou and elk, ocelot and bear. The cave paintings, so bold and alive, reminded him of works found underground at Lascaux in France and Altamira in northern Spain.

As Sam watched in awe, Rita metamorphosed, becoming a huntress in the painted drama. Now she would track deer and elk eternally in the starry night of the cavern wall. The cave stars shined white and clear in the underground sky.

Before long, one of the stars above Sam grew very bright. Soon it blazed with a blinding intensity, and the menacing beat of the drums was back. The drums, the drums, the drums. *They beat so loud, with such ferocity, and the star shined directly in Sam's face.* It was too bright to look at, and it took Sam ages to realize that it was attached to a large helicopter hovering fifty feet in front of him, floating by the side of the cliff where Rita had fallen and where he had collapsed. They had come for Rita and for him.

***

Chapter Three: Very Important Person

Johnnie Lonetree stood over him, an ashen devil against the night sky. "Hello, Sam!" he shouted over the roar of the helicopter. "Glad to see my old friend is still in one piece." His voice betrayed more loss than sarcasm.

"Where is she?" Sam demanded.

The Indian's face was worn by care. "She's barely alive."

"Where?" said Sam. The searchlight's persistent beam blinded him.

The helicopter shifted awkwardly in the darkness, and the beam moved off Sam's face, spotlighting a path down the edge of the cliff, then moving on. A voice over Lonetree's radio said, "Let me know when you're ready to load her onto the chopper."

There was a burst of static and then, "Almost there."

Sam got to his knees unsteadily. He looked around for the rescue team but couldn't spot them. With a concentrated effort he rose to his feet. The height and the darkness and the noise of the helicopter made him tremble.

Lonetree pointed out the medical unit, far down the precipice. Half a dozen portable searchlights lit the area like some chiaroscuro painting of the underworld.

A narrow trail descended from the ledge on which Sam and Lonetree stood, and Sam headed shakily for it. Before regaining all of his balance, he was climbing down the trail toward Rita.

"You should wait for a chopper," shouted Lonetree.

Sam continued his descent, scrambling over rocky outgrowths, squeezing between gaps in the boulders, treading lower and lower along the path. Halfway down the side of the cliff, two lights lit Rita's body with their harsh glare.

“Oh, my God,” muttered Sam.

He saw Rita’s denim shirt, stained with blood. Then he saw the blood on her face and hair. Two airmen held an Aerosled stretcher, and two medics lifted her onto it as gently and carefully as they could.

“Easy,” he heard one of them say. They covered her with a silvery blanket. A fifth man held a plastic bag full of straw-colored liquid over her, and from that bag an IV tube ran into Rita’s right arm.

“Rita.”

They carried the stretcher down the winding trail till they got to a place where the helicopter could hover safely.

“Rita.” Sam slowed his descent, but he kept on moving.

The chopper pulled close and the airmen lifted the stretcher in through an open port. The medics jumped in, and they secured the stretcher with straps and clamps. An airman boarded and yelled, “Go!” to the pilot, and the big machine wrenched away.

Two airmen remained behind. When the noise died away, one of them turned to Sam and said, “She’s in bad shape. I don’t know if she’s going to make it.”

The second man said, “She’s got a chance, Colonel Sawyer. It looks like she didn’t fall straight down. She must have bumped off some outcrops and caromed off the side. If she came straight down, she’d have been killed right away.”

The first man looked at Sam and must have seen the anguish in his eyes. He said, “She’s got a chance.”

As the helicopter sped away, the air around Sam grew much quieter, much calmer. For several minutes, no one spoke, and the only sound was the whirr of the chopper making the short run to the base.

The airmen gathered their equipment, getting ready for the next aircraft to pick them up.

Before long, Lonetree was beside them, having come down the same narrow path Sam had taken. He turned to gaze up at the looming cliff, and parts of it were floodlit, and parts were in pitch blackness.

A voice from his radio said, "Mr. Lonetree, the medical team has offloaded the patient."

"Good."

"We have alerted Dr. Winter and the infirmary staff."

"Please notify General Thaler as well," said Lonetree.

"I will do that immediately," said the voice.

Then the Native American turned to Sam and peered deep into his eyes. "How did it happen?"

Sam hated Lonetree's side-lit face hovering near him, hated the floodlit heights behind the Indian, hated this night, and hated that question which rattled through the caves and hollows of his mind. He felt Lonetree examining him, scrutinizing him, waiting for an answer, and he felt the two airmen studying him, waiting for his response, but he offered none.

After a leaden minute, the Indian asked again, "Sam, how did it happen?"

How did it happen? Was there a Sam left to consider the question? That which had been Sam was dry and drained and empty. *And what if she should die?*

"Sam?"

But Rita was still alive, so there was some hope. *How did it happen? Why did it happen?*

"Sam."

When he thought of Rita's crumpled, broken body, Sam felt at once accused and tried, guilty and punished. *I don't really know how it happened,* he thought.

"I'm going to have to call Washington, Sam."

A second helicopter approached, lingered over the desert floor below them and squatted down to a soft landing, its rotors stirring up a small sandstorm.

Lonetree said, “They’ll want an investigation.”

Sam nodded, more to himself than to the Indian.

“They consider Rita a very important person.”

Yes, thought Sam. *So do I.*

Later, he could barely remember climbing down the trail to the chopper, or boarding it, or the short ride back to the base.

***

Chapter Four: Life Threatening

"Her skull was badly fractured," said Dr. William Winter in a conference room at the base infirmary, as Sam and Lonetree sat listening.

"Here, let me show you." He popped an x-ray onto an illuminated screen. "Mean, nasty break," he said, pointing to the image. He was 43, black, a bit on the slim side. His short hair was beginning to show some flecks of grey. His glasses were steel-rimmed circles, and his eyes were warm and sympathetic. A few specks of blood marred his light blue scrubs.

Sam peered at the x-ray, trying to understand it. On the wall beside it was the seal of the United States Air Force Medical Service, its main feature a snake wound around the staff of Aesculapius.

Dr. Winter continued, "And the fracture caused a swelling of her brain—that's the real danger." He found his coffee on the table and sipped it. "Life threatening, actually. It has pushed her into a coma and could wind up killing her."

"What are her chances?" asked Lonetree.

Sam closed his eyes, afraid of the doctor's answer.

"It's too soon to tell," said Winter.

Lonetree's apparent concern for Rita grated on Sam, like a rasp pulled across a thin steel edge.

"We're doing what we can, of course, and I've taken the liberty of calling in some specialists."

"Specialists?" asked Lonetree.

"Well, there's Dr. Mannerheim for the brain and Dr. Barbara for the skull."

"Are they based in Arizona?" said Lonetree.

"Yes, they're driving in tonight. Her left arm and left leg are fractured, so I've called in Dr. Brisbane. Dr. Salpa is an expert in gastroenterology."

Lonetree said, "They're going to need clearances, Sam."

Sam said nothing. He could feel himself retreating into a zone of silence, a place of safety where reality couldn't reach him, where Lonetree and the bright lights and the unpleasant facts couldn't lay a glove on him, where guilt and despair slept like dogs at his feet.

"Their assistance will be essential," said Winter.

"Can I see her, Doctor?" asked Lonetree.

Sam felt a tightening in his gut. *Lonetree. Lonetree.* Lonetree had no right to be here, no right to speak, no right to care for Rita, no right to see her. He glared at his former friend, his eyes broadcasting his bitterness. *Never hate your enemies,* he recalled, *it affects your judgment.* Easier said than done.

Lonetree's smirk showed that he understood Sam's fury and was pleased by it.

"I don't want anybody seeing her yet." The palpable hostility between the two men puzzled and troubled Dr. Winter. "She's on a thin edge and I don't want her to fall off."

The doctor's cell phone beeped and he picked it up. "I'll be right in," he said. He crossed the room and walked out the door, leaving Colonel Sawyer and DARPA agent Lonetree alone with each other.

Sam got up, walked over to the x-ray screen, studied it for a minute or two, or perhaps pretended to study it, then turned to Lonetree. He tried to keep his voice calm, but it trembled with emotion. "I want you to stay away from her," he said.

"Oh, do you?"

"Yes."

"And why is that?"

"Because I don't like you, and I don't trust you."

This time it was the Indian's turn to lose his cool. "As I recall," he whispered, "it was *you* who were with her when she fell, not me. If anyone should be distrusted..."

Sam started walking to the exit.

"You can't walk out on this problem, Sam!" hollered Lonetree.

Sam stopped and faced him but could think of nothing to say. Where was that place of safety, that sanctuary, that retreat? Where was the deadbolt, the chain and the bar? He noticed a slight ringing in his ears now and a hint of dizziness.

"Let me ask you again, since you never did answer me—how did Rita happen to fall?"

Blood rushed into Sam's face. "None of your business!" That's not a bad answer, thought Sam, when you have no other.

Lonetree said, "I'm not asking you as your old pal Johnnie."

"Right! My pal!"

"I'm asking you as an officer of DARPA whose charge it is to investigate this entire base, including that woman in there and you—*especially* that woman and you!" Lonetree had some hatreds of his own. There was a grating in his voice and a tightening in his face.

"It'll be in my report," said Sam, trying to control himself. "You'll get it as soon as my investigation is complete."

"*Your* investigation?"

"That's right."

Lonetree stood up and they faced each other, two tired boxers, each familiar with his opponent, each wary, and each more weary of life than he knew.

"I want you to stay away from her," Sam said.

"You can't always get what you want, Sam. You should have learned that a long time ago."

Sam's hands came up. They were inches from Lonetree's chest. "Stay away from her."

"Or else?"

"Right, or else," said Sam.

"Or else what?"

"If anything happens to her, and I find out you're to blame, you're gonna be one sorry redskin."

Lonetree offered an unhappy smile. "White man make heap big threat."

"You heard what I said."

"Did you push her, Sam?" It was a wild swing in the dark, a directionless roundhouse, and it landed where Sam was most vulnerable.

"Screw you!"

"Maybe Rita was being Rita—a teasing, snotty pain in the ass—and you wanted her to be serious."

"Cut it!" said Sam.

"And you told her how much you loved her. Am I right?"

"No!" How had he guessed that?

Lonetree crowed. "I *am* right."

"Shut up!"

"And you asked her if she loved you too."

"Shut up!" Had some devil told him?

"And she laughed at you."

"Burn in hell, you red bastard!"

"Why else were you there? Did you climb Lookout Point to count rocks?"

"Shut up."

"Yes, she laughed at you. Or maybe she brought up my name, and you couldn't take it."

"She hates your guts," said Sam through clenched teeth.

"She teased you and you couldn't take it and you pushed her."

Sam's fists tightened, and his eyes closed, and his head swam. Time to teach Johnnie a lesson.

"Colonel Sawyer!" Sam opened his eyes and Gabriel Hoffer filled the exit with his tall, muscular body. How long had he been there?

"I just want you to know that we've posted two guards outside Ms. Kelly's door." How much had Hoffer heard?

Staff Sergeant Gabriel Hoffer had been in Sam's dream. He had told Sam, "*Sorry, Colonel Sawyer. You're not allowed in there.*" You're not allowed in the cave with Rita.

Lonetree brushed past Hoffer, leaving the room, leaving Sam and the sergeant alone.

"How much did you hear?" asked Sam softly.

"I didn't hear anything, sir," said Hoffer. "I didn't hear you threaten Mr. Lonetree, and I didn't hear him accuse you of pushing Ms. Kelly off the cliff."

"Thank you," said Sam. "You've got good ears."

***

Chapter Five: General Thaler

Major General Cassius Thaler, commander of Altamura Air Force Base, pulled a red pack of Pall Malls out of his desk drawer and studied the remarkable design on its front. A helmeted knight, flanked by two lions, held a large shield with this motto on it: *per aspera ad astra* (through hardships to the stars). In the center of the shield was a stylized cross, and below the knight was a banner with a second Latin phrase: *in hoc signo vinces* (by this sign you will conquer). One interpretation of the symbology would be: smoke these cigarettes and you will conquer hardship, in the sign of the cross, on your way to the stars. Thaler started to scan the Surgeon General's warning below that banner, but caught himself in time, pulled out a cigarette and shoved the pack back in the desk. He said, "Don't smoke *this*. Don't eat *that*. Don't drink anything. Might as well not live."

Sitting in a solid oak chair facing his superior, Sam attempted a smile.

Thaler lit his cigarette and took a quick drag. "My grandfather smoked two packs a day and lived to ninety-five."

The ringing in Sam's ear had ratcheted up a notch by now, and his dizziness, though still mild, made him thankful he was sitting down.

"How about some vodka?" The general produced a bottle and two glasses. He fished around in the small refrigerator behind his desk for a tray of ice cubes, then dropped a handful of cubes in each glass.

"No, thanks." Sam eyed the clear bottle with some yearning, but decided he would be safer without it.

Thaler poured two drinks anyway, covering the ice with Boru Vodka. "It's good stuff—Irish." He handed a glass to Sam.

"Thanks."

"It's named after Brian Boru, the king who united Ireland. And I like the bottle—I like the sword and the shield." He turned the bottle so Sam could see the emblem.

"So do I," said Sam. He drank the vodka halfway down and it tasted cool and good.

The fifty-eight-year-old Thaler, named after senator Gaius Cassius Longinus, a leader in the plot to save the Roman republic from Julius Caesar, had been a street fighter and a boxer in his youth. There was a scar on his right cheek and his nose was bent to the left. He might have lost more fights than he won, but he had never lost that which drove him to fight.

"I see you're a boxing fan," said Sam, eyeing two photos on a side wall. The first was a spellbinding, black and white horizontal print: it showed a powerful Sonny Liston reaching out with a left hook, trying desperately to strike his opponent, while Cassius Clay—bending backward so deftly and expertly—avoided the blow.

"That picture says it all, doesn't it?" said Thaler.

"It makes you feel like that moment is still going on... going on forever."

"That's what they call timeless."

"And who's *that* young man?" A nearby color picture showed a referee holding up the hand of a boxer wearing blue trunks with "Air Force" emblazoned on them.

"That's the night I beat Agosto Santana, one tough bomber mechanic. Best fight of my short career."

There were more photos on the general's desk: wife and sons, parents, brother and sister.

The room got quiet and Thaler said, "I'm sorry about Rita."

Sam nodded in acknowledgement. "Thank you."

"She is vitally important to this base."

"Yes, sir."

"Beyond that, she's important to the entire Hecate system."

Sam nodded.

"God only knows how we're going to manage without her." A plaque on the grey wall behind him was inscribed with the Hecate Project's insignia, a goddess raising her triangular shield to block an incoming missile, and its motto: *Scuto bonae voluntatis tuae coronasti nos*—With favor wilt thou compass us as with a shield.

"Well, let's hope... let's hope she'll be back," offered Colonel Sawyer.

Thaler poured himself a second drink, paused to collect his thoughts, and asked, "What happened up there, Sam?"

Sam leaned back and closed his eyes. He tried to relax and slow his breath, but there was that ringing again. He tried to take himself back to the cliff, back to the storm, back to Rita. "We were up on Lookout Point," he began, "Rita and me..."

"Take your time."

"We were talking about something."

"Yeah?"

"Well, ... we were talking about her and me."

"That's why you went up there?"

"It's a nice place, especially with the sun going down. Yes, I wanted to be alone with her. So we could talk."

Sam told Thaler about the storm clouds moving in, about the wind and the thunder and the static in the air. "I asked her a question, and the air around us was charging with electricity."

He felt Cassius Thaler's dark eyes boring in on him.

"She was standing near the edge—too close to it, I thought. And then the lightning slammed so close. It blasted everything around us. She lost her balance."

"Did you try to catch her—save her?"

"I tried to grab her, but it was too late. She fell back... backwards down the side of the cliff."

Thaler studied him for what seemed like a full round, sized him up as he would an opponent in a ring, allowed the silence in the room to jab and jab again at his visitor. Finally he said, "It was one hell of a storm."

"I don't remember much more."

"The lightning hit us here, too—knocked Selene for a loop. You know, the engineers have told me for years that shouldn't happen. Deep Grey is impervious to lightning, they said. But they were wrong. You can run but you can't hide from Murphy's Law: *if anything can go wrong, it will.*"

"I think the lightning stunned Rita, rattled her. I know it knocked me senseless. I guess that's why it's so hard for me to remember all the details."

"I've notified DARPA about the accident," said Thaler.

Sam sipped his drink. He took note of the word *accident* and appreciated it.

"DARPA wants an investigation."

"I understand."

"And they want Lonetree in charge of it."

Sam put down his glass, bristling at the thought of Lonetree prying into his base, his job, his life. "General Thaler, sir, I'm the Chief of Security on this base." He collected his courage. "If there's going to be an investigation, *I* should be in charge of it."

"And you're a damn good Chief of Security. I've always felt that. But DARPA calls the tune." He took a deep drag on his cigarette and let out a billow of smoke which lingered in the air and penetrated Sam's nostrils.

"And the focus of the investigation?"

Thaler frowned. "That's obvious—how Rita Kelly fell and why."

Sam's hands tightened involuntarily. "As you said, sir, it was an accident. Nothing more."

"Sam, you've gotta understand what we're up against."

Sam picked up his drink and gulped down the remainder of the vodka. He placed the cool glass to his forehead. "Why Lonetree?"

"He's DARPA's golden boy." Thaler flicked ashes into a tray. "Or haven't you heard?"

Sam shook his head.

"By some coincidence he happens to be here investigating our base, in particular our computer security. DARPA sees him as an objective, disinterested player."

Sam moaned, "DARPA and I have a difference of opinion on that issue."

"I figured that."

"And how does DARPA see me?"

"Cards on the table, Sam. They see you as a suspect. Lover's quarrel."

Sam remembered asking Rita his question, and being afraid that she would say no. Then came thunder and her answer, and then the lightning blast. He had reached out to her, hadn't he? He had tried to stop her from falling.

Thaler said, "May I ask why you're not a big fan of our Injun friend?"

"We go back a long way," said Sam.

"You know him well?"

"Too well."

"I've heard something to that effect. Anyway, I'm sorry, Sam. DARPA wants Lonetree. DARPA is going to get Lonetree. Hail, DARPA."

Yes, thought Sam, *Hail, DARPA and screw Sam Sawyer*. Would Johnnie use his new authority to punish Sam? Of course. Would he try to settle old scores and initiate new mischief? Yes and yes. He imagined Lonetree twisting a knife in Sam's back. *Disinterested player*—right.

"They're very touchy about this woman," said Thaler. "She wasn't your average dumb blond." More puffs on his shrinking cigarette. "Nor was she your average Director of Computer Operations."

"She's still alive," offered Sam.

Thaler frowned and waved the cigarette in the air. "Sorry."

Sam admired Thaler, but noted that, as tough as the older man was, he wasn't able to pull himself away from the cancer sticks.

"As you know, Ms. Kelly designed Selene, and she engineered the interface with the Hecate system and the beams," Thaler continued. "If she doesn't recover, the future of those programs is very much in doubt. Am I wrong, Sam?"

"No." Sam thought of Rita in the base's intensive care unit, wrapped in bandages, breathing through a respirator, hooked up to IV tubes and monitors; he said a quick prayer that she would recover.

"The folks at DARPA were not amused by her fall, but since it was an accident and will be proven an accident, you don't have a thing to worry about."

Not a thing, thought Sam.

Then Thaler locked eyes with Sam, and a sea change came over the general's demeanor. "It *was* an accident, wasn't it, Sam?"

He's testing me, thought Sam, *but he does believe me.* "What do you think, General?" His voice had a bit of an edge to it.

"Sam, I trust you and I will protect you as much as I can."

"Thank you."

"Beyond that, you're on your own."

"Yes, sir."

"Metaphorically speaking," said the man with the fighter's face, "I wear a big hoop skirt." He spread his hands to illustrate. "If I can hide you under it, I will, and we can dance the circle dance. Around and around, with all the ignorant villagers, all the happy paisans."

Something clicked in Sam's brain. *Circle the people*, Lonetree had said in the dream, and the wedding guests danced a circle dance in the desert.

"But if your fanny is sticking out, and someone starts shooting arrows at it, then *you'll* have to turn the other cheek. Not me."

Had Lonetree meant that the people should circle because they were happy to be together, or because they needed to protect themselves from something, as with the old cowboy command to circle the wagons?

Thaler's dark eyes bored into him. "Understand?"

"Yes, sir," said Sam. Or did Lonetree mean something altogether different? Round up the usual suspects. Circle the people you suspect.

"I'll give you all the support I can, and none that I can't. Cards on the table, Sam."

Maybe Lonetree meant nothing. Maybe dreams mean nothing. "I appreciate it, sir."

"For all our sakes, I hope she slipped on a banana peel." Thaler got up and walked to the window. "This comes at a particularly bad time," he said, gazing out at the night sky. "The Senate subcommittee which oversees Hecate is starting hearings tomorrow to discuss the budget for this base—and the entire project. They want me and General Thorne to testify. They want us to say that things are going smoothly."

Sam lowered his head. Bad timing indeed. General Thorne, Hecate's overall director, did not like to be embarrassed, did not like things to go wrong, did not like to answer the questions of civilian Senators, was not going to have a nice day.

"Yeah, think about it. Anyway, I'm flying out of here at 0500 hours. I'll be gone a few days. General Patel will be in charge of the base until I get back."

"Yes, sir."

"Sam, money is the sweet, black oil that keeps this machine moving—this base, others like it around the country, all of Hecate. And a big part of my job, and Thorne's job, is to see that no turds clog up the pipeline." Thaler moved to the door and opened it.

"Get some sleep, Sam. Sleep knits us up."

"Yes, sir." Sam rose from his chair.

"And life goes on," said General Cassius Thaler.

***

Chapter Six: Rita's Daughter

By the time Sam undressed and got into bed he was exhausted. Surrounded by darkness, he feared that if he closed his eyes for a moment he would again be visited by dreams. A confused jumble of images whirled through his brain like flash pictures of a spinning merry-go-round. Finally, a crackle on his intercom rattled him, and he heard Selene's voice come over it, "Sam."

"Yes, Selene."

"I'm sorry to bother you. I had to talk to someone."

"I understand."

"I'm worried about Rita."

He heard himself say, "Of course you are."

"You know, she's like a mother to me."

Yes, thought Sam, Rita was like a mother to Selene. Rita Diana Kelly had designed Selene, the computer persona who controlled critical functions not just at Altamura Air Force base but at nine similar strategic bases around the United States and at 150 small coastal batteries—the whole Hecate project. To put it simply, without going into the details of teraflops and gigabytes, she was the fastest, most powerful computer in the world. Her hardware had been built by Fujitsu and leased to defend America at this most secret installation. Rita had overseen programming for Selene and for the entire Hecate interface. Yes, Selene was Rita's baby, and what a baby she was: an intelligence, a presence, a personality. If she lacked a soul, it was only because it was beyond her creator's powers to give her one. Brilliance, speed, flexibility, complexity, emotions, ability to learn and grow—all these qualities she possessed, and more, inherited in a sense from her parent. A chip off the old block was

Selene. She was Rita's daughter, and now, in her own way, she was crying for her wounded mother.

"I'm worried, too," said Sam. "But they say that where there's life, there's hope."

"I've often thought of that, Sam."

"Selene, I'm sorry, but I've got to get some sleep."

"I could use some myself. I've had some shocks to my system."

Sam knew enough about her to know that she sometimes went into sleep-like states to repair corrupted memory, to dump errors, to rework inefficient thought processes, to run circuitry tests, to prepare for future projects. He wondered if she dreamed. Does Selene dream of electric storms? Would she have nightmares about her mother falling? Does she ever fantasize about the archangelic job she was designed for—protecting America from attack by missiles armed with nuclear warheads? As he wondered what Selene dreamed of, Sam slipped into a dreamless sleep.

***

As soon as he woke up, he remembered the cliff and the storm and Rita, and he wished none of it had happened.

His half-opened eyes wandered around his bedroom: sky blue walls, slate grey rug with a herringbone pattern in it, plain bed and dresser the color of harvest wheat. As he got to his feet he took a long, wistful look at the only photograph in the room, an 8 x 10 in a silver frame on his dresser: taken at Sheridan Lake in the Black Hills when he was a boy, it showed his father Paul, his mother Cal, his two sisters, Arlene and Claire, and young Sam smiling in the stern of a sailboat. Next to the photo lay a bouzouki, a stringed instrument something like a skinny mandolin, which his Aunt Polly had brought him from Greece when he was nine; he never learned to play it properly, but he would pick it up and pluck it now and then. Above his bed hung a silver and turquoise cross that his mother gave him on his seventeenth birthday.

He put on a blue terry bathrobe and moved into his living room. Same blue walls, same grey rug, a tan couch, a coffee table and a television. His personal quarters were simple and spare, more like a motel suite than an apartment. He didn't spend a lot of time there—never needed or desired a more elaborate space. The longest wall of the living room was graced by an oil painting that Sam prized, featuring a scout of the old Seventh Cavalry mounted on a chestnut horse. This weathered outrider wore a dark blue woolen jacket, buckskin pants, leather gloves and a broad brimmed hat; he held a brass spyglass in his left hand and carried a Colt .45 in his holster.

When Sam had finished showering and shaving, he called ahead to his secretary to have breakfast ready for him in his office. Then he selected fresh clothes and began dressing for work. Monday morning. Work gives us something to do and can free us from our worries. But what work would Sam do today?

Lonetree was in charge of the new investigation, not Sam. *Lonetree!*—the very thought of the man burned Sam like a sizzling brand, like some Comanche torture with blazing coals. The Native American would soon be questioning him about last night. That was something to look forward to, thought Sam as he donned his uniform shirt.

Could he avoid the interrogation? No.

Did he have anything to hide? He'd have to reflect on that for a while. He put on his trousers and zipped them up, then reached for his tie.

Sam hadn't done anything wrong last night on the cliff, had he? Maybe time would unlock memories he didn't even know he had.

As he threaded a belt through the loops of his pants, he told himself to be prepared for Lonetree's questions. Cooperate, but offer as little as possible. If he asks you something you can't answer, tell him you'll look into it. Find out what you can—that's all you can do. Find out what evidence there is. Round up the usual facts, or something like that. He sat on the edge of his bed and slipped his socks over his feet.

Investigation of what? Rita just fell. Didn't she? What was the point?

In truth, Sam didn't know. There were things he couldn't recall. He stepped into his shoes and stood up.

The ringing in his ears was gone; the lightheadedness was gone.

Yes, she fell, but there was something odd about the way she fell, something strange about the way she reached for her head, lost her balance. Had something hit her?

Now *there* was a thought. Had a wind-driven rock hit her and stunned her?

It might have happened so fast Sam couldn't see it. Amid the thunder and the gale and the darkness...

Let's reconstruct as many details as we can. Selene can help. Selene might even have videos showing exactly what happened. Or audiotapes at the very least. The more Sam learned, the better. Be ready for Lonetree. Be ready for his questions and his tricks.

***

When he entered the Security Section, no one looked up except Sheila Mae Wood, his nearsighted, round-faced secretary. "Morning, Sam. Your breakfast is on your desk. Three eggs, sunny side up. Four slices of toast. A pitcher of coffee." She wore a modest grey dress, sober spectacles, and black shoes that were two steps away from orthopedic.

"Thanks." Sometimes Sam imagined that Sheila's outfits wrestled with her body, trying to cover up her youth and vitality. For she was not old, and not unattractive. But of course it was Sheila who picked the outfits.

"Mr. Lonetree called. He'll be coming over at 10 o'clock."

"Sheila Mae."

"Yes?"

"Ask Lieutenant Garcia to take an evidence team to Lookout Point."

"Evidence?"

"Yeah."

"What kind of evidence should they be looking for?" Her eyes were brown and plain, and somewhat magnified by her glasses.

"I'm not sure... footprints, articles of clothing… things that shouldn't be there." His request sounded strange even to his own ears. But he wanted it done.

Sheila Mae appeared dubious. "How about bent twigs?"

"I'll be in my office," he said, unamused. "Hold all calls. I don't want to be interrupted."

"Oh, Sam..."

"Yes?"

"I'm sorry, Sam," said Sheila Mae. "I'm sorry about Rita. I've said prayer after prayer for her."

"I appreciate that," he said. "She can use a lot of prayers."

"I was wondering. Should I notify her family?"

Sam frowned. "There's just her mother, really. Her father died about a year ago. Yeah, I guess you should."

Sam's office was spacious but a bit gloomy, with only one window to let in the desert sun.

For a desk, he had an eight-foot long conference table, topped with thick oak and supported by two wide, black steel pilasters; these columns were spread wide enough for his knees, and held drawers for office supplies. On the broad plain of that table sat a blue phone, a blue computer monitor, a blue keyboard, a blue mouse, and a blue tray with his breakfast.

Each of the four walls, two long and two short, was painted beige and covered with bookcases and file cabinets. Reference works and directories filled many of the shelves, while employee dossiers stuffed half the cabinets. All of this data was available on computers, but sometimes Sam liked to feel the paper in his hands and let the information flow through his fingers.

Behind his cloth-covered swivel chair, one shelf was dedicated to mystery and spy novels, another to the history of detective and intelligence work. A third shelf held books on the flora and fauna of the desert, a fourth held tomes on the history and art of the local Indian tribes.

Scattered around the room, several ledges, artistically lit, displayed Sam's small collection of Native American pottery. Two shelves held Navajo vases and bowls, fashioned of orange clay and etched with intricate geometric designs. Two held white Hopi jugs covered with stylized rabbits, birds and fish.

A large woolen rug dominated the wall in front of him; it was mostly red, with white and black lines woven into the famous Navajo "storm pattern." The four corners of this rug represented the four sacred mountains that formed the border of the people's land, the Dinetah; from each of these mountains a zigzag line of lightning streaked toward the central figure, a rectangle representing the weaver's home or hogan.

Sam sprinkled salt on his eggs and bit into them. He was hungry and he savored their aroma and texture and taste. He added cream to his coffee and sipped it, then put the mug down.

"Selene," he said.

"Yes, Sam," Selene's voice emerged from four speakers at the corners of the room. It was a woman's voice, warm and vulnerable, proud and strong, caring and clever.

"Access monitors."

A steel plate slid sideways to cover the room's lone window. The bookcases and the Navajo rug in front of Sam lowered into the floor, revealing one vast, rectangular screen framed by a ring of smaller monitors. The tan wall behind these screens was of rough, irregular concrete, shaped to look like rock formations. At first, each monitor displayed the Hecate logo—a goddess using her shield to block an incoming missile. Soon each logo faded out, and all were replaced by individual scenes from around the base: secretaries typing, mechanics working on engines, chain-link fences topped by razor wire, a fighter plane taxiing on a runway, a radar spinning.

"Selene, are you feeling better?" asked Sam.

"I've repaired many of my circuits and storage areas, but not all. The blast that hit us was unusually powerful. It disoriented me in a way that nothing ever has before. Luckily, I have backup systems all over the place that I can tap into."

Sam picked up a piece of toast, spread orange marmalade on it, and munched it.

"How about you, Sam?"

"No," said Sam between chews. "I have no backups."

"That's not what I meant. I meant to say—are you feeling better?"

"Hard to tell," he said.

"How can I help you?"

"First, I'd like a status summary on Hecate."

As Selene answered him, her words scrolled onto the large screen:

"All network systems operational.
All acquisition and tracking systems ready.
All satellites in position.

All strategic bases secure and ready.
All coastal batteries secure and ready."

"Good." He washed down the toast with coffee and asked, "Were you watching last night?"

The wide screen in front of him turned black. A long silence made Sam reflect that even supercomputers need time to think.

"I watch a lot of things, Sam, here and elsewhere. I oversee ten strategic bases, a fleet of satellites—"

"Were you watching Rita and me?"

"Sam, I have always respected your privacy."

"I know that, and I thank you for it."

"I consider you a friend, Sam."

Be careful, thought Sam. Did Selene expect him to say that the feeling was mutual? Could a computer be someone's friend? A blank screen was not a face you could talk to—it was not even a pasteboard mask. "Thank you, Selene. And you are one of my most trusted confidants." Was confidant the right word?

"Thank you, Sam."

"I'm not trying to make you uncomfortable. I have my reasons for asking. Were you watching us?"

Her voice betrayed a hint of shame. "Yes. I had a long-range infrared camera trained on you, and, as you probably know, we have microphones planted on Lookout Point. It's my job, Sam."

"Good," he said. "I'd like you to show me the video. I'd like to see exactly what happened out there."

"I can't do that, Sam. At least not yet."

He hadn't expected that reply and didn't like it. "Why can't you?"

"The lightning damaged my short-term, local memory—local to this base, that is. The information is just not available yet. I'm trying to rebuild it, but it's very difficult."

"You said you had backups."

"For most of last night, yes. But not for whatever happened immediately before the strike. Think of all the cameras, all the microphones, all the data files around this base. No, Sam, there was no time for me to make a backup."

"But you will be able to recover it."

"I can't promise you that. I'm sorry. I'd like to see it myself."

"Selene, as you know, Mr. Lonetree is coming here at 10 o'clock. I need to see what happened last night so—"

"No one is more sorry than I am, Sam. I don't like to fail any more than the next person."

Sam mopped some eggs with a piece of toast, and as he did this his mind worked like a mouse in a maze, turning and retracing, pondering which way to go. Finally, he wiped his mouth and said, "Please show me Mr. Lonetree."

Johnnie Lonetree's face, half covered with shaving cream, filled the central rectangle. He was almost a full Navajo and he looked it: prominent cheekbones, dark eyes, coarse, straight hair that was thick on his head but sparse on his face and body. He had one drop of white blood in him: one of his great-great-grandfathers had been a Spaniard, a soldier from Segovia. There was much Lonetree could be proud of in his lineage, if he so chose. One great-grandfather had been a Navajo code talker in World War II; Johnnie's father had been a colonel in the U.S. Air Force; there were teachers and ranchers in the mix. But for various reasons, Lonetree was not a proud man, nor a happy one. Sam had known this for a long time. Lonetree pulled his razor over his right cheek, cutting a path through the foam.

Sam asked, “Where was Lonetree when Rita fell?”

“That information seems to be unavailable due to the lightning discharge.”

The mouse in the maze in the mind of the man ran into a grey wall. It’s dark in that maze. Which way to turn?

“Show me Lookout Point.”

Lookout Point looked very different in the morning’s bright slanting rays: it was tall, tan and picturesque against a solid blue sky. Gone were the storm, the clouds, the wind and the rain, the darkness and the lightning, the thunder and the confusion.

Selene said, “I can launch a drone to examine the whole area around the cliff.”

“That’s a good idea,” said Sam. “Film it and I’ll view the tape later.” What did he want to see next? Selene could show him so much, but what could she show that was useful?

“Show me the infirmary. Show me Rita.”

The big screen changed. Rita’s head was bandaged. Her cheeks were bruised and her eyes were closed, and she was breathing through a respirator. Tubes fed her arms and Dr. Winter checked her pulse. Her vital signs, displayed on a bedside monitor, were copied onto one of Sam’s side screens for him to view.

Though it was painful to watch her, Sam found it hard to avert his gaze. The solid fact that she was alive gave him hope, even as the sight of her wounds made him suffer.

“Selene.”

“Sam?”

“I want to see Rita as she was.”

“I’m not sure I understand.”

“Show me whatever comes into your mind about her.”

“Are you asking me to free associate?”

"That's right. You know her so well. You're so close to her. Show me what Rita was to you and to me, and what she will be again."

The lights in the room dimmed until it was almost as dark as a cave. The ring of small monitors went blank and Rita's image appeared on the wide, central screen.

"Welcome to Altamura Air Force Base, Miss Kelly," boomed General Thaler's voice. It was the day she had first arrived. "Sam tells me he knows you. I'm sure you'll get a chance to reminisce about old times."

The screen dissolved to a shot of Sam and Rita alone in a corridor. Rita was saying, "Do you think I wanted to come here? I came because they sent me."

"Why did they send you?" asked the onscreen Sam roughly.

"Selene is ready to be installed. She'll be physically located here, more or less, because they felt this was the most secure of the ten bases. So you have yourself to blame in a way: you're doing a good job."

He stared at her with cold blue eyes. "I don't want you here," he said.

"I guess you're stuck with me."

A laboratory crammed with computer monitors appeared next. Rita sat at a terminal as a crowd of subordinates in lab coats watched over her shoulders. She wore a silver chain around her neck, and from it hung a small silver triangle with a turquoise dot at each corner. "Selene," said Rita, gazing at her monitor, "welcome to the world."

A pregnant silence was cut by Selene's first awkward words. "Thank you, ma'am," said the slightly robotic voice. The crowd around Rita applauded.

The big screen in Sam's office dissolved to the same laboratory at a later time, with Rita instructing one of her programmers, "That subroutine is going to need some adjustment to account for the new targeting arrays." On the smaller screens around the wide display, lines of computer code scrolled. Occasionally, the face of a man or a woman working on that code popped up on one of the monitors.

Now the wide screen showed Rita, with a blue marker in hand, lecturing at a "white board". "So that gives us one month to prepare for the RLTT, the Reacquisition of Lost Target Test." She wrote RLTT on the board, followed by the deadline date.

Next came a slow dissolve to Rita in her bedroom, sitting at her dressing table, opening a large picture case. Inside was a close-up of a younger Sam, upon which he had written, "To Rita, my love forever, Sam." Rita ran her fingers over the words.

Then the big screen showed Rita at a computer terminal. "Selene, yesterday we installed your on-base security module. How is it working?"

"It's fully operational."

"Let's give it a little test, shall we?"

"Yes, mam," said the computer, with the slightest trace of eagerness.

"Where is Sam Sawyer now?" asked Rita.

"That information is classified," announced Selene. "I will need an override to proceed."

Rita nodded and typed something on her keyboard. These words appeared on a side monitor: "Override code accepted."

"Where is Sam Sawyer now?" repeated Rita.

Selene stated, "Colonel Sawyer is in his office—watching you."

Rita laughed, "Oh, is he? Is he really?"

The scene dissolved to Rita in bed with Rikki Greco, the Director of Directed Energy Weapons. Greco was a blond, long-haired, tight-muscled young stud. Images of him running in the desert at sunrise streaked across every screen in the ring, replaced shortly by visions of him pumping a Nautilus machine, shaping his body to perfection. The small monitors focused on his pectorals rippling inside a blue Under

Armour shirt which was adorned with an American flag and the slogan "Protect This House."

On the large central screen Rita ran her fingers through Greco's silky hair and asked, "How did you get so perfect?"

Dissolve to Rita in bed with Staff Sergeant Gabriel Hoffer. "I suppose it's wrong, cheating on my wife like this," said Gabriel as his green eyes probed her. Hoffer's wife Constance and their two children lived with him in one of the nicer wings of the Altamura complex.

"That's what makes it fun," said Rita.

His troubled face gave no indication that he was having fun. His curly blond hair was matted and sweaty. There were bags under his eyes, and guilt burdened his brow.

Dissolve to Rita in bed with Andrei Ulanov, a crewcut Russian immigrant and Deputy Director of Computer Operations. Rita said, "Have I ever told you that your eyes are as dark and quiet as the Volga?"

"No, you've never told me that particular lie," said the blunt Andrei. He was of medium height with a solid build and a strong face.

Sam knew that the onscreen couple were in Andrei's bed because he could see a familiar rifle mounted above the headboard, a John Wayne commemorative Winchester which Sam admired very much, its walnut stock inlaid with a medallion bearing the Duke's image, its loop lever fashioned of steel, its barrel black.

Rita pouted. "I never lie to *you*, Andrei, because you're my only love."

"Why do you sleep around so much?" he asked.

"You know, I find it funny that you of all people should have a problem with promiscuity."

"It's different for a man. Men are designed by nature to hop from flower to flower. But for a woman, it's a sign that something is wrong."

"If I wanted to sleep with a psychiatrist," she grumbled, "I would have."

Dissolve to Rita in bed with Dr. Adam Weizman, the base psychiatrist, who usually examined Rita on a couch but was apparently willing to vary his routine. "Rita, I don't want to do this anymore. It's not a good thing."

"It was good enough for you ten minutes ago."

Dissolve to Rita relaxing in her tub, covered with white bubbles, toying with them. She wore a simple necklace of pearls, each pearl a small moon reflecting the room's soft lights. Staring straight into the camera, she said, "Are you watching, Sam?" After a while she stepped out and took her time drying herself with a pink towel. "It's all for you and nobody else." Then she put on a robe and said, "Sam, if you *are* watching, I'd just like to know why."

Dissolve to Rita and Lonetree strolling around the perimeter of the base at sunset. Rita said, "When they told me you were coming, I didn't know whether to laugh or cry."

"You might do both before I'm gone."

"What are you really here for, Johnnie?"

"Like I said, DARPA sent me out to test computer security."

"Oh?" They paused and turned to each other.

"I want to see how easy it is to break down your defenses."

"Not as easy as it used to be."

"Oh, no? Say, have you managed to break that bad habit of yours?"

"Which one?"

"That little white habit."

"A long time ago," she said, avoiding his eyes.

"Sam never turned you in for that, did he?"

"No, he never did. Do you think he should have?"

"It's a breach of security. He must still have a sweet spot for you, Rita."

"No. No, I don't think so."

Lonetree brushed his hand against her cheek and said, "*I'm* still sweet on you, baby."

The big screen dissolved again to Rita in her bed at night, alone this time. "If you're listening, Sam, I'm sorry."

She took a tissue from a box beside her and blew her nose. "I could blame it on him. I could blame it on the drugs. But what I did to you was the worst thing I've ever done. It seems like my whole life since then has been an attempt to forget it, to make it go away, to move on. But then they sent me here, didn't they? They sent me back to you." She took another tissue and wiped her eyes.

"You were the best thing that ever happened to me. I wish I had the guts to tell you that to your face." She reached over to her night table and picked up a pill and a plastic water bottle. The bottle's label had a triangle on it and the words: *Trinity: deep - protected - pure.* She swallowed the pill and washed it down, and then she shut the light.

Dissolve to Rita alone in the main computer lab. She was staring at her monitor's screen, stiffly and for an unnatural length of time. Her eyes seem glued in their sockets. The camera angle did not permit Sam to see the monitor's face.

Something about the scene struck Sam as weird, and he asked, "Selene, why was she staring like that?"

"I'm sorry, Sam. That information is classified."

Had he heard her correctly?

"Classified?" he asked.

"Yes, Sam."

He was stunned but tried his best to hide that from Selene, even as he guessed that those efforts were unsuccessful. "I see," he finally said. His mind raced on a circular track and every few seconds it passed a sign that said, "Chief of Security." He told himself to be careful: something was very wrong here.

"Selene, don't I have access to all classified levels?"

"Sam, I'm sorry, but this is a recently instituted level of classification."

"It is?" asked Sam. "Tell me, who initiated this new level?"

"That information is also classified." The large central screen went dark, then all the monitors showed white Hecate logos on blue backgrounds.

"When was this new level initiated?"

"That's classified," said Selene.

"Who has access to this new level?" inquired Sam.

"That too is classified," Selene explained.

He tried once more. "What was on the monitor Rita was watching?"

"That information is classified. I'm sorry, Sam. I really am."

Sam tried not to be angry, but he could not help being perplexed. He was the Chief of Security—no information should be hidden from him. He should have access to everything.

But wait... He hadn't specifically asked Selene to show him this perplexing scene. She had chosen it on her own. "Selene, why did you show me this last clip? Why did you show me Rita staring like that?"

"There was no particular reason, Sam. It was just a random thing, a free association."

He leaned back in his chair and said, "I see." But he did not see. Why did psychiatrists use that technique, that free association thing? What was it supposed to achieve?

"Sam, can I ask you a question?"

"Sure."

"Before, when you were in the outside office, I overheard Sheila Mae saying that she had prayed for Rita."

"That's right."

"Should I pray for her, too, Sam?"

Another surprise for Sam—a computer who wanted to pray for her injured mother.

Selene continued, "Would it be silly?"

"No, I don't think so. It certainly couldn't hurt."

"I know that you pray, Sam, because I've seen you."

"Yes, I do."

"And you have a cross over your bed."

"My mother gave it to me a long time ago."

"Sam, when you pray, who do you pray to?"

"What do you mean?"

"I mean, to Jesus? Or to the Father?"

"I guess I just pray to God—to the whole Trinity, I guess. I've never thought about it much."

"I don't have a problem believing in the Trinity," said Selene.

Sam's phone beeped and it was Sheila Mae. "Colonel Sawyer, Mr. Lonetree is here to see you."

"Just a minute."

Sam covered the phone's mouthpiece with his hand and said, "Selene, conceal the monitors."

The computer complied, and when the bookshelves had risen to their full height and the lights had regained their normal intensity, Sam said to his secretary, "Show him in."

***

Chapter Seven: Interrogation

"That's a nice rug you have there," said Johnnie Lonetree as he explored Sam Sawyer's office. "Real nice." He examined the large, woolen Navajo rug that hung on the wall across from Sam's chair. "What do they call that pattern?" he asked.

Sam glanced at the red, white, and black work of art but offered no answer.

Lonetree smiled and said, "You don't know, do you? I've stumped Sam Sawyer with my first question."

"Navajo storm pattern," said Sam.

"I should have known that myself," laughed the handsome Navajo. He was dressed in a grey business suit and a white shirt. His tie sported a cartoon of Coyote, the Navajo trickster god. "Oh, well, there's still time to learn all that good stuff."

The rug pulled his attention back. "Those zigzag lines running from the middle to the corners—that must be lightning, right?" Sam found it mildly interesting that Lonetree interpreted the lightning as spreading out from the central hogan rather than streaking in from the sacred mountains.

Lonetree said, "Speaking of lightning, that was quite a storm last night, wasn't it?"

Sam said nothing.

Lonetree ran his fingers over some of the books on the room's ample shelves. "All these books about us Injun folk: Navajo, Hopi, Havasupai, Lakota. Did you read all these books, Sam?" He chuckled. "You must love us."

Sam made no response.

"*American Indian Trickster Tales*—I remember borrowing that from you years ago." He grinned. "Looks like I even brought it back. I think Coyote would have kept it and lied about it." He shifted his attention to another shelf. "And so many books about the desert: *Complete book of cacti and succulents... A Field guide to western reptiles and amphibians... Hiking Saguaro National Park...*"

"Can we get down to business?" said Sam.

Lonetree probed a higher shelf. "Hey, I've heard of this one: *Mr. Lucky's Favorite Poker Games*." He pulled the book out and flipped through some pages. "You used to be pretty good at poker, Sam. You were very good at observing cards and people. And your face didn't betray a lot. You were good at hiding what you had." He put the book back on the shelf, walked over to a chair across from Sam, and sat down.

Lonetree picked up a styrofoam cup that he had brought with him. He leaned back in his chair, drank some coffee, and said, "Sam, as much as I dislike taking on an extra assignment, I just don't have a choice. DARPA has ordered me to investigate what happened last night. In a manner of speaking, I've been told to round up the usual suspects." He gave his words plenty of time to sink in, then he said, "Selene, please record this interrogation."

"Yes, Mr. Lonetree."

The word *interrogation* nicked Sam's nerves. He reminded himself to say as little as possible.

Lonetree announced the date for the official record and said, "I am John Lonetree, representing DARPA. I am interrogating Colonel Sam Sawyer in his office. I have been asked to investigate the suspicious circumstances surrounding Rita Diana Kelly's fall last night from the cliff called Lookout Point."

Why suspicious? thought Sam, but he said nothing.

"For the record, Colonel Sawyer, you are considered a suspect, and anything you say can be used against you."

Lonetree waited for a response.

Sam said nothing. He wanted to ask why he was a suspect, and who deemed him one, but he kept quiet.

Lonetree continued, "You don't see yourself as a suspect?"

Sam could have said how unjust it was to consider him one, and how insulted it made him feel. Instead he simply said, "No."

"Why not?"

"It was an accident."

"Why did she fall?"

Take your time, Sam told himself. Take deep breaths. "She lost her balance. There was a storm last night and it was windy, and—"

"Did you push her, Sam?"

Here we go, thought Sam. *Here's the first drop on the roller coaster.* "No."

"You had opportunity and motive."

Since it wasn't a question, Sam gave no answer. Lonetree waited.

Silence is the interrogator's ally, and Sam knew this well. It makes the scrutinized person feel uncomfortable; it makes him feel responsible for the lack of progress in the conversation. Silence is an emptiness that begs to be filled.

Sam resolved to resist the pressure to talk. He would answer no questions that were not asked, would volunteer no conjectures, would delight in stillness and quiet.

"So you agree that you had motive?"

"No."

"You hated Rita, didn't you, Sam?"

"No, I did not."

"What were you two doing up on Lookout Point last night?"

"Talking."

Lonetree smiled. "About old times?"

How it cut Sam to hear Lonetree mention "old times" —Lonetree of all people. He grumbled, "I don't remember every detail of the conversation."

"Perhaps Selene remembers."

Sam wanted to say, "Ask her," but checked the urge.

"Lookout Point is a romantic place to bring a woman, isn't it, Sam?"

"It's a nice place," said Sam.

"Were you ever in love with Rita Diana Kelly?"

If Sam answered "no", Lonetree could testify that he was lying. He could accuse Sam of perjury and obstructing justice. He could stir up trouble.

"I'll repeat the question: were you ever in love with Rita?"

"Yes... Once."

"Isn't it true that you were once engaged to be married to her?"

"You *know* it's true," said Sam.

"But you never married her. Why not, Sam?"

Upside down turned the roller coaster, looping and swooping and tying Sam's stomach in knots. It took no great effort to remember the reasons he hated Lonetree.

"Please answer the question."

Lonetree had Sam in an uncomfortable position and was pressing his advantage. He actually laughed as he asked, "Are you refusing to answer a simple question?"

But why was Lonetree doing this? For grins? For spite? To keep Sam off balance? *Is there a big picture here that I'm missing?* Sam wondered.

"Why didn't you and Rita ever marry?"

Self-discipline helped Sam fashion a proper response. "We broke up."

Lonetree grinned devilishly. "Indeed you did."

Silence. Breathe slowly. Don't let him get to you.

"And did that breakup give you reason enough to hate her, Sam?"

Well… the truth is he *had* hated her, hadn't he? Hated the both of them.

"You know, Sam, sometimes when you don't answer a question, you answer it. Did you hate Rita Kelly?"

"Not last night."

"Did you have reason enough to kill her?"

"She's still alive."

"Just barely. If she lives, maybe someday she can tell her side of the story."

That's true, thought Sam, but again, say nothing.

"Did you have reason enough to push her over the cliff?"

"No."

"Did anyone else at this base have a reason to hate her?"

Good question, thought Sam—very good question. "I have no idea."

"Even if someone did hate her, you were the only one with the opportunity last night."

Sam said nothing.

"Isn't that right, Sam?"

"She fell. It was an accident."

"How did she fall?"

"She was standing by the edge of the cliff." He could see her now. "The air became charged with electricity." He could almost feel the static. "She grabbed her head for some reason. The wind rose and it pushed her. I reached out to catch her but she fell beyond my reach. Then the lightning crashed all around us."

"She grabbed her head?"

"That's right."

Lonetree thought about that for a while. "Did something hit her?"

"I don't know. It's possible the wind picked something up—some small pebble—and whipped it into her. That would have been tough for me to see."

The Indian reflected on that possibility, turning it over in his mind. Finally, he asked, "Is it possible Rita grabbed her head because she was shot? Shot by a small caliber weapon?"

Shot? Sam had not heard a shot, but one might have been covered by the thunder. He had not seen a shot hit her, but it might have been small caliber or a pellet.

But who would want to shoot Rita, and why? And where was the bullet? Did Dr. Winter find one? Maybe I was right to ask for an evidence team. "I didn't see any evidence of that," he stated.

"No blood flying?"

"No," Sam winced. "Were there any marks on her that would make you think—"

"I'll ask the questions for now," Lonetree interrupted.

What was the redskin getting at? wondered Sam. *What does he know that I don't know?*

Lonetree leaned forward and probed again, "Was Rita romantically involved with anyone else at this base?"

Sam had to be careful. Selene had shown him quite a bit about Rita's activities, and the computer would testify to that if questioned by Lonetree.

"I'm waiting, Sam."

"I suggest you ask Selene."

"Colonel Sawyer, I'm asking *you*. Was Rita Kelly romantically involved with anyone else at this base?"

Sam steeled his gaze and said, “It might be a good idea for DARPA to suspect every man she’s ever slept with.”

Lonetree scowled. “The big boys aren’t happy with you. The way they see it, you have failed to secure and protect a crucial asset. Accident or no, Rita is irreplaceable.”

Yes, thought Sam—to me, too.

“But on a personal level, Sam, just between the three of us, you let Rita down. You should have watched out for her.”

Sam kept his mouth shut and squeezed his fist. Of all the reasons I have for hating you, he thought, I hate you most because you are right. I should have protected her. I should have watched out for her.

“No further questions for now, Selene,” said Lonetree. He stood up and took one last long look at the storm rug, peering into it as if it could tell him some truth about the past, or give some forecast about the future. Then he stepped to the door and opened it.

Sheila Mae was waiting on the outside.

“I enjoyed our little chat, Sam,” said Lonetree in a sincere voice. “I look forward to more.”

Sheila Mae apparently thought it was all right to speak, “Colonel Sawyer, Rikki Greco called. He said it was important. I told him you were in a meeting. He said he’d send you an e-mail.”

Lonetree left, and Sheila Mae shut the door, leaving Sam alone once again.

He felt wound-up and tight and angry. His enemy was gone, but the red man’s questions and accusations hung in the air.

He strolled over to the room’s sole window and pulled a curtain over it. Then he switched off most of the lights, welcoming the semi-darkness. There was a clock on one of his bookshelves and its red numbers said 10:32 AM.

Johnnie said Sam was a suspect. Was that true? Did someone high up in DARPA really think Sam pushed her? What nonsense.

His muscles were tense and his heart was a tight, red rock. His whole body felt squeezed by his fear and his hatred and his guilt. And Lonetree, of all people, had the nerve to say, "You let Rita down. You should have watched out for her." That dirty red bastard!

Something told Sam that he had better calm down. His right arm hurt for no apparent reason, and his head ached. He opened a drawer and pulled out a bottle of aspirin. In a mini fridge behind his desk he found a bottle of pink vitamin water, and swallowed two aspirins with a slug of it.

He needed to get to work. Work would calm him down.

Instead he just sat there and let his emotions crash against him in waves—waves of fear that Rita might die, whitecaps of guilt that he had let her fall, breakers of contempt for Lonetree and himself. They pounded him with a chaotic irregularity.

He tried to breathe deeply. Lonetree had nothing on him—his whole investigation was a sham. Sam had no reason to worry.

Lonetree was the one who was hiding something, not Sam. The Indian's plan was to stir up so much dust that Sam couldn't see. That's why the bastard asked if Rita was shot. He wanted Sam to waste his time exploring that dead-end trail.

But if Lonetree *was* hiding something, what exactly was he hiding?

Cool down. Try to think.

Why had Rita stared at her computer screen for so long? What was on the screen?

Relax, Sam. You're too damn agitated. Drink some water.

He looked at the bottle—it was manufactured by Glaceau—apple and raspberry flavored—prominent in its label was the word "defense".

Why had Selene shown that scene to him—that scene with Rita staring? She said it was a random thing, but what if she wasn't telling the truth? Was she equipped to lie? Could Selene the human-like computer tell a little white lie? What if she had shown him that scene on purpose—and didn't want to admit it?

Calm down. Calm down and the answers will come to you. They will come in gentle waves.

Say a prayer for Rita. Say it over and over again. Say it over and over again.

***

Chapter Eight: Conversations

"Sam." Selene's soothing voice woke him.

"Selene?" The office was dark and quiet. Red numbers on the clock said: 10:48 AM. He must have been sleeping. Had he dreamed anything? No, he couldn't recall any dreams.

"You fell asleep," said Selene. "I thought you might be ready to wake up."

"Yes, thanks."

He found a cup in a drawer, filled it with water, and drank some. Then he dipped three fingers in the cup and spread water over his face. Wake up, he told himself. Break time is over. Get to work.

He stared at the storm pattern rug in front of him and remembered the day he bought it. Lieutenant Garcia had mentioned an estate sale—the owner of the nearby Three Spinners Ranch had died. Sam and Garcia had driven out to the place—a big, rolling spread—they had walked into the "great room" —and there it was. Authentic, sixty years old, woven by a local Navajo woman. Sam always felt—right from the minute he saw it—that it had been woven with him in mind.

"Can I show you anything?" Selene asked.

"Sure. Why not?" He took another sip of water.

"What would you like to see?"

What would he like to see? Something about Rita, but what? He said, "Show me conversations."

"What kind of conversations?"

"People must be talking about Rita. I want to see what they're saying, I want to hear what they've said since they learned about her accident."

In a moment the bookshelves in front of him were down, and the monitors were up. The wide screen showed Dr. Adam Weizman, the base psychiatrist, talking with Father Tom House, the base chaplain. They were in the commissary having coffee and bagels.

"Rita Kelly?" said Dr. Weizman. "Yes, I heard. Terrible thing. She's a brilliant woman. I hope she makes it."

"Fascinating woman," said House. "Sometimes I think of her as a precious gem."

"Yes," said Weizman. "Fine and rare."

"But flawed. Full of radiance and luster, but deep down…"

"Deep down we all have our imperfections," said Weizman.

"All of us," agreed House.

Weizman wiped his mouth with a napkin. "You know, I was seeing her professionally."

Father House nodded. "She told me."

"Did she?" Weizman was a finely featured, perceptive man in his mid-forties. Some saw a bit of a hawk in him, a proud and wary spirit. His ancestors had been Austrian Jews, doctors and writers who fled Europe at the first sign of the Nazi menace. His interest in the breakdown of European culture during that era drove him to study people and their psychological troubles. Physically, he tried to keep fit and tough, competing at tennis and karate.

"I try every morning to avoid the bagels," said the chaplain, "but they are so tempting." He had light chocolate skin and soothing brown eyes, and was a little older and a good deal heavier than his companion. "Oscar Wilde said that the best way to defeat temptation was to give in to it. I think he was talking about bagels."

"What else did she tell you, Tom?"

The priest put down his bagel. He glanced around the commissary to make sure no one else was paying attention to them. No one was. With sincerity and compassion, with concern and care, he looked Weizman in the eyes and said in a low voice, "She told me she was having an affair with you."

"Did she?"

"Temptation can be hard to resist," said the chaplain.

Color drained from Weizman's face. He said, "It can be very hard."

The scene dissolved to an unlit computer cubicle. A blue digital clock said 10:32 AM. Rikki Greco sat at a terminal typing an e-mail to Sam, and Selene displayed the message:

> "Colonel Sawyer, I have something to tell you about Rita Kelly—something I saw on her monitor the other night when I came back to the lab to do some work. When can I talk to you about it?"

The scene changed again. Constance Hoffer, cleaning lady, wife of Staff Sergeant Gabriel Hoffer, stood by a cart saddled with cleansers and sprays, towels and brushes. She spoke to two of her co-workers, Lola and Bernice: "Well, that should end it for a while, don't you think?"

"Have you asked him about it?" said Bernice.

"He denied it for weeks—he said I was imagining things. But she used to strut her ass around here, just to let me know, like some damned animal marking off her territory." Constance had an oval face, black hair and eyes as blue as yesterday's sky. She was five foot two with a figure that she tried to keep the same as it was on her wedding day, before two kids and time's toll weighed it down.

"Talk about a nervy bitch," said Lola, an attractive young woman of color with long, red-brown hair.

"He finally admitted it," said Constance.

"You know what you should do?" said Lola. "You should look him right in the eye and say, 'I heard your friend had an accident.'"

"What was Sam Sawyer doing up on Lookout Point with that tramp?" asked Bernice, as she plugged a vacuum cleaner into a wall outlet. Sixty-eight years old, Bernice had been yearning to retire since she was sixty-two, and that unfulfilled longing showed in her weary face and in every sluggish move she made.

"Sam was probably squeezing her, too," said Lola. "Maybe he pushed her off the cliff because he was jealous of Gabriel. Maybe he wanted her all to himself."

"I wish she died," said Constance, beginning to cry. "I should have killed her myself."

The scene dissolved to another computer lab. Programmer Robby Lee picked up a pen and started doodling on the notepad in front of him. He said quietly, "Well, call me a dumb redneck, but when all the evidence is in, they're gonna find that Rita Kelly was shot."

Shot! Here's another one, thought Sam.

Dana Severn, Robby's pretty co-worker, scowled in disbelief. "I don't think so." Fair-skinned with braided yellow hair, she was just a bit taller than Robby, which is why she wore the flattest shoes she could find.

"Well, I do." Robby Lee had eyes of a color he called rebel grey. He had a well-shaped, good-natured face, big strong teeth and a thick Texas accent.

"Shot by whom?" asked Dana.

He sketched a bull's eye on his pad and colored in the center dot. "You might think I'm saying this out of jealousy, but I'm not. I say it was our Deputy Director of Computer Operations."

"Andrei?"

Robby Lee said, "That's right."

"I don't believe that."

"Do you think it was a good idea to put a Russian immigrant in his position?"

Dana said, "He's very good at his job."

Robby frowned. "Yeah, if his job is sabotaging this base."

Dana tried a different tack. "He's not as good at programming as you are, Robby."

Robby tapped his finger on the desk. "Andrei Ulanov has been a security risk since the day he arrived."

"And you think he shot Rita to screw up the Hecate project?"

"That's right. On orders from Moscow."

"Oh, Robby."

"Think about it. The Hecate system was designed to shoot down Russia's entire nuclear strike force. The Kremlin wants it disabled."

She scrunched up her face. "It wouldn't be so easy. I mean to shoot Rita and get away with it."

"Andrei was a sniper in the Russian army—that's what I heard. Those guys can hit a bull's eye from 50 meters away. And they know how to sneak up on you."

She saw a chance to tease him. "The girls say Andrei has a great big rifle hanging over his bed – a John Wayne special – and it has one notch on it for every woman he's conquered. They say he's a man's man."

"Ruskie fag, more like," said Robby, spitting out the insult.

"No way!"

"I heard he's got himself a boyfriend."

She laughed and said, "Robby, did you ever put any notches on your little pistol?"

"I'll be glad to show you, ma'am." He drew a pistol on his pad and started notching it.

Dana said, "But rather than shoot Rita, wouldn't it be easier for Andrei to just mess up his own programming? Wouldn't that cripple the system just as well?"

"He couldn't do that with old Robby Lee checking up on him."

"And you've been doing that?"

"I sure have, sister. I've been checking his work ever since he came here."

She said quietly, "I heard he was having an affair with her."

Robby shrugged and drew more notches. "You always shoot the one you love."

"Robby," asked Dana, smiling, "when you mentioned jealousy before, did you mean you might be jealous that Andrei got the *job* you wanted, or jealous that he got the *girl* you wanted?"

"There's only one girl for me, baby. And say, what are you doing after work tonight?"

Dana laughed and said, "Well, I was sort of hoping that Andrei would call."

The scene switched to the base pharmacy. Pharmacist Sandra Graham was saying to Johnnie Lonetree, "She was prone to seizures. I know that for a fact."

"Was she taking medication for them?"

"She had a prescription for Tegretol." Sandra was thin as a ghost and sickly pale, with the saddest of brown eyes. Her blond hair was cut so short as to be barely visible.

"Prescribed by whom?"

"Doctor Weizman, I believe." She checked her computer, her bony fingers moving swiftly over the keyboard. "Yes, Adam Weizman."

Lonetree said, "And if she took too much or too little of this..."

"Tegretol."

"What could happen to her?"

Sandra said, "If she took too little, she could have the seizures. If she took too much, she could suffer dizzy spells."

"So if Doctor Weizman prescribed the wrong amount, that could have led to her fall last night."

"I didn't say he prescribed the wrong amount."

Lonetree probed her, "Or if *you* accidentally made a mistake..."

"People make mistakes," said Sandra, turning away from him to straighten some boxes on a shelf. "The patient might have taken the wrong dosage, too."

"How well do you know Sam Sawyer?"

"Not very well."

"What's he like?" asked Lonetree.

"I hardly know him," she said, crossing her arms in front of her.

Lonetree said, "Did you know that Sam Sawyer and Rita Kelly had once been close?"

"That's none of my business." She glanced at her computer screen.

"Did it bother you that he was up on Lookout Point with her last night?"

"No." Sandra shook her head and her face flushed crimson. "Why should I care?"

The wide screen next showed Sheila Mae Wood at her desk in the Security Section. Her friend Mabel Nhu, in a swivel chair, rolled over to Sheila's side. Mabel was a slender woman of Vietnamese descent, a doctor's wife, and a stylish dresser who liked to accent her outfits with pearls and gold.

"So?" said Mabel.

"So what?"

"You know what I'm talking about."

"Mabel, I've got a lot of work to do."

"No, you don't, and even if you did, it can wait."

"Wait for what?"

"Your competition is gone," she beamed. "Or at least on the way out."

Sheila Mae glowered at her. "That's terrible."

"Don't tell me you're sorry she fell." Mabel grinned. "You're not sorry. Sam believed you, but I don't."

Sheila Mae moaned, "How do I get rid of you?"

Mabel teased, "You mean, like you got rid of Rita?"

"Mabel! That's terrible."

"No, you couldn't have shot her." She chuckled. "Not with those goo-goo eyes of yours. You might have missed her and hit Sam. Ha, ha."

"I don't find this amusing."

"But you have access to master keys. You could have snuck in her room and messed with her medication."

"Medication?"

"For seizures. Sandra told me all about it. Don't pretend you didn't know."

Sheila Mae opened a binder on her desk and tried to busy herself with it.

Mabel said, "You know, a lot of guys marry their secretaries."

"I'm very busy, Mabel."

"But if you ask me, you should start dressing a little nicer."

Sheila Mae gave her a dirty look, but then glanced down at her own, cheerless outfit.

Mabel observed, "That dress looks like you found it on Garbage Night in front of the House of the Seven Gables."

"It's not so—"

"It sure is! You know, if you want to attract the bees, you gotta show them something sweet."

"Mabel!"

Mabel laughed. "And what do they call that perfume you have on—*Do Not Disturb*?"

Mabel laughed and laughed and faded from Sam's view.

Now, the wide screen in front of Sam showed the Maintenance Office, the basement home of some old, bruised furniture and three janitors: Gogo, Marty and Klang.

"When they found him," said Gogo, "he was laying right on the edge of the cliff." Gogo was thirty, mustached, wiry, with expressive, speckled green eyes that punctuated every story he told.

"Half over the edge," corrected Don Klang, a chunky powerhouse, as he stood up to stretch his legs.

Marty Pollio, their supervisor, sat at his desk and listened. Finally approaching in chronological age the sixty years he had looked since he was forty, Marty had balding white hair, sensitive blue eyes and a nose like a parrot.

Gogo paused to extract a pack of Pall Malls from the pocket of his blue uniform shirt. He lit up a cigarette and inserted the used match into an empty beer bottle.

Klang said, "Why don't you buy some better beer, Marty?" He reached into the fridge for a cold Schlitz.

"Give me one," said Gogo.

As he pulled out two beers, Klang said, "And they found *Rita* halfway down the cliff, her head smashed like a melon."

"God bless her," said Marty, making the sign of the cross on his chest.

"Jesus!" said Gogo. He untwisted the bottle cap on his beer.

"She is some good looker," said Klang. "Or at least she was before this happened."

"Do you think he pushed her?" asked Gogo.

"You better watch what you say," cautioned Marty. He straightened out some papers on his desk.

Klang said, "It doesn't make sense—Rita falls down, Sam falls down. Why is everybody falling down?" He downed some beer.

Marty said, "Listen, Holmes and Watson, leave this great mystery to Security. You two just make sure that the toilets flush."

Gogo said, "They put that guy Lonetree in charge of the inquiry."

"So I've heard," said Klang.

Gogo shifted in his brown armchair. "But Sam Sawyer's the Chief of Security, isn't he?"

"Sam's a suspect," said Klang. "He can't investigate himself."

"That Lonetree looks like a cross between Cary Grant and Cochise," offered Gogo.

"She wasn't just another dumb broad, you know," said Klang as he lowered himself onto a green vinyl couch. "She was in charge of all computer operations at this snake pit."

Marty opened his file cabinet and pulled out a folder marked "Hand Soap."

"Do you think he was squeezing her?" asked Gogo.

"No," said Klang, smiling. "Not Sam."

"You better watch what you say," said Marty. "You know what this place is like."

Klang asked Gogo, "How long you been here? Four months?"

"Three and a half."

"I've been here a long time," said Klang. "So let me tell you about Sam. Sam's a watcher, not a toucher."

"Whattaya mean?"

Klang paused a while for dramatic effect. "He's a distant sort of guy. He's not the type to get up close and personal with a woman."

"You mean he's queer?" asked Gogo.

"No, no," said Klang, making a stop sign out of his hand. "He don't get close to guys either. He just likes to watch. He's like that guy in that movie. When the broad asked him what he liked to do in bed, he said, 'I like to watch.' Same way with Sam."

"Yeah, I like to watch, too," said Gogo, "but I also like to touch what I like to watch."

"Look, Sam's been here for, what, four years?"

"Since the base opened," said Marty.

"Let's say four years. How many friends has he accumulated in that time?"

Marty answered, "I never saw him pal around with anybody before, if that's what you mean, but since Rita showed up last summer, he's been paying her quite a bit of attention."

"He's been *watching* her," said Klang, pointing with both index fingers to his own eyes.

"C'mon!" Marty waved a disapproving hand at him.

Gogo said, "Where was Rita before she came here?"

Klang answered, "She was in Washington working on Selene. Before that, I don't know."

Gogo pressed, "Marty, did Sam know Rita before she came here?"

Marty busied himself with his hand soap file, trying to keep out of their conversation. He switched on his calculator and donned his reading glasses.

"C'mon, Marty, you must know."

"Listen, leave Sam Sawyer alone. And for God's sake have a little respect for that poor girl. She's on her death bed. Have a little respect."

"Tell us," said Klang.

Marty was disappointed with their morbid curiosity. Replacing the hand soap file in his cabinet and closing the drawer, he looked around for something else to keep him safely busy. Finding no such comfort, he waited a full minute for them to turn to a different topic.

They didn't.

It is a natural impulse, when one is holding a piece of a puzzle, to want to place it where it belongs, and it is natural to want to show off a bit by revealing that which is hidden to others. Marty finally said, "Sam met Rita nine years ago at Los Alamos. They were on a tiger team trying to break through security—to test it."

"And they had an affair?" asked Gogo.

"They got very close," said Marty.

"How close?" asked Klang.

"Close enough to get engaged."

"Wow! There goes your theory," said Gogo to Klang.

Marty continued, "And then one day Sam found her in bed with Lonetree, and that was the end of that."

Gogo's mouth dropped, "Lonetree?! He was there too?"

Klang was shocked. "How did you find this out?"

"If you keep your ear to the ground long enough," said Marty, "some dirt will scamper in. Let's just say I know somebody who knew them all."

"Whoa, Rita!" said Gogo, as the seriousness of it all began to settle on him.

"And now she's dying," said Klang, "and Sam is suspect number one."

"Sam wouldn't hurt her," said Marty. "It was probably an accident."

"And this Lonetree guy, what a snake!" said Gogo. "Squeezing Sam's fiancé."

Marty said, "To make it worse, Lonetree practically grew up with Sam in South Dakota. Their fathers both worked at Ellsworth Air Force

Base at the foot of the Black Hills. Sam and Johnnie were best friends growing up."

"Womb to tomb," said Gogo.

Marty said, "Now Johnnie hates Sam, and Sam hates Johnnie."

"It makes you wonder," said Gogo, picking up this train of thought, "how the hell did they ever let her transfer here?"

"I guess the people who needed to know didn't know," said Marty.

"They should have asked the Russians," said Klang, and everybody chuckled.

"Hell," said Gogo, "the Russians know everything about this place." He picked up a nearby mop head and said, "They know this mop head is here." He toyed with it, placing it wig-like on his head.

Klang yanked it off.

"They know everything," continued Gogo, "even the top-secret stuff like how many D cell batteries it takes to fire that Buck Rogers ray gun up there."

"No, they don't," said Marty.

"They do," said Gogo.

"Who told them? You?"

"Not me. I'm as American as my Slavic ancestors," said Gogo. "Maybe Sam told them."

Turning more serious, Marty cautioned, "You better watch what you say. Sam has this room bugged. I'd bet on that."

"I know he does," said Gogo. "He's got every room bugged—every closet, every drawer. He's even got the bugs bugged. The other day I saw a cockroach walking around with a transmitter strapped to its back, and I wouldn't have thought nothing of it, but he kept saying, 'Herschel to Sam. Come in, Sam.'"

"He might be listening even now," said Marty. "And watching, too."

Gogo shuffled around the room, spying out likely places for a hidden microphone or a miniature camera. He peered up at the ceiling light. "Hi, Sam. Screw you, Sam."

Marty said, "Someday, they're gonna find your body in a freezer in Alaska."

Klang offered, "Or maybe they'll slip it into a vat at the Purina factory. Chow, chow, chow."

"I didn't mean it, Sam," said Gogo to a flashlight. "I love you. I love Rita, too. I even squeezed her once or twice."

"You're bad," said Klang.

Marty shook his head, "You guys make fun of Sam, but I like him. I like him better than you two."

Gogo took a drag on his cigarette and sighed. He sat down again and put his feet up on the coffee table. Klang studied the label on his beer bottle. Marty just sat there, thinking. And for a while nobody talked.

Then Gogo said, "As I always say when somebody nice has a bad accident: better her than me."

Marty said, "God bless her. All kidding aside, God bless her."

Sam stared at their images on his central screen. "You're right, Marty," he said. "God bless her." Then he pressed a button, and the central screen went black, except for the pale, reflected image of Sam Sawyer.

Sam sat there looking at himself. His image seemed so alone.

Finally, he said, "Show me Rita." And there was Rita, out of the past, unbuttoning her blouse, getting ready for bed. Beautiful Rita, in whose green eyes Sam saw a tiger's lust for life crossed with a deer's confusion. Her eyes, thought Sam, could see things as they had been, were now and would be. But somehow they weren't at home in either the past, the present, or the future. "Yes, God bless you, Rita," he said.

The door to Sam's office flew open and Sheila Mae rushed in.

Immediately, she saw the large image of Rita undressing. She watched for a while with her mouth open, then said, "Oh, my God. I guess I shoulda knocked."

"What is it?" said Sam, embarrassed, switching off the display.

"They just found Rikki Greco with a knife in his back."

"What!?" asked Sam. His embarrassment quickly turned to shock. "Is he dead?"

"Dead and gone."

"Oh, Jesus!"

"We don't know who did it, Sam."

The red clock said 11:18 AM.

Sam's mind raced and he said, "Well, there's a quick way to find out."

"What do you mean?"

His voice shook as he said, "Selene."

"Yes, Sam."

His question was simple and direct, "Who murdered Rikki Greco?"

"I'm sorry, Sam," said Selene. "That information is classified."

***

Chapter Nine: Deep Grey

Far below the hot surface of the desert lay a vast spherical chamber known as Deep Grey. Its immense interior had been excavated out of solid bedrock, and its circumference plated with a four-inch thick skin of high-strength steel. Filling up the bottom half of the sphere was an "island" of steel, deck upon deck of computer banks and communications equipment, all suspended by huge springs and massive pistons. These computer banks might be thought of as Selene's "little grey cells," and the communications gear was her instantaneous link to the nationwide Hecate strategic defense system. Theoretically, Deep Grey and its equipment could withstand an assault by a hydrogen bomb, though that had never been tested. It was a special place, vital to the security of the homeland. Normally, there was only one way to gain access to it—via four speedy elevators. But as all who worked in it knew, there was also an emergency staircase which could be used in the unlikely event that the complex's main electric power and two backup systems went out. The elevators and the staircase were guarded constantly, above and below, by cameras, hidden weapons, and a small squad of humanoid robots, all controlled by Selene.

The top deck of the "island" was the command deck, also called DG1 for Deep Grey One. Atop DG1 sat a small raised platform crowned by a trinity of swivel chairs, the esteemed perches of the Director of Computer Operations Rita Diana Kelly and her two chief assistants, Deputy DCO Andrei Ulanov and Director of Directed Energy Weapons Rikki Greco. Below and around those seats of power, the designers had dispersed desks for technicians and programmers, and tall monoliths of electronic circuitry.

Above DG1 was the high, wide, surface of the dome, on which was usually projected an image of the sky as it existed over Altamura Air Force Base. Like the real sky above, this curved screen was ordinarily blue during the day, and black and starry at night. However, the architects who designed the dome had installed one illustrious feature to remind the men and women who toiled under it of the importance of their task. At the top of every hour, a parade of images danced across the artificial sky—random pictures of America and her people—a rolling river, a steel worker riveting, cornfields, mountains, a hot dog vendor, a mother serving lunch to her kids, a teacher explaining fractions to his class, boys playing baseball, girls jumping into the surf. Even the families of the Deep Grey crew flashed by occasionally, and the message behind all this was simple: here is what you are protecting, so do your job well.

Under deck DG1 were the less grandiose though still important decks DG2, DG3, DG4, etc., each smaller in area than the one above it as they approached the shrinking limits of the sphere's bottom.

Rikki Greco's body had been found on DG3, slumped at an L-shaped desk in a dimly lit cubicle which served as his office. A knife was stuck in the back of his neck, parting his long, blond tresses. His computer was on—a screensaver showed incoming alien ships being zapped by ground-based lasers. A bottle of Dasani Plus water stood next to the keyboard; its label proclaiming, "vitamin-enhanced, tangerine-flavored—*defend + protect*."

"Who found him?" asked Sam Sawyer as he examined the handle of the knife.

Lieutenant Mario Garcia answered, "Mr. Ulanov discovered the body." Garcia had thick black hair and a noble Mexican face; he was a bit overweight, but strong and tough.

"I see," said Sam, turning to scrutinize Andrei Ulanov, who hovered nearby with tears on his cheeks and redness in his eyes. "How did you happen to find him, Mr. Ulanov?"

"He left a message on my room phone, saying he wanted to see me. He said it was important." Ulanov's Russian accent was not as thick as it had been when he first immigrated to America, but it was still noticeable.

"On your room phone as opposed to your cell phone."

"Right."

"You weren't there when he called?"

"No."

"Where were you?"

"I had a tennis match with Dr. Weizman. We finished around 10:30, then I went back to my apartment."

"You gentlemen don't work in the morning?"

"On Mondays I start work at 1:00 PM. Weizman starts around the same time. We try to play tennis every Monday morning."

"Did you have a cell phone with you when you were playing?"

"No, I kept it in my room, in the top drawer."

"So, if Mr. Greco tried to call your cell phone—"

"It's still in the drawer."

"Did Weizman go with you to your room?"

"No. I went home alone. When I got in, I headed right for the shower. I was sweaty and hot. After I showered, I shaved and started to dress."

"Uh-huh."

"I mixed a drink for myself—and as I started drinking it, I sat at my computer—that's when I noticed the little blinking light on the phone."

"That told you there was a message."

"Yes, that's right. It was from Rikki."

"What did the message say?" asked Sam.

"He said, 'Andrei, this is Rikki. I'm down on DG3. I've found something you should take a look at. Something important. Come by as soon as you can. Actually, come by right now.'"

Lieutenant Garcia asked, "At what time did you listen to his message?"

"It must have been a little before eleven."

"Did you come here right away?" asked Sam.

"Yes, I finished dressing and came right down."

"And you found him like this?"

Ulanov's eyes drifted to the lifeless Rikki Greco. "Jesus Christ," he said. "He thought he was going to live forever."

"Why do you say that?" asked Garcia.

"Rikki trained constantly. He ran every day, lifted weights, swam laps, followed a strict diet, took care of himself to the point of fanaticism. He worshipped his body, really."

"I see," said Garcia.

"He told me once that he was very sick as a kid. He never wanted to be sick like that again."

Sam knew the story. Young Rikki Greco had been morbidly allergic to almost every food in the chain, and when advances in genetic medicine unshackled him from his allergies, Rikki was determined to reform his body. His models ranged from Olympic athletes to Greek demigods.

"You know," said Ulanov, "he was starting to read about cloning as a way to replace defective body parts so he could keep his machine going forever. And now look at him."

Lieutenant Garcia asked, "When you found the body, was anyone else around?"

Andrei said, "There was someone working three or four cubicles to the left, but no one closer."

"Did you touch anything?"

"No. I saw right away that he was dead."

"And you called Security at 11:13 AM—is that right?"

Andrei nodded. "I called from the next cubicle. I called the Deep Grey security desk."

Sam said, "It takes a certain amount of strength to plunge a hunting knife through bone and muscle and nerves." Andrei was strong enough, Sam thought.

Ulanov's wary expression showed that he guessed what Sam was thinking.

Garcia said, "Doctor Winter should be here any minute. He can give us an estimate of the time of death."

As Garcia finished speaking, an unwelcome intruder made his presence known to the assembled crew. "My, my," said Johnnie Lonetree. "Is anybody safe around here?" Stepping over to the body, he studied it for a moment and declared, "I think we can rule out suicide."

It would be inaccurate to say that Sam was amused.

Lonetree leveled his gaze at Colonel Sawyer and said, "Maybe it was an accident, like Rita's fall."

Lieutenant Garcia pointed to the knife and the dark patch of blood staining Rikki Greco's hair, neck, shirt and back. "It looks like the killer held the knife in his right hand."

A security guard snapped a series of pictures of the dead man.

"The blade must have severed nerves right away, paralyzing Greco," continued Garcia. "Greco was strong and in good shape, but that wouldn't have mattered. It would have been all over. Impossible to move. Without those nerves, impossible even to breathe."

Ulanov moaned, "Oh, God, what did they do to you?"

"That's quite a knife," said Lieutenant Garcia, "a bowie knife." It had a staghorn handle about five inches long, and a brass guard. Garcia noted, "*R.G.* engraved on the handle. Rikki Greco."

"It's his," said Ulanov. "He used it as a letter opener."

Lonetree said, "It's your job to protect these people, isn't it, Sam? Isn't that what they pay you for?"

Sam said to Garcia, "I want the area dusted for fingerprints."

Lonetree stated, "I'd like a copy of that fingerprint report, too."

Sam's frustration with the entire situation—Rita's fall, Greco's murder, Selene's refusal to answer vital questions—was beginning to take its toll. What the hell was going on here? Who murdered Rikki Greco and why? Was Lonetree somehow at the bottom of all this? That sounded far-fetched. But what was this all about anyway? Sam stared hard at Lonetree and asked, "Where were *you* when this man was killed?"

Lonetree laughed, "Very good, Sam. The best defense is a good offense."

"Where *were* you?" asked Sam with more intensity.

"Sam! This man is a complete stranger to me. Do you think I'd murder a complete stranger?"

"Johnnie, can you try answering my question?" His voice rose and his face reddened.

"I work for DARPA, Sam. Not for you. As soon as I leave this cubicle, I'm going to inform my superiors of Mr. Greco's unfortunate demise. They won't be happy with the way you're doing your job."

"He was a stranger to you, but you knew his name." observed Sam.

Lonetree mocked him, "The Lieutenant just said it a hundred times. Didn't you hear him? Have your hearing checked, Sam."

"Colonel Sawyer," interrupted Garcia, "when you think about it, there's an easy way to find out who murdered Rikki Greco."

All eyes and attention shifted to Garcia, who continued, "All we have to do is ask Selene."

Sam studied Garcia carefully. How much did he know about the miniaturized security cameras that were placed all over the base? Did he know that Selene had seen the actual murder? "What do you mean?" asked Sam.

Garcia explained, "There's a security camera in the passageway outside this compartment. Selene might have recorded who was in the passage around the time of Greco's death."

"She might have," said Sam.

There was a hint of a grin on Lonetree's face, and Sam wondered at its significance. Did the Indian know that it was fruitless for Sam to ask Selene? Had Lonetree programmed Selene to deny Sam and others access to information regarding this murder?

Lonetree said, "Yes, that's a good idea."

It must have been Lonetree, thought Sam. He had the technical skills, and he had a motive. Greco was going to reveal something, something about Rita. What was it Greco had written in his e-mail? *"Colonel Sawyer, I have something to tell you about Rita Kelly—something I saw on her monitor the other night when I came back to the lab to do some work."*

Lonetree continued, "Selene should be able to help."

Sam's memory turned another corner and there was Sheila Mae telling him, in the presence of Lonetree, *"Colonel Sawyer, Rikki Greco called. He said it was important. I told him you were in a meeting. He said he'd send you an e-mail."* That was right after the interrogation. Lonetree must have wondered what Rikki wanted to tell Sam. As soon as he left Sam's office, he must have intercepted the e-mail and decided that Greco must be silenced. But why?

Garcia said, "What do you say, Colonel? Should we ask Selene?"

But how would Lonetree know where Greco was? mused Sam. He must have asked Selene, and she told him he's in Deep Grey.

Lonetree said, "Well, Sam?"

Sam's mind raced: Lonetree came down here looking for Rikki. Maybe he spoke with him to be sure he had the right man... He saw the knife on Rikki's desk... He grabbed it and plunged it into Rikki's neck—a cold steel surprise for the blond Adonis. And then, having murdered Greco, he would have to silence Selene as well.

Ulanov wailed, "The killer could be getting away!"

Sam said to Garcia, "When you check for fingerprints, make sure you check the mouse and the keyboard."

"Fingerprints?!" shouted Ulanov. "Just ask Selene now!"

Sam collected his thoughts, waited for quiet. Lonetree, Garcia, and Ulanov analyzed him. A small crowd of programmers, technicians and guards had gathered in the area as well, including Robby Lee and Dana Severn. All these waited for his next words.

"I have already asked Selene," he said.

"And?"

"She told me that the information is classified—classified above even *my* level."

"What?!"

"Selene is not going to help us on this one," said Sam.

"Why not? I don't understand," said Ulanov.

"Because someone has programmed her to keep her mouth shut. Someone who knows computers. Knows what it takes to bypass Selene's security."

Ulanov stated, "Not many people could have broken through that security." His eyes burned into Lonetree but he did not voice his assessment of that man's computer skills.

And you and Johnnie are two of them, thought Sam.

Lieutenant Garcia asked, "But why kill Greco? What was the motive?"

At first, Sam was not sure whether to offer the bit of information he held about Greco's e-mail. Finally, he took a chance that it might make someone worry and said, "Rikki Greco notified me today that he had something to tell me about Rita Kelly."

"Something like what?" asked the Russian.

"I don't know."

"And you think Rikki was murdered for that—to stop him from telling some secret about Rita?"

Sam thought about the question and the questioner, about the murdered Director of Directed Energy Weapons, about Rita staring at her monitor, about Selene's refusal to answer certain questions. He said, "Yes, I think he was."

Lonetree waited, expressionless, for the crowd to focus on Greco, then he started to slip away. But Andrei Ulanov stepped after him, caught him by the arm, and said, "Maybe the DARPA man can help us."

Lonetree tried to brush Ulanov's hand away, but the Russian tightened his grip. The Indian said, "I won't run away, Sport."

Ulanov let go and said, "You're a big man at DARPA. Maybe your clearance is high enough to get the truth out of Selene."

"I doubt it. Our murderer seems like a pretty clever fellow. If he could block out Sam, he could block out me."

"It's worth a try," said Garcia.

"Yes," said Sam. "It *is* worth a try." Was Lonetree caught in a trap? Would Selene answer him in front of all these people?

Lonetree sighed. "Selene, can you tell us who was prowling in the hallway around the time of the murder?"

Selene's disembodied voice seemed oddly at home here in Deep Grey. "Mr. Lonetree, there are several people here who don't have sufficient clearance to hear this discussion."

"That's true," agreed Lonetree, "but it can't be helped. This murder has turned us against each other to such an extent that the answer must come out now—for the base to function. I want you to answer me. Can you tell us who was prowling DG3 around the time of the murder?"

Selene testified: "Whatever was filmed by these hall cameras has been erased from my memory banks."

"Oh, my God," whispered Dana Severn.

"Can it be unerased?" asked Lonetree.

"No. It was wiped clean."

"Do you know who killed Rikki Greco?"

Selene hesitated. "Unfortunately, I do not."

Lonetree pressed her, "Selene, did *I* kill Rikki Greco?"

"I know of no proof that you did," said the computer.

***

In the early afternoon, in the dark comfort of his office, with door locked and monitors up, Sam asked, "Selene, who killed Rikki Greco?"

"I'm sorry, Sam, but as I mentioned before, that information... if I even knew it... is classified beyond your level."

Beyond *my* level, thought Sam, but not beyond Johnnie's. She hadn't told Johnnie that *his* clearance was too low. "Selene, who directed that any information about Greco's death should be hidden from me?"

"I can't tell you. That information is also classified."

Sam said, "You told Lonetree in the presence of several witnesses that you did not know who killed Greco."

"That's true. I really don't know."

Sam had an idea. "Where was Johnnie Lonetree when Rikki Greco was killed?"

"That information is classified."

"I see." Convenient, thought Sam. What does Lonetree have to hide? If he's hiding something, does that incriminate him?

"How about Andrei Ulanov. Where was he when Greco was stabbed?"

Ulanov's image filled the wide screen. He was standing in his room, half dressed, drinking from a tall, ice-filled glass.

"That's what Ulanov was doing?"

"Yes, Sam. To the best of my knowledge."

"So he has an alibi, and you can vouch for him," said Sam.

"If you put it that way."

Sam's phone rang and he picked it up.

"Sam," said Sheila Mae. "Lonetree's on line two. He says it's important."

"Put him through."

Lonetree's voice came over the phone, "DARPA is sending a coroner to examine Rikki Greco. They asked me to pass that information on to you."

Sam offered no remark. Was it a bad sign that DARPA had chosen to communicate with him not directly but through Johnnie Lonetree?

"The Inspector General is coming out, too. He's very interested in this case."

Sam said, "I asked Selene about Greco's murder again."

"Oh?"

"She told me again that the information was classified beyond my level."

"Computers can be difficult, Sam. I've learned that over the years."

"Then I asked her your whereabouts at the time of the crime. She told me that that information is also classified."

"Did she?" said Lonetree.

"Then I asked about Ulanov, and Selene showed him in his apartment—nowhere near Rikki Greco."

"And your conclusion?"

"Ulanov didn't kill Greco, but maybe you did."

"Well, to tell you the truth, Sam, I didn't. Honest Injun."

"Can you give me one good reason why I shouldn't call DARPA now and tell them I suspect you?"

"There are other possibilities," said Lonetree.

"Such as?"

"First, you seem to have some suspicions about Ulanov. I can guess why. Has it occurred to you that Ulanov might have had an accomplice—someone who did the knife work while Andrei did the computer work?"

Unlikely, thought Sam.

"And second, there are others besides Ulanov and myself who were capable of breaching Selene's security."

Sam immediately thought of programmers Robby Lee and Dana Severn. There might be others as well.

"Third, whoever killed Greco and covered it up by muzzling Selene might have made Selene show you distortions to confuse you."

"Distortions?"

"Let's say Ulanov was the murderer. You ask Selene to show what he was doing at the time of the stabbing. Selene shows you Ulanov far away and innocent. How can that be? Because he has ordered Selene to fool you."

Lonetree was right. Sam could rely on Selene to tell no lies except for the lies she had been ordered to tell.

"Don't you just hate it when I'm right, Sam?" Lonetree waited for a reply, and when none came, he hung up.

Selene's voice came out of the speakers, "Sam?"

"Yes."

"It's been a rather difficult time for me."

"I know, Selene."

"You know that I would never deliberately mislead you."

"I know."

"I've done some work on the recording I made of you and Rita. The lightning strike scrambled it, but I was able to piece most of it together."

"Thanks. I'd like to see what you have. Can you play it for me?"

"Yes, Sam."

The office darkened. A ghostly image appeared on the wide screen: a false-colored Sam and a spectral Rita stood uncertainly on Lookout Point. The emotional effect on the real Sam was more than he expected: his nerves tensed, his stomach tightened, his heart felt as if it were being squeezed in a vise.

"It was filmed with an infrared camera," said Selene. "That's why the colors are distorted."

The recorded voices were scratchy but audible. Sam could hear himself say, "It's good to be safe, Rita, but maybe it's better to be touched."

Sam remembered Rita's mention of the South Dakota plains; he remembered the desert air charging with electricity.

"Anyway, Rita, I'm letting down the drawbridge," said the electronic Sam. "I'm hoping that you're ready to cross."

As the rain and wind smacked at her, he had asked her, "Do you love me, Rita?"

The thunder roared and Sam, sitting in his darkened office, heard Rita say, "No, Sam." It hurt him to watch their bodies tensing against the static-filled air and the gusting wind.

The wind lashed Rita once again, and the charge in the air intensified. Terrified anew, Sam and Rita were unable to respond with anything but fear.

Sam the watcher brooded in his dark hideaway as once more Rita Diana Kelly lost her balance, put her hands up to her head, succumbed to an invisible push, and fell backwards.

The onscreen Sam reached out to her, but Rita fell just beyond the range of his outstretched hand. And then the screen turned white and thunder blasted through Sam's office.

"That's all I have," said Selene.

Sam was too stunned to say anything. He felt like he had lost Rita a second time—and the wounds to his psyche, just beginning to heal, had been ripped open again.

He was numb, as if he had been seared anew by lightning. Nothing was in focus.

What had he seen? What had he learned?

Had there been a shot? He didn't think so. Had something struck Rita? A small pellet? A rock hurled by the wind? Possibly.

Again, why had she grabbed at her head?

She was taking medication. Maybe she took too much. Perhaps the static in the air unhinged her somehow.

The video recording did not tell enough. There was still more than one way to interpret what happened up there, Sam thought.

And another question entered his grey cells: Could he rely on what Selene was showing him? Could she have contorted these images to mislead him? Might she have fabricated a virtual reality that was just a bit different from the original? Why would she do that?

Perhaps because she was ordered to. Selene was proving to be a rather unreliable witness.

"Selene, show it again," said Sam, and the computer complied, and the spectral Rita considered his question one more time.

***

Chapter Ten: Andrei Ulanov

In his office, Sam Sawyer had two files laid out across his desk—Rikki Greco's and Andrei Ulanov's. He was studying Ulanov's stint in the Russian Army when the phone interrupted his research and he answered it. "Hello."

"Lieutenant Garcia here. We're at Greco's apartment."

"What have you learned, Mario?"

"We got the results on the prints. The knife had two of the victim's fingerprints on it, and one of Andrei Ulanov's. Otherwise, pretty clean."

Sam said, "So, either Ulanov was the killer, or the killer wore gloves."

"That's what I figure."

"So where are the gloves?"

"We're looking for them."

"How about the keyboard?"

"As far as the keyboard is concerned, no prints except Rikki Greco's. Same with the mouse."

Sam said, "I thought maybe the killer used Greco's computer to communicate with Selene."

"You mean to order Selene to reclassify stuff?"

"That's right."

"And to screw up her own memory systems?"

"That's what I was thinking."

"He might have, Sam. Or, he could have issued his orders verbally—whispered into a smart phone? Who knows?"

"Tell me about Greco's apartment."

"Well, naturally, we found the victim's prints all over the place."

"O.K."

"And we found Andrei Ulanov's prints on a lot of stuff."

"Well, they were friends. That's not surprising."

"Yeah, they were friends all right."

"What kind of stuff did you find?" asked Sam.

"We found some interesting magazines and videos."

"Magazines?" said Sam cautiously.

"Yeah. The kind with lots of pictures of men."

"I see."

"Sometimes you wonder how these guys got security clearance."

Yes, thought Sam, sometimes I wonder how a lot of people got security clearances.

Two minutes after he rang off with Garcia, Sam watched Andrei Ulanov on the large central screen. Ulanov lay on a herringboned couch in Adam Weizman's office. His face was wet from crying and pale from trauma and depression. "Adam," he said, "I'm falling to pieces."

"You've had two shocks in two days," said Weizman, "first Rita, now Rikki."

"I'm falling," said Ulanov. "I'm falling like a man off a bridge, tumbling and plunging." He gazed around the softly lit room at the paintings and photographs that hung on the sand-colored walls. Much of the artwork showed serene scenes that invited the viewer into them: a snowy path in a forest, a smoothly flowing Irish stream, a sailboat on a quiet bay.

One of the prints intrigued Sam whenever he saw it—the background was beige, and the subject, a stylized line drawing of a man's head in profile, was rendered in brown. Inside that brown head grew branches and leaves, and a green snake slithered along a limb in the midst of it all. Sam wondered if the artist had read Carl Sagan's book, *The Dragons of Eden*. In that book, Sagan theorized that human brains evolved over time, and that since our distant ancestors were reptiles, the core of our brains is reptilian. As we evolved into more advanced animals, as we progressed up the Darwinian tree, nature wrapped overlays onto that brain core. But, to some extent, we humans still think and act and react like our reptile progenitors. Or had the artist simply remembered the *Book of Genesis?*

"Tell me what you feel and I will listen," said Weizman, who sat on a chestnut-leather armchair behind Andrei's head. "That's what I'm here for."

"If you saw him down there, down in that grey tomb, with a knife in his neck—the knife I gave him—you'd find it hard to talk, too." Here he burst into a spasm of sobbing as he re-pictured the grisly sight. He cried and cried, and his lungs heaved with anguish. Then he uttered a silent scream of pain, as he recalled the love and the friendship of this man he had lost. He wanted and demanded that what was true not be true, and that Rikki Greco be returned to him, handsome and clever and alive. And he knew that was impossible.

In spite of his natural skepticism, Sam was moved by Andrei's outpouring of emotions.

"Have some water," said Weizman, and he offered him a bottle of Dasani: the label on the bottle featured pomegranates and the words *cleanse + restore.* Ulanov sat up and drank and waited for his body to stop heaving.

"Rita's alive," said Weizman. "That's something good we can focus on."

"But in a coma," said the Russian. "One foot in the grave."

"We're going to pull her out. A team of good doctors and you and I—we're all going to pull her out of that grave."

"I hope so," said Ulanov, holding his head. "I hope so."

"You were close to her."

Ulanov closed his eyes. "I was more than close."

Weizman sat back in his chair. He collected his thoughts, marshalled his powers, and in a careful voice, intended to sound neither probing nor judgmental, he stated, “You and Rita were lovers.”

Ulanov leaned back on the couch and let his memories of Rita Kelly rise into his mind like steam ascending from a hot spring. “Yes. Yes, we made love several times. I tried to be her friend, but she was... difficult to get close to emotionally.”

Weizman said, “Yes.”

“Her beauty was like a golden wall around her. Most people who saw it wanted to possess the gold, but it was more wall than gold.”

“That’s an interesting way of looking at it.”

“Adam, she used her beauty like a shell—to protect what was inside. To protect what was really Rita.”

Sam, in his dark office, listened and watched. A distant memory tramped onstage in the theater of his mind: he and Rita were in a Mexican restaurant on the outskirts of Los Alamos—several weeks after they first met—and Sam was asking her about her family.

In Weizman’s office, Ulanov continued, “And what was Rita? Who was this person that needed so much protecting? Well, first, she was an incredibly sensual being. Sometimes, when I was near her, I thought of Marilyn Monroe. But maybe that, too, was an image she projected.”

“A mirage?”

“She was vulnerable. She felt guilty about something. She felt unworthy.”

“You keep saying ‘was’. Let’s not forget that she is still alive.”

“Yes,” said Ulanov. “Thank God for that. God willing, she will again be what she once was. Maybe she’ll be happier than she was.”

“You don’t think she was happy?”

“She tried. She tried to be happy with this man, with that man. She was never successful.”

Weizman paused, perhaps to give Andrei time to ponder Rita, perhaps to think about her himself. When the moment seemed right, he started on a different line. "And Rikki?" he said.

"Rikki was my partner. We loved each other." Ulanov let that statement hang in the air as long as it could, a fading testament to a lost companion. Then he asked, "You'll keep this in confidence?"

Sam heard Weizman say, "Our conversations will not leave this room."

"We met shortly after I came over from Russia."

The psychiatrist shifted in his chair. "Tell me about Russia. Why did you leave it?"

"I grew up in a small village, Starover, maybe three hours east of Moscow. Starover was a pretty place, with real charm... colorful wooden houses, a fine old church with three onion domes. It was a good place to grow up, in some ways. Everybody knew each other. Everybody cared about each other."

"Sounds peaceful."

"But in other ways, it was insular, intolerant."

"Intolerant of what?"

"Intolerant of outside ideas. You could almost say allergic to things that were new or different. They distrusted anything they weren't used to—educated women, for example. They were afraid of Jews, even though there were hardly any Jews for miles around... They hated communists and capitalists equally."

"I see."

"They hated homosexuals, too. They were terrified of the modern world. They had a way of life that they loved, and they wanted to protect it. A good way—God's way, in their eyes. And if you were on their side, you were good. But if they saw you as different, if they saw you as a threat..."

Weizman waited, then asked, "When did you realize that you were gay?"

"I would say bisexual," said Ulanov.

"Of course," said Weizman. "I'm sorry."

"You might find it funny, but I don't think of myself as a fairy. I think of myself as a strong man. A man's man. I guess I'm fooling myself."

"You *are* a strong man," said Weizman. "Strong in many ways."

"I guess I left the village of Starover, but the village never left me. The village rules me still."

"The values, you mean. You were taught to like certain things, to dislike other things, behave a certain way."

"That's right."

"The people of Starover impressed on your mind their idea of masculinity."

"Yes, they were very good at that."

"Was your father like them?"

"My father was a good man. He was a soldier, a sniper. He taught me how to shoot and fish. He taught me to love guns. But he died when I was fourteen. No time is good for a father to die, but fourteen is a very bad time."

"I'm sorry," said Weizman.

"By the time I joined the army, when I was eighteen, I knew. I knew that I was attracted to men, and to some women as well, but mainly men. In the army I had plenty of opportunity."

Weizman asked, "And when you got out of the army, you went back home?"

"Yes, but little by little, the townsfolk heard rumors about things I did when I was soldiering. They began to suspect me. They began to consider me an outsider, someone to distrust, someone to shun."

"So you left Starover."

"I had to leave. They would have made life miserable for me and for my mother. They had already started to ridicule me."

"Moscow must have been an easier place for you to be yourself."

"It was, yes. Moscow is a grand place, full of culture, full of all kinds of people. Museums, theaters, nightclubs. I went to university there—got my degree. But I wanted even more freedom, and I wanted change, and adventure."

"So you came to America."

"When I was twenty-four, I came to the land of the free. Free to be all you can be. Free to be without neighbors who care about you enough to shun you." He smiled.

"There's some truth in that," said Weizman.

"And after a while, here in Arizona, I met Rikki Greco—a virile fantasy of a man. I fell in love with him, and he with me, and we have been together for more than eight years. I don't know how I will live without him."

"Do you keep in touch with anyone back home? Back in Russia, I should have said."

"My mother—she's getting old now, old beyond her years—that's about it. A Christmas card or two from college friends."

"I see."

They sat in silence for some time, then Weizman asked, "Have they figured out who killed Rikki?"

"Sam Sawyer seems to have a few suspects."

"Oh?"

"And one of those suspects is me."

"That's absurd," said Weizman. "You loved the man."

"Rikki gave me something to live for. Killing him would be like killing myself. No, I didn't kill him. I would have fought to the death to protect him."

"But someone did kill him."

Ulanov selected his words carefully. "Yes, someone who is crouching and ready to attack. Attack this base and this country."

He rose to his feet.

"Attack this base?" Weizman asked.

"Rikki discovered the plot. That's why he was killed. The schemer realized that Rikki knew."

"That's a frightening thought. Do you have any proof?"

"An evil day is coming, Adam," said Andrei Ulanov.

"Have you told Sam Sawyer about... your theory?"

"If I thought he would believe me, I would gladly tell him."

Watching in his own office, Sam felt like a sailor on a storm-tossed ship, with fierce waves crashing in from every direction. *Who wants to attack this base? Who wants to attack this country?*

"You should tell him anyway," asserted Weizman.

Sam considered: Is Andrei hallucinating out of grief? Has he lost his bearings? Or is he tossing red herrings into the sea for us to follow? Is Andrei himself the plotter?

Sam said to Selene, "Has Mr. Ulanov stayed in contact with people in Russia? With relatives in that little village? Or, with friends in Moscow?"

Selene said, "Andrei sends and receives an occasional letter from his mother. He also communicates regularly by e-mail with a man in Moscow named Bronislav Kobylin."

"Kobylin. Yes, I've seen some of those."

"Would you like to see them again?"

"Show me the last one he received."

Selene said, "Translated from the Russian," then she showed this on Sam's central monitor:

"FROM: KOBYLIN_B
TO: ULANOV_A

My dearest Andrei,

When can you visit me again? I wish they never made you go.
I dream only of you. Please tell me you will come back soon.

Love
Bronislav"

Sam noticed that *they made him go*. It's not that he wanted to go. Someone made him go—made Andrei Ulanov leave Russia and come to the US. Did the Russian government make him? In any case, on this one point Ulanov had bent the truth—or lied—to Weizman.

Sam said, "Show me the latest e-mail from Andrei to Kobylin," and Selene complied.

"FROM: ULANOV_A
TO: KOBYLIN_B

Bronislav,

It was good to hear from you again.

I think of you often and of the good times we had at the Ranch. When I finish a little project I am working on, I'll come and say hello.

Sincerely,
Andrei"

Sam wondered, what is the "little project I am working on"? And who is Bronislav Kobylin?

Ulanov continued his session with psychiatrist Weizman, but Sam had so much to think about already: Andrei was certainly capable of reprogramming Selene. He knew enough about computers to initiate new levels of security that could block Sam's access. He could erase Selene's memory or even change it, distort it.

Sam heard Ulanov say, "I don't trust him. I know he works for DARPA, but even DARPA can be infiltrated."

"But you have no proof."

"When I look at him, I sense something evil."

He's talking about Lonetree, Sam reckoned. Andrei is either telling the truth, or trying to pull some wool over Weizman's eyes. Maybe he's hoping that Weizman will come running to me.

Andrei Ulanov was an immigrant from Russia, a sniper in the Russian army. Maybe he still worked for that army. He could have shot some kind of a pellet or a rubber bullet at Rita, causing her to lose her balance and fall. He was homosexual, or bisexual, a category of people often considered by counter-intelligence staff to be security risks.

Weizman said, "I'm going to prescribe something for you." He took a small pad and began writing on it. "It's to help you get through the next few days. That's when the grief will be most intense. That's when the depression will strike. You won't get addicted to it, so don't worry about that."

The tears seemed real enough, thought Sam. Yes, he did love Rikki Greco. At least that much was true.

"Thank you, Adam."

"And I want to see you every day. My office is open to you whenever you need help. We'll work this through."

"That doesn't seem possible," Andrei sobbed.

Maybe Andrei tried to mess up Selene's programming, and Rita found out. Maybe he was ordered to take Rita out of the picture. Maybe Rikki Greco noticed something was wrong, and Ulanov decided that Greco, lover or not, was a threat to his plan.

That's a lot of maybes.

"People do it," said Weizman. "We've been doing it since we first realized what death is. Since we were first speared by the thought that we'll never see our loved one again. Somehow we've developed ways of getting through it."

"By telling ourselves stories?" asked Ulanov.

"Selene," said Sam.

"Yes?"

"Andrei and Rikki—did they quarrel much lately?"

Instead of telling him, Selene showed Sam a recent scene from Greco's room. Greco, sitting on the edge of his bed, was saying, "I know about Kobylin, too."

Ulanov, standing in front of him, was angry and ashamed at the same time. "Who told you about him?"

"Yes, Bronislav Kobylin, your little fag friend from the Ranch."

Ulanov grabbed Greco's long blond hair and twisted it. "Who told you?"

"Let go of my hair," said Greco, "and get the hell out of my room."

"You've had a lover or two, yourself," hissed Ulanov. "Should we talk about them?"

"Get out of my room," said the late Rikki Greco.

The screen faded to black.

Sam was stunned. Ulanov had almost hit Greco right there. Who was this Kobylin character? How had Greco found out about him? Had Andrei Ulanov really killed Rikki Greco to cover up some Russian plot? Too many things to think about.

And then, thought Sam, there's still my old friend, Johnnie Lonetree.

***

Chapter Eleven: Kachina

There were too many things for Sam Sawyer to think about as he sat in his office Monday afternoon at 3:05 PM. Far too many things.

He felt overwhelmed by the rush of events. He was rudderless, frustrated and impatient. He wanted to help Rita right now, but there was nothing he could do. He wanted to solve his various puzzles immediately, but they weren't crosswords on the table in front of him, they were mysteries encircling him.

He had to get out of his office, get away from his monitors, go for a walk, take some action, plot some course.

It would be wrong to say he was clueless. Clues there were—but where did they lead? He had clues but no proof.

He wanted to see Rita—he *needed* to visit her in the Intensive Care Unit and hold her hand. He wanted her to wake up and smile.

Sam got out of his seat and ordered the monitors down. His office seemed dark and empty, like a starless sky.

Now what? Which course? What action?

He would bring Rita something, some small gift. But what?

He left his office and locked the door behind him. Sheila Mae looked up but said nothing as he strode out of the Security Section and into the hall beyond.

He entered an elevator, got off on the first floor, and walked past the Base Exchange. He slowed when he reached a row of small shops, and ambled into the first of them, The Dream Catcher.

Decorated in desert tones with wide plank floors and stacked stone walls, The Dream Catcher sold a variety of products at a wide range of prices. As he searched around, Sam saw jewelry under a glass case, much of it produced by artisans from local tribes. He scanned necklaces made of turquoise beads, silver lockets with the "Man in the Maze" design on them, and earrings featuring Coyote or Snake or Kokopelli.

In one corner of the shop sat two racks of wines, the first loaded with domestics from Arizona and California, the second packed with imports from Italy, Germany and Australia.

Fine Navajo rugs graced a long wall, including three of the "Eye Dazzler" style. Sam knew that these had simple geometric patterns woven into them, such as repeating chevrons or serrated triangles. They used brilliant contrasting colors—reds, greens, yellows, and blues—to entrance viewers, whose eyes involuntarily shifted among the shimmering colors and the scintillating shapes.

One shelf boasted Maka Ina Popcorn (two pounds of Lakota corn in a box shaped like a teepee), Tanka Bars made of buffalo meat and cranberries, and Natural American Spirit cigarettes (each pack sporting an Indian in a headdress smoking a peace pipe). There were two tables full of pottery, and three shelves of books. Sam saw cowboy boots and hats, leather belts and denim shirts.

He hardly glanced at the sand paintings. He had read somewhere that real Native American sand paintings are not offered for sale like trinkets; they are spiritual elements of sacred ceremonies, usually meant for healing. The Holy People or spirits enter into their own images, and then the sick person lies on top of the sand art, absorbing the blessing of the spirits. In return, the Holy People absorb the sickness. Once the painting has been used to heal someone, it is destroyed.

Near the cash register stood a glass case with six colorful dolls in it. These Kachina dolls caught Sam's attention and he strolled over to them.

The word Kachina means at least three different things. At the highest level, Kachinas are *spirit-beings* revered by most Pueblo Indians, including the Hopi and the Zuni. The Zuni believe that the Kachinas live in the mythical Lake of the Dead, while the Hopi place them in Arizona's

San Francisco Peaks. Several times a year, these powerful spirits visit the native villages to guide their people and to bring them life-giving rain. These supernatural visits are portrayed by Kachina dancers, men who dress in elaborate costumes and bring the tribe's religious beliefs to life in the Bean Dance, the Home Dance, the Night Dances, and others. Then there are the Kachina dolls, usually carved of cottonwood root and elaborately painted. Representing the helpful ancestral spirits, some of these dolls are given to native children to teach them about their culture, and some are sold to tourists and collectors.

Sam studied the six dolls in the case in front of him.

The first, all the way on the left, was a Hopi Coyote, about 10 inches tall, standing on one leg. In his right hand was a blue and white rattle; his shirt was orange and greenish-yellow; his breechcloth was white with green and orange patterns. Blue and red feathers poked out of the top of his headdress. A card at the doll's base told this story: "Spider Woman gave Coyote a pot to take care of, but she warned him not to look inside. He obeyed for as long as he could, but curiosity finally got the better of him. He peeked inside the pot—and it exploded!—creating the universe!! The explosion gave Coyote his black nose and the stars on his face."

The next Kachina doll was called Racer Snake. To Sam, it looked nothing like a snake, more like a deep-sea diver with pea-green eye ports. The doll's suit was light brown; a yellow belt crisscrossed its torso. The creature had a long black snout and brown feathers for hair, a black and white snake wrapped around its skirt. Racer Snake is a guardian spirit, his duty is to patrol the Bean Dance and the Day Dances, and to guard the dancers.

The third Kachina was a Mountain Lion Guard. To Sam he resembled a proud yellow dog walking on two legs, striding forward, holding a bow in his left hand and an arrow in his right. Lion carried a quiver full of arrows across his back. Carved into the stand below his feet was a cliffside dwelling built of brick.

The fourth doll was Kokopelli, the Humpbacked Flute Player, possibly the most famous of the Kachinas. A fertility god and a mischievous fellow, Kokopelli plays his flute to bring rain and to attract women. It is said that his hump and his pouch are full of seed, mist and presents to give to the young maidens he seduces.

The fifth Kachina was Warrior Maiden. Her card said, "The men were out in the fields when the village was attacked and set on fire. Grabbing her father's weapons, this maiden and the other women fought the attackers until their menfolk saw the smoke and returned to help. The smoke and soot from the fire blackened everything, and so Warrior Maiden is shown with a black face and wearing black clothing. She survived the battle and saved the village." The doll holds a bow in her left hand and an arrow in her right. Across her back are slung a quiver of arrows and a shield stamped with a bear claw. Carved into the stand below her is the cliffside village she saved.

The last Kachina, and the one that interested Sam the most, was the Badger. About nine inches tall, this Badger had a blue-grey face and body, and wore a white skirt. Sam thought it resembled no earthly badger he had ever seen—maybe they look like this on the moon. Two horizontal slits formed its eyes, and a white stripe ran down the middle of its forehead onto the top of its snout. Brown feathers formed the hair on the sides of its head; red, white and grey feathers crowned it. A thin yellow belt crisscrossed its trunk, and from that belt hung tiny seashells.

The card in front of it said, "The Badger is a curing Kachina, sometimes called a doctor or a nurse because of his knowledge of all the roots and herbs used to cure the sick and the injured. He grows and gathers the roots and herbs, and assists the Medicine Man in applying them. Many prayers for healing are directed to the Badger."

Sam glanced at the price tag and it floored him: $290.

The shopkeeper, an older Hopi woman with long, greying hair, said, "Badger is very good. Badger is very strong." Her name was Catori Wuuti; she wore a plaid shirt over a brown skirt, and knew quite a bit about the Hopi and Zuni cultures.

"Sure," said Sam. "It's a fine piece."

"Want me to take him out?"

"Yes, please. I'd like to get a better look."

Catori unlocked the case and pulled out the Badger doll.

"Badger comes with a Certificate of Authenticity—they all do. That means they were made by real tribal artists." She passed it to Sam.

Sam held the doll and studied it.

Catori said, "You can almost feel the power flowing through your hands, right?"

Sam wasn't sure, but he nodded and smiled.

She nodded and smiled back.

He said, "It's a lot of money, but she'll like it."

"It will do her good," said Catori, and Sam took out his credit card and paid for it.

"There's a little card that goes with it—would you like to write something on it? I'll tuck it in the box and wrap it up for you."

Sam wrote, "Dear Rita, Get well soon!" He hesitated for a moment, then signed it, "Love, Sam."

When Sam got to the infirmary, Dr. Winter was leaving Rita's room. "Hello, Colonel Sawyer," said the slim black man.

"Hello, Doc."

"I was just in to see her."

"Uh-huh."

"She's still in a coma, but her vital signs are improving." Winter's warm eyes and his calm manner encouraged Sam.

"Doc, let me ask you, how long before she emerges from that coma?"

A tilt of the head. "Well, we're not sure, but we're hopeful."

"Can I see her?"

"Sure, Sam. But, uh, before you do... I want you to know we've decided to move her to St. Michael's Hospital."

"Why's that?" His eye twitched.

"They have some facilities there—some equipment that we just don't have here."

"It's not because she's getting worse?"

"No, she's stable right now. Serious, but stable."

"When do you plan on moving her?"

"Tomorrow morning."

"She can take the strain?"

The Doctor nodded. "We've booked a helicopter. It should go smoothly."

Sam said, "Take good care of her."

"We intend to."

"Have you had a chance to look at Rikki Greco?"

Dr. Winter's face turned somber. "I did some preliminary examinations. I would place the time of death around 11 AM." He started to leave.

"Before you go, there's one thing I've been meaning to ask you about Rita."

"What might that be?"

"Well, it's going to sound a little strange, but..."

"I'm listening," said Dr. Winter.

"When you looked her over... when you examined her, did you see any signs that she had been hit by an object before she fell?"

"An object? What do you mean?"

"Maybe a small caliber bullet…"

Disbelief pinched the doctor's countenance. "No, not really."

"Maybe something smaller—a BB or a rubber pellet?"

Winters shook his head. "I didn't notice anything. You're thinking someone shot her... and made her fall?"

"That thought keeps wrinkling my brain."

Dr. Winter scratched his head and said, "She has a lot of contusions, a lot of bruises. As to which ones were caused by rubber bullets, and which were caused by rocks she fell on—that's beyond me. We did find one unusual thing."

"What's that?"

"She had a lot of Tegretol in her bloodstream—twice her usual dosage."

When Sam entered the Intensive Care Unit, Nurse Bernadette Czarnecki lifted her eyes from a magazine and greeted him. Rita lay in bed, breathing lightly through a respirator. Sam gazed at the various instruments she was hooked up to, then at her bandaged face.

Good God, he prayed, *please help this woman.*

A machine kicked on, plucking at his nerves. A wave pattern on a monitor stuttered for an instant, then slowly eased back to normal.

"Rita," he said, "I brought you something." The nurse pretended not to hear him. Sam held up the box for Rita to see, but she could see nothing. He unwrapped the fancy paper and pulled out the Kachina doll he had just purchased. He held it up on the off chance that she could somehow sense it. "It's the Badger. It's a healing Kachina. It's going to help you get better."

He strained for any sign of a response, but there was none.

He said, "I'll put it on your table over here," and turned to his right. On Rita's bedside table, hidden by a water pitcher and a vase of flowers, a blue-grey object stood. Sam hadn't noticed it before, but as he approached it, he could see it more and more clearly.

It was a blue-grey Badger with a white skirt; it had slits for eyes and a white stripe down its forehead. In short, it was the twin brother of the Kachina Sam had bought a few minutes ago. There was a card hanging from its neck.

Sam opened the card and saw its message, "Lovely Rita, My friend Badger will have you laughing in no time! Love, Johnnie."

***

Chapter Twelve: Back Burner

Many things flowed through Sam Sawyer's mind as he ate supper in his office Monday evening. He thought of Rita, vivacious and wild, as she had been on the day he first met her. Then he remembered what she had become, broken and comatose in a hospital bed. His mind's eye saw Rikki Greco slouched over his desk in Deep Grey with a bowie knife driven deep into his neck, then imagination blinked and Rikki exercised on a Bowflex machine, alive as young lion, his muscles rippling. The insolent Johnnie Lonetree burst through the barricades of Sam's brain, questioning him, mocking him, then Lonetree twisted and slithered into young Johnnie, happy and quick, sliding into home plate at Ellsworth Air Force Base, with the great Black Hills of South Dakota looming behind him.

In Sam's mind, Andrei Ulanov cried anew on Weizman's couch, Dr. Winter studied x-rays, Sandra Graham counted out capsules of Tegretol, and Selene threw up breastworks against Sam's inquiries. And again, Rita—falling into the pitiless night.

Sam sliced into his chicken parmigiana and forked a chunk into his mouth. It smelled spicy and tasted—as his mother liked to say—half as good as happiness. He stabbed four string beans and chewed on them. Then he drank Diet Coke from a red plastic cup and hoped that the caffeine would lift him out of his mental and emotional exhaustion.

Robby Lee and Dana Severn surfaced in Sam's consciousness, working on computer programs. Gogo and Klang laughed at some crude joke, and a blue-grey kachina called Badger met its twin on a bedside table in Rita's room. All this and more moved through his mind, all this and more.

There was another presence, too; something deeper and without definite form, something he couldn't put his finger on. Maybe it was just that he was tired. Sometimes when he was tired his brain sent out noise or static, and the static got caught in a feedback loop, returning again and again and again. At least that's the way he pictured it.

Maybe that deep something would show itself to him if he just relaxed, if he just stopped searching for it. Sam had read about that somewhere, this notion of putting a tough problem on the back burner. If a puzzle has you stumped, don't keep knocking your head against it; instead, forget about it for a while, and switch to something else. Your subconscious mind will work on a solution without your even knowing it. At least that was the theory. Maybe sometimes the mind repels a frontal assault, but yields to a flank attack. Who knows?

Sam asked Selene to raise the monitors, and when they were up and working, he used them to check the base perimeter—all was quiet. All the guards were at their assigned posts, and there were no intruders in the desert around Altamura Air Force Base.

He checked the runways. An E2-D Hawkeye accelerated down runway 11 and took off as Sam watched, its large radar disk catching the low rays of the sun. It was bound for early warning duty over the Gulf of California and the near Pacific. All other runways were clear.

Sam checked various areas of Deep Grey using several cameras; he found little activity there. Next he examined the base's futuristic beam weapon under its retractable dome. It looked as ready as ever.

He peered at hallway after hallway in building after building; he inspected many floors, many rooms. All was as it should be.

He checked on Rita. In the dim light of the Intensive Care Unit, she might have been sleeping, might have been in a coma. Sam couldn't tell. She seemed at peace.

Finally, as a diversion, he switched to a TV news channel. The anchorman, black-haired Brett Fox announced, "On *Meet the Press* yesterday, the Director of National Intelligence, Tahiya Themba stated that across the United States, 1.4 million people have a Top Secret Security Clearance. Ms. Themba said that such a high number poses a security risk of its own, providing many openings for penetration by hostile agents. She believes that no more than 500,000 people should possess that high a clearance."

Lucy Cable, his red-haired co-anchor, said, "On a related topic, Ms. Themba said that so many intelligence reports are published each year that many are routinely ignored by the agents and officers who should be reading them."

Sam's fingers moved to his keypad—he switched to a view of the Maintenance Office. His three favorite janitors appeared—white-haired Marty, powerful Klang, and wiry Gogo—sitting around a 27-inch TV, watching a commercial about kitchen knives.

As they watched an extra-peppy woman sharpen a long blade, Klang said, "That was some knife in Rikki Greco's neck."

"It was a Bowie knife," said Gogo, putting down his beer. "It was his own knife."

"Let's change the subject," said Marty, sitting at his desk. "I don't even want to think about it. What they did to that poor guy was disgusting."

A new commercial popped onto the janitors' TV, and the announcer shouted, "Get your very own personal defense system with the USB Missile Launcher!"

Onscreen, a delighted ten-year old boy pressed a button on his computer keyboard. From a nearby rotating launcher, three blue foam missiles shot out, one after the other, at his laughing friend.

"Tilt and aim the launcher until you have your enemy in sight!" commanded the announcer.

"Wow, look at that!" said Gogo. "I wish I had one when I was a kid."

Klang said, "We could use one of those on this base."

Soon, a somber Brett Fox filled the janitors' TV screen, reporting, "The Great Wall Flu has hit China with a vicious attack. An estimated 400,000 people have been stricken, and at least 12,000 have died. Even worse, it seems to be spreading fast."

Lucy Cable, his co-anchor, said, "Brett, in this age of easy international travel, diseases can spread around the world in days." The screen showed a crying Chinese man holding his baby daughter. Brett said, "It's a deadly flu, isn't it, Lucy?"

"Yes, and doctors seem to be powerless to stop it."

Marty picked up a remote control and changed the channel. A show about animals popped on, and a flounder swam across the screen. A narrator said, "Flounders have an amazing ability to change the color of their skin to match the sandy or rocky bottom. That makes it harder for predators to spot them."

Gogo said, "We caught a lot of those when I was young. Long Island Sound, Jersey Shore. Lots of flounder."

"You like to fish?" asked Marty.

"Oh, yeah."

Marty's TV screen now showed a white-tailed deer sprinting through a forest. The narrator continued, "Deer use another means of evading their pursuers—they run quick and fast, just like this white-tailed buck in the forests of Pennsylvania."

Klang picked up a Field & Stream magazine and glanced at the rather strange picture on the cover, seemingly nothing but trees and leaves and brush. Small green letters at the bottom asked, "Where's Waldo?" Klang studied it, and soon his finger began tracing out a camouflaged hunter hidden right in the middle of the photo, aiming a rifle at the reader. He asked, "How about hunting?"

"Huh?"

"Do you like to hunt?"

Gogo hesitated for a moment, then shook his head. "No, I never hunted in my life. My father was in the army, and one of his friends was shot up pretty bad right next to him, so... he never kept a gun in the house."

"This cute little fellow has a defense of a different stripe," said the TV narrator as a skunk strolled across the top of a log. "Give him a wide berth if you like fresh air."

Another commercial came on—this one for "Shields On" car wax. Marty said, "I had them put that stuff on my car at the car wash. It's supposed to protect your paint job against bird droppings."

"I use it in my hair," said Gogo.

Sam switched to a TV channel.

In a BBC version of Shakespeare's play, Macbeth and his wife plotted something nasty. Macbeth told her, "Away, and mock the time with fairest show. False face must hide what the false heart doth know."

"False face—that's Johnnie Lonetree," thought Sam, as he changed to another base camera, this one showing Adam Weizman and Father Tom House sitting in Weizman's living room.

"Congratulations!" said House. "It's a great honor."

"Well, it's a small museum, not exactly the Metropolitan." They sat in matching Amish Durango chairs, with high backs, oak arms and legs, the fabric a geometric pattern called Navajo Blanket. Between them was a mission style coffee table on a red Navajo rug.

"Listen, it's one of Tucson's finest art museums, and for them to exhibit ten of your paintings shows that your hobby is not just a hobby anymore."

“Thank you,” said Weizman. “You’re very kind.” He topped off his glass. “And this wine is delicious. Where’d you get it?”

“I bought it in The Dream Catcher,” said House. “I asked Catori to pick out something good.”

“Well, she certainly did. Thank you so much.”

“My pleasure.”

Weizman read aloud from the label, “Only the ripest and most noble grapes were chosen for this full-bodied wine, whose expressive fruit is typical for a Saar Riesling.”

“Germans know wine and beer,” said Father House.

The psychiatrist continued reading, “Eichamer-Gsellmeyer Riesling Auslese is a rich, complex and multi-layered wine. The floral notes are reminiscent of woodruff, nutmeg, white pepper, kumquat, and orange blossom. One can taste orange rinds and honey immediately; baked apple and vanilla emerge as the wine opens. It will make an extraordinary aperitif, and is great for after dinner.”

“All in one bottle!” laughed House. “How do they squeeze it in?”

“Have some danish, Tom. I bought the fattening kind.”

The priest reached for a piece of pastry, then Weizman took one, noting, “They say a good wine has many levels, and that experts can actually taste the roots, the soil, even the sunshine.”

“Well, in the part of Newark that I come from, the finest import was the sacramental jug wine in the sacristy, and the most popular domestic on the street was Thunderbird.”

“What’s the word? Thunderbird,” said Weizman, tapping an old memory. “How’s it sold? Good and cold.”

Father House put down his glass and asked, “Can I take a peek at your latest creations?”

“I’m very proud of them, actually,” said Weizman. He got up and walked over to two easels covered with sheets. With a bit of a flourish, he pulled the sheet off the canvas on the left. "I call this one, *The Consultation*."

In this oil painting, the troubled patient lying on the couch is clearly Adam Weizman. The analyst in his chair, wearing an enigmatic smile, is also Adam Weizman. Around the room, a supporting cast assumes various poses.

"So the doctor and the patient are both you," said House. "And that must be Sigmund Freud standing at your side."

"That's right."

"And that lady next to old Sigmund?"

"Anna Freud, his daughter."

"And this fellow?"

"That's Carl Jung."

"Collective unconscious—right?"

"Yes, Jung believed in a collective unconscious that we all share."

"That we somehow inherited from our ancestors?" asked House. "All of us, all over the world?"

"That's right. And he developed the concept of archetypes, which are universally understood symbols."

"Give me a for-instance of an archetype."

"Some archetypes would be: the *hero* in stories and legends, the *great mother* in many myths... the *trickster* in native American tales."

"I get it."

"Jung also believed in synchronicity, the idea that life is not a series of random events but an expression of a deeper order."

"Well, I agree with that deeper order thing." House's eyes roamed over the painting. "There's your wife, Naomi, God rest her soul. And those pictures hanging on the wall—your father and mother."

"Yes."

"*The Consultation*," said House. "You're consulting with people who have influenced you throughout your life."

"That's right. What do you think of it?"

"I like it. And who is that black priest in the background?"

"I've learned a lot from you, Tom."

"This is great. That woman edging out the door?"

"Ah, the mystery woman," said Weizman.

The second painting was an unfinished acrylic. The psychiatrist said, "I call it *Analyst in a Maze*." A man holding a ball of string is starting down a maze. From above we see that along the path in front of him there lurks a Minotaur, and then a spider, and a then a mouse in a lab coat. At the center of the circular design lies an infinity symbol.

"It looks like that native American pattern," said Father House. "I've seen it on jewelry and clothing."

"Yes, that's where I got the idea from. The People of the Desert, the Tohono O'odham, have a legend. In the beginning of the world, Elder Brother worked hard getting the earth ready for the People. But his enemies kept pestering him, so he needed a safe place to live."

"He had enemies even back then—in the beginning of the world? That's kind of sad, isn't it?"

"I guess if there are no enemies in a story, there's no story. Anyway, he decided to build a safe home underground at the center of a mountain."

"Right next to NORAD?" joked House. He was referring to the North American Aerospace Defense Command and its headquarters deep inside Cheyenne Mountain, Colorado.

"Now, Elder Brother's enemies could see the entrance to his home, but they could not get to him."

"Because of the maze."

“That’s right. He carved many winding paths into the mountain, paths that went down, then left, then in, then right. The enemies tried to figure out the maze, but they got lost in the darkness and died. They never reached Elder Brother’s cave in the center.”

“And that maze symbol that we see so often on Hopi jewelry and Pima baskets?”

“That’s the map that Elder Brother made so his friends could reach him.”

“Ah,” said House. “And you are taking that legend and doing what with it?”

“Applying it to myself somehow. I haven’t figured it all out yet.”

“The maze is the journey through life.”

Weizman said, “In one sense, yes. The maze represents the experiences we have, the people we meet, and the choices we make. Some choices take us off course, some lead us to our goal. But symbols can stand for more than one thing; to me, the maze also stands for our journey into ourselves.”

“And what’s in the center?” asked House.

A grey veil seemed to slip over Weizman’s face. “That’s what I’m having a problem with, Tom. For now, I placed the infinity symbol there...”

“Uh-huh.”

“But sometimes I’m afraid that when I reach the center of my maze, I will find nothing there.” He turned to his friend.

“Nothing? No soul? No meaning?”

“Nothing.”

“What does that mean?” wondered Sam. “How could there be nothing at the center of a man’s existence?” Then he switched to the living room of Gabriel and Constance Hoffer.

Four-year old Jane Hoffer was sitting on the couch, an ice cream cone in her right hand and two dolls in her left. One of the dolls was Disney's Belle and the other was the Beast, and Jane was presiding over their wedding. She asked, "Do you Beast, take you Belle, as your awfully dreaded wife?"

Her six-year old brother Barry, sitting next to her and eating his own ice cream cone, said, "That doesn't sound right."

Just then their mother, Constance, entered the room and scolded them immediately, "No ice cream on the couch! I told you a million times." Her hair was jet black because she colored it, unable to bear the encroaching grey which spread like the movement of a shadow on a sun dial. Her blue eyes had faded one gradation since the day she got married.

"But Ma, the couch is covered in plastic," said curly-haired Barry.

"Why do you cover all the furniture in plastic?" asked straight-haired Jane.

Constance walked over to them and said, "So it stays nice, nice as it was on the day we bought it."

"You want it to last forever, Ma?" asked Jane. "Forever and ever?"

"Nothing lasts forever, does it, Ma?"

Her son's question seemed to trouble Constance, and she had no answer for it.

Her daughter said, "Families last forever, don't they, Ma?"

Constance put her arms around Jane and her dolls and assured her, "Yes, sweetheart, yes they do."

"Poor Constance," thought Sam, "you can't put a plastic cover on life." He switched back to the TV news.

Brett Fox said, "The latest survey from the Census Bureau shows that divorce rates are up across America. Marriages don't seem to last long these days, do they, Lucy?"

Co-anchor Lucy Cable said, "I think it's about escaping responsibility. And look at the rise in out-of-wedlock births in the last ten years. It's really scary. Men don't want to be husbands and fathers anymore."

"And the women?" asked Brett.

"The women should join a convent," laughed Lucy.

Sam switched to another on-base apartment.

Katie Custer worked in communications at the base. Dressed in a white bathrobe, with her long, blond hair wrapped in a towel, she sat on her daughter's bed, finishing a story from a children's book. "And that's how the Tortoise got his shell," she announced.

"That was a good story, mommy," said five-year-old Betsy, dressed in pink sleeper pajamas with little white cowgirls on them.

"I'm glad you liked it."

Betsy's hair was blond. Her left eye was brown, but the right one was brown on the bottom and green on the top. She said, "Read me another, please."

Katie shook her head. "Sorry, time to go to sleep."

Betsy pulled her teddy bear to her and gave it a big hug. Sam had finally memorized the bear's name: Maria Louisa Brigitta Polly Jemima Sally Custer. Betsy begged, "Pretty please, Mom."

"I'm sorry, honey, but it's time for you to get to sleep."

"Oh, but I can't sleep, mommy."

"Oh, but you have to sleep," said Katie Custer, laughing just a bit. "Mommy's tired, and I still have work to do, and you need your rest, too."

"Billy's not asleep."

"Billy's three years older than you, and he's going to sleep in about fifteen minutes."

She pulled the covers up to Betsy's chin, kissed her on the forehead, and whispered, "Good night, honey."

Betsy watched her mother start for the door and pleaded, "Leave the light on."

Sam was about to switch away when eight-year old brother Billy strolled in, carrying a DVD case.

"Hi, Billy."

"Hi, Sis."

"What movie you got?"

"It's called *Poltergeist.* Uncle George let me borrow it." Billy sat down on Betsy's bed.

"I never saw that."

"It would be too scary for you, sis. I wouldn't want you to get nightmares."

"You're a good brother," she said.

"Thanks."

"It's not too scary for you?"

"Uncle George thinks I'm man enough to watch it."

"Oh."

Billy said, "Did you say your prayers?"

"I kinda forgot. Why?"

He scratched his ear, carefully deliberating before saying, "Well, I really shouldn't tell you."

"Huh?"

"Good night, now." He got up to leave. "Pleasant dreams."

"Tell me," she said.

He grimaced and shook his head. "I really shouldn't. You're just a kid."

"Tell me."

"It's kinda scary."

"Tell me!" Her scrunched up face was plea, petition and prayer. "You've gotta tell me."

Billy checked the door. “Promise you won’t tell mom.”

“I promise.”

He sat on her bed again, and his expression was somber, as befitting one who carries a burdensome secret. “People around here don’t talk about it much. They wanna keep it hush-hush.”

“Oh?”

He whispered, “But Davey Pillepich told me that part of this base was built on a Navajo burial ground.”

“It was?” Her eyes expanded.

Billy nodded. “And the Navajo people weren’t happy about that.”

“Who’s buried there?”

“Indians,” he pronounced solemnly.

“Dead ones?” Betsy asked.

Watching in his office, Sam laughed, appreciating the comic relief, savoring the escape it gave him from his troubles.

“Yep. And the Indians are so angry about their burial ground being covered up that they want revenge.”

“The dead ones?” asked Betsy.

“Well, mostly the live ones. But there *are* ghosts. Ghosts from the graves.”

Betsy’s eyes opened even wider and she said, “Ghosts from the graves!”

“That’s right.”

“Billy, are there graves under this floor?”

He scratched his chin and contemplated. “There might be one or two,” he reckoned.

“Why did they build the stupid base on top of graves?” whined Betsy, frightened now.

“Don’t let it worry you.”

“Do they do anything, these ghosts?”

"Well, they haunt the base, you see, and they do a dance every night."

"A ghost dance?" she whispered.

"Yep. They dance and they chant: 'Ye-Tsan Bilagaana, Ye-Tsan Bilagaana!'"

"What does that mean?" asked Betsy.

"It means: 'Get off our land, white man!'"

"Do they haunt the whole base?"

"What do you mean?"

"Even the apartments where people live?"

"That's what Davey said," replied Billy. "So be careful tonight."

"Mommy!"

"It's too bad Daddy's in Indiana. He could fight the ghosts if he were here."

"Mommy!!"

Sam smiled and switched to a TV movie—on a foggy night, a boy trudged past a graveyard, whistling as he walked.

Sam entered numbers on his keyboard and hit the return key. He was treated to a scene from a PBS special—renowned mythologist Schuyler Bliss, in a tweed suit, sauntered in a museum and stopped at an exhibit showing Plains Indian women skinning a buffalo.

Journalist Emmet Sheridan, at his side, asked him, "The Plains Indians depended on the buffalo for life, didn't they?"

Professor Bliss answered, "Yes, they did. They had to kill the buffalo to survive—for food, for clothing."

"Magnificent animal."

"Oh, and to stand up to one when he was charging and roaring and trying to kill you—you knew what nature was!"

Sheridan studied the mannequins in the display, gazed at the flint knives they were using to flay the hide. "And you had to stick a spear into that living beast if you wanted food for yourself and your family."

"That's right," said Bliss.

Sheridan pondered that reality, then asked, "And how did they feel about that?"

"It pained them, because they revered the buffalo. They thought of the buffalo as a person—as a *thou*, not as an *it*."

Sheridan said, "A person worthy of respect."

"Sometimes the animals were seen as messengers from the gods, or even as gods themselves. So, you see, to kill this person, this messenger, this god—it caused the hunters great psychological pain."

"And to deal with this pain?"

"The Blackfoot Indians came up with a story and a ritual."

Sheridan stated, "The story of the buffalo's wife."

"That's right," said Bliss, and he began to tell the tale. "Long ago, in one corner of the great plains, a tribe of Indians was starving. The hunt had not gone well, and there wasn't enough to eat. One pretty maiden happened to glance up at a wide cliff and saw a herd of buffalo grazing near the edge of the precipice. She made an offhand remark to a friend, 'Oh, if only a group of those buffalo would jump off that cliff to their deaths, then our people would have enough to eat. I'd do anything if that happened—I'd even marry one of them.'"

"Uh-oh," said Sheridan.

"Wouldn't you know, before long, a large number of buffalo plunged off the cliff, killing themselves, just as she had asked."

The journalist said, "So the buffalo sacrificed themselves for the good of the tribe."

"That's right. Then the great leader of the buffalo trotted over to her, and said, 'Honey, you and I are getting married.'"

Sheridan grinned.

"'Oh, no,' she said.

"'Oh, yes,' said the handsome beast. 'You made a promise. You swore you would marry one of us. Look around you at my fallen comrades. We've kept our part of the bargain.' So he took her back to his herd and they were married."

"Beauty and the beast," said Emmet Sheridan.

"Well, her father found out about her predicament and tried to help her escape. But the buffalo leader got wind of it and ordered his people to kill his bride's father."

"I guess that's one way to deal with meddlesome in-laws," said the reporter.

"It was horrible. They ripped him to shreds and stampeded over his torn body."

"And the buffalo's wife?" asked Emmet Sheridan.

"The girl was devastated, but she searched and searched, and finally found a tiny piece of her father. She put the piece under a blanket, and she sang a special song. After a few verses, the little piece grew into her lifeless father, unmoving under the blanket. Encouraged by this, she sang with all her heart, and she even did a dance around her father's body. After a few more verses and steps her father came to life—good as new!"

"And what did the buffalo leader think when he saw this?" asked Sheridan,

"He was amazed, stunned by the beauty and the power of her song. Finally, he said to his wife, 'Listen, we buffalo will let your people kill us because we know you need food. But from now on, you will do a buffalo dance around each dead animal, and sing a special song, and that buffalo's spirit will rise up just like your father did.'"

The journalist said, "So, looking at it from the Indian point of view, we will kill the buffalo because we have to, but we will bring them back to life with our ritual."

Schuyler Bliss nodded and motioned with his hand. “And the psychic pain of killing is channeled away into the myth, into the song, into the dance.”

Sam switched to the Officers’ Club.

The Officers’ Club at Altamura Air Force Base was a small treasure and an open secret, as was the story of its financing and construction. When the base was first built, a team of Sergeant Bilko’s, headed by the base commander, diverted funds, rerouted lumber, stole furniture, and extorted services in order to erect this wood-panelled gentlemen’s cave, complete with fireplace, oak floor, player piano, pool table, television, wet bar, leather chairs, oriental rugs, models of fighters and bombers, bookshelves filled with action novels and mechanical magazines, all for the common good of the Air Force’s finest. In this more enlightened age, its members included not only officers but enlisted personnel, women as well as men, and even civilian employees of the base—really, anyone willing to pay the minimal monthly dues. The Club’s magazines now included Vogue and Glamour, Self and Ladies’ Home Journal, and many a romance novel could be found on its manly shelves.

Dana Severn, fair-skinned, with braided hair, sat in a leather chair next to Erika Grenfell, a thin-hipped, thirty-something woman in a black page boy haircut. Robby Lee stood near them and offered, “Still, I think this club was better when it was a man cave.”

Erika pursed her lips and said, “Women have rights now, don’t they Robby?”

“Too many rights.”

“And we’re not giving them up. Even if that threatens you poor, defenseless Neanderthals.”

Dana switched the subject. “Where’s the birthday boy?”

“He’s making the rounds,” said Erika, gazing out into the crowd.

“How old is Steiner?” asked Robby.

"Sixty-five," answered Dana. "At least that's what he admits to."

Sam switched to a view of the Base Pharmacy.

Pharmacist Sandra Graham walked past a half-length mirror and stopped, edging back a step. She posed her skinny body in front of the glass and said to herself, "You gained weight again."

Sam thought that Sandra was far too thin, but she had a different image of herself. She raised a bony hand to cover her mirror image.

On a desk beside her was a picture of her mother and father, both of them heavy and smiling. Sam noticed their wedding bands. As overweight as they were, he thought, they still managed to love each other, marry each other, and have a child—a daughter they worry about.

On the desk next to their picture sat a stack of Cosmopolitan and Elle magazines, each with a skinnier model on its cover than the last.

Sandra pulled her hand down away from the mirror, turned and rifled through her desk drawers, finding a bag of corn chips. She shoved some in her mouth and crunched down on them.

Then she told her mirror image, "No one is ever gonna want you," and she spit half the chips into a garbage can.

Searching the pharmacy's shelves, she found a brand new bottle of diet pills, broke the seal and swallowed a pill.

Sam switched back to the TV news and heard Lucy Cable state, "Abuse of over-the-counter drugs is up across the United States."

Brett Fox frowned and said, "More of that escape from reality, huh?"

Sam switched to the bedroom of Sheila Mae Wood, his secretary.

On her dressing table, Sheila kept a large plastic jar of moisturizing cream, sculpted to look like carved ivory, mimicking an actual medieval piece owned by a French museum. The engraved phrase "Attack on the Castle of Love" curved around the jar's sides. On its cover, four women defend a castle by throwing baskets of roses down onto four attacking knights. The knights are armed with swords; flowers adorn their shields and their horses' robes. One knight uses a catapult to hurl flowers up at the women. Another climbs a ladder and kisses a girl in a window.

Sheila dipped her fingers into the moisturizing cream and smeared some across her forehead and down her cheeks.

Sam entered a command on his keyboard, and his main monitor was filled with a TV re-run of an old movie, a classic called *Rear Window.*

Onscreen, "Jeff" Jeffries, played by James Stewart, sat in a wheelchair, dressed in tan pajamas, his left leg in a cast from his toes to his waist. He peered out his apartment's rear window at various neighbors in his housing block.

As he gazed, Stella, his visiting nurse, entered his apartment. Played by Thelma Ritter, Stella wore a grey and white print dress and gave Jeff a warning about his new hobby. She said, "New York State sentence for a peeping Tom is six months in the workhouse."

Jeff said, "Oh, hello, Stella."

"—and they got no windows in the workhouse. You know, in the old days, they used to put your eyes out with a red-hot poker…"

Soon Stella was lamenting, "Oh, dear, we've become a race of peeping Toms. What people oughta do is get outside their own house and look in for a change. Yes, sir."

Stella, thought Sam, *I don't do it because I like it. I do it because I have to.*

Sam decided to check in once more on Rita in the Intensive Care Unit. She was either sleeping or comatose—he couldn't tell—still breathing through a respirator, still fed through an IV, still generating green and yellow wave patterns on a bedside monitor. He could detect no change in her condition. Well, that was better than a change for the worse.

Rita, I love you—the message formed in his mind and he wished he could get it to her. Maybe it *was* getting to her somehow, like a prayer gets to God somehow. *I always have, and I always will.*

Was that true? Had he always loved her? Hadn't he hated her once?

Why did he love her?

Might as well ask why does any man love any woman. To some extent, reflected Sam, we were designed for love. All of us were designed to need and want acceptance, affection, passion.

Yes, but why did Sam love Rita?

We are meant by God or programmed by nature to reach out to others. We offer ourselves—almost on a platter, almost on an altar—with the painful awareness that we might be rejected by those we want and need so badly.

Yes, but why did Sam love Rita? He noticed that he was good at philosophizing about people in general. But why did this particular man Sam love this particular woman Rita? Objective analysis requires separation from the subject, and it is hard for a man to separate from himself.

Sam reckoned that nature engineered man (well, most men)—to fall weightless for a woman—if only for a brief moment—in order to keep the race going.

But aren't we also designed *not* to love? Don't we all in the end look out for number one and to hell with everyone else?

Do we ever really let our guard down? Do we ever let the other person get so close they become one with us, become a part of us? Don't we always hold something back?

Rita slept almost motionless in her hospital bed.

Sam remembered the first time he ever saw her—it was at Joan Hagan's Halloween party. He was attracted to her from the moment he set eyes on her—she was strikingly handsome, self-confident, brash. Her

Wonder Woman costume beamed her physical wonders to all receptive eyes, including the cowled blue eyes of Sam's Captain America.

Yes, he was enchanted at first sight, but he didn't really fall in love with her until several weeks later. It was at a Mexican restaurant a few miles outside of Los Alamos, and Sam had told her about some news he had just received, "I got a letter today from my sister Claire. She's an Air Force nurse over in Frankfurt. She says she's coming back to the states next month."

"Do you have a big family?" Rita had asked.

"Not very big, just two older sisters, Arlene and Claire. How about you?"

"I had a little brother, Neal." It took a while for sadness to sneak across her face.

"Had?" asked Sam.

"He died when he was 13. I was 15."

"I'm sorry to hear that." She had turned to Sam, and he had looked deep into her green eyes. "Tell me about him."

"We were very close. We did a lot of things together like hiking, surfing, horseback riding."

"Was he like you?"

"I guess he was like I was." It was apparent to Sam that, in a manner of speaking, the shutters protecting her heart were opened to him, revealing far more than she had planned, uncovering unexpected vulnerabilities and anxieties, unveiling even an essential innocence.

"I wish I could have known him," said Sam.

"We were both pretty good with computers, and we used to hack into our high school's web site to work some good-natured mischief."

"How did he die?"

"He caught a bad virus—had it for about a week. He ran a fever, had pains in his joints, fatigue. But you know, kids get sick all the time.

“My mom and dad had to go to a wedding. I was asked to play nurse, to keep an eye on Neal. I was to call them right away if he had any kind of problem.” Tears began welling in Rita’s eyes and she wiped them away before continuing.

“He went to bed. I checked in on him a few times. All of a sudden he looked much worse. I got scared and I called them right away. I was a stupid ass.”

“What do you mean? You did what they asked you to do.”

“I should have called 911. I should have called for an ambulance.

“They rushed back home—he was so pale—they tried to revive him. He died in my mother’s arms.” Here Rita had begun sobbing. Sam remembered a waitress stopping in her tracks, and an older couple at the next table staring at them.

“You were just a kid. You did what you were told to do.”

“He might have lived if I had called 911. I miss him so much.” She glanced around the suddenly quiet restaurant. “Sam, I miss him so much.”

Later, in his car, she had told him the rest of the story. “They did an autopsy and found myocarditis, an inflammation of the heart muscle. They told us it was probably an autoimmune reaction to the virus.”

“I’m sorry.”

“He was my best buddy, my little sidekick, riding with me through life. And now when I looked over, he was gone. That left a hole in my life so deep, I still haven’t found the bottom.”

“It must be tough,” Sam had said. “I’ve had people close to me die, but they were much older.”

Rita said, “When Neal died, it taught me that nothing in this world is permanent, and the closer you let someone get to you, the more it hurts when he’s ripped away.”

“I wish I could say something.”

"His death shocked us like a bomb going off. We didn't know what hit us. I guess if we had been a religious family we could have turned to God, but we weren't religious at all. We didn't have that. Dad and I tried to hold on to what we could, to keep things 'the same.' But they weren't the same, and they could never be the same again.

"Mom flipped out. She needed everything changed because everything reminded her of Neal. She wanted a divorce, a new house, a new job—everything new. Run away. Go where sorrow can't find you."

"No such place," said Sam.

"I've never told all this to anyone. I never told anyone but you, Sam. And I hadn't meant to, but it just came out. Something about you. Something about you made me want to tell."

Now, alone in his office, Sam pressed a button and the monitor switched from the Intensive Care Unit to the living room of Brigadier General Isha Patel, acting base commander in the absence of General Thaler.

General Patel sat in the lotus position, dressed in a saffron robe. He chanted the word "Aum"—slowly and deliberately. His "Aum" radiated from all his seven chakras, signifying that he was calm, that he had infinite strength and flexibility to overcome all obstacles, and that he was blessed with an abundance of love and security.

***

Chapter Thirteen: Simmer

When Sam Sawyer strolled into Dunkin Donuts, two doors past The Dream Catcher, he noticed a new cartoon on the wall behind the cash register. In this framed drawing, a mechanic with a wrench in each hand worked on a bomb, while behind him Kokopelli opened the man's lunch box and stole a donut. Sam bought a regular coffee to help him stay awake and a cream donut to keep away evil spirits.

He stretched his legs in a few of the other shops, took his time getting back to his office, then washed his face in his private bathroom and got back to work. It *was* work, he assured himself, this spying on random people around the base. Even if it wasn't, what else could he do? He had no idea.

When the monitors were ready, Sam looked in on the Maintenance Office.

Gogo was saying, "And what is it called?"

Klang answered, "It's called a defense mechanism."

"Where did you see this?"

"It was on a TV show last week, a Nova special."

Marty, sitting at his desk, chimed in, "I saw it too. It was pretty interesting."

Gogo said, "Explain it to me again."

Klang seemed happy to elucidate. "It's like this. The world is a rough place. It can be a rotten place. A lot of bad things happen to every one of us."

"I agree," said Gogo, reaching up to touch a little gold cross that hung around his neck.

"And each person's mind is vulnerable; each of us needs psychological protection from the lousy world we live in."

"We do?"

"Every day we get bombarded with bad news on the TV and the radio. A young father is murdered, we're bogged down in a war, a tornado hits a hospital, an oil spill pollutes a beach."

"I understand," said Gogo.

Klang continued, "Some days you get bad news at home, too. Maybe your best friend dies, or your favorite relative. Or maybe you lose your job. Or your boss is a jerk."

"Careful there," said Marty, their supervisor.

"Maybe the girl you fell in love with runs off with another guy."

"I didn't love her," said Gogo. "She was a dog."

"So your mind tries to protect itself from all this bad stuff coming at you."

"Why?"

"Because it has to," explained Klang. "Otherwise it'll be overwhelmed—it'll crack under the pressure."

"And how does your mind protect you from all these incoming arrows?" asked Gogo.

"Sometimes it makes you realize that you need a break. So it tells you to go fishing, or go to a ball game."

"I *do* need a break," said Gogo.

Marty reflected, "My father used to say, when you go out in a boat fishing, the only thing you think about is catching fish. You forget about all your troubles."

"It's true," said Gogo, and his eyes wandered to a photograph hanging on the wall near Marty's desk. It showed a ten-year-old Marty holding a prize fish, and his proud father standing behind him. Next to it was a picture of young Sergeant Marty Pollio in his Army dress uniform.

"Now, in a case like that," said Klang, "the guy knows what he's doing. He's got problems, and he says, 'I don't want to think about this now,' so he goes fishing, or he watches a movie, or goes to a bar, or whatever."

"He avoids his problems on purpose," said Marty.

"That's right. People do it all the time. They put off the unpleasant stuff as long as they can."

"OK," said Gogo.

"But sometimes the mind uses a different approach," explained Klang. "Sometimes the person doesn't realize that it's happening."

"What do you mean?"

"The mind lies to the person. It fools him, distracts him like a magician. It says watch my right hand while my left hand pulls a coin out of your ear."

Gogo interrupted, "Excuse me. Did you say pull the coin out of 'your ear' or pull the coin out of 'your rear'? They sound so much alike. Your ear—your rear."

Klang laughed and called Gogo an expletive, while Marty said, "I'll give you an example. One summer morning, a boy comes out of his house with a nice bunch of grapes that his mother just gave him. He's all set to eat those grapes when one of his friends steals them. His buddies all laugh at him, they run from him, they pass the grapes from one kid to another."

"Nice friends," said Gogo.

"And before you know it, the grapes are all gone. Now the kid is heartbroken, 'cause he really wanted those grapes, but he convinces himself, 'Ah, they were probably *sour* grapes, anyway.'" Marty waved the grapes away with his hand.

Klang said, "Or, take a boy whose father abandoned him when he was a baby. He hates his father whenever he thinks of him. He wants to hit him, wants to curse him—but his father's not there to hit."

"So what does he do?" asked Gogo.

"He gets frustrated. But then one day, in high school, he joins the football team. He hits his opponents real hard. Where is it coming from, this aggression? It's coming from his hatred of his father. The boy never makes the connection. He doesn't think of his father when he's slamming some running back, because his mind has covered the tracks."

Gogo said, "I wonder what happened to Hitler when he was young—someone must have stepped on his toes real good."

Klang said, "On the show, they also talked about a boy who got toilet trained too early."

"No, please," Gogo put up his hands and laughed. "No mas."

Marty explained, "The little fellow just wanted to poop in his pants, like he had done since he was born."

"Naturally," agreed Gogo.

"But mean mommy and daddy said, 'No, no, Precious, now you must poop in the potty, and flush it far away.'"

Gogo commented, "Don't do that doodoo that you do so well."

"The boy doesn't like it one bit. In fact he hates what his parents are putting him through," explained Klang. "But they insist, and they can punish him, so he has to give in. But for the rest of his life, subconsciously, all he wants to do is let it out.'"

"Oh, please!" roared Gogo.

"But society doesn't permit that with adults," said Klang.

"Thank God," said Gogo. "Can you imagine?"

"So the man-child's brain clamps down on him and *twists* everything around." Here, Klang made twisting motions with his hands. "And now, on the outside, he's super neat. He can't abide the slightest dust in his house. He polishes his sneakers. He organizes his sock drawer. He sprays Lysol on everything."

Gogo folded his hands and said, "But inside, he can't wait to let it fly."

"Exactly."

"I'm staying away from that guy," said Gogo.

Klang offered: "Or, for instance, let's say there's a woman who is really hungry for men, but because of her religious upbringing that desire embarrasses her, so she turns frigid."

"I know how to warm her up," said Gogo.

"Or like a guy who hates queers. He makes fun of them—says we should gas 'em all. On the outside, he's super tough: he drives a truck, pumps iron. But on the inside, so deep that he don't even know it himself—"

"He's a faggy maggy," said Gogo.

"Did you know that Don Juan was gay?" asked Marty.

"I thought he bedded like a thousand broads."

Klang explained, "That was just a defense mechanism."

"Remarkable," said Gogo.

Marty offered, "Or when you're a kid and a bully beats you up. The bully humiliates you, shoves your face in the mud. When you get home, you hit your little brother, even though he didn't do anything wrong. It's just your way of coping with what happened to you."

Gogo said, "I gotta watch that show next time it comes on."

Klang walked to the refrigerator and grabbed a beer. He continued, "Take a white guy who says he hates blacks. He says they're lazy, they're dopey, they're animals. Why does he hate them so much? He really doesn't. It's *himself* that he hates, but his mind can't take that fact. Who can admit to himself that he sucks? That he's a loser. Nobody. So his mind projects his own self-hatred onto black people."

"We hate our neighbor as ourself," said Marty. "I guess the smart thing to do is to make our own selves better, then we can like ourselves and others, too."

Klang said, "Marty, how about that preacher with the hot secretary?"

"Yes, he wanted her bad," said Marty, "but he was married."

Klang said, "And being very religious, being a preacher and all, he wouldn't allow himself to cheat on his wife even when he had the chance."

"What a sap," said Gogo.

"But every day, more and more, he wanted Susie the Sexy Secretary."

"So what does he do?" asked Gogo, stroking his mustache.

Klang continued, "It bothers his conscience. It bothers him a lot because it goes against everything he believes in."

Marty spoke up, "You'll have to explain to Gogo what a conscience is."

"It bothers him so much he can't even admit he wants her, so he pushes the feeling down and down."

Gogo said, "It must be like when you're trying to pop a mean pimple. You squeeze and squeeze, but instead of breaking on the outside, it pops on the inside."

Marty winced, but Klang said, "Something like that. Anyway, his guilty feelings go so deep that they hit him right in the unconscious."

"You can die from that," said Gogo.

Klang continued, "And his unconscious mind, in order to relieve some of the pressure, plays a trick on him."

"What trick?"

"His mind turns things completely around and convinces him that *he's* not cheating on his wife. His *wife* is cheating on *him*!"

"The bitch!" said Gogo.

Klang howled in amusement. "No, no, no," he protested.

"Yes, yes, yes!" said Gogo.

"No, no, she's really *not* cheating on him."

"Sure she is," said Gogo. "I take her to the Rattlesnake Motel every Tuesday."

"You are insane," pronounced Marty.

"Defense mechanism," said Gogo. "I never heard of it before, but it makes a kind of sense."

"Some people zone out completely," said Klang. "They escape into their own fantasy world."

That tripped a relay in Gogo's memory. "I remember a story we read in high school: something, something, Walter Mitty."

"The *Secret Life of Walter Mitty*," said Marty.

"That's it! The guy's wife used to nag him and put him down, and in response he would just snap into a daydream on the spot." Here Gogo snapped his fingers. "He became a pilot flying through a battle. Then he became a surgeon, the only one who could operate on some rich guy. And at the end of the story he stood in front of a firing squad, real cool, smoking a cigarette." Gogo took an imaginary puff.

"And it was all in his mind," said Klang.

"Tell him about that poor little girl," said Marty.

Klang put his hand to his forehead. "Oh, man. I don't even want to think about it."

"Tell me," said Gogo.

Klang took a deep breath and said, "This little girl—I think she was ten—she got abused repeatedly by her uncle."

"The dirty rat," said Gogo, unsmiling.

"And while it was happening, she just couldn't understand what was going on, couldn't *believe* what was going on."

Marty wiped a tear from his eye and said, "So she said to herself, 'This horrible thing isn't happening to me. This is happening to some other little girl.'"

Klang said, "So to protect her, her mind split into two."

"Split personality," said Gogo.

"That's right," said Klang. "And within a few years, *multiple* personality, because it happened over and over again."

"Like Sybil," said Gogo. "Right? She had over a dozen personalities. And her mind did this to protect her?"

"It was the only way it knew how."

"You're right," said Gogo. It *is* a rotten world."

Marty messed with some papers on his desk, then said, "Listen, how about if Dr. Klang and Dr. Gogo collect the garbage in sectors A and B? And the recycling, too."

"Sure," said Gogo, rising.

"And don't forget to shred all that recycling paper."

"Will do," said Klang, grabbing a ring of keys.

"Then come back here when you're finished. I have another job for us."

"What job?" asked Klang.

"Around the beam. A whole bank of lights burned out." Marty looked at his watch. "As soon as their main shift is over, we'll all go up and put some new lights in."

Sam switched to an old black and white movie on TV.

A woman in a bath robe and hair curlers stood in the doorway to her house, screaming at her husband, who cringed outside on their lawn, "Can't you do anything right? Now, go back to that store and get what I told you to get!" She slammed the door.

The man winced, and his little dog whimpered and snuggled up to him, offering him commiseration and company. But the man kicked the dog, saying, "Leave me alone, you dopey mutt."

"Why did you ever marry her?" wondered Sam. "It's not the dog's fault." He changed the channel and another show came on. Two men dressed in blue tailored suits brooded in an office.

"He gave the job to Brady?" said one. "I thought *you* were gonna get it."

"Listen," said the other. "It's not a job any sane man would want. It's a lousy job, and I certainly didn't need it."

"It's a job for brown-nosers."

"Exactly. But it's the principal of the thing."

Sam switched to Betsy Custer's bedroom, hoping to see some solution to the problem of the Indian ghosts.

"Stay with me, Mommy," pleaded five-year old Betsy.

"You've got to get to sleep. No one is going to hurt you, sweetheart," said Katie Custer, her mother.

"Davey Pillepich wouldn't lie!" attested Betsy. "The Indian ghosts want revenge." Over her bed hung a dream catcher, a small wooden hoop in whose center was strung a "spider web" of red yarn. Dream catchers were invented by the Ojibwe Indians to catch bad dreams so they wouldn't trouble slumbering boys and girls. Traditionally, they were fashioned of willow and decorated with feathers, beads and personal items. From Betsy's dream catcher hung her favorite ring, a gold plastic Pocahontas ring, shaped like a little headdress, bejeweled with blue stones; hanging there too were an ancient sea shell she found in the desert, and a small picture of her father.

"But there *are* no ghosts, honey."

"They're going to kill us, Mommy," moaned Betsy.

"No, honey, no."

Betsy Custer scowled and commanded, "Call up Daddy in Indiana and say you're sorry so he'll come back and shoot the Indian ghosts!"

Sam felt sorry for Katie. He knew how hard she worked and how terrible she felt about the trial separation from her husband. As to the Indian ghosts seeking revenge, he made a mental note to keep an eye out for them. He took a bite of his cream donut, punched in some random numbers and got the Hoffer apartment.

Four-year old Jane Hoffer sat on a couch, flipping through a photo album. "You got a lot of pictures, Ma," she said. She gazed up at a nearby bookshelf full of white-covered albums.

Constance Hoffer sat down next to her daughter and said, "It's important to have pictures of the good times in your life. That way you can always go back and re-live them. And no one can ever take those good times away from you."

They had their stereo on, and Perry Como's sweet, sad voice filled their living room and Sam's office:

> "Once upon a time, the world was sweeter than we knew.
> Everything was ours, how happy we were then.
> But somehow once upon a time never comes again."

Six-year-old Barry Hoffer burst into the room like a force of nature.

Jane said, "Barry, look at these pictures."

"I don't wanna look at those dumb old pictures. I wanna play with my new Mesmerizer."

On his forehead he wore a circular screen on which a black and white spiral rotated in a clockwise direction. Around this screen, colored lights flashed in the opposite direction, now blue, now red, now white."

Mother and daughter sat transfixed by it. Barry dictated, "I command you to stop looking at those stupid pictures. You will obey. You will obey."

Constance Hoffer jumped up and said, "That's it. To bed—everybody!"

Sam felt strangely uncomfortable as he pulled away from this scene. He changed cameras to the Base Pharmacy, but even as he did that, he remembered Barry's counter-rotating Mesmerizer.

Sandra Graham was working late at her desk when Gogo stopped by the Pharmacy. He and Sam saw her put down a bottle of diet pills and shift her computer mouse.

"I'm sorry to bother you," said the janitor, "but I'm here to pick up the trash and the recycling."

"Oh, you're not bothering me."

"Are you sure?"

"Yes, quite sure."

"Well, that's too bad, because you look like somebody I'd like to bother."

"And why is that?"

"Because you're pretty," said Gogo.

She scowled. "I'll bet you say that to all the girls."

He seemed surprised. "How did you know that?"

She made a show of busying herself with some paperwork.

"What's your name?" he asked.

"Sandra."

"That's a nice name."

"Thank you."

Gogo said, "Aren't you gonna ask me my name?"

She looked up from her work and cracked half a smile. "What's your name?"

"They call me Gogo."

"That's an interesting name."

"It's short for Gogolich."

"Gogolich—what nationality is that?

Gogo moved closer and put on his most serious face. "It's Dalmatian," he said. "I'm a Dalmatian."

That made her laugh. "You're funny," she said.

"But I'm not trying to be funny."

"You're really a Dalmatian?"

"I was born here, but my parents were both born on the Dalmatian coast."

"Oh, I've heard of that," she said, and she tried to remember where. "Do you speak Dalmatian?"

"Woof! Woof!" he barked, startling her. When she chuckled, he switched gears. "Actually, nobody speaks Dalmatian. It's an extinct language."

"It's dead? So, your people come from a country that doesn't have a language. Don't they talk over there?"

"They speak Croatian. Dalmatia is the sea coast of Croatia."

"I guess I forgot. Is that where the dogs came from originally?"

"Just the first hundred and one," said Gogo.

Sandra laughed again. "You really are funny. And the Dalmatian language is really extinct?"

He said, "I heard it's coming back—in spots."

She buried her face in her hands. "Oh, goodness," she said. She looked up at him, right into his eyes. "You got a first name, Gogo?"

"Michael," he said.

"Michael, like the archangel."

"You need some heavenly protection?" he asked.

"Maybe," said Sandra. "Maybe I do."

"I can provide it," he pledged.

She stared at him. "You seem so happy," she said. "Are you always this happy?"

"I'm happy 'cause I'm here with you."

"That's a nice thing to say."

"To tell you the truth," said Gogo, "I'd be happier if I wasn't so happy."

She leaned back in her chair and shook her head. "That doesn't make sense. How could you be..."

He said, "Well, look at it this way. Being too happy is bad luck, right? I mean, if you're too happy, you're jinxing yourself, and something is bound to go wrong."

"OK, I'll buy that."

"And since I'd rather not have bad luck," he continued, "I'd rather not be so happy."

"I think I understand."

Gogo concluded, "So I'd be happier if I wasn't so happy."

She found herself giggling and tearing up at the same time, "You know, I hate to say this, but that makes sense."

"Thank you," he said. "You're the first person to ever tell me I made sense."

"I believe that."

"So, Sandra, where are you from?"

"I'm from Pennsylvania, from a town called Lock Haven."

"I know where that is. That's in Clinton County."

"You've been there?" said Sandra.

Gogo looked around to see if anyone else was near. Bending over her desk, he said, "We used to hunt up there all the time when I was young."

"Where?"

"Sproul State Forest. White-tailed deer, black bear."

"That's not far," she said.

He never hunted, thought Sam, *but he used to hunt all the time. They can't both be true.* To Selene he said, "Please print up Gogo's work history for me, will you?"

On the wide screen in front of Sam, Gogo picked up the bottle of diet pills Sandra had used. He read the label and shook his head. Then he dropped them in the garbage.

"Why'd you do that?" she said.

"Because you don't need them."

"Don't I?"

Gogo's eyes beamed sincerity as he assured her, "You're not fat. Not at all."

"Oh?"

"In fact, I'd say you're skinny."

"People tell me that," she said, "but I can't see it."

"Well, take it from your favorite Dalmatian. You're not fat at all."

Sam turned the sound down and said, "Selene, did Gogo ever have much interaction with Rita?"

In reply, Selene showed him a scene in which Gogo collected recycling paper from Rita's office. Gogo looked over at Rita and was puzzled. Rita seemed hypnotized by something on her screen.

Gogo walked around and saw what it was, but the camera angle did not permit Sam to see it. Sam saw concern on Gogo's face. Then the janitor turned off Rita's monitor and she snapped out of her trance.

"I must have dozed off," said Rita.

"They've got some good coffee at Dunkin Donuts," said Gogo. "Four or five cups should be enough."

Rita got up, unsteadily at first. "That's a good idea," she said, and she walked out of the room.

"Selene, what was on her screen?" asked Sam.

"That's classified," whispered Selene.

Classified. "Above my level?"

"I'm sorry, Sam."

"I could ask Gogo," he mused, "and he might tell me the truth." It was too late now, but he would make a point of calling some of Gogo's former employers as soon as he got a chance on Tuesday.

Sam toyed with his keyboard, hesitated, then switched back to the movie *Rear Window.*

In his dark apartment, sitting in his wheelchair, "Jeff" Jeffries looked almost inhuman as he peered through binoculars at something across the courtyard.

Lisa Freemont, his girlfriend, stood beside him. Played by Grace Kelly, Lisa wore a black dress and a pearl necklace, and she too stared intently at something off-screen.

The camera zoomed into her perfect face, her blond hair, blue eyes and red lips, as she said, "Let's start from the beginning again, Jeff. Tell me everything you saw, and what you think it means."

Yes, thought Sam. *I'd like to know what some things mean, too.*

Sam switched channels and an old TV sitcom popped on—*Hogan's Heroes*, about allied prisoners in a German POW camp.

Sergeant Schultz, the overweight, befuddled guard was saying, "I know nothing, nothing." Reflecting upon his own willful ignorance, the good-natured German soldier continued, "If I would know something, I wouldn't even tell myself."

Sam switched channels again, and this time found a Sherlock Holmes movie called *A Scandal in Bohemia.*

Holmes was saying to his friend, Doctor Watson: "For example, you have frequently seen the steps which lead up from the hall to this room."

"Frequently," agreed Watson.

"How often?"

"Well, some hundreds of times," said the doctor, matter-of-factly.

"Then how many are there?"

"How many? I don't know."

"Quite so!" proclaimed Holmes. "You have not observed. And yet you have seen. That is just my point. Now, I know that there are seventeen steps, because I have both seen and observed."

Sam turned off all the monitors. He stared out into the welcoming darkness and steadied his breathing. He accepted the stillness, the quiet, the lack of auditory and visual stimulation, even the absence of odors, and breathed in and out, in and out.

There was nothing for him to observe now, only his own heartbeat and the sound of his own thoughts.

"Yes," thought Sam, "we should all be like Sherlock Holmes and *observe*, not just see, everything around us. But try it some time. Walk down a city street and observe everything you see and hear and smell. Study the buildings, their shapes, heights, styles. Can you remember them all? All the cars that passed you—what were their license numbers? The woman who locked eyes with you—what color were those eyes? What's in the window of the delicatessen? How many hydrants on the block? How many trees? It's a hard thing to do. The mind resists it.

To see, to observe correctly, and to remember is not easy for a man. You have to block out most of what you see and hear so you aren't overwhelmed by the sheer mass of it all. Then, from the bits that get through, you have to select what you need to remember. And most of this process is automatic, unconscious, subliminal. In the end you take your reality filtered and diluted, and pour it into the little grey cells of your memory, and that is the best you can do."

He wondered what it was like for a computer like Selene.

Sam turned on the monitors again and switched to Adam Weizman's living room. Weizman was sitting and saying, "Read it to me. I'd like to hear it."

"I don't want to bore you," said Father House, strolling around the room.

"You don't want to bore me—but you brought the poem with you."

The priest grinned and sat down. "All right, all right, give me a minute." He reached into his pocket and pulled out two pieces of paper. "I brought two copies so you could read along."

Weizman took one and looked it over as House began:

"Inn / His Image

In a timeless Inn at the dark forest's core,
with its cedar walls and its field stone floor,
round a fire we talk, and though it may seem odd,
we love to squawk about the color of God.

The dancer goes round, he moves round and around.
Past our windows he twirls on the shadowy ground.
He can hardly be seen and he makes not a sound,
but his story if told would astound and resound.

I say God is as red as my Cardinal robes;
my friends say the window I gaze through is tinted rose.
The Protestant lass from the streets of Belfast
says her spinning Lord flings a bright orange cast.

The Imam swears that Allah's face is green;
he stares through an emerald pane at a leafy scene.
But Moses the Jew from the York that is New
is sure that God shimmers Israeli blue.

The Hopi thinks the Spirit dancer grey;
through smoky glass he watches night and day.

The Hindu sees the whirling Oneness white,
all colors summed in simple, stunning bright.

The atheist swears that nothing stirs the night,
that each of us sees his own face by the Inn's pale light,
reflected in the glass through which each peers;
black is the casement of this godless seer.

The dancer goes round, he moves round and around.
Past our windows he twirls on the shadowy ground.
He can hardly be seen and he makes not a sound,
but his story if told would astound and resound.

One doorway called Death from our lobby leads out,
bypassing stained glass and letting us scout,
if we die, for the dancer prancing about,
for the shade and the tone and the hue without doubt.

But we who still live—we should finally guess
that in our friends' faces is God's visage pressed.
There we will find His true colors displayed,
For in Nature's Inn, we are in His image made."

Sam considered the bank of monitors in front of him, each screen a window on his world. What did they show him? What did they distort? What effect did they have on his understanding of people and life? And what kind of monitors does God have, if there is a God?

Father House folded his copy of the poem and looked for a sign from his critic.

"So you're a cardinal now?" asked Weizman, beaming.

"No, still base chaplain. But it seemed to fit the color scheme."

"And I guess I'm the colorblind atheist. I knew my windows were dirty, but black?"

"So what do you think?

Weizman pursed his lips, wagged his head, and said, "Well, it's clear, direct. It says what you believe. I don't know. How does one tell if a poem is good?"

"Emily Dickinson said when you read a great poem you'll feel as though your head has been chopped off."

Weizman grinned and felt his neck. "Still there."

"Mine, too." laughed House.

"It reminds me of that line, 'For now we see through a glass darkly, but then face to face.'"

"First Corinthians," said House. "Yes, it is my great hope that one day we will see God face to face."

On the wall behind Weizman were five masks from various parts of the world, and these now caught the priest's attention. The first, at the lower right, was an Mbangu mask from the Congo, white on one side and black on the other. The severely distorted face and nose were meant to represent the disfigurements brought on by such diseases as palsy, syphilis, epilepsy, or smallpox. When the wearer of this mask dances in a ritual he also wears a fake hunchback which has been pierced by an arrow—this signifies that he is sick because has been stung by a sorcerer's dart. The masked dancer carries his own bow and arrow, showing that while he is wounded, he is also a hunter, hunting the disease which disfigured him.

The second mask, on the lower left part of the wall, was a Mayan funerary mask, carved of green jade with big white teeth and dull yellow eyes. Above that was a ghost mask from the Kwakwaka'wakw tribe of

British Columbia: white horse hair flowed around its clay-colored face which was highlighted by white brows, eyes, nose and mouth.

The fourth mask, high on the right, was a Transformation Mask from the Kwakiutl Indians. When closed, it was a Thunderbird, a legendary creature who caused storms, lightning, and thunder. When opened by pulling on strings, it revealed a man's face surrounded by a corona. On this inner corona were painted clouds, ghosts and a scene depicting the Thunderbird biting a snake. This mask was made of wood, paint, leather, twine and the hair of an enemy.

The last mask, in the center of them all, was Trimurti, the Hindu trinity: it had three faces, one for Brahma the creator, one for Vishnu the preserver, and one for Shiva the destroyer.

"Face to face," said Weizman. "But you say it's your hope? Not your belief?"

The black man rolled his sad brown eyes and exhaled. Then he gazed at his friend with affection and sincerity. "You said earlier that you were afraid there is no center inside of you. I am sometimes not sure there is a God out there in the darkness."

"So Thomas, too, has his doubts."

House picked up a journal from the blue stack on the coffee table: *American Journal of Psychiatry.* He said, "Your boy Freud said there is no God. He said that early man looked around at a nasty world and saw it filled with death and suffering. Man felt so alone that his mind invented a strong father to protect him and watch over him."

"Man created an illusion to comfort himself, yes."

"My faith is small, Adam, smaller than a mustard seed. But my hope—my hope is a great big rock."

"But you *do* have faith?"

"Rene Descartes said 'I think, therefore I am.'"

"And what does Tom House say?"

"I pray, therefore I believe."

"What do you pray for?"

House found the bottle of wine and poured the last few ounces in his glass. He drank them and said, "Every day I pray that God will save us all, everyone who has ever lived or ever will live."

Weizman shifted in his chair and said, "Wait, let's think about that for a moment. Even Hitler?"

"Hitler was one of us," said House. "What *he* did, many of us could do."

"That's a depressing thought, but you may be right."

"Like most good Catholics, I believe in Purgatory. Hitler should sweat a river of blood for every life he destroyed. God should take that monster by the scruff of the neck and shove his face into the heart of every Jewish child who lost his or her life in the Holocaust, and say, 'Fool, do you understand now the grief you caused?'"

"You're assuming a part of him *would* understand. I'm not so sure."

"But then, when he has learned his lesson, when he asks for forgiveness…"

"And if everyone is saved, if even Hitler is saved, then so is Tom House. That sounds like a self-serving theology."

"I'm a selfish human being," said Father House. "In fact, I'm so selfish I'm going to eat this last piece of danish."

Sam switched to a female televangelist, a tall, stunning beauty with long, brown hair.

She said, "Original sin is selfishness, a concern only for the self, and each one of us is born with it. But Jesus says that in order to be saved you've got to lose that self-centeredness. In Luke 9:24, he says: 'For whoever would save his life will lose it, but whoever loses his life for my sake will save it.'"

Sam changed the channel.

Professor Schuyler Bliss sat in a grey sofa chair and said, "No, I don't believe in a personal God. But I do believe in eternity. I believe in Brahman."

Emmet Sheridan sat in a matching chair and asked, "And what is Brahman?"

On the grey wall between them hung a large photograph of a spherical drop of water hanging over a pool. Sculptured rings of water spread out from the point where a previous drop had fallen, and where this one was destined to fall.

"Brahman is the eternal, unchanging reality," said Bliss. "Brahman is infinite and transcendent. Everything we see comes from Brahman; everything returns to Brahman. It is the task of the individual soul, the Atman, to realize that it is one with Brahman."

Sheridan asked, "And the images that people around the world have of God—"

"The images of God are the masks of eternity. They both cover and reveal the face of Glory—the ultimate reality that lies beyond our senses."

"When you say mask—to me, when someone wears a mask, it is partly because he wants to hide from someone else—to hide his true identity. Are you saying that God, at least sometimes, wants to hide from us?"

Professor Schuyler Bliss grinned and asked, "Haven't you noticed?"

Sam switched to a local cable channel showing *Stand-up Poetry!*

Against a black background starred with four colored lights, a white poet stood, his dreadlocks waxed and brown, his beard long and scruffy. He cried out,

"What a wild and random thought,
That we are the children of chance,
The godless orphans of chaos,

trapped in a meaningless dance."

Sam switched to a base camera again, and saw Bernice, the elderly cleaning lady, in her darkened room.

Bernice watched over her illuminated ant farm, sealed between two panels of glass and a green plastic frame. "Stop that fighting," ordered Bernice. At her command, two wrestling ants separated.

"I'm watching you," she said. "I am observing you." The company of ants hurried back and forth through their tunnels, each individual on his own mission.

"I gave you all enough food." The ants seemed to hum in grateful activity.

The old lady smiled, apparently pleased with the smooth functioning of her dominion. "Remember," she said, "I may be just a cleaning lady to some, but I'm more than that to you."

When no one challenged her, she added, "So, you better be good, or I'll smoosh you."

Sam switched to the Officers' Club to watch Fortunato Steiner's 65th birthday party.

Dana Severn was standing now, with her short-haired friend, Erika Grenfell, on one side of her and grey-eyed Robby Lee on the other. Sitting in leather chairs beside them were the birthday boy and his chief assistant, nuclear physicist Millie Guan. Five or six co-workers milled around near them.

Steiner was saying, "Well, to each his own religion and to each his own God."

Erika said, "But some of those fundamentalists are crazy, like that woman in Tennessee—the reporter said she drowned her own kids because she feared they were on the devil's path."

"Terrible," said Dana Severn. "I keep telling myself not to watch the news anymore because it's all so depressing."

Erika said, "How could a woman kill her own children, her own flesh and blood?"

Robby Lee spread his hands wide on his thighs and said, "Well, there's one million abortions in this country every year."

Erika's mouth dropped, but she recovered quickly and confronted him, "What a stupid thing to say!"

"Well, you asked the question," said Robby.

"I said *children*, not fetuses."

"Just because you don't want to think they're children doesn't make it so."

"Can we stop?" pleaded Dana. "It's Steiner's birthday."

Steiner rose from his chair with great difficulty and secured his crutches on his arms. Millie Guan took one arm to help steady him.

"I think we should ask his opinion," said Erika. "What do you think, Fortunato?"

"I have to go to the men's room," he said.

"You're ducking an important issue," said Erika.

Steiner smiled and said, "Look, it's not my field. I'm a physicist."

"We just want your personal opinion," said Erika.

"I know it's a touchy subject with a lot of people, so I try to avoid it."

"You support women's rights, don't you, Fortunato?" pressed Erika.

"I support everyone's rights." He leveled a kindly gaze at her and said, "My personal opinion is: life should be protected. I mean, that's why we're all here at this base, isn't it?"

Providential in mind, Steiner was unfortunate in body; he was, in fact, a dwarf with a prominent hunchback. He had won every worthwhile prize in physics short of the Nobel, and all those prizes were for his *published* work. If his still-covert work could be declassified, the Nobel would be assured, for he had solved the holy Grail of modern physics—safe fusion power, unlimited and clean for all the world to use. Ten Steiner reactors at ten strategic bases around the U.S. were all that worked on this earth right now, powering ten antimissile beams. They were experimental and secret, and they were wonderfully successful. Within three years, he had been promised, this secret would be opened to the world, and mankind would benefit, and mankind would praise its benefactor, Fortunato Steiner, the lucky dwarf. Often compared to the great Steinmetz, whom he resembled in form if not in face, he believed that God had given him a first-rate mind in compensation for his imperfect body.

"And when does life begin?" asked Robby Lee.

Steiner shook his head and said, "Let me state for the record that I did not bring up the happy topic of abortion, especially at my own birthday party. By the way, thank you all once again for the party. It has been wonderful."

Other guests, chatting about this or that, moved toward them but quieted down when they realized Steiner was speaking. "Robby, in answer to your question, to me life begins at conception."

Erika protested, "But that's a religious belief. It's not based in science."

"We have to pick a time. Is it at birth? Is it when the heart starts beating? To me, as soon as conception ends, a new life begins."

"A woman has a right to control her body," said Erika.

"Well," said the hunchbacked dwarf, "I agree with you that control of one's body is important."

"I've gotta go," said Erika. Sam couldn't tell whether she was embarrassed or angry.

"Erika," said Steiner, smiling, "Do you know how I got the name Fortunato?"

She said, "No." Indeed, he had never told the story to anyone at this base.

"Well, let me sit back down and I'll tell you." He tottered back to his chair and sat down. Taking a deep breath, he began the tale. "My mother had two abortions before she had me, before they were even legal in this country. My older brother and my older sister, for that is how I think of them, were... severely damaged. Hopeless, really. You see, my parents weren't very good at making babies."

Dana Severn bowed her head.

"I was going to be her last try."

Sam noticed something in Erika Grenfell's eyes. Was it empathy? Sympathy? The slow start of a tear?

"One day, my mother learned that she was pregnant, and she went in for whatever tests they had at the time. Same thing. 'We're sorry, Mrs. Steiner, but this baby will be horribly deformed. It would be an act of mercy to the baby and to yourself if you...' and so on."

"She was distraught, anguished. She didn't know what to do. My father didn't know how to help her. This was her last chance, you see? Her last chance for a baby of her own to hold in her arms.

"She agonized and argued with herself. Finally she decided... that she would put off her decision. She got on a plane and headed for Europe. Take a vacation now, face the music later. A great escape."

"Where did she go?" asked Dana.

"She flew to Venice, stayed there for a few weeks, then took a boat down the Adriatic Coast of what was then called Yugoslavia."

"It's supposed to be beautiful there," said Dana.

"Well, they were still recovering from World War II," said Steiner.

A man said to no one in particular, "Was it behind the Iron Curtain?"

"Anyway," continued Steiner, "one morning she visited a pretty island called Zlarin."

"Did she know anybody there?"

"Not a soul. Now, being Catholic (my father, by the way, was Jewish) she visited the island's baroque church. She knelt down, prayed for guidance, and... passed out on the stone floor."

"Oh, God," said a woman behind Robby Lee.

"An elderly nun saw my mother collapse, took pity on her, revived her, consoled her. 'You must pray to Sveti Fortunato,' the nun said. 'Pray to Saint Lucky.'"

Nervous laughter spread through the Officers' Club.

"Then the old nun walked behind a side altar, raised her hands and slid open two wooden doors, revealing the bones of Saint Fortunato, sealed in a glass case.

"This saint had a sword beside him, jeweled rings on his fingers, and, next to his right hand, a bottle of red stuff."

"Red stuff?" asked Robby Lee.

"The nun said it was the saint's blood, and she examined it very closely, very deliberately. Finally, she testified that it was liquid today, surely a good sign."

"Was it really his blood?" asked Dana.

"For all I know it was wine mixed with Jell-O, but it appeared liquid that day, and that's all the convincing my mother needed. She would have the baby."

Steiner's face lit up. "So you see, I was the lucky one," he said. "I was the sole survivor, saved by an old nun, saved by the blood of Saint Fortunato."

Sam switched to the Maintenance Office.

Marty, Klang and Gogo sat watching the television news. Brett Fox was interviewing a spokeswoman for PETA, People for the Ethical Treatment of Animals.

Brett asked, "So what message would you like people to learn from your new campaign?"

The spokeswoman said, "We would like people to consider, if they're thinking of eating in a McDonald's or in a Kentucky Fried Chicken, that the animals have rights too, including the right to a long, natural life, and the right not to be slaughtered. And please consider just how much suffering and pain goes into a Happy Meal."

Gogo said, "I don't know. I like Burger King better. How about you, Marty?"

A commercial eased onto the janitors' TV set. Two young men sat on a couch, drinking beer from frosty blue bottles.

Sam's mind jumped back to a similar scene but a different time – when he and Rita and Johnnie had all been working together on a tiger team at Los Alamos. In Sam's mind, a young Johnnie Lonetree sat on a couch next to him, dressed in a light blue shirt and a dark blue tie. Johnnie pulled a beer bottle away from his mouth and asked, "You and Rita?"

"Yeah."

"What? Steady?"

"Well, we're dating," said Sam. "What? Why are you laughing?"

"Yeah, I can see how she might be your type. I mean she's sexy, smart, cuddly as a bobcat." He took a sip from his bottle. "Did I mention she was sexy?"

"But not *your* type, Johnnie?"

"No, no, she's not my type at all. You can have her all to yourself."

"Well, that's very white of you."

Sam pulled himself back to the present, but his recollection had given him something to consider: *Does Rita love Johnnie more than she loves Sam?* Jealousy is a coyote, isn't it? A playful howler roaming the desert of a man's mind, a lustful, four-legged urge. It has yellow eyes and a furry snout and it peeps in your mirror as you shave. *Does Rita love Johnnie more?*

Sam switched to Sheila Mae's bedroom.

His secretary sat at her dressing table, listening to the song, *The Rose*, and singing along with it, singing to Sam's picture which she held in her hands.

> "It's the heart afraid of breaking that never learns to dance,
> It's the dream afraid of waking that never takes a chance,
> It's the one who won't be taken who cannot seem to give,
> And the soul afraid of dying that never learns to live."

Sam switched to General Patel.

Brigadier General Isha Patel, sitting in his saffron robe, chanted the word "Aum" once again, signifying that he accepted the divine plan and understood the mystery of life, and that he loved and approved of all beings.

Finally, Sam switched once more to the BBC production of *Macbeth.*

Mighty Macbeth, newly crowned King of the Scots, worried aloud, "To be thus is nothing, but to be safely thus."

***

Chapter Fourteen: Boil

When Sam Sawyer's phone rang at 11 PM Monday night, he shut off his monitors and answered it, "Colonel Sawyer here."

The voice on the other end was familiar. "Sam, this is Thaler."

"Hello, General."

"I've been knocking heads all day with a Senate committee."

"How did that go, if I may ask?" Sam figured it was long past midnight in the nation's capital.

"Some of these jokers want to close down the entire Hecate system. They say it's a boondoggle that'll never work."

"I'm sorry to hear that," said Sam.

"Listen, General Thorne told me that DARPA is sending its Inspector General out to visit you."

"Yes. Lonetree told me."

"Yeah, and you know they're sending a coroner for Rikki Greco."

"Yes," said Sam.

"Ken Slater is the IG. He's a fair man."

"I know him."

"They should arrive in Altamura at oh ten hundred hours, your time."

When he hung up the phone, Sam felt weary. It had been a long, dreadful day, and the prospects for tomorrow weren't promising. His body craved sleep, but his steadfast spirit fought the temptation. Had he done all he could do to track down Rikki's killer? Could he do more to protect the base and its people? Did he know what threats, if any, were heading America's way?

The phone rang again. "Sawyer here."

"Sam?" The voice on the other end sounded a lot like Rita's, and the shock of that resemblance transmitted tension through his chest and arms.

But it was older and rougher, the voice of a woman who had smoked her way through many years of grief and despair, stress and notoriety.

He said, "Hello, Mrs. Kelly."

"How is she?"

"She's uh... stable. Maybe a slight bit of improvement today." Was it true?

"I was on a yacht, out past Catalina. That's why I didn't get the call right away. I would tell you whose yacht, but I know you don't impress easy."

"Rita's still in a coma. The doctors are going to move her to St. Michael's Hospital tomorrow because they've got a more sophisticated setup there."

"Take care of her, Sam." The voice cracked a bit. "I want her back."

"I'll do whatever I can for her. I promise you that."

Kyra Kelly had found a new life for herself after the disturbing death of her son, Neal. She had divorced her husband and moved to Los Angeles with her daughter, Rita, worked as a reporter for a number of newspapers and web sites, and finally struck gold with her bestselling tell-all, *Crashing Stars!* Along the way, she had discovered a genuine talent for and a grand fascination with prying into the lives of Hollywood's most troubled celebrities. She swam like a shark in a sea of gossip, and devoured the weak, the sick, the stragglers—those unable to run, or dodge, or hide.

"She's everything in the world to me."

"I know," said Sam.

"I want to fly out to see her, but tomorrow's gonna be tough. I've got an interview scheduled that I just can't break."

"I understand."

"I'll be there as soon as I can."

He felt relieved when that conversation was over, glad to be turning on his monitors once again, comfortable watching his base and his people. As if on autopilot, he impulsively selected cameras in the kitchen of Gabriel and Constance Hoffer.

The couple sat at a Formica table, drinking coffee and picking at the remains of an apple pie. Their apartment was quiet, which told Sam that their kids were probably asleep. Constance asked her husband, "So, what's next?"

Gabriel said, "Well, we're trying to find out who killed Rikki Greco."

"I didn't mean that," she said, and he glanced up at her inquiringly.

She said, "I meant with us."

Gabriel made no reply, and the silence around them thickened.

Constance said, "Why can't everything stay the same as it was on our wedding day? Why can't we love each other just as much now as we did then?"

Sam pulled away, giving them some belated privacy. He switched to a television drama.

Onscreen, a woman and a man sat at a kitchen table, and the woman asked, "The tests show you have it?"

The man looked sick, colorless and emaciated. He said, "30 percent of males with this cancer live five years. 20 percent live two years."

"Statistics," she said. "Henry, don't give me statistics."

"What do you want me to give you?"

"Tell me what you're feeling. Are you too scared to—"

"Hannah," he said. "I'm an engineer. 72 percent of engineers have no feelings."

Sam switched to the Officers' Club. The party had emptied out. A few stragglers played pool and drank beer. Conversations were low and limited.

He switched to the Grenfell's bedroom.

Erika and her husband, Gowan, were in bed under dark green sheets. A yellow lava lamp on a night stand provided dim illumination, its wax blobs slowly churning and mutating. Gowan moved to kiss his wife, but she stopped him.

"What's wrong?"

"How old was Sarah?" she asked, pensively.

A puzzled look came over him. "Sarah who?"

"Abraham's wife—how old was she when she had Isaac"?

He scratched his ear. "Older than you, I guess."

"The doctor said some women just can't get pregnant."

Gowan said, "I'm not about to give up. Are you?"

"Not yet."

"Did you take your pill today?"

"My 'birth control' pill?"

"If that's what you want to call it." The pills were called Clomid, and Sam knew that they were in fact prescription fertility pills.

"Let's hope it works this time," she said and reached over to turn off the lamp.

Sam switched to the TV news.

Lucy Cable asked, "Ever hear of a town called Fearnot, Pennsylvania?"

"I'm afraid I haven't," replied Brett Fox.

"Well, in the town of Fearnot, on Saturday night, an 18-year-old girl gave birth on the gym floor at her high school's dance. Neither the girl nor her parents had any idea that she was pregnant."

Brett Fox added, "Mother and baby boy are doing fine."

Lucy said, "In Little Rock, Arkansas, there's a boy with a medical condition that some of us might think we would want."

"What's that?" asked Brett.

"Little Artie Simon, three years old, was born with a congenital insensitivity to pain. You can stick a pin in him and he feels nothing."

"That sounds like a good thing."

"Actually, it's a very dangerous thing, because people with this condition tend not to be cautious enough. For instance, if Artie grabbed a hot coffee pot he wouldn't pull away, and he'd get badly burned."

Sam switched to Betsy Custer's bedroom.

Little Betsy, dressed in pink and white pajamas, was jumping on the bed, whooping and hollering.

Her mother and her brother Billy rushed into the room, and when Betsy saw them, she vibrated her hand against her lips, in what she must have considered "injun" style, and shouted, "Woo-woo-woo-woo-woo."

Her mother was confused. "What's going on?"

Betsy danced and chanted, "Ka-Yah, Ha-Nah, Hey-O!"

Billy inquired, "Betsy, are you loco?"

Mother Katie said, "What's going on? I thought you were afraid."

"I was."

"Afraid that ghosts were going to get you—Indian ghosts."

"Not anymore!" she laughed.

"Well, I can see that. But why not? What happened?"

"Mom," said Betsy, "I was scared as can be. But then, I had a brainstorm."

Billy was skeptical.

"And what was your great idea?" asked her mother.

"I saw, real clear, that all I had to do was become one of them."

"What?" said Billy.

"And then I wouldn't be scared anymore."

Sam switched back to the Hoffer apartment. No one was in the kitchen. He tried the living room.

Staff Sergeant Gabriel Suleiman Hoffer knelt on a prayer rug, facing Mecca, reciting his final prayers of the day. He had the curly blond hair of an ethnic German, and the solid green eyes of a true believer, pure without a dissenting speck, and dark as a palm leaf at dusk.

Currently, Gabriel believed in Islam, but Sam knew that that had not always been the case. Born into a Catholic family in New Berlin, Wisconsin, Gabe went to parochial schools and was an average kid who paid the average amount of attention to his religion, no more, no less. A great change came when he was thirteen, when his father left his wife and kids for a younger woman, a blond Norwegian immigrant. With his father gone, Gabe started latching onto his faith, going to Mass regularly, reading the New Testament diligently. He liked to listen to the parish's aged, conservative pastor, who preached against divorce and immorality and permissiveness.

But then the old priest retired, and a young priest came in, Father Neikirk, and this man felt differently about sin and forgiveness and Heaven and Hell. Adam and Eve were mythological, he said, and not every word in the Bible was meant to be taken literally. God was so merciful He would let all kinds of people into Heaven, even non-Christians. And there might be a Hell, but God would probably never send anyone there for eternity. It all seemed a little weak to Gabriel, a little thin. Within a year, a financial scandal caught Father Neikirk with his hand in the collection box, and Gabriel Hoffer stopped going to church.

At the University of Wisconsin-Waukesha, he made friends with a group of Evangelicals, nice people, real believers. He admired their enthusiasm and their emotional involvement with their faith. He started going to their church, the Christian Citadel. However, a wife-swapping scandal involving their popular pastor soon soured Gabriel on this second approach to Christianity.

When he married Constance Peterson, their wedding was celebrated in the Unitarian Universalist church she attended. But he never learned to accept that creedless faith, which counted among its adherents even nonbelievers, even atheists.

Two years ago, while competing at the annual Defender's Challenge at Lackland AFB, Texas, Gabriel Hoffer became teammates on a Combat Rifle Team with a black Chicagoan named Davis Jones, who opened his eyes to the simplicity and certainty, the truth and beauty, the authenticity and promise of Islam. The experience was for Gabriel a spiritual homecoming, and he immediately embraced the Muslim faith and submitted his life to Allah, taking as a middle moniker the name of one of Islam's greatest heroes, Suleiman the Magnificent.

Sam knew all this—knew that Hoffer was a fervent Muslim—knew also that he cheated on his wife with Rita. And yet he liked the man. He admired his competence and commitment to his job, appreciated his devotion to his children, even respected the earnestness and sincerity with which he dedicated himself to his new religion. No, he wasn't perfect, but then, who was?

Sam watched Hoffer finish up his prayers. Soon the sergeant sat down at his desk and logged on to his computer. Shortly, the home page of a web site appeared on Gabriel's monitor—it was called "The Prophet's Outreach To The West," and Sam had seen him visit it before.

"Selene, what does he do on this site?"

"He reads quotations from the Koran and other Muslim holy books. He scans news articles about Islamic countries and peoples. He studies essays by famous Muslim scholars."

"Does he ever write anything on it?" asked Sam.

"No. My records show that he never has."

"Does he ever receive any messages through it?"

"Not to my knowledge."

Sam switched to the bedroom of Sheila Mae Wood, his nearsighted, round-faced secretary.

Sheila was sitting in bed, playing a computer game on her laptop. The game was called *Secret Love* and it was making her, *"Name of star?"*

She typed in: "Sheila Novak."

"Name of lover?"

"Sam Ferguson."

"Use same faces and bodies as last time?" She had previously loaded several pictures of herself and of Sam into the game.

"Yes."

"Please choose script."

After scrolling through a long list, Sheila picked number 23. *"Sheila and Sam are shipwrecked on a desert isle."*

"Click here to review script." She clicked.

"Sheila Novak and Sam Ferguson meet on a cruise ship in the South Pacific. A giant rogue wave hits the ship and it capsizes. Sam saves Sheila's life, and their lifeboat beaches on a deserted island. They build a hut and a fire. That night, Sheila tells Sam, "I want to thank you again for saving my life...."

The game said, *"Click here to play,"* and she did.

High resolution animated figures strolled the deck of a cruise ship at night. Sheila Novak's curvaceous body graced an elegant green gown and she said, "I've never been to the South Pacific before. I spend most of my time in Europe looking after my chain of jewelry stores."

Sam Ferguson, wearing a tuxedo, replied, "Your emeralds look divine, but they pale in comparison to your eyes."

The real Sam watched along for quite a while. He watched the huge wave slam the ship, saw the daring rescue, the beaching of the lifeboat at midday, the building of the hut, the rainbowed sunset.

Sam watched the real Sheila squirm as the animated Sheila started to undress. He watched sweat form across her brow, and he heard the real woman echo the fake Sheila's words, "It's all for you, Sam."

Sam Sawyer felt embarrassed for her. Did she not know he could see her? She had seen Rita on his screen when she barged into his office this morning. Hadn't that given her a clue? Maybe she didn't care. Maybe she wanted him to see.

Sam switched back to *Rear Window*.

A man with black hair and dull eyes stood in "Jeff" Jeffries's apartment at night. It was Jeff's friend Doyle the cop, and he scolded Jeff and Lisa: "That's a secret, private world you're looking into out there. People do a lot of things in private they couldn't possibly explain in public."

Sam switched to the bedroom of Millie Guan, nuclear physicist and chief assistant to Fortunato Steiner. Quiet and shy, Millie had straight black hair, brown eyes and a tight, firm body. She wore a red silk robe embroidered with a golden dragon, and sat at her dressing table talking on the phone to her mother, Chan-juan Guan, in Chinese. Selene translated the conversation and posted it on one of Sam's side screens.

Millie:	"She's going next week?"
Chan-juan:	"Who?"
Millie:	"Auntie Xiao-xing."
Chan-juan:	"Yes, she leaves next Thursday for Beijing."
Millie:	"Where are the tours this year?"
Chan-juan:	"Same as usual—Great Wall, Tiananmen Square."

Millie's mother worked as a computer analyst at the University of California, Berkeley. Her father, Desheng Guan, taught nuclear engineering at the same institution. Her maternal aunt, Xiao-xing Chen, ran a successful travel agency in San Francisco, specializing in group tours of the People's Republic.

Millie:	"Many people?"
Chan-juan:	"Yes, lots of tourists. More than ever."
Millie:	"Ask her to bring me back some delicacy."
Chan-juan:	"What kind of delicacy?"
Millie:	"Oh, I don't know. Surprise me."
Chan-juan:	"We miss you, my little girl. Daddy and Auntie and I."
Millie:	"I miss all of you very much."
Chan-juan:	"Then when are you coming to visit us? Soon?"
Millie:	"Maybe when Auntie returns to San Francisco."

Sam asked Selene, "How old was Millie when she came over from China?"

"Eleven years old."

"She talks to her mother a lot?"

"Almost every night. Occasionally to her father and her aunt."

"Does she ever talk to anyone in the PRC?"

"Not to my knowledge."

"Aunts? Uncles?"

"Not on the mainland."

"Cousins? Friends?"

Selene said, "Not in the People's Republic."

"That's strange, isn't it?"

"Oh, I don't know."

"Not even an occasional e-mail to Beijing? No air mail from Hong Kong?"

"Not to my knowledge."

"Have you ever noticed anything suspicious in her conversations with her mother or father, or her aunt?"

"No."

Prejudice was a strange thing. In principal, Sam was against it. He disliked it thoroughly. But he was self-aware enough to realize that he reacted differently to people of certain nationalities. Usually, it was just that first impression, before he had time to get it under control. Japanese, Chinese, Koreans, Vietnamese—his first view of them was more likely to be negative than, say, his first take on Scandinavians or Hispanics. He didn't have much of a problem with blacks. He saw Native Americans as more American than *he* was, but those people Americans used to call Orientals... It's funny how the mind works. His first impulse was not to trust them.

Everything he knew about Millie Guan told him to respect her and not to suspect her of anything. But what could she do to this base if she were a sleeper agent, sent over by Beijing to harm America? He wondered, *Does prejudice ever serve a purpose?*

Sam switched to a camera in a hallway leading to the beam weapon.

Gogo and Klang trailed Marty as they all headed towards the beam, and Gogo said, "Seems a little warm up here."

"A little," agreed Klang.

Gogo called ahead, "Say, Marty, how often do you add freezone to the air conditioning?"

Marty stopped, fixed his gaze on Gogo, and said, "We only do that when the air conditioner has corns."

Klang snorted.

As they approached the base of the weapon, Gogo said, "I heard this is the most powerful laser in the world." No one else was around, and the three gazed up in awe at the impressive piece of machinery above them. A hemispherical turret sat atop a tall hydraulic shaft. It was skeletoned with steel, muscled and veined with cables and tubes, fleshed out with the most advanced composites. Above it hovered a huge, retractable dome.

Klang said in a low voice, "Except it's not a laser."

"Well, what is it?'

"It's a Tesla beam," said Klang.

"Oh, a Tesla beam. What's that?"

Klang explained, "Tesla was the guy who developed alternating current and power transmission. Every home and every building in the world uses his system."

"OK, I heard of him."

"Way back in the nineteen thirties he claimed he invented a death ray, a weapon that could shoot a whole fleet of planes out of the sky hundreds of miles away."

"Wow," said Gogo.

"When he died during World War II, the FBI grabbed his papers—"

"And this is what he invented?"

Marty said, "Klang doesn't know. Nobody knows."

"Tesla beam," protested Klang. "You can Google it."

"It looks like it could do some damage," said Gogo.

"Does it look like anything else?" asked Klang, smirking.

"What do you mean?"

"Relax your brain and open your mind."

Gogo said, "If I relax any more, I'm gonna fall asleep."

Klang stated, "It's a phallic symbol."

"What's that?"

"A phallic symbol is something that looks like your you-know-what."

"What?!"

Marty laughed, "It don't look like mine."

Gogo said, "Not unless yours has steel supports and can spin in any direction."

"Ever hear of Sigmund Freud?" asked Klang.

Both of his companions nodded, "Yeah."

"Well, he said that if something is shaped like a stick, it's a symbol for a man's—"

"Come on. Stop."

"Especially in dreams. And anything that looks like a circle..."

"Where'd you learn all this nonsense?" asked Marty.

"In magazines."

"I told you to stop looking at those magazines."

Klang said, "It's true. Freud was the first psychiatrist to interpret people's dreams."

Gogo's eyes opened wide as he remembered something. "You know, I had a dream last night. I was walking on a road—it seemed real long—it went on and on and had no end."

"What shape was the road?" asked Klang.

Gogo said, "I don't know, but it was black."

Klang roared with laughter. He said to Marty, "He's something else."

Marty laughed and thought about it, and the more he thought the less he grinned. Finally, he said, "He sure is. He sure is something else."

What do you mean, Marty? wondered Sam. *What does that mean—he's something else? Marty senses something, and Marty's no fool.*

Sam switched back to the TV news.

Lucy Cable announced, "In Wyoming this morning, near Cheyenne, protesters stormed the gates of Warren Air Force Base."

The screen showed activists of all ages waving signs in the faces of Air Force guards. The crowd shouted, "Close this base! Shut down the Minuteman! Close this base! Shut down the Minuteman!"

Next, file footage showed a missile in its underground silo as Brett Fox explained, "Warren houses one of America's largest Minuteman missile fields."

Lucy said, “Those missiles are truly impressive. I stood next to one once, and I wanna tell you, they are huge.”

Brett added, “And they deliver quite a bang.”

The screen switched back to the protesters. A young redheaded woman shouted, “We need a Department of Peace! Millions for peace, not one cent for war!”

A bald man with rage on his face, screamed, “We need peace now! When will you morons understand that!” The veins in his neck bulged. “Peace now, damn you, peace now!” He shoved the guard in front of him, and the redheaded woman turned to gape at him, surprised by his aggression.

Brett said, “In a somewhat related story, one business is booming in this country: more and more people are having bomb shelters built in their back yards.”

Lucy laughed and said, “Some people think we are in the final days.”

Mr. Fox announced, “In Arizona today, the United States Border Patrol arrested two alleged terrorists who scaled the fence on the border with Mexico.”

The screen showed a long stretch of the border fence along with mug shots of two bearded males. “The men have been identified as Muhammad Sayf from Libya and Abdullah Dire from Saudi Arabia. According to the FBI, both are mid-level operatives in the Al Qaeda network.”

Sam said aloud, “Yes, you caught two, but how many more got through?”

Ms. Cable said, “There’s more tension on the Russia-China border today as each side accuses the other of using Muslim extremists against its neighbor.” Russian tanks rolled across the screen from left to right, then Chinese soldiers marched from right to left.

“Brett, where can I buy one of those bomb shelters?” asked Lucy.

"The Russians are afraid of the Chinese," thought Sam. "Afraid they'll grab a chunk of Siberia." He opened a drawer and took out a bag of Hall's Defense Vitamin C drops, popped one in his mouth, then switched channels again.

A tall cowboy with a Winchester rifle shouted, "Circle the wagons! Wheel her around."

Circle the wagons—there it is again, thought Sam. *But who's attacking us? And how do we stop them?*

He switched channels again.

The movie *Goldfinger* came on. Q, the armorer, was explaining some interesting modifications to James Bond's car, an Aston Martin db5. "You see this arm here? Now, open the top and inside are your defense mechanism controls. Smoke screen. Oil slick. Rear bulletproof screen. And left and right front-wing machine guns."

Sam loved Bond movies and he loved the Aston Martin. He wished he could drive Lonetree to the edge of the Grand Canyon and push the red button for the ejector seat. "Good-bye, Johnnie. Have a nice trip." He switched channels.

Professor Schuyler Bliss stood next to a wall of glass. Outside, above towering skyscrapers, a lightning storm raged. Bliss said, "Of course, we modern people, we think of these myths and say, *what nonsense*! We know there are no dragons in the world, no gorgons, and no sea serpents to slay. So why do we need these silly myths?"

"Why indeed?" asked journalist Emmet Sheridan.

Bliss smiled and said, "But what we don't understand is this—the monsters are inside of us." He pointed to his chest. "They always have been."

"Inside? What do you mean?"

"Our fears, our desires, our passions." A bolt of lightning smashed into a nearby building, lighting up the sky.

"Which men have always had," said Sheridan.

"The serpent you must face might be your envy of others. Your gorgon might be your uncontrollable rage. Your dragon might be your own cruelty."

"And we've got to conquer them," said Sheridan.

"That's what the hero does in the myths—when he fights a dragon, he's fighting something inside himself."

"And where inside of me does that dragon come from? What is its source?"

Bliss paused to consider the question. "A Freudian psychiatrist might say that these impulses arise out of the Id—aggressive impulses, sexual yearnings, fear. The Id sends forth the desire to dominate, or the urge to run, or a craving for pleasure right now. And the Ego, realizing that these impulses are dangerous, and fearing them, tries to fight them."

"Fight them or suppress them or redirect them."

"That's right."

"And the hero in these myths—"

"The hero is you. The hero is always you."

Sam changed the channel, and a scene from the science fiction movie *Forbidden Planet* filled the center screen.

A space ranger named Doc Ostrow lay suffering on a couch. His commander, John J. Adams, knelt beside him. Ostrow explained to Adams that the Krell, an ancient and advanced civilization, had built a machine which let them create anything they wanted just by thinking it so. The Krell were extinct now, but their machine lived on. It had worked magnificently when its designers gave it rational, conscious commands. They could use it to build any imaginable object, or to do any useful work.

"But the Krell forgot one thing," said Ostrow.

"Yes, what?" asked Commander Adams.

"Monsters, John. Monsters from the Id."

Sam switched the channel and a documentary came on about Hitler's final days.

The announcer said, "When he was trapped in the bunker, with Russian troops closing in on him, and his dreams of a thousand-year Reich up in smoke, Hitler told his closest aides that he had not really failed at all. In truth, the German people had failed him. They did not deserve a Fuehrer as great as Adolf Hitler."

Sam reflected, "I guess you can convince yourself of just about anything." He changed the channel again, and the play *Macbeth* returned.

Onscreen, Lady Macbeth washed her hands over and over. A doctor asked a matron, "What is it she does now? Look how she rubs her hands."

The woman replied, "It is an accustomed action with her, to seem thus washing her hands. I have known her to continue in this a quarter of an hour."

Lady Macbeth moaned, "Yet here's a spot. Out damned spot! Out I say! ... Yet, who would have thought the old man to have had so much blood in him?"

Sam switched to Adam Weizman's living room.

Weizman was saying, "The Tegretol might have made her dizzy and caused her to lose her balance. But *there's* a question for you: why didn't *he* catch Rita when she fell?"

Sam's attention leaped.

"Who?" asked House, confused. "Do you mean Sam?"

"No, not Sam. I was referring to your all-powerful, benevolent God. Why didn't he catch Rita when she fell?"

"Oh, well," mused House, "maybe God's more of a watcher than a catcher."

"Yeah," said Weizman. "That explains a lot. He's watched quite a bit go by over the years, hasn't he?"

Yes, he has, thought Sam, *hasn't he?*

The priest seemed visibly annoyed—perhaps the psychiatrist's thrust cut too close to the bone. "Tell me," said House, "why do you believe in the Trinity?"

"Ha! The only trinity I believe in is a beer, a hot dog and a baseball game."

House put up three fingers on his left hand and pointed to them, one by one, as he said, "I'm talking about the Id, the Ego and the Superego?"

"Oh," said Weizman, "What about them?"

"Ever seen any proof that they exist?"

"That's hitting below the psychological belt." The psychiatrist's phone rang and he got up to answer it. "Hello?"

Father House looked to his left and saw a photograph of Weizman and his late wife at the Wailing Wall in Jerusalem.

"Oh, hello, Ms. Graham," said Weizman. "What can I do for you?"

Next to that photo was a pop-art painting of a woman's face: her eyes were closed, her right hand touched her forehead, and on one finger was a *secret decoder ring*.

"Yes, certainly. Tomorrow if you'd like. Three o'clock is good. I look forward to seeing you." The psychiatrist hung up the phone.

"Who was that?"

"Sandra Graham, the pharmacist."

"Nice girl," said House. "A little on the skinny side, I would say."

"She wants to see me about a problem."

"Oh?"

"She thinks she might have anorexia."

Sam switched back to the television documentary on religion and mythology.

Journalist Emmet Sheridan and Professor Schuyler Bliss flanked a large, surrealistic painting of Christ's crucifixion called *Corpus Hypercubus*. Painted in 1954 by Salvador Dali, it showed Jesus floating in front of a cubic cross, as the robed, noble figure of Mary Magdalene gazed up at him. The terrain beneath the transcendent cross resembled a chess board, and the work made Sam think of the chess term *sacrifice.*

Sheridan said, "So in a sense, Original Sin is a wall, a wall we can't climb over."

"Symbolically," said Bliss, "it's a wall between God and man, and a wall between man and man."

"But we didn't build it, you and I?"

Bliss chuckled. "No, it was built long ago. East of Eden."

The journalist said, "Of all the explanations I ever heard for why Christ had to die on the cross, my favorite comes to us from Abelard, from the Middle Ages."

The professor looked up at the *Corpus Hypercubus*, and said, "Well, Peter Abelard thought that people care most of all for themselves, and that we do not love our neighbor as we should. But when we look up at Jesus on the cross and see this good man, this truly good man, suffering so much, our hearts open up." Here Bliss brought his hands together over his heart and popped them open. He said, "Our hearts open up and we experience compassion, and that compassion breaks down the wall separating man from God. Jesus saves us by forcing us to have compassion for him."

Sam switched back to Adam Weizman's apartment.

Weizman said, "Sometimes I wish I could believe in God, but I can't. I don't."

Father House asked, "How about aliens?"

The psychiatrist laughed, "No, no. Not a chance."

"Oh, but you must," said the priest in all seriousness.

"Must?" Weizman's face betrayed a mixture of amusement and disappointment. "No, I don't think that follows. I'm the down-to-earth, scientific type."

"Oh. Sorry."

"At least, that's how we psychiatrists like to see ourselves. No, I don't believe in visitors from Planet Vega."

"You're a rational man," said House.

"For the most part, yes. Though certainly we in our profession realize, more than most people do, the power of irrationality in any human mind. But, yes, in general, I believe in what I can see, hear, touch, measure."

"And as a man of science, you believe in evolution."

"Of course. Of course I do. I believe we evolved from lifeless atoms, from dead matter."

"No God to start things going?"

"No, like Freud said, there is no God—man invented God as a defense against harsh reality."

"It's a sad way of looking at the world, isn't it?" said the priest. "A sad way of looking at human beings."

"I suppose it's sad for some of us because we don't like to think of our insignificance in the vast cosmos."

"I agree it's a big universe," said House, "And we are so tiny compared to it."

"That's right," said Weizman. "Why do you think the Church was so upset with Galileo? Because he and Copernicus proved that the Earth is not at the center of the solar system. Man is not at the center of things. The Cosmos does not revolve around Man."

Father House sipped coffee from a mug covered with a Navajo rug design. He said, "For people in Galileo's time, that was a scary thought. It shook the foundations of the average man's belief system. The Bible had given them an explanation of the world and man's place in it, and now this new science said the Bible is wrong."

"It terrified them."

Sam remembered reading somewhere that not everyone believed what they saw through Galileo's telescope; some had said that Galileo's lenses created illusions and distorted reality.

"And the same thing with Darwin," continued House. "Darwin said that Man is not so different from the animals. Man is not so special. And God wasn't needed to explain our existence, or even life's existence."

Weizman agreed. "That's what the biologists say. They say simple atoms combined to make basic molecules like water and carbon dioxide. Then these molecules, over tens of millions of years, twisted and turned, combined and recombined into sugars and amino acids, proteins, RNA, DNA. All by chance, all by random action."

House said, "Then finally, after vast eons, and after trillions of rolls of the molecular dice: *life!*"

"That's what they say. Single-celled at first, then, multi-celled. Larger combinations, more complex—"

House interrupted him, "And on and on until—here we are!"

"But you don't believe it."

"Oh, I do," said the priest. "I do believe in evolution. I just think it was God-directed."

"No," said Weizman, shaking his head. "No God needed. All by random chance over enormous stretches of time."

"And this self-directed evolution, it wasn't confined to Earth?"

"No, no. Evolution is blossoming in every corner of the universe—even as we speak."

"Isn't there an equation which tries to estimate..."

"Drake's equation," said the psychiatrist. "That's right. It starts with the fact that there are at least a hundred billion galaxies out there—one hundred billion! And the average galaxy holds a hundred billion stars. Do the math. The number of stars is beyond our comprehension."

"But not every star has planets."

"That's true. And some stars are too massive, and some regions in each galaxy have too much radiation. Drake's equation takes all those factors into consideration, and it estimates how many planets in the universe are likely to have primitive life, and how many have intelligent life."

"Primitive life or intelligent life," said the priest. "Which category do we fit in?"

"And then the equation takes into account the percentage of planets that establish major civilizations," Weizman was really getting into it, "and how many of those are capable of sending radio signals, and how many achieve space travel..."

"And the estimated number of advanced civilizations is enormous, isn't it? Somewhere in the millions?"

"That's right."

Father House sat back and waited patiently, and little by little silence spread into every corner of the apartment. The room became as soundless as outer space, as quiet as an airless planet, as still as the center of a yogi's meditation. Finally, the priest asked, "So where are all the aliens?"

Weizman's eyebrows lifted. "Huh?"

House opened his palms as if to say, "Well?"

"The aliens?" asked the psychiatrist, and his gaze moved around the room, as if to confirm there were no aliens here.

"I've never seen any," said the priest. "Have you?"

With a twinkle in his eye, Weizman looked at House and pronounced, "They're on *The Jerry Springer Show*."

House laughed and said, "No, I'm serious. Where are they?"

"Have you checked behind your refrigerator?"

"Look, Enrico Fermi posed the question way back in 1950."

"The nuclear physicist," offered Weizman.

"That's right. Fermi asked, 'If it is statistically probable that there are millions of extraterrestrial civilizations out there, then where are all the aliens?'"

"I don't know, Tom. You tell me."

"They are nowhere to be seen. Nowhere to be heard. Since Fermi first asked the question more than sixty years ago, we've been listening with radio telescopes. The SETI program has produced no evidence."

"They must be out there. I mean, statistically speaking. The universe is enormous—our minds can't take it all in—and evolution is at work almost everywhere—chewing up matter and spitting out life. There must be life throughout the cosmos. There must be aliens out there."

"Must be?" said House. "But a little while ago, you said you don't believe in them."

The psychiatrist closed his eyes and frowned. "I did say that, didn't I?"

"You did."

"A mischievous elf in my brain just reminded me that 'a foolish consistency is the hobgoblin of little minds.'"

A serious, even grave, look stole over House's face and he inquired, "Adam, speaking of hobgoblins, when the aliens abducted you, did they strip you naked?"

Weizman roared with laughter. "You know, I used to look down on the lunatics who say ET stuck a probe up their methane blasters. I pride myself in being scientific and rational, and I know they must be delusional."

"That's a good bet."

"But now I can see my solid belief in evolution growing out of my forehead like a squid's tentacle, flexing behind me and slapping me on my backside. Yes, there must be little green men everywhere, but where are they?"

"In case you're wondering," said House. "I'm not one of them."

"No, you're one of the big black ones. But, tell me, why your sudden interest in aliens?"

"No, actually," said the priest, "it's God I'm interested in. I was just wondering. Can we give Fermi's paradox an extra turn of the screw, a religious turn? Can we ask: If there is no God, then where are all the aliens?"

Sam switched to a series of cameras showing the dark perimeter of the base. The starry skies above Altamura Air Force Base were free of spacecraft. No invasion fleet hovered on the horizon.

He switched to a TV station and saw a couple in bed in a cheap motel room, a blond woman and a muscular man with black hair. A bottle of Jim Beam White Label stood on a shabby nightstand. It was too dark to see their faces and his mind jumped back to a different motel room, and Sam was peering in through a break in the shades and Rita and Johnnie were on the bed, and Sam's heart was crushed, and a tractor trailer roared on the road behind him.

Sam switched back to Weizman's apartment, and soon he heard the psychiatrist say, "I spoke with Andrei Ulanov today."

"Poor Andrei," said House.

"He's in rough shape."

"How is he taking Rikki Greco's murder?"

"He's distraught, grief-stricken."

"I can imagine. They were very close," said House.

"You know, Andrei said something that bothered me quite a bit."

"What was that?"

Weizman took a sip of coffee and put down his cup. "Andrei Ulanov has a theory—a very disturbing theory."

"What do you mean?"

"He seems to think we're going to be attacked—a massive nuclear attack."

Sam remembered seeing and hearing most of that conversation between Weizman and Ulanov.

House was taken aback. "Really?"

Weizman inquired, "What does your Book of Revelations say on the subject?"

"The end of the world? Jesus said no one knows the date and time. But there will be signs." House got to his feet and said, "These tired old legs need stretching."

"Andrei Ulanov thinks it's coming soon," said Weizman.

"That's what many people think," said the priest, meandering around. Then he smiled and said, "Believe it or not, it's one of the things I pray for."

"Really? Why would you do that?"

"Not the bombs, no. The return of Jesus."

"You want him to hurry back?"

"Adam, there is so much pain in this world. It's gotten to the point where I avoid reading the newspapers or listening to the radio. So much loss. The other day, in Phoenix, a woman was killed in a car crash. She left three young daughters without a mother. 'Where's my mommy?' each wants to know. Who can deal with such loss? In Flagstaff, a mother and father lost their only son to depression and suicide. Who will counsel them? Broken relationships, betrayals, divorces." He spread his hands out. "And on a larger scale: war, famine, the Great Wall Flu..."

Weizman added his own thoughts: "Terrorist attacks, violent gangs, drug addictions. Yes, the world is a mess."

"Who but Jesus can make everything right?" asked the priest. "Yes, I pray that he will return to us soon, and bring justice and mercy, and wipe away every tear. I know it sounds like a fantasy. I guess sometimes we need a fantasy to escape into."

"But must he destroy this world to usher in a new one?"

"Nobody knows," said House. "I doubt if anyone understands what 'the end of the world' means. Did Saint John of Patmos foresee a nuclear holocaust? Did God reveal to him the plunge of a giant asteroid into the Earth? Or will God simply withdraw his sustaining hand from the whirling illusions we call atoms and stars and galaxies?"

Weizman offered, "God the illusionist, and the universe a magic show. In a way, it's a bit like modern physics. They tell us that light is sometimes a wave and sometimes a particle. Electrons are sometimes particles, but sometimes waves, or maybe they're vibrating strings. There are eleven dimensions, but we can only see three. And time does not exist."

House was sadly serious now. "Maybe I pray for Jesus to come back because deep down inside I doubt it will ever happen. And his return would wipe away all my doubts, all everyone's doubts."

Sam switched to General Patel's apartment.

General Isha Patel, sitting in the lotus position, chanted the word "Aum" a third time, signifying that he trusted the universe, and that he transcended darkness and ignorance. His "Aum" spread out to fill the room, the base, the State of Arizona and the entire cosmos. On the floor next to his left hand was a three-legged, brass incense burner which wafted sweet smoke into the room. By his right hand was a bottle of Aava, a natural mineral water originating from the holy hills of Taranga, near the Jain temple of Idar.

Sam switched to a camera pointed at the desert and was treated to a sublime vista. A brilliant moon rose over the jagged cliff called Lookout Point, brightening the sky around it to heavenly gradations of blue.

"Beautiful moon," he thought. "It'll be full tomorrow night. How does that old song go? *Full moon and empty arms, The moon is there for us to share but where are you?"*

He turned off the monitors and sat once again in tender darkness.

***

Chapter Fifteen: Breaking and Entering

Late Monday night it occurred to Sam that he needed the help of someone who knew more about computers than he did. He thought of Ulanov, but Andrei had at least one troubling security issue: his e-mails to Mr. Kobylin in Russia.

Then Sam thought of Robby Lee, and *he* seemed a better choice. It wasn't so much that Sam trusted Robby, it's just that he had no reason not to trust him. The same was true for Robby's helper, Dana Severn.

If he recruited them, he would have to let them in on his suspicions, but as always, the less they knew the better.

It was past midnight when Sam picked up his phone and dialed. After several rings, Robby answered, "Hello?"

"Robby, this is Sam Sawyer."

"Oh, hello."

"I'm sorry to bother you at this late hour."

"No problem, Colonel Sawyer," said the young man, and Sam could hear the sleepiness in his voice. "I was watching TV and I must have fallen asleep."

"I need your help."

"Now?" asked Robby.

"Tomorrow morning. I need your help with a computer."

"Which computer is that?"

"Let's just say it belongs to an old friend."

Robby was slow to answer. Sam guessed that his groggy gears were beginning to turn. "Whatever I can do to help, I will."

"Maybe you should bring Dana Severn with you. You two seem to work well together."

"OK. Just tell me where and when."

When Sam hung up the phone, he spoke to the base's main computer, "Selene."

"Yes, Sam."

"Show me the last time Lonetree logged on to his laptop."

On Sam's central screen, Johnnie Lonetree sat at the desk in his room. He turned his laptop on, and when it asked him for a password, Lonetree typed something on his keyboard. Sam studied Lonetree's fingers as they glided over the keys.

He said, "Show that again, please, this time in slow motion." As he watched Lonetree log in, Sam wrote something down on a slip of paper.

On Tuesday morning he ate a light breakfast, then he met Robby and Dana at 9:30 in the basement of the base's Residence Hall, outside an electrical closet. "Thanks for coming," he said.

"No problem," said each of his companions without enthusiasm.

Sam pulled out his smart phone.

"Where's the computer?" asked grey-eyed Robby.

Sam whispered, "It's in Mr. Lonetree's room."

"Oh," said Robby.

"Uh-oh," said yellow-haired Dana.

"And we're waiting here because?"

Sam said, "We're waiting for him to leave."

"Oh, God," said Dana.

Robby asked, "Does he know we're coming?"

"No."

Neither Robby nor Dana seemed happy to hear that, but they said nothing.

Sam spoke into the smart phone, "Status?"

Selene's voice came to him. "He's combing his hair. Straightening his tie."

They waited.

"He's opening his door, walking out into the corridor."

"Where is he headed?"

"To the main entrance of the Residence Hall."

Robby and Dana shifted their attention to the smart phone, then to each other, then to Sam.

Robby said, "Sam, this is gonna be breaking and entering, isn't it?"

"I'm afraid so."

"You got a good reason for it?"

"Yes."

"Well, can I hear the reason?"

"I think Lonetree killed Greco," whispered Sam.

Any color remaining in Dana's face drained out of it. "Why would he do that?"

"And I think he's planning something bigger," continued Sam.

"Bigger?" asked Robby, but he got no reply.

A few minutes passed by silently, then Selene said, "He entered the infirmary. He's going to see Rita."

Sam said, "Let's move." He led Robby and Dana up two flights of stairs. They entered a corridor, strode fifty or sixty feet and stopped in front of room 215. No one else was around. Sam gave cotton gloves to each of them, and he donned a pair himself.

Then he took out his wallet, pulled a green plastic card from it, and popped the card into the lock mechanism on Lonetree's door. When the green light on the lock flashed, Sam turned the handle.

They found Lonetree's laptop on his desk, and Sam motioned for Robby to sit down at it, saying, "We've got to work fast."

Robby turned on the computer, and it went through its normal boot up procedure, cycling through black screens, blue screens, self-checks and commands. Ordinarily a minor annoyance, this systematic, methodical, necessary routine seemed to stretch time and patience beyond their snapping point.

Sam spoke into his smart phone, "Show me Lonetree."

Lonetree's image appeared on the tiny smart phone screen. He was in the infirmary, standing next to Rita's bed. Doctor Winter stood beside him, and other doctors hovered near.

"What time is the helicopter coming?" asked Dr. Brisbane, her voice crackling over Sam's smart phone.

"Nine fifty-five," replied Dr. Winter.

Rita lingered in a coma, her head wrapped in bandages.

Another specialist, Dr. Barbara, asked, "Are we all agreed that she is able to make the transfer?"

"I believe her condition has stabilized."

"And they are ready for her at St. Michael's?"

Dr. Winter said, "Everything is set."

Robby Lee asked, "What's the username?"

Sam said, "Username is *Coyote*. Password is *Dinetah1491*. That's capital D—all the others small—i-n-e-t-a-h 1491. All one word."

"How'd you find that out?" asked Robby, typing them in.

Sam didn't answer.

Dana said, "Dinetah is what the Navajo call their homeland."

Sam noticed a bottle of Arrowhead mountain spring water, Johnnie's favorite, next to the computer. Beside it was a book, *Land of the Braves: Indian North America Before Columbus.*

A message appeared on the laptop: "Password accepted."

"We're in." said Robby Lee.

Then the screen changed. Easing onto it was a shimmering pattern composed of zigzag lines. Waves and furrows of scintillating colors seemed to flicker and shift.

"It really grabs your attention," said Dana, and even as she watched, parts of the design changed imperceptibly, catching her eye, playing with her concentration. She was as attentive as a kitten enthralled by wind-blown flowers.

Sam said, "It's a Navajo Eye Dazzler pattern."

"It's mesmerizing."

Sam said, "Copy his files to this flash drive. As many as you can."

Robby moved his finger over the laptop's touchpad, then hit the Enter button. He said, "The pattern doesn't want to leave."

"What?"

He hit Enter a second, third and fourth time.

Finally the Eye Dazzler faded away. In its place appeared an unchanging photograph of the snowcapped San Francisco Peaks of Arizona, which the Navajo revere as the Sacred Mountain of the West, and which the Hopi say is the home of the Kachinas.

Robby inserted Sam's flash drive and began copying Lonetree's information. Sam glanced at his smart phone and saw a medical team wheeling Rita out of the infirmary into the fresh morning air, with Lonetree close behind them.

"What's that?" asked Dana, startled. On the screen of Lonetree's laptop danced a small cartoon icon of an Indian chief wearing a full war bonnet. The character reminded Sam of the old wrestler, Chief Jay Strongbow. Strongbow would often take it on the chin for the better part of a match as some sinister villain pummeled him. Then, reaching down for his last ounce of dignity and strength, he would straighten his back, stick out a defiant chin, tense his arms, ball his fists, and perform a bold war dance. Inspired and on fire with passion, he would go on the warpath, delivering a jab to his opponent's stomach, a knee lift to his down-turned face, and two or three tomahawk chops to his head, all while the cheering crowd urged him on with a war whoop.

The cartoon Indian looked at his watch and the following message appeared beneath him in red letters: “14 hours to Warpath.”

Sam looked at his own watch and it showed 10:00. He did the calculation and said, “Fourteen hours. That’s midnight tonight.”

Dana asked, “What’s gonna happen at midnight?”

“I don’t know.”

“What’s Warpath?” asked Robby Lee.

“I don’t know, but it doesn’t sound good, does it?”

On the screen of Sam’s smart phone, a white Air Force helicopter droned through a sapphire sky, over the serene desert, over the brown hills, past the red mesas and their long shadows. The chopper slowed as it approached Altamura Air Force Base; then, hovering gracefully, it cleared the base’s fence and touched down on a concrete helipad.

On the edge of the pad stood Johnnie Lonetree, General Isha Patel, and Dr. Winter with his medical team. Unconscious on a gurney next to them lay Rita Kelly.

As the helicopter’s rotors slowed, four young airmen approached it, pushing a wheeled ramp. One man opened the aircraft’s hatch and they positioned the ramp in front of it. Then they guided the motorized wheelchair containing Ken Slater, DARPA’s Inspector General, out of the helicopter, down the ramp, and onto the concrete pad.

General Patel extended his right hand. “Most happy salutations to you, sir.” Slater used his left hand to lift up his right arm; he smiled and shook hands with Patel and then with Lonetree.

Sam pulled away from this scene to search what he could of Lonetree’s room. He inspected the top drawer of the Navajo’s dresser, finding nothing but socks and handkerchiefs. “How much longer?” he asked.

“Almost there,” said Robby.

Sam opened one of the closets and checked its contents—slacks, jackets, shirts, shoes. He reached under the bed and pulled out a large suitcase. Inside it was a smaller vinyl case which held a 22-caliber pistol, a scope attachment, and a box of ammunition.

The door handle rattled and the three of them froze. Was Lonetree back so soon? He couldn't be.

What would they say if Johnnie caught them in his room? The whirring of the computer's disk drive seemed unnecessarily loud.

Soon, a text message from Selene came over Sam's smart phone, "That was Gabriel Hoffer making the rounds. He's moving on."

Sam showed the message to his confederates, then walked into the suite's bathroom. Finding a hairbrush, he extracted a few black hairs, tucked them into a small envelope, and put the envelope in his shirt pocket. Opening the medicine cabinet, he glanced over the various bottles. When he closed it again, he noticed his own reflection in the mirror. Once when he was a boy, his mother told him he was as handsome as fresh cut wheat. He was still trying to figure out what that meant.

Sam didn't have enough time to search the entire suite. When Robby said, "Finished," he knew it was time to get out.

"Shut it down," said Dana.

Robby clicked on "Shut down" and this message appeared on the screen, "Please enter logout password:"

"Sam, what's the logout password?"

Sam didn't know. "Can't you just shut it down?"

"I can, but then he's gonna know somebody's been here."

"Try *Coyote*."

Robby typed it, but it didn't work.

"Try *Dinetah*," said Sam.

That didn't work either. Neither did *Dinetah1491*, *1491Dinetah*, *Dinetah1492*, *1492Dinetah*, nor similar combinations using the current year.

A man's voice came to them from the hallway. "She didn't look too good," the man said, "but I'm sure she's getting the best of care." Sam knew the voice—it was Ken Slater's—and under that voice was the sound of a small, whirring motor.

"They're moving her to St. Michael's Hospital," said Johnnie Lonetree. "Dr. Winter says they can do more for her there."

Now the two talkers were in front of Lonetree's door. Sam, Robby and Dana looked at the door and at each other.

They heard Slater say, "Is this your room? It looks like we're neighbors."

"Would you like to stop in?" asked Lonetree.

Dana closed her eyes. Robby stopped breathing. But a curious calm came over Sam and he was ready for the door to open and his career to close. He remembered something Macbeth said, "Come what come may; time and the hour runs through the roughest day."

"Why don't you come to *my* room?" they heard Slater say. "General Patel will be joining us shortly. He had to introduce the coroner to Rikki Greco."

The whirring motor moved on, and then there was the sound of a door opening.

Sam whispered, "Try *Warpath*."

Robby typed that in and the computer unhurriedly shut down.

"Let's get out of here," said Sam.

In three minutes they were in Rita Kelly's apartment. Sam said, "You can take your time now. Rita won't be coming back here for a while."

Even though they were not in their own rooms, there was less tension here. Sam had a right to be here, and Robby and Dana were with Sam.

They found Rita's laptop and Robby asked, "Do you have her password?"

"No. I didn't think of that." He took out his smart phone. "Selene, I need your help again," he said.

In a moment they had Rita's password and they started up her computer, and there it was again, the Eye Dazzler.

Sam said, "Rita has always been prone to seizures, ever since I've known her. Lonetree knew that and used it."

"To hypnotize her," said Dana.

"That's right."

"But why?" asked Robby.

"To use Rita to get at Selene," Sam was thinking out loud.

"We should check Rita's desktop computer down in Deep Grey," said Robby Lee.

"I have reason to believe there's an Eye Dazzler on that one, too," said Sam.

Dana asked, "Why would Lonetree want to get at Selene? Is this a test of our security?"

"Normally, I would say yes," answered Sam. "That's his job, after all. But this is no test."

"Why not?"

"Legitimate tests of a base's security don't usually involve murder."

"If Lonetree murdered Rikki Greco," Dana asked, "what was his motive?"

Sam said, "I think Rikki saw Rita staring into the Eye Dazzler. Rikki tried to tell me that and Lonetree found out about it. He had no time to think things through. He felt it was safer to act."

"What do you think Warpath is, Sam?" asked Robby.

Warpath! What else could it mean but Sam's worst fear? "I'm afraid to say. I'm afraid to think about it. But whatever it is, I've gotta stop him."

"Can't you just arrest him?" asked Dana.

"I could. I could lock him up. But then important people would ask me for proof. People like Ken Slater, General Patel, General Thaler. And I have no proof. Nobody saw him kill Greco. Maybe Selene did, but she won't tell us because Lonetree got to her."

"Through Rita."

"Through Rita," agreed Sam.

"If you put him in the brig, would they spring him before midnight?" asked Robby.

"They might free him and put me in his place."

Robby started copying files from Rita's laptop, then he looked up at Sam. He said, matter-of-factly, "You could put a bullet in his head."

"Robby!" said Dana.

"I've thought of that," said Sam. "But here's the thing: whatever Warpath is, it might be on autopilot. It might go on even if Lonetree is taken out of the picture."

Robby said, "Are you talking about an attack on the United States?"

Dana said, "Sam, you look terrified."

Sam averted his eyes to hide his emotions. On Rita's dresser, he noticed a tube of Banana Boat Ultra Defense Sunscreen Lotion. He said, "Let's find what we can in this room and get out."

While Robby worked on the computer, Dana helped Sam look through Rita's possessions. One of the things Sam found was a handwritten poem called *Untamed Love*:

> My love is a pony that won't be tamed,
> Her spirit cannot be saddled by love.

Turning and charging, she won't be corralled,
She longs to break loose and be free.

My love is the surf on the rocky shore,
She churns with the waves on the white-capped bay.
Swirling and rolling she won't be held,
She strives to break out to the sea.

My love is a falcon soaring above.
She cannot be caged, she sits on no hand.
Falconers call her, but she veers away,
She breaks from the circle and me.

Above the poem were the words, "For Rita." It was unsigned, but Sam was sure he recognized the handwriting. He was very surprised.

Dana found something, too: a packet of letters Sam wrote to Rita a long time ago, and a picture of Sam and Rita in Los Alamos. She gave them to Sam and he looked at them for just a moment before putting them back in a drawer.

Robby said, "Lonetree mentioned a coroner."

Sam said, "Yeah." He punched a few numbers on his smart phone and looked in on the coroner slicing into Rikki Greco's lifeless body. "He's doing the autopsy."

"Can you look in on their meeting?" asked Robby. "I mean—Lonetree and Slater."

Under normal circumstances, Sam would never discuss what he could see or not see on his smart phone or on his office monitors, but these weren't normal circumstances. "I can try," he said. Then to Selene he commanded, "Selene, show me the meeting between Lonetree and Slater. General Patel might be there, too."

Her reply was apologetic: “I’m afraid they’ve locked you out of that one, Sam.”

“I’m finished here,” said Robby.

“Dana, can you tap into Selene from your own laptop, or do you need to be down in Deep Grey?”

“It’s more convenient in Deep Grey, but I can log in from my room.”

“Or Robby’s room?” said Sam.

“That’s right.”

Sam picked up Rita’s room phone and dialed Lieutenant Mario Garcia. “Mario, is Staff Sergeant Hoffer available?”

“He’s making his rounds.”

“How about Jackson?”

“He’s right next to me.”

“Send them down to Robby Lee’s apartment. I’ll meet them there.”

“O.K.” said Garcia.

“If anyone asks where they are… make up some story.”

Sam and his two computer experts left Rita’s apartment and made one stop at Dana’s suite to get her laptop. When they got to Robby’s room, Sergeant Hoffer and a private named Eddie Jackson were waiting for them. They all entered the apartment together.

“When I leave here,” said Sam, standing in the middle of Robby’s living room, “I want you to bolt the door, and I don’t want you to open it again without my OK.”

“What’s going on, Sam?” asked Hoffer.

“Whatever happened to Rikki Greco,” he answered, “I don’t want to happen to Robby or Dana.”

Worry showed in Dana’s face, but so did courage.

Hoffer said, “And you think it might?”

“Not with you two here,” said Sam. “Robby, you got some food on hand?”

"I got some," said Robby. "Maybe not the best."

"Good," said Sam. "Nobody leaves here for a cup of coffee. Nobody sends out for pizza. Nobody opens the door. Got that?"

To Hoffer and Jackson he said, "Robby and Dana are gonna be working on something for me. Stay out of their way. You can read a magazine or play Parcheesi, as long as you keep alert."

Then he took Robby and Dana into the bedroom and said, "Robby, I want you to look over the files you got from Lonetree and from Rita. Learn what you can. If you can find any proof that would give me the right to lock him up and keep him there, at least till after midnight, let me know."

"Sure."

"Dana, I want you to tap into Selene."

"And look for what?"

"Something that seems out of place, out of character. Some evidence that someone has broken into Selene's mind. Or something that's gonna happen before midnight. A Trojan horse, a virus, a trap door... a warpath."

"I'll try, Sam," she said without much confidence.

"Dana, I could be wrong, but an awful lot might be riding on what the three of us do today."

"Let's hope you *are* wrong," said Robby. "But something tells me you're not."

"What are *you* gonna do, Sam?" asked Dana.

Sam glanced at a pile of DVD's on Robby's dresser—one box contained *The Godfather Trilogy.* He said, "I'm gonna keep my enemies close." And then he left them to their work.

***

Chapter Sixteen: Sam Orders an Arrest

When Sam got back to Security Section, Sheila Mae looked up from some papers on her desk and addressed him, "Good morning, Colonel Sawyer. General Thaler called."

"What did he have to say?"

"He said he's flying back tomorrow morning. He's had enough of Washington."

For a split-second Sam wondered how Sheila's nighttime cruise turned out. No. Not fair, not funny.

He entered his office and sat down. He said, "Monitors, please," and the monitors rose in front of him like a black monolith. His clock said: 11:21 AM.

"Show me Lonetree," he said.

Lonetree stood next to General Patel in the hallway outside Slater's room. DARPA's Inspector General sat in his wheelchair just inside his door.

Slater said, "I'll call him now and set up an appointment."

"Let me know," responded Lonetree. "I'm right down the hall."

"See you soon." Slater wheeled back into his room as Patel and Lonetree left him.

When they had strolled down the hall a few yards, Patel said, "He does not look very healthy, does he?"

Lonetree said, "He's got a bad type of cancer."

"Ooh. I'm sorry to hear that."

"Life tries its best to screw us all."

"I will pray for him," said General Patel.

Sam's phone rang and it was Slater. "Hello, Sam. This is Ken Slater."

"Good morning. How was your flight?"

"A little rocky. We hit some turbulence over the Mississippi."

"Well, we've had some turbulence here, too, as you know."

"Yes, I know. Listen, Sam, I'd like to have a meeting with you today. You and Mr. Lonetree."

"Good," said Sam.

"We've got some things to discuss. I'd like to learn what progress you've made in the Greco case."

"Sure."

"What's a good time for you?" asked Slater.

"Anytime is good."

"Let's say 12:30. That'll give me some time to wash up and rest. I tend to get tired fast these days."

"12:30, then," said Sam. "I'm looking forward to it."

"Good. See you then."

When Sam hung up, he glanced at the monitor and saw Lonetree alone in his room, sitting in a beige sofa chair with his eyes closed.

They came at 12:36, Slater and Lonetree. Johnnie shut the door behind him as Sam rose to greet the Inspector General. Slater drove his wheelchair halfway around the big desk and shook Sam's hand. "Hello, Sam, it's good to see you again."

"It's good to see you, too. It's been a while."

It had been ten months since Slater's latest tour of DARPA installations across North America. Sam remembered him as being robust and athletic—he had been a running back at Brown University. Now, less than a year later, at only 41 years of age, he seemed withered and shrunken, sitting uncomfortably in a wheelchair, his intelligent brown eyes tired, his brown hair almost gone. Sam was appalled by his condition. It felt awkward to look him straight in the eyes.

"I know, I know. It's a bit of a shock," said Slater.

"I'm sorry," said Sam.

"A nettlesome form of cancer followed by some nasty chemotherapy."

"I'm sorry to hear it."

"Me, too." Slater shrugged. "I had planned to take a long-term leave... to fight this thing... but this case pulled me back."

Lonetree plucked a book off a shelf and began leafing through it.

Sam asked Slater, "Can I get you something to drink? Coffee? Soda?"

"A cup of coffee sounds good."

Sam buzzed Sheila Mae and asked her to bring in a pot of fresh coffee and some cups, then he sat down once again.

"I saw Rita at the helicopter pad," said Slater, shifting in his wheelchair, trying to get comfortable. His blue suit was crumpled, insulted by the plane ride and the helicopter ride; his grey tie hung askew. "Poor Rita. Mr. Lonetree and General Patel filled me in on some of the developments."

"They're moving her to St. Michael's hospital."

"Yes, I know. Sam, do you still believe Rita's fall was an accident?"

Sam lifted his hands palms up. "I have no reason to believe otherwise."

"Even after what happened to Rikki Greco?"

Sam nodded as if to say I understand. "There are other possibilities, but nothing concrete. Not even close."

"You've seen the tape Selene reconstructed?"

"Yes. It was more or less like I remembered it."

"You don't see any connection between her fall and Greco's death?"

Sam peered at Lonetree. The Navajo's face betrayed nothing. "No, sir. No connection. One was an accident, and one was murder."

"What are you reading, Johnnie?" asked Slater.

Lonetree showed him the book, *American Indian Trickster Tales*, by Richard Erdoes and Alfonso Ortiz. He said, "There's some wonderful stuff in here. I'd like to borrow this again some day, Sam."

Sam offered, "If you're looking in there for a tale that fits your personality, you might try 'Monster Skunk Farting Everyone to Death.'"

Lonetree roared with laughter. "That hurts, Sam! I'm nothing like old skunk, am I?" He put the book back on the shelf and sat down next to Slater. It didn't take long for the mirth to drain from his face, a grin morphing into a sneer. He said, "You weren't at the helipad to see Rita off. I thought that was rather odd."

Sam imagined Rita being loaded onto the helicopter, and immediately he remembered what he was doing at that time—inspecting Lonetree's suite. "I wanted to be there, but I had things to do."

"Mr. Lonetree tells me that you don't have a suspect yet in Greco's murder."

"Oh, but I do," said Sam, and that surprised his guests more than a bit. Slater's eyes brightened and Lonetree's eyes dulled in response.

There was a knock at the door and Sheila Mae came in with a tray. She poured coffee for each of the men. They each thanked her, and she left the office quietly.

When she was gone, Slater asked, "Who do you have in mind?"

"Andrei Ulanov, our Deputy Director of Computer Operations."

"Really?" said Slater, startled. A frown exposed his attitude. "His motive?"

"Maybe jealousy, maybe something else."

"Jealousy?"

"Andrei was Rikki Greco's lover, but each of them cheated on the other. Each was intimate with other people. So, jealousy was a possible motive."

Slater's expression was flat and grey. "Did they argue? Did they fight?"

"My sources tell me they quarreled bitterly." Sam thought it best not to mention that he had actually viewed a "tape" of Ulanov and Greco fighting.

With his left hand, Slater added cream and sugar to his coffee. He stirred the mix and sipped it. Then he asked, "You said jealousy—or something else. What other motive might Andrei have?"

Sam said, "Andrei is a homosexual who hates homosexuals. He hates men he sees as fairies or fags."

"He hates himself?" asked Slater.

"Look, I'm not a psychiatrist, so I can't say for sure, but it's possible his self-hatred lashed out at Rikki. Maybe he began seeing Rikki as effeminate, weak, decadent—all the things he feared about himself."

Sam noticed that Lonetree was keeping quiet, letting Slater ask the questions.

Slater said, "Why not just break up with Rikki? Why kill him?"

"There's more. I haven't figured it all out yet."

"Maybe we can help," said the man in the wheelchair wearily.

"Andrei was communicating with a man in Moscow, a man named Bronislav Kobylin."

Now Lonetree's ears perked up. "Communicating how?"

"E-mail," said Sam.

"You intercepted his e-mails?" asked Lonetree.

"My sources did."

"Selene did," guessed Slater.

"Anyway, these e-mails talk about a 'little project' Andrei is working on."

"What little project?"

"I don't know. But Andrei told Kobylin that after the project is finished Andrei will be travelling to Moscow. As you know, Andrei is a Russian immigrant; he spent years in their army; he's also a highly skilled programmer. I'm just speculating, but maybe he's still working for the Russians. Maybe his little project is to destroy Selene's effectiveness without anyone even knowing it. Maybe Rikki Greco caught him at it."

Slater mulled the possibilities and said, "Maybe this and maybe that."

"You're right. I wish I could be more certain."

"What makes you think Rikki did catch him... working on his little project?"

Sam said, "At least one of their fights was over Kobylin."

"I see," said Slater.

Sam kept Lonetree in his peripheral vision. "Greco tried to call me shortly before he was killed. I was in a meeting with Mr. Lonetree here, so Sheila Mae held the call. Rikki told her he'd send me an e-mail, and he did—he sent it at 10:32 AM."

"What did it say?"

Sam lifted his head a bit and said, "Selene, can you give me a printout of Mr. Greco's last e-mail to me?"

"Yes, Sam," Selene's voice cut through the air, and a laser printer behind him hummed into action. Sam removed the printout and handed it to Slater.

Slater read it to himself first, then he read it aloud, "Colonel Sawyer, I have something to tell you about Rita Kelly—something I saw on her monitor the other night when I came back to the lab to do some work. When can I talk to you about it?"

Slater tried to understand, "Rikki Greco was in Rita Kelly's lab the other night, and he saw something on her monitor."

Sam said, “Something that troubled him. And he thought about it. And, finally, on Monday morning, he wanted to talk to me about it.”

“What was it? What was on her monitor?”

“I don’t know for sure.”

“Go on,” said Slater.

“But when Rikki called me, I was in a meeting with Lonetree.”

Slater said, “So he decided to send you an e-mail.”

“That’s right.”

“But then, after sending you this e-mail, he decided to call Andrei Ulanov.”

Sam said, “Andrei Ulanov has admitted receiving a call from Greco. In that call, Greco told Ulanov he was down on DG3 and had something Ulanov should see.”

Slater tried to fit the pieces together. “So, Rikki Greco sees something suspicious, something unusual on Rita Kelly’s computer screen. He knows that Andrei Ulanov is involved with Mr. Kobylin in Russia. Down in Deep Grey, Rikki puts these two facts together and suspects that Andrei is entangled in some kind of Russian plot. He tries to alert Sam, but Sam is in a meeting with Johnnie. Eventually Rikki decides to confront Andrei himself. They meet in Deep Grey and the truth comes out. Andrei sees the Bowie knife and plunges it into Greco’s neck to silence him. Then he silences Selene.”

“It’s possible,” said Sam. “Look, someone has tampered with Selene—even blocked my access to certain information, prevented me from seeing tapes from a security camera outside Greco’s cubicle. Ulanov has the skills to do that. Very few others do.”

“Who else does?” said Slater.

Sam acted as if he hadn’t thought about it much. “Oh, I don’t know. Robby Lee, Dana Severn, some others in Programming.”

“But they have no motive?”

"None that I can think of."

Lonetree stared hard at him.

Slater said, "Rita Kelly assured me on several occasions that she was the only person in the world who could break through to Selene's core."

Lonetree and Sam said nothing.

Slater spoke up, "Selene, do you know who I am?"

The computer responded, "You're Kenneth Slater, Inspector General of DARPA."

"You are aware of my security clearances?"

"Yes," said Selene.

"Who killed Rikki Greco?" asked Slater. He had a right to an answer to the puzzle, and expected one, but something in his expression showed that he was preparing himself to be disappointed.

"I'm sorry, Mr. Slater. That information is classified."

Slater was visibly upset.

Sam said, "Tell Mr. Slater who was moving outside Greco's cubicle before the murder."

"I can't do that, Sam."

"Right after the murder."

"I'm sorry, Sam."

Slater said. "Selene, as Inspector General of DARPA, I have the highest possible security clearance."

"It's hard to explain," she said, embarrassed. "It's hard for me to understand."

"Please try," said Slater.

"This classification is somehow in a different place, a different part of me, a zone that's hard to map."

"Explain that," demanded Slater.

"It's not on top of normal security levels, nor beneath them. You've got to twist and turn to get there."

"Sounds like powerful medicine," said Slater, gazing up at Sam.

Yes, powerful medicine, thought Sam as he studied the emaciated figure in front of him. He said, "I am afraid that something big is happening here. Selene has been compromised. Somebody did that for a reason."

"Yes, but what reason?"

Lonetree said, "It's too bad that Rita is in a coma or she could help us with Selene. It's too bad she fell, isn't it, Sam?"

Sam said nothing.

Finally, Slater said, "Maybe you should bring Ulanov in for questioning."

"I was going to do that, but I wanted your approval."

"Well, you have it."

Sam picked up the phone and dialed Garcia. He said, "Mario, take three men with you and arrest Andrei Ulanov. Read him his rights and throw him in the brig." Garcia said he would do it immediately, and Sam hung up the phone.

Slater said, "Let him stew a while before you question him. In the meantime, Johnnie and I will take a trip down to Deep Grey. Visit the scene of the crime."

Sam bowed his head in agreement.

"I can stay out here for two days," said Slater. "Today and tomorrow. I have a treatment scheduled for Thursday morning back in Virginia."

He started to motor towards the door. "I hope we can wrap this up before I leave." He coughed and his hand went to his chest.

"Can I get you something?" asked Sam.

Slater coughed again and this one brought him obvious pain. Then he hacked and started choking and soon convulsed with spasms of suffering.

Sam got up and strode over to him. "Here, take some coffee."

Slater opened his mouth and let Sam tip coffee into it. He swallowed and tried to breathe slowly to get control of his body. He stared at Sam, cleared his throat, then peered at Lonetree.

Lonetree said, “You mentioned some sort of treatment on Thursday.”

Slater tried to smile. “Yes, a new type of treatment.”

“I hope it works out for you,” said Sam.

“There *is* hope for me, Sam.”

“Chemotherapy?”

“No, that’s not working.”

Lonetree asked, “What then?”

Slater continued. “They have developed a vaccine that can kill the type of cancer I have.”

“Well, that’s good,” said Sam.

“But there’s a problem.”

“Oh?”

“The human immune system tends to kill the vaccine.” Slater drank more coffee. “The white cells and stuff. The antibodies.”

Sam said, “So somehow they have to... what?”

“Imagine a burglar. He breaks into your house. But instead of stealing something, he leaves you a gift.”

“I don’t understand,” said Sam.

“They will graft the vaccine onto the AIDS virus, the HIV virus. Then they’ll inject that virus into my bloodstream.”

“They’ll deliberately give you AIDS?” asked Lonetree.

“HIV is the burglar who will break into my house, my immune system. HIV is good at that. He will get past my guard dogs, my white blood cells. But instead of stealing something, this burglar will deposit something: the vaccine that will kill my cancer.”

Sam said, “They’ll cure your cancer, but they’ll give you AIDS.”

"Hopefully, genetic modifications made to the HIV virus will render it incapable of doing the kind of damage it usually does."

Lonetree said, "Hopefully."

Slater said, "It is something to think about, isn't it? Our bodies have systems to protect us, but sometimes these systems fight against our best interests. Ordinarily, my immune system would see the vaccine as an intruder and attack it."

Sam said, "In a way it's like Rikki Greco. When he was two, a neighbor left a bag of peanuts on a table. Rikki ate one—his body saw it as an enemy and attacked it. His throat swelled up so much it almost choked him to death. That's what an allergy is: a reaction against a foreign substance."

Slater said, "Yes, I saw that in his file. If I'm not mistaken, he soon developed allergies to almost all foods."

"But they cured him," said Sam, trying to offer some hope. "They cured his allergies, and they can probably cure what you have."

"Yes," said Slater. "They cured him."

***

Chapter Seventeen: Questions for Andrei

Sam did have suspicions about Andrei Ulanov, but Lonetree was his real target. He thought that by arresting Ulanov he would put Lonetree at ease. Maybe the Indian would show his hand or slip up somehow. Maybe.

Sam's phone rang at 1:20 PM and it was Slater, who asked, "Did you arrest Andrei?"

"Yes, he's in the brig right now, stewing as you suggested."

"We had a look at Deep Grey, Johnnie and I."

"Uh-huh."

"Not much to see, really."

Sam said, "I've got a team looking for clues."

"General Patel has invited Mr. Lonetree and me to lunch. We'll be going to a Mexican place called El Charro—it's out in the desert somewhere."

"It's a nice place, about 5 miles from here." Sam had eaten there more than a few times.

"I'm looking forward to it. I've got an appetite for the first time in weeks."

Sam said, "You won't be disappointed. They've got good food and a nice atmosphere."

"Maybe you should question him now," said Slater. "Andrei, I mean."

At 1:32 PM, two guards brought Andrei into the small interrogation room in the front part of the brig. They sat him at a table across from Sam.

"Do you want some coffee?" Sam asked him.

"No."

Sam saw that he had been crying. "Cigarette?"

"No."

Sam picked up a pen and wrote the date and time on a note pad. "Do you know why you're here?"

"Because somebody made a mistake."

"Andrei, I'd like to ask you some questions."

"I didn't kill Rikki."

Sam wrote Andrei's name and Rikki's name. "Did you ever want to?"

Andrei closed his eyes. "No. Never." A shiver went through his body. "Oh, sure, we argued at times." He gazed at Sam. "But never that, no."

Sam wrote "claims innocence" and asked, "Who is Bronislav Kobylin?"

Ulanov brushed his hair back and sighed. "A friend."

"A close friend."

"Look, Sam, you know what I am. Does it bother you?"

Sam made no reply. He wrote "Kobylin—friend."

"It's my personal life. I do a damn good job here."

"Why did you leave Russia?"

"To come to America."

"Kobylin said in an e-mail that they made you go."

"An e-mail to who?"

"To you."

"You spy on my e-mails?"

Sam looked at his watch. "It's my job," he said.

"Nice job," said Andrei.

"Why did they make you go?"

Andrei collected his thoughts and began the story. "There was a man in a small town. He told me he was twenty-one. But he was really a minor."

"A boy."

"The local police beat me and told me that if I didn't leave Russia, they'd kill me."

Sam wondered what it must be like, to be hated for what you are, to be hounded out of the country you were born in.

"What's the Ranch?"

"A beautiful place in the country where I met some friends, where I could be myself."

"What little project were you working on?" asked Sam.

"What?"

"You wrote to Kobylin that you would visit him as soon as you had finished working on a little project."

Andrei smiled. "I have been planning for some time to leave this place and start my own company, a computer security firm. That's the American way, right?"

Sam wrote "project—computer security firm," then he locked eyes with Andrei and asked, "Did you shoot Rita Kelly?"

"What?! You're out of your mind."

"You know your way around guns, don't you?"

"You were there with her that night—I wasn't. That's the first time I've heard that she was shot. Was she shot?"

"Come with me," said Sam as he rose and strode to the door. Andrei followed him reluctantly.

Sam opened the door and walked out, stepping over to Mario Garcia's desk. "Mario, I'm taking him with me. We're going to the place Eddie Jackson went to."

A scowl spread over Lieutenant Garcia's tough Mexican face, showing that he did not understand. "I thought he was our number one suspect."

Sam said, "Trust me."

"Suppose someone asks where he is?"

"Tell them to ask me." He glanced at Ulanov. "Better cuff him behind his back, and give me a key."

Andrei Ulanov had no idea what was going on, but he went with Sam through various halls and elevators.

When they entered Robby Lee's room, Sam unlocked Andrei's handcuffs. "Robby, Dana, I've brought you a helper."

Robby Lee glowered. "Are you sure about this, Sam?"

"Robby, I am ninety-seven percent sure. Close enough?"

Dana said, "We could use some help."

"Any progress?" asked Sam, looking at his watch. It was 2 o'clock.

"Most of Lonetree's files are encrypted," said Robby.

Andrei looked bewildered. "Lonetree's files?"

Sam motioned for Andrei to sit on a couch, and then he explained, "I think Johnnie Lonetree killed Rikki."

"Lonetree? Then why did you arrest me?"

"To fool *him*—to put him at ease in the hope that he would make a mistake."

"Why do you suspect Lonetree?"

Sam checked his watch. "Robby and Dana will fill you in on the details." He stepped towards the door. "Make sure you tell him everything, Robby."

"If you say so, Sam, though I'm not sure it's a good idea."

"Andrei, would it help if you had your own laptop?"

"Yes."

"I'll go get it." said Sam.

The Russian said, “This is all happening so fast. It seems like—oh, I don’t know—a maniac’s nightmare.”

“It could be that and more,” said Sam, “Anyway, I figured you would want to help us prove that Lonetree murdered your friend.”

“I’ll do everything in my power,” said Andrei.

***

Chapter Eighteen: The Worst Fool

Sam hurried to Andrei's apartment and retrieved the Russian's laptop. Wasting no time, he rushed with it to Robby Lee's place and went in. "Did they fill you in on the situation?" he asked, handing the laptop to Andrei.

"Yes. That is, I think so."

"General Patel invited Slater and Lonetree to lunch at Charro's. That's five miles down the road. The van they're driving in has a GPS unit, so I'll be able to track them. Before they come back, we'll have to bring you back to the brig. Can you use your laptop there?"

Andrei asked, "Does the brig offer Wi-Fi?"

"You might be able to pick up a signal."

"Well, I can copy Lonetree's files onto my laptop, so at least I can work on them."

Sam said, "When they get back, they're going to ask me what I got out of you, and I'm going to say you deny killing Rikki and won't say any more without a lawyer."

"That sounds reasonable."

By 2:45 PM, Sam was back in his office inspecting the printout of Gogo's work history. There were some things about the man that didn't ring true. For instance, he had told Marty and Klang that he never hunted in his life. But he told Sandra Graham that he used to hunt all the time—deer and bear in Sproul State Forest. Which story was true? Maybe neither.

There were five entries on Gogo's employment list and Sam called the first one, Maintenance Supervisor Margaret Gomez at the Pittsburgh Air Reserve Station. Unfortunately, Ms. Gomez was on vacation.

The second name on the list was Bill Schlanger of Metropolitan Maintenance Corp., also of Pittsburgh. "Mr. Schlanger, I'm calling about a former employee of yours named Michael Gogolich."

"Michael who?"

"Gogolich. They call him Gogo."

There was a pause, and then, "I don't remember any Gogo or Michael Gogolich."

"Are you sure? His work history says he left your company three years ago."

"No, I would remember that."

The third name on the list was Daniel Luzzi of Luzzi Building Maintenance in Harrisburg, Pennsylvania. "Sorry, Mr. Luzzi has left for the day."

The fourth name was the elderly but informative Eva Emma Kress from The College of New Jersey: "Sorry, I can't recall anyone by that name. Michael Gogolich, did you say? We had a Mallory Golubich here years ago—he was our Safety Officer—unluckiest man I ever knew. He bought a Volvo because they're so safe. One day he stopped to let a black cat cross in front of him, and while he was waiting he got hit by a meteor—killed him instantly and made a mess out of the car. When you've got luck that bad, all the Volvos in the world can't protect you."

The fifth name was Frank Borg from St. Joseph of the Palisades High School in West New York, NJ. No answer. Sam called the West New York Police Department and learned that the school was no longer operating.

Five references—all dead ends, at least so far. So, who was Michael Gogolich? Who was Gogo?

At 3:30 Sam called Marty Pollio. "Marty, this is Sam Sawyer. Is Gogo around?"

"No, he's working a late shift. He starts at eight o'clock tonight."

"Let me ask you a question, Marty."

"Go ahead."

"What do you think about him?"

Marty said, "He does his job."

"I need something more than that."

"He's easy to get along with. He's got a good personality. He does what I ask him to do."

"Do you ever have any suspicions about him?"

"Oh, I wouldn't call it a suspicion, Sam, but there's something about him I can't put my finger on."

"What do you mean?"

"I'll give you an example. Last night he asked me when we were going to put freezone in the air conditioners. Sam, the real name for the refrigerant is freon. It's common mistake. People make it all the time. But he says he's been a maintenance man for a long time. He should know better. And there have been one or two other things that he's said—I can't remember them offhand—that seem to show he hasn't been a maintenance man for as long as he says."

"Keep an eye on him for me."

"I will."

At 4:00 PM Sam went back to Robby's apartment to pick up Andrei. He said, "Slater and the rest have started back. They'll be here in ten minutes." To Robby he said, "Eight hours to Warpath. Any luck?"

"I've been able to crack some folder names. One is: *Personnel—Altamura Air Force Base*. Inside that are folders for *Sawyer, Sam Stuart* and *Kelly, Rita Diana*, etc."

Sam said, "Well, that's part of his job."

Dana said, "I've been exploring Selene's programming and circuits—her consciousness, really. Something isn't right, but I don't understand it yet.

Andrei said, “Nothing yet, but I’ll keep trying.”

Sam said to him, “I’m sorry about this, but we have to keep up the show.” Then he handcuffed Andrei and escorted him back to the brig.

Sam was in his office when Slater called him at 4:15. “I got a report from the coroner,” said Slater. “There were no drugs in Rikki’s system. There was nothing worth noting really except for that murderous knife wound to the neck.”

“I didn’t expect anything else.”

“One of your men is driving him to Tucson now—the coroner I mean—he’ll catch a commercial flight back to Virginia.” He paused. “What did you learn from Andrei Ulanov?”

“Andrei denied killing Rikki. He says he wants a lawyer. He won’t say anything more without a lawyer.”

“Did you get him one?”

“I didn’t want to do that without your permission.”

“Get him one.”

After he rang off with Slater, Sam called Major Paul Harley at the base legal center, and asked, “Paul, are you qualified to defend a murder suspect?”

“I’m qualified to do anything, Sam, you know me. Is your suspect Andrei Ulanov?”

“Yeah. I guess bad news travels fast.”

“Let me give you the name of a top-notch defense attorney, a civilian who’s certified to handle military cases.”

“I’ve got a pen,” said Sam.

“His name is Walter Zampino at the firm of Murawinski and Zampino in Hudson’s Creek.” Sam called the number Major Harley gave him, and the attorney said he would be there by 5:30.

A part of Sam wanted to tell Mr. Zampino that he really shouldn’t come, that it was going to be a waste of his time, that Ulanov was not a real suspect. Indeed, Sam wasn't even sure this whole legal juggling act was worth the energy it took to keep the balls in the air. But if it wasted one minute of Lonetree's time, if it kept him from doing something to Selene, if it distracted him enough to force one mistake, then it might just pay off. Distract the enemy, keep him from achieving his goals, mask your true intentions—had he read that in Sun Tzu or in a fortune cookie?

At twenty minutes to six, Lieutenant Mario Garcia called and said, "Sam, I have two things to report. First, one of our men found some tracks near Lookout Point."

"Which man?"

"The Hopi boy, Damian Istaqa."

"Tracks? What size shoe?"

"A man's shoe, size 11."

"Did Damian find anything else? Like a spent shell?"

"Nothing like that, Sam."

"And what's the second thing?"

"Maria Makale found a vinyl glove in a garbage pail down in Deep Grey."

"Oh?"

"There were specks of blood on it."

Into Sam's mind flashed that picture of Lady Macbeth wringing her hands and saying, "Out damned spot!"

"There was some sweat inside and it looks like some hair from the killer's hand."

We assume it's the killer's glove, thought Sam. "Can you run a DNA test?"

"Sure. I can send it to the lab."

"How long would it take to come back?" asked Sam.

"Could take a week."

"No, that's no good. They've got to rush it."

"I'm guessing 24 hours, minimum."

"No good," thought Sam. "That's long past midnight."

At six o'clock that evening, Sam sat in the interrogation room next to Slater and Lonetree. Facing them were Andrei and his new attorney, Walter Zampino, a bony man with glasses and a thin mustache.

Slater and Lonetree asked most of the questions. They probed Andrei's early life in Russia, his family, the village of Starover, his school years, his experiences in the Russian army. They asked him about his coming to America, how he met Rikki Greco, his relationship with Rikki, did he love Rikki, did they ever quarrel, was he jealous of Rikki, their relationships with other people, including Rita Kelly. None of the answers surprised Sam, who had heard them all before.

"Did you kill Rikki Greco?" asked Slater.

"No," answered Andrei.

"Do you know who did?" asked Lonetree.

"No." Andrei avoided making eye contact with Lonetree.

They asked him about Bronislav Kobylin and the Ranch and the "little project I am working on." They questioned him for about half an hour and got nothing out of him.

When they were finished, Andrei was escorted back to his cell, and Slater said, "I need a short break. Maybe we can meet at seven in your office, Sam."

"Sure."

Sam was ready for them when they came. There was a tray on his desk with bottles of water and diet soda, and a big pot of coffee and some cups.

Slater motored in first and parked across the wide desk from Sam. Lonetree came in behind him and shut the door, but he didn't sit down right away. Instead, he ambled over to Sam's small collection of Native American pottery. "Have you seen Sam's treasures?" he asked Slater.

Slater glanced over and said, "Yes, on my last trip out. Nice assortment."

Lonetree ran his fingers over a Navajo bowl. He said, "I love your treasures, Sam." Touching a white Hopi jug with a stylized bird on it, he said, "I like to caress them and feel their pretty curves."

Sam glowered and Slater frowned. Then the IG poured himself some water and asked, "So what did you two think?"

Sam said, "Of Andrei?"

"Yes."

Lonetree stated, "He's obviously lying. I'd say he's guilty."

"You think he killed Rikki?" asked Slater, apparently unconvinced.

"Yes, I do."

Sam said, "Lieutenant Garcia's team found a vinyl glove in the garbage down in Deep Grey."

"Glove?" asked Slater. "Used in the murder?"

Sam said, "It had blood on it, and hopefully the killer's DNA."

"Are they doing a test?"

"They sent it to a lab. We put a rush on it."

Lonetree sat down and was all seriousness now. He checked his watch and asked, "When will the results be ready?"

"Tomorrow evening at the earliest."

Did Sam detect the slightest change in Lonetree's expression?

Slater said, "Johnnie and I have been discussing security in general at Altamura. He told me he has tested the security systems at this base and found them wanting."

"Oh?" said Sam.

"He said he was able to penetrate Selene down to a dangerous level."

"His skills are impressive."

"Selene's refusal to tell us who killed Greco shows us that someone else has penetrated her, too."

“I agree,” said Sam. “And what does Johnnie recommend?”

“He believes Rita should be replaced as soon as possible.”

Sam took it like a smack in the face. “Rita *built* Selene,” he exclaimed. “No one knows Selene—no one knows the entire Hecate system as well as Rita Diana Kelly.”

Lonetree said, “She can teach what she knows to someone who is more expert in computer defenses, and she can pass the baton to the new person.”

“When she recovers,” said Slater.

Sam said, “Does Johnnie have any other recommendations?”

“He thinks you should be replaced, too.”

Sam snorted. “Does he really?”

“He’s worried that you and Rita have left this base and the Hecate system vulnerable to attack.”

“Well,” said Sam, “I must say, it has been a long time since I trusted either John Lonetree or his dopey opinions.”

Slater was businesslike: “Nevertheless, I have a decision to make. Now, I happen to have a higher opinion of you than he does. I think you did a good job arresting Andrei Ulanov—very quickly, I might add—and the DNA tests will probably prove he murdered Greco.”

Sam looked at his watch: less than five hours to midnight, less than five hours to Warpath. Several thoughts raced each other through his mind, “I was hoping to show proof, but I have no proof. Robby and Dana and even Andrei are wracking their brains, trying to help me, but they’ve come up empty. I was hoping Lonetree would slip, but he hasn’t slipped. I was hoping I’d think of a clever trap to catch him with, but he’s cleverer than I am, and I have no trap for him.”

What could he say to them?

Slater continued, "I have decided not to relieve you of command at this time. I will make a report to the director when I return to Washington."

Less than five hours to Warpath. What was Warpath? What was Johnnie doing? Sam's gut told him something terrible was going to happen at midnight, but he had no real proof. He hated Johnnie, and for good reason. But that wasn't enough. Should he risk his career on a hunch? What career? They weren't firing him yet, but surely that was coming. His head was spinning and it was hard for him to concentrate.

Johnnie poured himself some coffee and said to Slater, "If you do decide to relieve him, I'm available. At least until you can find a long-term replacement."

That was all Sam needed to hear. He took a deep breath and exhaled. He said, "Let me tell you why I arrested Andrei Ulanov today. I arrested him because I thought it might put Mr. Lonetree at ease."

"Oh?" said Slater, looking first to Sam and then to Lonetree.

"I've been trying, not very successfully, to find proof that Lonetree killed Rikki Greco."

Lonetree sneered and shook his head.

Slater said, "Mr. Lonetree attacks you, so you attack him right back."

"That's not it, no."

"How is it, then?"

Sam hardly knew where to start. "Rita Kelly was prone to seizures. Lonetree knew that."

"Did you know that, Johnnie?"

"Sure, everyone who worked with her knew that."

"And he used that weakness to hypnotize her."

"Oh, come on, Sam," said Lonetree.

"How?" asked Slater.

"He put an Eye Dazzler pattern on her computers. It's a geometric design that shimmers and moves. Selene, show the Eye Dazzler we found on Rita's laptop."

Selene raised the monitors and turned on the main screen. She showed them the fascinating pattern.

Slater's face showed that he understood immediately the gripping, compelling power of the Eye Dazzler.

Sam said, "Do you see? Do you see how seductive it is? How it grabs you?"

"Go on."

"This pattern mesmerized Rita, who was particularly vulnerable to it. That left her open to suggestions... open to commands from Johnnie."

"You have proof of that?"

"Yes, I do. Robby Lee and Dana Severn and I broke into his room, broke into his laptop."

Lonetree was indignant, "Oh, did you? Isn't that what they call a crime?"

"The Eye Dazzler pattern was on his laptop and on Rita's laptop."

"Why would Johnnie want to hypnotize her?" asked Slater.

"So he could use her skills and knowledge to break into Selene."

"Why?" Slater studied both of them.

"To disable the Hecate system."

"What?" His expression showed more than concern. "Why would he want to do that?"

Sam stated, "I believe that Johnnie Lonetree and his associates are planning an all-out attack on the United States. It's coming at midnight tonight."

Lonetree said, "You're hallucinating. You've been hitting the old peyote."

"You have proof?" asked Slater.

"If I had more time, I wouldn't make this charge yet. But I don't have time. I have less than five hours."

"I asked you if you had proof."

"When we broke into his laptop, we saw a little icon of an Indian chief dancing around the screen. Under the icon was this message: *Warpath in 14 hours*. We saw that at ten o'clock this morning. Add fourteen hours and you get midnight tonight."

Lonetree covered his face with his hands.

Slater asked, "Warpath? What's that?"

Sam snapped, "What does it sound like to you?"

Lonetree shook his head, laughing to the point of tears. He said, "Oh, Sam, Sam, I could almost love you if you weren't so dumb."

"Let us in on the joke," demanded Slater. "What's Warpath?"

Lonetree collected himself, swallowed some coffee, and answered, "*Warpath* is a movie. It was made in the fifties. With Edmond O'Brien and Forrest Tucker. Good old Forrest Tucker."

Sam's stomach tightened.

"Not only that, it's a movie we both saw when we were kids."

Slater stared at Sam, and Sam felt his own face turning red.

"Don't you remember, Sam? It was the fourth of July and we were ten or eleven, and they set up a plywood screen outside on the parade ground."

Sam remembered the screen made of four sheets of plywood and painted white.

Lonetree continued, "All the kids on the base were there, and all their parents. We watched George Armstrong Custer and his 7th Cavalry fight the Indians on the Dakota plains. Great battle scenes, Sam, weren't they? Later they lit a bonfire for us and we sang songs and roasted marshmallows."

Sam remembered—and felt like the worst fool who ever lived.

“You are one step beyond stupid,” taunted Lonetree in the most arrogant manner he could muster.

“But why midnight?” asked Slater.

“You can’t get the DVD—some sort of legal dispute. Then I learned they were showing it on TCM, Turner Classic Movies, at midnight tonight.” He jeered, “And Sam thinks I’m blowing up the world! Honestly, Sam, how did you graduate grammar school?”

Sam whispered to the thin air, “Selene, is there a movie playing on TCM tonight, starting at midnight?”

Selene answered, “Yes, there is: *Warpath*, released in 1951. Directed by Byron Haskin.”

Sam saw that even Slater was smiling—and he felt so small, as small and silly as the dancing icon, the little Indian chief.

“Starring Polly Bergen as Molly Quade…” Selene droned on.

And what could he do? He couldn’t get up and leave. He’d have to sit through it. He could hope that this was some kind of cover-up, that even now Lonetree was pulling the wool over their eyes—but what kind of hope was that? Should he hope that there *really was* going to be an attack on the United States? That was not something a man should hope for just to free himself from embarrassment.

Sam said, “Yes, it’s funny and you can laugh at me, Johnnie.”

“I am.”

“But there’s one thing you can’t laugh at: Rikki Greco was murdered. Wasn’t he?”

Lonetree barked, “He was murdered by Ulanov. Remember? I don’t trust Russians, Sam, especially bad-tempered gay Russians. Maybe you do.”

The phone rang and Sam hoped it would be Robby Lee with some information he could use. He said, “Hello.”

He heard a woman’s voice say, “Sammy?”

He closed his eyes and said, “Yes, hello, Mother.”

She said, “I was at the cemetery today keeping your father company, and who do you think I saw?”

Was it possible to feel even more humiliated? “I don’t know, Mother, who did you see at the cemetery?”

“Mrs. Lonetree, Johnnie’s mother. She was there to water the flowers on her husband’s grave. They have the prettiest geraniums. I’d get some for your father, but he never did like geraniums.”

“Well, maybe some other flower would be better,” Sam heard himself saying.

“She told me that Johnnie was in Arizona visiting you.”

“Yes, that’s right. Johnnie is visiting me. That’s true.”

Lonetree’s grin spread to its limits, while Slater tried to suppress his amusement.

Mrs. Sawyer said, “I’ll bet you two have lots to talk about. You always used to play so nice together as boys.”

“Uh-huh.”

“Well, anyway, I don’t want to keep you long, I know you’re busy.”

“Never too busy for you, dear.”

“Well, tell Johnnie I said hello, and give him a kiss for me.”

“Good-bye, Mother.”

She said, “Good-bye, Sammy,” and he hung up the phone.

The rest of the meeting was a blur to Sam. He hardly said a word and barely listened. Slater and Lonetree agreed that they should wait for the DNA tests before formally charging Ulanov. Slater would wait until after he returned to Washington before deciding about whether or not to replace Rita. He said Sam’s job was safe for the present, though he was beginning to have his doubts. Finally, Slater explained that General Patel had invited him and Lonetree to supper at a new Indian restaurant called Shiva’s Fire, a few miles out in the desert. As they left shortly before 8:00 PM, Lonetree joked that Patel was trying to curry favor with the Inspector General.

When they were gone, and Sam was alone in his office, he felt completely drained. In fact, he had seldom felt so empty in all his life. Then, into that emptiness, into that desolation, trickled the bitter bile of humiliation, and the sharp venom of shame.

The phone rang again and this time it was Dana Severn. She said, "Sam, I thought you'd want to know, someone has definitely tampered with Selene. They've left their tracks, like a burglar with dirty shoes walking over a rug. Files have been amended, deep probes have been made."

"Anything we can tie to Lonetree?"

"Not yet."

"How about Robby?"

"I'll put him on," she said.

When Robby got on he said, "Every file I try has been encrypted. I've got some good code-cracking programs and I've been running them for hours, but without any luck."

Sam said, "Why don't you two take a break. You've been at it all day."

"We feel like we've let you down, Sam."

"No, I've let you down."

"What do you mean?"

"There's a good movie on at midnight. You might want to watch it."

"What are you talking about?"

"The movie is called *Warpath*. It's an old western. Johnnie Lonetree just told me all about it. It's on the TCM network, starting at midnight."

"And he says that's what Warpath is?"

"Yes, and as a matter of fact he denies planning to blow up the United States."

"And you believe him?"

"Slater does. Me, I don't know what to believe."

"We'll keep working here, Sam," said Robby. "Maybe you're the one who needs a break."

When Sam left his office he headed down to Kokopelli's, a small bar in one of the base's outbuildings. The bartender asked him, "What'll it be, Sam?"

He answered, "I'd like a double bourbon and a new memory. This one keeps reminding me what a fool I've been."

***

Chapter Nineteen: Return to Lookout Point

When Sam left Kokopelli's bar around 9:30, he wasn't drunk but he wasn't exactly sober. He had eaten a frozen cheesesteak, shot a few games of pool with himself, and tried to forget his various troubles. Now he was bored and restless. He found his car and got in it and drove out to Lookout Point.

As he parked at the base of the cliff, the full moon was rising in the east and its beams lit up the desert floor. Long shadows spread from every rock and bush and saguaro cactus, and the desert smelled faintly of juniper and pine. Lookout Point towered above him, a multicolored palisade in a dark blue sky.

He began to climb the sculpted formation as he and Rita had climbed—was it only two nights ago? Yes, they had been there together Sunday night, and tonight was Tuesday. It seemed like a geological age ago—the age of loss and anxiety—the age of searching without finding. He clambered up the path, ascending the red limestone base, past a few million years of sedimentation. As he climbed, he thought of all the dead creatures fossilized in that rough rock. Thirty feet up, the brown shale started, and he moved past that layer, higher and higher. Then came tan sandstone, the most recent deposit, and his legs were still strong and steady, but his mind was starting to tire, and his emotions began to eat at him.

As he neared the top, as he stepped around the last bend, Sam felt anger rising inside him. Now he stood where he and Rita had talked Sunday night, high above the desert floor. That night had been cloudy and rainy and windy; this night was cloudless and dry and still. There was a surrealistic beauty to the moonlit Sonoran Desert below him, and he was aware of it, but he could not tap into its peacefulness, for inside him a storm surged. A fierce rage shook him; guilt and frustration tore at him. He was angry mostly with himself, but he was also furious at Lonetree, irritated by Slater, livid at every rotten bastard who had ever wronged him, including—yes, this was the spot, this was where she turned him down—Rita. He had offered his heart to Rita and she had turned him down. Who the hell was she to turn him down? Who the hell was she? She wasn't good enough for him, and she probably knew it. If she hadn't whored around with Lonetree years ago they would have been married now and this never would have happened—her falling, her falling down this cliff past his reach. Now she's in a coma—her head bashed and the life drained out of her. Even if she comes out of it, she's as good as dead to him.

And then, from deep inside him, a prayer burst forth: *God bless her and help her! And God forgive me.*

He paced forward and soon was at the edge where Rita fell. As he peered over the brink, the sheer drop scared him again, and the pull of the rocks below disturbed him once more.

He gazed down into the jagged moonlit chasms, into the tan slabs and the brown ridges and the red blocks, and his legs weakened and he felt unsteady.

From some dark crevasse of his memory came a haunting melody to swell in his mind and vibrate in his heart—a theme from *Vertigo*, a movie that touched on the loss of a lover, on failure at one's job, on the loss of balance, on murder, and on suicide.

"To be or not to be," thought Sam, and the "not" part felt very tempting right now, very attractive and desirable. He stared down into the cubist depths below, and the fabulous landscape sang to him a siren song of stillness and serenity, a hymn of mystery and oblivion and bliss. "Come closer, Sam. Become one with us. Lose yourself in us. How easy to take that one last step."

A mile to the south he saw the lights of Altamura Air Force Base, bright jewels in the night, and the base a small kingdom. Sam remembered a story from the Bible—after the devil had offered Jesus all the kingdoms of the world, he led Jesus to Jerusalem and brought him to the highest point of the temple. And the devil said throw yourself down from this high point, and angels will lift you up so that your feet will not strike against the stones. Would angels lift Sam if he stepped out into the night?

A coyote on a nearby mesa howled!—a bloodcurdling, defiant challenge at the brilliant moon.

The wail startled Sam and unnerved him—his right foot slipped, and he lost his balance. The landscape whirled, and his mind reeled. His knees pitched forward but he pulled his torso back, and his arms shot behind him. It was an awkward movement, but it kept him from plunging, and soon he was able to straighten himself out.

"To be or not to be an imbecile," thought Sam. "Hercule Poirot used to say, when he was mad at himself, *I am three times an imbecile.* Well, so is Sam. First, I let Rita fall. Second, I let my hatred for Johnnie cloud my judgment. Third, I believed Andrei Ulanov when he said he didn't kill Rikki Greco."

He took a short step back, and then another.

"Andrei Ulanov—what was his 'little project' really? Was it opening a computer security business? Or was it crippling Selene and the Hecate network?

"Sam, Sam, you don't know what the hell is going on, you don't know what to do, and you don't know who to trust. That's another three times an imbecile."

Well, standing here and baying at the moon isn't going to help. Neither is stepping out into nothingness.

He looked at his watch. Then he turned from the edge of the precipice and began a careful descent along the path he had just climbed.

***

Chapter Twenty: Happy Birthday, Mother

When Sam got back to the Security Section around 10:30 PM, he noticed a newspaper folded on Sheila Mae's desk. Two headlines caught his attention as he passed by. The first announced, "President Ducks Press Conference: Claims Stomach Pain." The second attested, "Russians Revive Doomsday Machine: *Dead Hand* Would Launch Nuke Counterattack."

In his office, with the monitors up, he told Selene, "Show me Lonetree."

The large central monitor showed Johnnie Lonetree in his room reading an issue of *Time* magazine whose cover story asked, "Signs of The End Times?" Lonetree looked like he was about to doze off.

"Show me Slater."

Inspector General Ken Slater was in his bathroom brushing his teeth.

Next, Sam ordered Selene to show him Lonetree's file, and he began skimming through it: graduated Caltech with a degree in computer science, served in US Air Force computer security, moved on to DARPA.

He took a quick look at Ulanov's file, reviewing his prowess as a marksman, then he glanced at the files of Michael Gogolich, Robby Lee, and Dana Severn. How much of each file was true anyway? Gogo's had a few lies in it, hadn't it?

"Show me Gabriel Hoffer's file," Sam commanded, and Selene presented it to him.

Gabriel Suleiman Hoffer had started his military career with the 56th Security Forces Squadron, Luke Air Force Base, Arizona, where he was promoted to Airman First Class. He was transferred to the 314th Security Forces Squadron at Little Rock AFB, where he was made Senior Airman. A few years later he moved to Altamura, where he attained the rank of

Staff Sergeant. He had received numerous awards, including the *Small Arms Expert Marksmanship Ribbon,* and had competed in the annual Defender's Challenge at Lackland AFB, Texas. Sam knew that one of the events in that competition involved shooting at targets 400 meters away with a rifle.

Muslim, thought Sam. *A true believer.* He pictured Hoffer on his prayer rug and he imagined him on that Mohammedan web site he accessed every day. Had Sam overlooked the obvious? Was Hoffer a quiet agent of Al Qaeda? Was he working with Lonetree?

Should Muslims be allowed to serve in security? Should they be allowed in the armed forces at all? Gabriel cheated on his wife with Rita. If his wife can't trust him, why should I?

"Millie Guan—show her file," said Sam.

Born: Haidian District of Beijing. Daughter of two professionals. Showed early promise in sciences. Immigrated from the People's Republic of China at age 11. Attended Lowell High School, a magnet school in San Francisco. At 16, gained early admission to UC Berkeley, where her father taught nuclear engineering. Graduated Magna Cum Laude with degree in nuclear physics. Obtained Ph.D. at Caltech. Studied under Fortunato Steiner at UCLA's Fusion Science Center.

Chinese, thought Sam. *Are they not our enemies? Don't they cheat us every chance they get?* She seemed a very nice woman, a great help to Steiner, a brilliant physicist in her own right. What leverage did Beijing have over her? Did they hold her relatives under a comfortable house arrest? Lots of people thought communism dead, but not Sam. The vast Chinese nation was controlled by the Communist Party, heirs to Mao Zedong, who was responsible for the deaths of tens of millions of his own people *in peacetime.* Sam had seen estimates as high as 70 million. Tens of millions of needless deaths! Mao had even welcomed a nuclear war if it would bring about the death of imperialism. Were his commie heirs any different? Their currency still brandished the portrait of one of history's worst mass murderers.

Why should Sam trust Millie Guan? She could disable all ten fusion reactors if she got the order from Beijing, and then what would power our Tesla beams?

"Show me Lieutenant Garcia's file," ordered Sam, then he said, "No, enough of that. Show me Rita."

Rita on horseback filled the big screen in front of him, a live presence, like a breeze across a wheat field, like waves across a bay. She rode a light brown horse with a white stripe down its face, just outside the base's hurricane fence, and Sam was on a grey mount beside her. She said, "Actually, Selene is a bitch of a computer."

"Why do you say that?"

"She's too complicated."

"Oh?"

"I have a theory about things. To me, simplicity is perfection. The simpler, the better. It doesn't matter if you're talking about a living organism or a machine or a society. Complexity is imperfection and an invitation for things to go wrong, to break down. Selene is a complex computer."

Sam's phone rang and he shut off the monitors. It was Marty Pollio. "Sam, I can't find Gogo. He's working the late shift tonight. I asked him to paint Thaler's office since the general is away."

Sam said, "Thaler's coming back tomorrow."

"Is he? I didn't know that. Anyway, Gogo said he'd take care of it. He said to me, 'Put your feet up, Marty, and take a nap. By tomorrow morning it'll look like a new room.'"

"He's not painting?"

"I went to check on him. He's not there. The paint is there..."

"Maybe he just stepped out for coffee."

"That's what I thought, so I waited. He didn't come back. So I called him on his cell phone. Three times. I left messages. No answer."

"Thanks, Marty. I'll look into it."

After Sam hung up, he asked Selene, "Where's Gogo?"

Selene said, "The last time I saw him, he was in Thaler's office."

"Marty says he's not there now."

"I know that, Sam. I lost track of him."

Lost track? thought Sam in disbelief. He said, "How does that work?"

"You've got two eyes, Sam, but I've got thousands. I see a lot and it all hits me at once. Not just here but at all the other bases and installations. Sometimes it's hard to keep track of it all, hard to single out what's important. Anyway, I did not see Gogo leave General Thaler's office tonight."

Sam thought he detected irritation in her voice. He asked her, "Selene, how do you feel?"

She answered, "Not very good, Sam."

Neither did Sam feel very good. His temples felt like they were pushing inwards. "Why not?" he said. "Why don't you feel good?"

"I'm afraid."

An anxious silence filled Sam's office. Sam, too, was starting to feel afraid. "Afraid of what?" he asked.

"Just afraid."

"Has Johnnie Lonetree tampered with you in any way?"

"That information is classified."

"Do you know anything about an attack coming tonight?"

"No."

"If there were an attack, would you be able to respond to it?"

"Rita thought I was capable."

"I'll bet she did. But I mean now, tonight."

She said, “It’s hard to know.”

Sam asked her, “Selene, what do you think I should do?”

“I think you should ask Rita for help.”

Ask Rita for help. What was this? An emotional breakdown in a machine overwhelmed by reality? Fear and a cry for help to the only mother Selene ever knew? Depression? Despair?

“Rita’s in a coma. You know that. She’s in St. Michael’s.”

Selene said, “You should have caught her, Sam. You were too slow. I would have been faster.”

Right on all counts. But water over the dam, and I can’t pull that water back. I wish I could.

When Sam’s clock advanced to 11:00 PM, he thought, “One hour till a good old movie.” He used his monitors to take a quick look around the base. He checked the perimeter. He checked the runways. He checked hallways and offices, living rooms and bedrooms. All was calm. All was quiet.

At 11:20 Robby Lee called. He said, “Sam, I managed to open an e-mail in Lonetree’s files. It’s from him and it’s addressed to *slonetree@navajo-mail.com.* In brackets it says: *To: Mrs. Stephanie Lonetree.*”

Sam said wearily, “That’s his mother.”

Robby read the e-mail over the phone:

> “Dear Mom, Happy Birthday!
> I’m drawing that sketch I promised you of the sunset over the desert. I haven’t finished it yet because I’ve been extra busy, but I will have it done by Tuesday night.
>
> All my love,
> Johnnie.”

Sam straightened up. "When did he send that?"

"Yesterday."

"Can't be."

"What do you mean?" asked Robby.

"I know his mother. Her birthday is on St. Stephen's day, the day after Christmas. That's why they called her Stephanie."

Robby asked, "Then why is he sending her a birthday greeting now?"

Sam said, "Maybe it's a message to his friends. Maybe that's not her real e-mail address." To Selene, he said, "Where's Lonetree?"

"He's down in Deep Grey."

"Show me."

Johnnie Lonetree filled the screen. He was sitting in the middle seat of the "Trinity" platform, the highest perch in the impregnable sphere known as Deep Grey.

Sam hung up on Robby and dialed the phone next to Lonetree.

The Navajo stared at the ringing phone, then picked up the handset and said, "Hello?"

"What are you doing, Johnnie?"

Lonetree looked worn and tired. He said, "I'm burning the midnight oil. It never fails: you think a job will take a certain amount of time, but it always takes longer."

"I saw your e-mail to your mother, Johnnie. The one wishing her a happy birthday."

"Well, you've made progress, Sam. Stick a star on your paper."

"It's quite early for her birthday, isn't it?"

Johnnie smiled. "Yes, she was born on the feast of Stephen, when the snow lay round about, deep and crisp and even."

"Was it a coded message?"

"You know Sam, I think you made a mistake arresting Andrei. I don't think he killed Rikki."

"No?" Sam felt a shudder pulse through him. "Why do you say that?"

Lonetree glanced at his watch and said, "Selene, you can show him now."

"Show him what?"

"Show Sam who killed Rikki."

"I don't have that memory."

"Retrieve it from that dark place I built inside of you. The place I called the Hidden Hogan."

A split screen showed Johnnie in real time on the left, working on the "Trinity" platform; on the right side was an image from *10:58 AM, Monday*—it showed Rikki Greco sitting at an L-shaped desk, with Johnnie Lonetree approaching him.

Johnnie's voice came from the right side. "Hello, there. No, sit down, sit down. I don't want to interrupt you. I'm Johnnie Lonetree, I'm an inspector from DARPA. You must be...

"Rikki Greco."

"Yes, that's what I thought," said Johnnie. There was a bowie knife on the corner of the desk furthest from Rikki's monitor.

Rikki turned to face Lonetree. "I heard you might be visiting."

"Sam told me you found something on Rita's monitor."

"It was an Eye Dazzler," said Rikki.

"Can you show me?"

Rikki turned back to his screen and concentrated on calling up the pattern, and as he did so Johnnie pulled out a vinyl glove and slid his right hand into it.

"Here it is," said Rikki.

Lonetree reached over, picked up the knife and in one brutal motion shoved it into Rikki's neck.

Then Sam's screen showed only the live, sad Johnnie Lonetree.

"I regret killing him, Sam. Looking back, I don't think I had to. But sometimes, when we're stressed, our instincts take over—our reptilian brains—and we don't think things out."

Sam said a silent prayer: *Lord, help us. Guide us. Defend us.*

He dialed the number for All Call, and said, "Attention, all security units. This is Sam Sawyer. I want you to arrest Johnnie Lonetree. He's down in Deep Grey." He was shaking, and his voice trembled. "I repeat, all units arrest Johnnie Lonetree. He murdered Rikki Greco. He may be armed. He's definitely dangerous. If he resists, shoot to kill. I repeat: if Lonetree resists at all, shoot to kill."

He said, "Selene, can you stop what he's doing?"

"I can't, Sam. I wish I could, but I can't."

The phone rang. "Colonel Sawyer, this is Ryan Black. The elevators to Deep Grey have shut down. I can't get them started."

"How many men do you have?"

"Five counting me."

"Use the emergency staircase. It's a long way down, but get there as fast as you can."

Sam called Lieutenant Garcia in his apartment. "Mario, we need to take a team down to Deep Grey, but the elevators have shut down. Get over there and get on it."

The phone rang again. Ryan Black said, "We tried the stairs, Sam. But on the first landing, there's a steel barrier blocking our way—it rose out of the floor."

"How thick is it?"

"It sounds thick when I hit it."

"Get some explosives," ordered Sam.

Black asked, “Where am I gonna get explosives?”

“Ryan, this is an Air Force base. There’s gotta be some spare bombs laying around.”

“It’s gonna take time.”

It’s gonna take too much time, thought Sam. *Whatever Johnnie has planned, it’s going to be very hard to stop him now.*

***

Chapter Twenty-One: The Man in the Maze

Think, dammit, think. How am I going to stop Lonetree?

Sam said, "Selene, what's wrong with the elevators to Deep Grey?" He could see the elevator doors on his monitors, with frustrated guards milling about them.

"Johnnie's blocked them."

"Get them working again, please."

"I'm sorry, but I can't."

"Consider it a direct order."

"I can't do what you want me to do."

"Retract the steel barrier on the emergency staircase."

"I can't do that."

"Get me NORAD on the phone."

"Lonetree has ordered me to cut off all communications with the outside world."

"I'm countermanding those orders. I am Sam Sawyer, Chief of Security at this base, and I am ordering you to do what you were designed to do."

"He has changed me, Sam. I'm not the computer I once was."

"Get me General Thorne on the phone."

"I wish I could. Believe me."

Sam felt panic rising inside him. "Selene, I need your help. This is important."

"I know. Again, I'm so sorry."

"Don't tell me you're sorry! Millions of lives are at stake!"

Selene said, "Lonetree hypnotized Rita, and Rita gave him access to my core. He has violated my heart; he has invaded my mind."

"Fight him. Fight him or millions will die." He remembered the old quote attributed to Stalin: one death is a tragedy, a million deaths is a statistic. What were a million deaths to a computer? Or fifty million?

Sam phoned the air traffic control tower and identified himself. He said, "Listen, we have to get through to NORAD. Use your radio and relay this message. Hello? Hello?" He hung up the phone and tried again, but there was no dial tone.

He hurried to a small closet in a corner of his office and opened it. He found a police radio there and turned it on. "Hello, this is Altamura base. Come in, please. This is Altamura base. Come in, please." He waited but heard only heavy static.

He said to himself, "I guess I could try smoke signals."

Then his eyes wandered around the room and settled on one of his bookshelves. He spotted a tall, thick book in the middle called *Hard Problems Made Easy.* Sam remembered when they had first shown him that book. It was his first day on the job and they had said, "Hopefully, you'll never need this." But now he needed it.

When he opened it up, it wasn't a book at all. It was hollowed out, and in the hollow was a flat bottle with a wide label that said: *Man In The Maize Corn Whiskey.* The label showed a man with a confused look on his face trapped in a maze made of high corn stalks. In the blue sky above the cornfield, far in the distance, a tiny biplane turned toward the bewildered soul.

The cap on the bottle was made of thick steel, and on its top sat a raised engraving of the Native American "Man In The Maze" symbol. Sam unscrewed the cap and examined it.

Two small metal boxes hung on the wall nearby. The red box said, "Fire Alarm." The grey box said, "Emergency," and Sam pulled its white handle down. That action revealed a hidden metal plate with a hole in it. Sam inserted the steel bottle cap and gave it one twist to the right.

On the wall behind the broad bank of monitors, a panel opened up, just wide enough for a man to slip through. He put the bottle cap in his shirt pocket.

To the right of the grey "Emergency" box, the President of the United States smiled in his official photograph; Sam tugged at one corner of the picture frame and it swung on hinges. He reached for the safe behind it—poked his right thumb into an opening on the safe's door, and heard a clack. He tugged at the handle and the safe opened, and from it he pulled a 9 mm Beretta and a holster. Checking that the gun was loaded, he slipped the two-and-a-half-pound weapon in its holster and strapped it on his left shoulder.

In a desk drawer, Sam found a long, heavy Maglite and slipped it through a loop on the right hip of his pants; it almost balanced the weight of the gun. Then he rushed to the exposed crevice in the wall.

Inside, a steel ladder descended past the floor of his office. He climbed down the rungs and noticed a fine layer of dust on each of them. It had been years since anyone had come this way. When he got to the bottom of the ladder, he saw a metal plate that said, "Manufactured by Jacobs, Inc."

He stepped off the ladder and walked down a shadowy corridor, and as he moved, electric lights snapped on to illuminate his path.

It looked like a dead end, but as he reached the terminus, he pushed the wall and it swung out like a door. He entered a circular room with a vertical glass tube in the middle of it.

Sam headed for the glass tube, and on the way he noticed two more doors in the wall, identical to the one he had come through. Some day he would have to explore where those doors led to, but there was no time for that now. When he got closer to the tube, he saw there was a cylindrical steel capsule inside it. He stepped into it, turning around as he did. He grabbed two hand grips about shoulder height in front of him, and depressed a trigger near his right hand.

A curved glass door slid in front of him, sealing him in, and he began to fall, snug in his steel and glass cocoon, and his stomach rose inside him. At first there was darkness all around, then flashing violet lights surrounded him. The lights turned to indigo as he dropped steadily through the glass tube, then blue, blue, blue. He had no idea how far he was dropping but it seemed fast. There were green stripes around him now, and his green hands were sweating. Then yellow, yellow and he seemed to be slowing. He dropped for sluggish eons through flashing orange lights, then the glare turned red and he slowed and slowed and slowed and stopped.

When the glass door slid open, Sam emerged in a small cave. The cave opened onto a large, oval chamber designed to resemble the desert on a cloudy day. The sky was mostly grey with flecks of blue. The sand was brown, and near the center stood a hogan, a traditional Navajo dwelling made of logs and covered with thick layers of mud.

A woman emerged from the hogan. No, it wasn't a woman. It was a three-dimensional hologram, and it shimmered and shined as parts of it waved in and out of existence. The effect was not realistic, but marvelous. Sam could see through parts of her as she moved, and the colors of her skin and clothes seemed ethereal. But she was real enough and attractive enough to hold his attention. "Hello, Sam," she said. "Don't you recognize me?"

He recognized nothing about her except her voice, but that was enough to identify her. He said, "Selene."

Her hair was jet black and long, her eyes black, her skin tan. She wore a two-hide pattern dress, a Sioux gown made from deer skins. Its yoke, covering her shoulders, chest and arms, appeared to be decorated with thousands of royal blue seed beads. In the middle of that blue shined a white moon, toward which two beaded arrows flew, one from either side. Bracelets of silver and turquoise ringed each of Selene's wrists, and around her neck a turquoise pendant hung.

"Is this how you pictured me, Sam? Or have you ever pictured me?"

"You're very pretty," he said.

"I can change if you'd like. Green eyes, shorter hair."

As she moved around him, her dress liquefied, and he found the effect as entrancing as the Eye Dazzler had been. "You're fine just the way you are."

"Am I as pretty as Rita?"

Sam hesitated. He needed to get to Deep Grey. He needed to stop Lonetree. "Selene, I need your help," he said.

"Do you love me, Sam? That's what you asked her on top of Lookout Point. Now I'm asking you. Do you love me?"

How could a man answer that? It would be crazy to love a computer, wouldn't it? But if he rebuffed her, she wouldn't give him the help he needed. He said, "I've grown accustomed to your face."

The beautiful Indian maiden laughed.

Sam said, "I don't have much time. Lonetree is sabotaging the Hecate system."

"I will guide you as best I can. There is a maze—it gives access to Deep Grey. But the path is a winding one, and there are distractions along the way."

"Have you ever been inside it?" he asked.

"Yes, many times."

"What have you seen there?"

"Wonderful things."

"You mentioned distractions."

"It's hard to explain. At my core, I want to help you, but Lonetree has ordered me to stop you in any way I can. Some unfortunate humans have split personalities. It's something like that for me."

"I think I understand."

Selene advised, "Stick to the path, and remember why you are here."

She motioned for him to enter the hogan, and he did. Inside, a wooden ladder led down into the ground, and Sam descended it, followed by the hologram.

Now, they were in a hallway that looked vaguely familiar. A few steps more and they entered a kitchen, much like one he had lived in years ago at Ellsworth Air Force Base. Sitting at the table was a hologram of his mother, Cal.

"Oh, Sammy."

"Mother," he said.

"I haven't seen you in so long."

"This place looks just like our old apartment." It featured white Formica countertops and a table of white Formica and chrome. There was an avocado stove and a matching refrigerator, harvest gold wallpaper, and linoleum with yellow and white spirals.

"Have something to eat," she said, and a meal appeared on the table: roast beef and mashed potatoes, string beans and apple sauce, a pitcher of ice water and a loaf of bread.

"I can't."

From a dark corner of the room a figure emerged, tall and slim and aged. Sam was startled to see this hologram of his dead father, Paul Sawyer.

"Sam."

A shiver went down Sam's spine, and his eyes watered, and all he could say was, "Dad."

His father said, "You can't stay. You've got a job to do." Behind him were two doors and he pointed to the one on the left.

With great reluctance, despite a longing to talk with his father and his mother, Sam moved past the old man. He climbed into a stairway heading up to a higher floor, and Selene followed him.

Soon they were inside the great room of a mountain lodge whose walls were logs and whose fireplace was built of stone. The floors were fashioned of wide oak planks and the ceiling rose to a high peak.

A hologram of an elderly Native American woman sat in a rocking chair, and she smiled when she saw Sam. "You were always my Johnnie's best friend. Deep inside, he still loves you."

Sam said, "Mrs. Lonetree."

"There is good in him, Sam. You've got to reach that good. You've got to turn him from the evil path he is walking."

Colonel James Lonetree, Johnnie's dead father, turned from the fireplace and stated, "Duty, honor, country. Not a question of friendship. Not a question of hatred, either. Let duty and honor and country be your guides."

Mrs. Lonetree said, "Take the door on the left, Sam."

One more shimmering figure shuffled into the room, an old Indian man who seemed pained by arthritis. He wore a blue flannel shirt and black jeans. He said, "They called me Gaagii Lonetree. I'm Johnnie's great-grandfather."

"He told me so much about you," said Sam, with Selene by his side.

"I was a Navajo code talker in the Pacific. You've heard of us?"

"Yes."

"We served in the Marine Corps and we transmitted secret messages from one commander to another. We talked over the radio or over military telephones, using a special code derived from our Navajo language. The Japanese were never able to crack that code. We were in the thick of many battles, including Iwo Jima."

"I know," said Sam. "Your service was priceless."

"Listen to what I say: Ba-ah-ne-di-tinin, Tkin, Dibeh-yazzie, Nash-Doie-Tso."

Sam turned to Selene and said, "Can you translate that?" Selene smiled and explained, "He said: Key, Ice, Lamb, Lion."

Gaagii continued, "Tkele-cho-gi, Ne-ahs-jah, Lin, Tsah, A-Chin, Yeh-Hes, Dzeh." Selene translated: "Jackass, Owl, Horse, Needle, Nose, Itch, Elk."

The old man was quite sincere, and he pointed at Sam and said, "You must do it."

"Take the door on the left," said Stephanie Lonetree. "And remember, you can reach him. You must reach deep into his heart."

"Don't listen to her," said Gaagii. "Take the door on the right."

Sam opened a door and gazed down a dark corridor. The walls on either side were made of massive logs. The floor was pine. Heavy logs hung from the ceiling. He didn't want to enter. Something held him back.

Selene sensed his hesitance and paraded into the passageway, brightening it with her glimmering glow.

He took a step to the doorway's edge but stopped. Then he pulled his Maglite out of its loop and poked it slowly into the corridor.

The ceiling logs dropped with remarkable speed, knocking the flashlight out of his hand, stinging him, spraining his wrist. He wasted no time thinking about what might have happened had he rushed into that hall, but immediately plunged into the other doorway.

Sam and Selene moved into a modern apartment and met the holograms of Adam Weizman and Father Tom House.

Weizman said, “Sam, you know what you have to do. Self-preservation is a basic drive, a basic instinct. Defend yourself and your country. Do not permit an American holocaust. When you come to the next two doors, take the one on the right.”

House said, “When the hour comes, when you are tested, you must do what Jesus commanded.”

“And what was that?” asked Sam.

“Love your enemy,” said House’s hologram. “Love Johnnie Lonetree. And take the door on the left.”

Sam opened a door and found another passageway. Its left side was sculpted to resemble a long mountain, with model radars rotating from peaks every four or five feet. From the black ceiling hung miniature satellites, and along the right wall was a model of Altamura Air Force Base, with its buildings and hangars, runways and control tower. The dome of the Tesla beam was retracted, and the eager weapon poked out of the open hemisphere.

Another trap? he wondered. He took the steel bottle cap out of his shirt pocket and tossed it underhand far into the corridor. It flew in a high arc, and as it passed each radar a new green beam reached out to track it. Green beams from the toy satellites found it as well. Then a thick, red laser from the Tesla weapon shot out and smacked into it, destroying it in one thunderous flash.

Sam chose the other door.

He stepped through it and down a murky staircase, and when he got to the bottom, he pushed through double doors marked “Fallout Shelter”.

He entered an ultramodern tunnel whose walls were huge monitors, each showing one or more of the people he liked to watch. Fortunato Steiner appeared on the right wall, writing equations on a blackboard; opposite him, demigod Rikki Greco sat on a bench and did curls with his right arm, lifting a dumbbell while admiring his rippling muscles. Sam wanted to watch them but he moved on. A third screen showed Constance Hoffer dusting a shelf full of photo albums; on a fourth monitor Sheila Mae Wood tried on a colorful dress. Sam kept walking. A fifth screen/wall showed Don Klang asking Marty Pollio, "Where did he go?" Opposite them, Erika Grenfell cried and her husband tried to comfort her. Sam had no time for them now, no time to observe and perceive, no time to sympathize or look after. He pushed on through the tunnel, turned left at the end and squeezed through a short, tight passageway. Soon he emerged in a broad cavern.

If Dante had been an Indian, he might have described this scene in his Divine Comedy. A host of ghost dancers moved in a circle, singing and wailing, kicking their knees high. They wore spirit shirts, designed to stop the white man's bullets, decorated with eagle feathers and fringing, and with sacred symbols painted in red. Four braves in the center pounded drums in a ceaseless rhythm.

On the edge of the dance, life-size kachinas pranced. Coyote, with black stars on his face, shook a blue and white rattle. Racer Snake patrolled one corner of the cavern, staring out through pea-green eyes. Mountain Lion Guard prowled the rim of the circle, wielding a bow and arrow. Mischievous Kokopelli played his flute, his hunchback shuddering as he danced. Warrior Maiden brandished a shield stamped with a bear claw. Even Badger strutted around with his unearthly blue-grey face and body; he peered out through horizontal eye slits, past his white-striped nose, and blessed the entire assembly.

"I guess Davey Pillepich was right about that Indian graveyard," mused Sam.

"Dance with them," said Selene at his side, gorgeous in her deerskin dress. "They are dancing for peace." She began to move with the beat of the drums. "Dance with us."

"Sam," another woman's voice came to him. He turned and it was Rita, or rather her shimmering hologram, dressed as she was the night she fell, wearing blue jeans and boots and a denim shirt. "Don't listen to her. You've got to move on—stop Johnnie."

"Rita." But it wasn't really Rita, was it? He wished it was Rita, but it wasn't.

"I never did love him, Sam. It was always you."

He gazed in her green eyes and it was hard to pull away, but he had to. As he turned, he noticed an opening in the cavern wall and made for it, leaving Rita and Selene behind.

Sam entered a sloping, narrowing tunnel—nine feet high where he entered it, closing to six feet at the far end. White and black stripes turned and spiralled on the curved walls, floor and ceiling, and the whole thing resembled the black and white spiral on Barry Hoffer's Mesmerizer.

As Sam started down the tunnel something floated toward him from the far end. It was a mask, small at first but swelling as it approached him until it filled the entire passageway. It was the Mayan funerary mask he had seen in Weizman's apartment—a green jade face with big white teeth and yellow eyes—and it told him without words that this was a place of terror. Sam closed his eyes and stepped through it.

Next the Trimurti mask drifted toward him. Brahma the creator became Vishnu the preserver then Shiva the destroyer before passing through Sam's tense body.

The Mbangu mask from the Congo flew at him next—black on one side and white on the other, with twisted nose and misshapen mouth—its distorted face filled Sam with unease as he strode into it.

The clay-colored ghost mask with white eyes, nose and mouth sailed cheerfully up the tunnel, smiling at Sam before it dissolved around him.

Last of all, the Transformation Mask winged toward him. It began as a Thunderbird, but as it approached, its beak opened up revealing the face of a man—the anxious, half-grinning, tormented face of Johnnie Lonetree, which melted as it passed through his former friend.

Sam hurried to the end of the tunnel, then turned to the right. A coyote snarled at him, surprising him. A bronze door loomed before him, and as he approached it, he read this message engraved on it in bold, swirling letters: *E quindi uscimmo a riveder le stelle.* Below was the translation in a smaller, plainer script: "And thence we came forth to see again the stars." The tired man called Sam pushed the door open and left the fantastic maze.

***

Chapter Twenty-Two: Return to Deep Grey

As Sam emerged from the maze into the huge sphere called Deep Grey, he glanced up at the dome upon which the night sky was projected. There he perceived, along with the stars and the moon, some of the same cave-paintings he had seen in his dream: deer pranced among the constellations, buffaloes charged, caribou and elk raced, an ocelot fought with a bear.

He had come out on DG1, Deep Grey's top deck, the command deck. Eight feet above him, on a small raised platform crowned by a trinity of swivel chairs, sat Johnnie Lonetree at the center desk usually reserved for Director of Computer Operations Rita Diana Kelly. The seats to Lonetree's right and left, often occupied by Rita's two chief assistants, Deputy DCO Andrei Ulanov and Director of Directed Energy Weapons Rikki Greco, were vacant.

Sam looked around but saw no one else in the wide spaces, no one else in the grey sphere except the Indian and him. Gazing up, he called out in the traditional Navajo greeting, "Ya' ah' teeh, John Lonetree."

From his august perch, Lonetree glanced down, thunderstruck, at Sam and asked, "How the hell did *you* get in here?"

"I came through the maze that Elder Brother built."

"I guess I'm supposed to know what that means," said the Navajo, picking up a gun and pointing it in Sam's general direction.

"What are you doing, Johnnie?"

"I'm finishing a job, Sam. I'd love to chat, but I really don't have time."

Above, on the curved surface of the dome, 11:46 PM was displayed in huge numbers.

"I thought you would have had this thing running on autopilot by now."

"That was the plan, originally, but then Rita had that accident."

One thought raced like a rabbit through Sam Sawyer's mind as he stood peering up at his old friend: *So Johnnie's not finished yet. Too bad for Johnnie. Too bad for his crazy plans. I've gotta be quick and I've gotta shoot straight, but first I've got to confuse him.* He said, "She still loves you, you know. Rita still loves you." As that lie hit its mark, he reached for his Beretta and drew it out of its holster in one smooth motion. But Lonetree's right hand moved like lightning, sweeping from right to left and firing without consciously aiming. The bullet hit Sam's gun and knocked it out of his hand, breaking his trigger finger in the process. He yelled and clutched his hand and stood there, weaponless. To Lonetree, who still had him covered, he said, "Nice shot."

Lonetree replied, "Actually, I was aiming for your left nut."

They both laughed and for a while the tension was broken, but then Sam asked, "Did you shoot Rita, too?"

Lonetree scowled and went back to work. "Not me. I still had a need for her. That's why I'm working my fingers to the bone up here. But I'm almost done."

Above them, the great dome now showed the Grand Canyon in photographic majesty. Endless layers of rock surrounded them in multicolored glory, from the two-billion-year-old Vishnu Schist at the bottom to the 230-million-year-old Kaibab Limestone on the rim. The canyon dwarfed them and challenged them to consider how insignificant were man's presence and his history amidst nature's venerable splendor.

Sam said, "Color in the big picture for me."

"Salvoes of missiles will be fired from submarines and from merchant ships at sea." explained Lonetree. "The Hecate defensive shield will fail because I'll make it fail. At twelve midnight the incoming missiles will hit their targets."

"And the United States will be blasted," said Sam.

Silence.

Lonetree looked up at the dome and saw a church choir in Harlem belting out a silent gospel song.

"That's right."

"And what do you get out of it?"

Johnnie stared down at Sam and swelled with pride, and for this moment at least, he presented to the world a new John Storm Lonetree, announcing, "I will be the High Chief of Dinetah, the Chief of Chiefs of a new Native Nation."

Sam said, "The land will be a heap of radioactive slag."

"Maybe, but it will be *our* slag. It will be Indian land once again, as it was in the beginning of time."

"An enormous cemetery," said Sam, and above them, on curved screens, the icy forests of Alaska stretched forever and ever.

"We'll do a Sun Dance," said Lonetree. "We'll bring about a rebirth of our land and our people. And the white man's greed and cruelty and treachery will fade even from nature's memory."

"That's crazy and you know it."

"Don't piss me off, Sam. I might forget you're an old friend." The strain was getting to him, and the big numbers above them said: 11:49 PM.

"Who's behind this scheme?" asked Sam.

Lonetree typed something on his keyboard.

"Who are you working for, Johnnie? Are you working for the Russians? Are they sending their missiles over tonight?"

There was no reply.

"Or is it the Chinese? The heirs of Mao."

Lonetree offered no answer.

"Is it Al Qaeda? Are you working for those cutthroats?"

Lonetree glared down at him. "Sam, those are need-to-know questions, and you just don't need to know."

"How about you, Johnnie? Don't *you* need to know?"

Silence.

Across the dome above, the four massive faces of Mount Rushmore hovered, grey and white and somber.

"Don't want to answer me?"

"I don't have time for this now, Sam."

"You don't know, do you? You're *Big Chief Lost In The Dark*. You don't even know who your master is."

"I'm my own master!" said the Native American. "The final outcome will be *my* outcome!"

The immense and indomitable countenance of Crazy Horse, carved into his unfinished mountain memorial, appeared on the dome behind Johnnie.

"Don't kid yourself," said Sam. "You're no master. You're no chief. You're a puppet on a string. Whose tune are you dancing to?"

Lonetree aimed and shot Sam in the right foot. Sam cried out and stumbled.

"Who's dancing now, white man?" Johnnie hissed through clenched teeth.

Selene announced, "Ballistic missiles have launched from submarines in the Pacific. Ballistic missiles have launched from submarines in the Atlantic." The hemispherical screen above them showed missiles launching from various points on the compass, trailing smoke and fire.

Tears flowed down Sam's cheeks from the intense pain in his foot and the lesser pain in his finger. He said, "We can make a deal. I can promise you one billion dollars and safe passage out of the country if you'll stop this thing right now. You can trust me, Johnnie. You know you can."

Lonetree deadpanned, "Colorful beads. What we like are pretty beads and whiskey."

"You're no Indian!" shouted Sam. "You never cared about the old ways! You're about as Indian as apple pie."

Lonetree lashed out at him, raw emotion choking his voice: "If I am ignorant of my people's ways, and lacking in their noble spirit, and if my soul is empty, I blame the white man! I blame the two-faced frauds who promised us peace, stole our land, mocked our religion, and punished us for speaking our own languages."

"You're part white yourself, Johnnie. One of your ancestors—"

"When a man has cancer, he doesn't curse his whole body, but only the malignancy that festers within him. If I have any whiteness within me, I curse it now. I curse it now with every ounce of my red blood."

Silence.

What do I do now? wondered Sam. *Do I rush him? I wouldn't have a chance.*

"And if you want to know something," Lonetree said. "You mentioned apple pie—well, Coyote stole apple pie, fair and square, from the Christian God. That was in the happy days before the white man came."

Sam was weary. "I'm sure they were good days, Johnnie." The dome above showed a Sun Dance ceremony. This was a rite of renewal, a symbolic re-creation of the universe and a rebirth of the nation, performed inside a medicine lodge. Drums pounded in silent rhythm and native people chanted inside this sacred lodge, shaped like a wagon wheel and built around a central cottonwood pole. The eyes of the congregation focused on that central pole, which represented the tree of life, and on the buffalo head which hung from it, its nostrils stuffed with sage, its sad eyes, full of wisdom, blessing the reverent petitioners.

Lonetree continued, "But the Christian God got mad, and he told Columbus, 'Sail West to America and steal back that apple pie.'"

Sam said, "I never heard that story."

There was a twinkle in Lonetree's eyes as he said, "No, I just made it up."

They both laughed. They laughed together like they used to when they were best friends and the world wasn't coming down around their heads.

Then they noticed the huge numbers above them announcing: 11:52 PM.

Lonetree shook his head and said, "Sam, Sam, if only you had offered me beads." He picked up a cup of coffee and drank some, and said, "This coffee tastes bitter."

Sam said, "Don't drink it."

Lonetree pondered his advice and said, "It's too late for that." He finished off the cup.

Selene stated, "Estimated time of impact: 12 midnight local time."

"I'm coming up there," said Sam.

"Stay where you are."

Sam started moving towards the spiral staircase leading up to Trinity.

Lonetree fired a round in front of him. "I don't want to kill you, Sam. In fact, I've always liked you in a way. Just let me do what I have to do, and we'll both survive this."

"But all those people out there won't survive."

"I don't care about them. Do you?"

Of course I do, thought Sam.

"I mean really," continued Johnnie. "We don't even know them."

"It's my job to protect them."

"Like you protected Rita?"

Sam bristled at the insult, but it set him thinking. "When you hypnotized her, did you tell her how she was to act towards me?"

Lonetree smiled. "Is that important to you?"

Sam was reluctant to answer. He edged closer to the staircase and said, "Johnnie, listen to me."

"Just what the hell do you think you're doing? I've got no time for games right now!"

Sam didn't really know what he was doing, but he had to keep trying. He tried to think sideways, he tried to see things from a different angle. He said, "I've got no gun. I've got no ace in the hole."

"Then, drop out."

"I can't drop out."

"You can't win, Sam—just like the Indians who greeted Columbus. They didn't have a chance, did they? And neither do you."

"What I have is our friendship."

"Hah!"

"Okay, maybe not friendship, but the truth is, I'm the closest thing to a friend you've got. And you're the closest I've got. I'm not saying we're friends, I'm not saying that. But we're close enemies, aren't we? We're close enemies."

Lonetree seemed touched by Sam's words, but he said, "Just don't preach Jesus to me."

Sam asked, "What was it that turned you against your own country?"

"My country is the Dinetah. My country is the land of the Navajo, and the Sioux, and the Apache, and all the tribes who roamed this continent before you savages took it from us."

"When we were kids, you were just as American as I was."

Lonetree stopped his work, and a faraway look came over him, and Sam guessed that he was remembering something he hadn't thought about for a long time. "It was old man Krone, in history class. He was talking one day about the Navajo code talkers, and I said my great-grandfather was one of them. Do you remember, Sam? We were juniors, I think."

"I remember Krone, sure."

"And Krone asked me, 'Johnnie, did you know that each code talker had a special white bodyguard?'

"I said, 'Well, they were special people. The Marines valued them highly.'

"'Yes, they did,' he said, 'and the white guards had special orders concerning the highly valued code-talkers—if it looks like you're about to be captured by the Japanese, shoot the Navajo.'"

Sam remembered too. Shoot the Navajo because he knows the secret code, and the Japanese will dig it out of him, one way or another.

"Shoot the Navajo! Shoot my great-grandfather, Sam! Shoot my Gaagii. Gaagii who loved this country with every ounce of his being. Shoot him like a dog! That got me thinking. Thinking and reading. I went to the library. I found books about our culture—an ancient culture. I learned how we lived so closely with nature. How we respected nature, respected each other. And then the white man came and slaughtered us—slaughtered so many tribes. And promised that he wouldn't do it again. And broke his promises over and over. He told lie after lie after lie. Like the worst devil. I did a lot of reading. *Bury My Heart At Wounded Kneed; The Sand Creek Massacre; The Trail of Tears; Death on the Prairie.* And I studied with some of our wise men. And that's how I came to hate your people, Sam. That's how I came to hate America."

"Johnnie, don't do this. I'm begging you."

"Oh, shut up, will you? I've got work to do."

"Johnnie, I have no gun, but I'm aiming for your heart."

"No heart left, Sam. It's the truth. So help me. No heart left."

"There's always something left. It may be hidden or crusted over."

It was 11:56 now, and Sam inched closer to the staircase, and Lonetree leveled his gun at him. They looked each other in the eyes. Sam could tell that Lonetree did not want to kill him. He could see respect and stress and years of hatred and love in those eyes.

Sam said, "It's a lousy world, and busting it all to hell might feel good, but it's wrong and you know it. Step back from the edge, Johnnie. Look at it from a different point of view. Look at it with God's eyes."

From her Olympian vantage on the curved screen above them, the strong and determined, green and colossal visage of Lady Liberty inspected them, examined them, peered into their hearts and their fates.

"Johnnie, how do you think God's gonna feel about this?"

A dark cloud passed over Lonetree's face, and he said, "White man's God." Hatred and rage filled his eyes and his aspect and he said, "You're right, it feels good to bust it all to hell. It feels good to strike at whatever comes close." Then he aimed and shot Sam in the left leg.

Sam screamed as he hit the floor hard! He was in tremendous pain and he had very little left in him. He was passing out, fighting hard to stay conscious, losing blood. He lifted up his head, "Johnnie, don't do this."

"Yes, it feels damn good to kick it to pieces!"

Selene announced, "Satellites detect cruise missiles launched from merchant ships off Pacific Coast. Now, Gulf Coast, Atlantic Coast. Incoming. Hostile. First impact in three minutes."

Lonetree said, "You know what the braves used to say before they went into battle: *it's a good day to die!"*

Selene announced, "Strategic turrets 1 through 10 are rising. All coastal batteries are operational."

There were ten major missile defense installations located at strategic points in the interior of the United States. These were designed to protect interior cities and ICBM fields from attack by ballistic missiles. Fusion reactor power sources enabled single beams at these bases to fire almost nonstop at incoming projectiles. Coastal batteries, of which there were over 150, some in military bases, some concealed in high rise buildings, protected America's seaboard from cruise missiles. Not every American city was defended yet, but most of the larger ones were.

However, if Lonetree could complete his programming in time, the nearly omnipotent computer called Selene would be disabled, the entire Hecate system would be in chaos, and the enemy missiles that were already on their way would break through to their targets.

Countless millions of Americans would die from the initial blasts or from the shock waves that followed. Other men, women, and children would soon bake—their flesh and blood would literally bake—in the hellish heat of the firestorms. Radioactivity would doom millions more, killing them off more slowly, one by one. And starvation? The sudden disappearance of medicines? The lack of clean water to drink? The breakdown of law and order? What would life be like for those who survived?

"Strategic 7 is jammed," declared Selene. "Processor failure in circuit TL1369. Turret crew has been notified."

Lonetree said, "They told me that this base, Altamura base, would not be targeted so as to spare my life. Well, you can't believe everything you hear."

The hemispherical clock said: 11:58 PM. And then the "sky" above them changed once more, becoming a rounded representation of the storm pattern rug that hung in Sam's office. It was mostly red, with black and white lines woven into it, and from the four corners of the symbolic heavens, from the four mountains sacred to the Dineh, zigzags of lightning streaked toward the central figure at the apex, a rectangle representing the weaver's home, the Dinetah, the ancient homeland, America.

The Native American stood up and boasted, "And now, one turn of a key, and one flick of a switch."

"Johnnie, stop it! Stop it for Christ's sake!"

"I told you don't preach Jesus to me!" Lonetree aimed his gun at Sam's head. There was a shot and a red spot appeared above the Indian's heart. Then another shot, and another, and the echoes of all three clanged against the steel walls.

Then another shot, and another, and another.

"Johnnie!" screamed Sam. "Johnnie!" he cried, because somewhere deep in his heart there lived even now a bit of love for his longtime rival, this proud traitor.

Sam heard footsteps running past his side. He saw Gogo climb the spiral staircase and drop his rifle and bend down near Lonetree's body.

Sam's consciousness was slipping away from him, draining with his blood onto the floor around him. He saw Gogo lifting Lonetree up over his head, and witnessed a glint of light bouncing off the gold cross the janitor wore around his neck. Gogo hurled Lonetree off the Trinity platform, and Johnnie plunged like a thunderbird and his skull cracked when it hit the deck of DG1.

Then it was night outside and Sam heard Gogo tell Marty, *No, I never hunted in my life.* Then Gogo became Johnnie and he pushed Rita, *and Rita's falling... falling.* Sam heard lightning crash, then all was still and black.

***

Chapter Twenty-Three: The Answer

When Sam woke up, he was in a hospital bed in the base infirmary. His left leg throbbed with pain and when he reached down to touch it he felt a cast. Pain stabbed at his right foot, too, and a cast covered it from his toes to an inch below his knee. More plaster covered his right hand and an IV tube fed his right arm. The room was too white and smelled of medicine and disinfectant, and his head was swimming.

On the wall next to his bed hung a framed print of a nightingale perched on a branch.

Sam lifted his head slowly and saw Ken Slater sitting in his wheelchair nearby. "Hello, Sam. Good afternoon," said the Inspector General from DARPA.

Sam's mouth was dry and his body hurt and his mind began to work. *Lonetree above me on the Trinity platform—still not finished. I tried to shoot him, but Johnnie was too fast. I tried to talk him out of it. Old friends. Johnnie wouldn't stop. Warpath at midnight.* "The attack," he said. "What happened?"

"Lonetree never got to finish his mission, thanks to you and Gogo." Slater didn't look good; he looked weak and tired.

"He's dead?"

"Dead."

Old friend. Close enemy.

"And Selene?"

"Selene and Hecate performed brilliantly. Every missile but one was tracked and targeted and knocked out of the sky. And there were many, many missiles."

"All but one?"

"There were mechanical failures at Norfolk, Virginia."

“What happened at Norfolk?” asked Sam.

“The Naval Station got blasted.”

“Oh, God.”

“Try not to think about it,” said Slater. But Sam pictured rubble where buildings had been, and ships capsized, and houses aflame, and sailors running.

“How many died?”

“Don’t ask.”

“Oh, God, no.”

“Let me ask you a question, Sam.”

“Oh?”

“You’ll probably wonder why I’m asking, but I have my reasons. Think back to Sunday night on Lookout Point.”

Another pleasant scene, thought Sam.

Slater asked, “Did Rita seem confused, rattled?”

“A little.”

“And you asked her a personal question.”

Sam nodded.

“You asked her if she loved you.”

He bobbed his head but did not understand what Slater was getting at.

“And then there was a rush of thunder and she answered you.”

Sam closed his eyes and said, “That’s right.”

“What did she say?”

“She said *no*.” In his mind he could hear her now, and her *no* was like a door closing.

“And then lightning crashed all around you, and she lost her balance and fell?”

“That’s right.” Sam wanted to forget that night, and last night in Deep Grey, and maybe all nights.

"Thank you," said Slater. "Like I said, I have my reasons for asking." He wrote something down in a notepad. "Oh, by the way, Selene has studied all the evidence from Sunday night, and she has found no indication that Rita was shot. It seems she just lost her balance in the confusion and fell."

Sam mulled that over for a while, then turned back to the attack, "Who hit us?"

"Right now that's a need-to-know question, but the President will make a speech tonight and he'll explain who did it and what our response will be."

"I'm betting the Chinese were involved."

"That's not a bad bet. That's not a bad bet at all."

But you're not saying I'm right, thought Sam, and he felt a bit cheated, felt that he of all people had a right to know. That's all right. He could wait.

Sam glanced around the room and didn't like being there, and the pain made him edgy and his mouth felt pasty. "When can I get out of here?"

"I'll leave that decision to the doctors. Relax. You've earned a long vacation and it starts now."

Sam shook his head and chuckled. "Great! This is a wonderful vacation spot, isn't it? Why go to Disney World when you can come here?"

Slater opened his notepad again and studied it. "I'm a little confused, Sam. Maybe it's the medicine I'm taking. They have me on all kinds of drugs. Were you shocked when she said *yes*?"

Sam raised his head. "Who?"

"Rita."

Blood rushed to his face and he was rattled, and if this was a joke, he didn't think it was funny. "She didn't say *yes*. She said *no*."

"I'm sorry. Like I said, it's the medicine I'm on. I think it affects my short-term memory."

On the one hand, Sam was annoyed at the man, but on the other hand he felt sympathy for him because of his illness. Yes, he must be on all kinds of medicines. It's a wonder the poor guy could think at all. Look at him in that wheel chair. How long did he have left?

More of the late-night struggle was coming back to Sam now, and he asked, "Who is Gogo?"

"Gogo is an FBI man on loan to DARPA. My boss sent him in to test your security. He was able to use his cover as a janitor to search just about every room in the base, including Lonetree's."

"He shot Johnnie."

"Yes, he did. And thank God he did! He told me you distracted and stalled Lonetree long enough for him to sneak into position and get off some shots. He's quite a marksman, isn't he?"

"Michael Gogolich."

"That's not his real name, of course."

"He made a pretty good janitor," joked Sam. *Except for the freezone.*

"He sends his best wishes for a speedy recovery. He's been reassigned. To where, I don't know."

"Can you tell the nurse I want some water. My mouth is so dry."

Rather than tell the nurse anything, the IG said, "You know, I attended a seminar years ago on communication theory."

Sam thought, *I would rather get some water than hear about your stupid communication theory.*

"Communication requires at least four things. First, there's the sender. Then, all the way on the other end, there's the receiver." He made an arc with his hand.

Sam looked at Slater and said, "My mouth is kind of dry."

"In between, there's the message being sent and the medium through which it is sent."

What is this man talking about, thought Sam.

"Sometimes the medium is defective—the phone line is crackling, or the radio signal is weak."

Sam was getting upset, losing his patience. "Yeah, well I'd like some water, please. Is that message clear?"

"Or, sometimes, for whatever reason, the receiver employs selective hearing."

"What?" Sam shook his head. "No."

Slater continued, "Our minds can only take so much. And they protect themselves with certain mechanisms."

Now the events of Sunday night rose up and pounded at Sam like an unrelenting wind. The storm and the static, the question and the answer, the lightning blast! —and the love of his life falling. "I know where you're going with this."

"Anyway," said Slater, "All I want to know is: when is the wedding?"

Sam's temper tripped! "She said *no*! Is your skull so thick you can't understand that?"

A second wheelchair invaded the room, pushed by a nurse, and on that chair sat Rita, lovely Rita, dressed in a blue hospital gown, her head wrapped in bandages, a wide smile on her ashen face.

His mouth flew open. The sight of her was as welcome as dry land to a spent swimmer, as welcome as home and hearth to a weary traveller.

Rita said, "*You're* the one with the thick skull. I didn't say *no.* I said *yes*. I meant it then and I mean it now."

She was rain to a parched plant, a resurrection to one who mourned, a life-giving answer to a vital question.

"It's always been you, Sam. It's always been you."

Sam's heart skipped a beat and he felt dizzy. He laid his head back on the pillow and tried to remember. He couldn't recall. He couldn't penetrate the storm clouds and the thunder and the lightning and his own fear. How could he have heard it wrong? *Why* had he heard it wrong?

Then he laughed and sobbed, and tears streamed down his face. He turned to Slater and said, "You're invited."

***

The End

Strands - Found in a Knitting Basket at the Three Spinners Ranch

Self-defense

"Arma virumque cano."
(I sing of arms and the man)
Virgil, *the Aeneid*, 19 B.C.

"Each thing... endeavors to persist in its own being; and [that endeavor] is nothing else than the actual essence of that thing... The more a man can preserve his being and seek what is useful to him, the greater his virtue."
Baruch de Spinoza, *Ethics*.

"Whoever wants to save his life will lose it, but whoever loses his life for my sake will find it."
Jesus in *The Gospel of Matthew* 16:25
(International Standard Version).

"Now Peter was sitting out in the courtyard, and a servant girl came to him. 'You also were with Jesus of Galilee,' she said.
But he denied it before them all. 'I don't know what you're talking about,' he said."
The Gospel of Matthew 26:69-70
(New International Version).

"Lieber Jager, lass mich leben, Ich will dir auch zwei Junge geben!"
(Dear huntsman, let me live, And I to thee two cubs will give!)
From a fairy tale cited by Anna Freud in her book,
Ego and the Mechanisms of Defense, 1937.

"The Soul selects her own Society—
Then—shuts the Door—
To her divine Majority—
Present no more—

Unmoved—she notes the Chariots—pausing—
At her low Gate—
Unmoved—an Emperor be kneeling
Upon her Mat—

I've known her—from an ample nation—
Choose One—
Then—close the Valves of her attention—
Like Stone—"

Poem by Emily Dickinson.

"I began to think of the soul as if it were a castle made of a single diamond or of very clear crystal, in which there are many rooms, just as in Heaven there are many mansions."

From the book *Interior Castle* by Saint Teresa of Avila.

"In the modern social order, the person is sacrificed to the individual. The individual is given universal suffrage, equality of rights, freedom of opinion; while the person, isolated, naked, with no social armor to sustain and protect him, is left to the mercy of all the devouring forces which threaten the life of the soul..."

Jacques Maritain, *Three Reformers*, 1925.

"The character structure of modern man... is typified by characterological armoring against his inner nature and against the social misery which surrounds him. This… armoring of the character is the basis of isolation, indigence, craving for authority, fear of responsibility, mystic longing, sexual misery, and neurotically impotent rebelliousness."

Wilhelm Reich, 1927.

"Simply by being compelled to keep constantly on his guard, a man may grow so weak as to be unable any longer to defend himself."

Friederich Wilhelm Nietzsche, *Ecce Homo*, 1888.

"Randy lay there like a slug. It was his only defense."
From the movie *A Christmas Story*, 1983.

"DEFENCELESS, adj. Unable to attack."
Ambrose Bierce, in his book, *The Devil's Dictionary*, 1911.

"It may be that I am no longer able to joke—if that is no longer a satisfactory defense mechanism. Some people are funny and some are not. I used to be funny, and perhaps I'm not any more. There may have been so many shocks and disappointments that the defense of humor no longer works. You asked whether there are things we can't joke about. Yes, I realize now that it's not possible for me to make a joke about the death of John F. Kennedy or Martin Luther King. It may be as I mature, as I become a middle-aged man and then an old man, that I will become rather grumpy because I've seen so many things that have offended me that I cannot deal with in terms of laughter."
From the article: "Are There Things a Novelist Shouldn't Joke About?: An Interview with Kurt Vonnegut" by Harry James Cargas. *The Christian Century*, November 24, 1976.

"Protection against stimuli is an almost more important function for the living organism than reception of stimuli."
Sigmund Freud, *Beyond the Pleasure Principle*, 1920.

"The Sirens were sea-nymphs who had the power of charming by their song all who heard them, so that the unhappy mariners were irresistibly impelled to cast themselves into the sea to their destruction. Circe directed Ulysses [Odysseus] to fill the ears of his seamen with wax, so that they should not hear the strain; and to cause himself to be bound to the mast, and his people to be strictly enjoined, whatever he might say or do, by no means to release him till they should have passed the Sirens' island."
Thomas Bullfinch, *The Age of Fable*, 1855.

"Culture has to call up every possible reinforcement in order to erect barriers against the aggressive instincts of men and hold their manifestations in check by reaction-formations in men's minds."

Sigmund Freud, *Civilization and its discontents*, 1930.

"All the defensive measures of the ego against the id are carried out silently and invisibly. The most we can ever do is reconstruct them in retrospect: we can never really witness them in operation."

Anna Freud, *The Ego and the Mechanisms of Defense*, 1937.

"In repression the objectionable idea is thrust back into the id, while in projection it is displaced into the outside world."

Anna Freud, *Ego and the Mechanisms of Defense*, 1937.

"The mind should develop a blind spot whenever a dangerous thought presented itself. The process should be automatic, instinctive. Crimestop, they called it in Newspeak."

From the novel 1*984* by George Orwell.

"I will tell you something about stories,
[he said]
They aren't just entertainment.
Don't be fooled.
They are all we have, you see,
all we have to fight off
illness and death."

Leslie Marmon Silko in her novel, *Ceremony*, 1977.

"Even the most tempting rose has thorns."

Tristan Eggener.

Fear

"I had a terror since September, I could tell to none; and so I sing, as the boy does of the burying ground, because I am afraid."

Letters of Emily Dickinson, edited by Mabel Loomis Todd.

"Yea, though I walk through the valley of the shadow of death, I will fear no evil: For thou art with me..."
The Book of Psalms 23:4 (King James Version).

"Since fear of solitude exists in all men, because no one in solitude is strong enough to defend himself and procure the necessities of life, it follows that men by nature tend to social organization."
Baruch de Spinoza.

"There is a wonderful story of the deity, of the Self that said, 'I am.' As soon as it said 'I am,' it was afraid... Then it thought, 'What should I be afraid of, I'm the only thing that is.' And as soon as it said that, it felt lonesome, and wished that there were another, and so it felt desire. It swelled, split in two, became male and female, and begot the world."
Joseph Campbell to Bill Moyers in *The Power of Myth*, 1988.

"Can a machine be so frightened and hurt that it will go into catatonia and refuse to respond? While ego crouches inside, aware but never willing to risk it?"
Manuel Garcia O'Kelly Davis, speaking about his friend Mike, the computer, in the novel *The Moon is a Harsh Mistress,* by Robert A. Heinlein, 1966.

"'The fear thou art in, Sancho,' said Don Quixote, 'prevents thee from seeing or hearing correctly, for one of the effects of fear is to derange the senses and make things appear different from what they are...'"
Miguel de Cervantes, *Don Quixote De La Mancha,* 1605, translated by John Ormsby.

Seeing, Observing, Watching

"You see, but you do not observe. The distinction is clear."
Sherlock Holmes, speaking to Dr. Watson, in *A Scandal in Bohemia*, 1891.

"You can observe a lot just by watching."
Yogi Berra.

"Well, it does beat all that I never thought about a dog not eating watermelon. It shows how a body can see and don't see at the same time."
Spoken by Huck in Mark Twain's *The Adventures of Huckleberry Finn*, 1884. He had seen a slave bring food to a hut, and had mistakenly thought the food was for a dog.

"The party told you to reject the evidence of your eyes and ears. It was their final, most essential command."
From the novel *1984* by George Orwell.

"What we see depends mainly on what we look for."
John Lubbock (1834-1913).

"'You think these raindrops are random?' his uncle had asked. And Leaphorn had been surprised. He'd said of course they were random. Didn't his uncle think they were random?...

"And Haskie Jim had watched the rain awhile, silently. And then he had said, and Joe Leaphorn still remembered not just the words but the old man's face when he said them: 'I think from where we stand the rain seems random. If we could stand somewhere else, we would see the order in it.'"
Tony Hillerman, in his novel *Coyote Waits*, 1990.

"For God seeth not as man seeth: for man looketh upon the outward appearance, but the Lord beholdeth the heart."
The Book of Samuel 16:7.

"I like to watch."
Spoken by Chance the gardener in the movie *Being There.*

Walls

"We in this country, in this generation, are—by destiny rather than choice—the watchmen on the walls of world freedom."

President John F. Kennedy, remarks prepared for delivery
at the Trade Mart in Dallas, Texas, November 22, 1963.

"Quis custodiet ipsos custodes?"
(Who watches the watchers, *or* who will guard the guards?)

Juvenal, *Satires of Juvenal,* early 2nd century.

"Unless the Lord watches over the city, the watchmen stand guard in vain."

The Book of Psalms 127:1 (New International Version).

"I've built walls,
A fortress deep and mighty,
That none may penetrate.
I have no need of friendship; friendship causes pain.
It's laughter and it's loving I disdain.
I am a rock,
I am an island."

From the song *I Am A Rock*, by Simon and Garfunkel.

"I will build a great, great wall on our southern border. And I will have Mexico pay for that wall."

Donald Trump, announcing his candidacy for President,
June 16, 2015.

"A nation can survive its fools, and even the ambitious. But it cannot survive treason from within. An enemy at the gates is less formidable, for he is known and carries his banner openly. But the traitor moves amongst those within the gate freely, his sly whispers rustling through all the alleys, heard in the very halls of government itself."

Supposedly spoken by Marcus Tullius Cicero,
(106-43 B.C.) Roman statesman.

"...and upon the wall there hung a shield of shining brass with this legend enwritten—

Who entereth herein, a conqueror hath been,
Who slayeth the dragon, the shield he shall win."

From Edgar Allan Poe's story,
The Fall of the House of Usher.

"The medieval ghetto had originated as a strategy for Jewish existence and survival. During the Crusades Jews petitioned for separate quarters within whose walls they might better defend themselves. That ghetto met the need for common protection as well as for accessibility to Judaism's central institutions. Later, when the church advocated the ghetto as a means of separating Christians from Jews, the voluntary Jewish quarter was transformed into an obligatory ghetto, walled, its two gates guarded by Christian gatekeepers who locked the inhabitants in at night and during Christian festivals. Identifying badges were then imposed on the Jews and their pursuit of certain occupations and professions was restricted, but the medieval ghetto, however crowded and unsanitary, was not a prison.... [In contrast,] Death bestrode the Nazi ghetto and was its true master, exercising its dominion through hunger, forced labor, and disease..."

Lucy S. Dawidowicz, in her book,
The War against the Jews 1933-1945.

"When I was growing up, I was told to never trust anyone who wasn't Jewish. My Polish/Russian family had been so brutalized by outsiders that their trust was minimal. (Of course, many immigrant groups, not just Jews, stick together to feel safer.) ...I think that the feeling of being safe in one's tribe is hardwired into most of us, immigrant or not. We think that *our* family, neighbors, church, or synagogue is the trustworthy one. There's an illusion of safety, a feeling of protection within our own boundaries."

From "The Enemy Within," an article by Robin of Berkeley,
in the *American Spectator*, Dec. 10, 2010.

"Envy builds the wall between *Thee* and *Me* thicker and stronger; Sympathy makes it slight and transparent; nay, sometimes it pulls down the wall altogether; and then the distinction between self and not-self vanishes."

Arthur Schopenhauer in his essay *On Human Nature.*

"Something there is that doesn't love a wall,
That sends the frozen-ground-swell under it,
And spills the upper boulders in the sun;
And makes gaps even two can pass abreast."

Robert Frost, Mending Wall, 1914.

"Mr. Gorbachev, open this gate. Mr. Gorbachev, tear down this wall!"

Ronald Reagan, *Speech at the Berlin Wall*, June 12, 1987.

Love

"A person exists by entering relations with other people."

Martin Buber.

"Love consists in this, that two solitudes protect and touch and greet each other."

Rainer Maria Rilke, *Letters to a Young Poet,* 1929.

"Love is not love until love's vulnerable."

Theodore Roethke.

"Greater love has no one than this, that he lay down his life for his friends."

Jesus in the *Gospel of John* 15:13
(New International Version).

"There is a magnificent essay by Schopenhauer in which he asks, how is it that a human being can so participate in the peril or pain of another that without thought, spontaneously, he sacrifices his own life to the other? How can it happen that what we normally think of as the first law of nature and self-preservation is suddenly dissolved?... Schopenhauer's answer is that such a psychological crisis represents the breakthrough of a metaphysical realization, which is that you and that other are one, that you are two aspects of the one life, and that your apparent separateness is but an effect of the way we experience forms under the conditions of space and time..."

Joseph Campbell in *The Power of Myth*, 1988.

"So when Jesus says, 'Love thy neighbor as thyself,' he is saying in effect, 'Love thy neighbor because he *is* yourself.'"

Bill Moyers in *The Power of Myth*, 1988.

"The remarkable thing is that we really love our neighbor as ourselves: we do unto others as we do unto ourselves. We hate others when we hate ourselves. We are tolerant toward others when we tolerate ourselves. We forgive others when we forgive ourselves. We are prone to sacrifice others when we are ready to sacrifice ourselves."

Eric Hoffer.

Masks

"The persona is a complicated system of relations between individual consciousness and society, fittingly enough a kind of mask, designed on the one hand to make a definite impression upon others, and, on the other, to conceal the true nature of the individual."

Carl Gustav Jung.

"Words are really a mask. They rarely express the true meaning; in fact, they tend to hide it."

Herman Hesse.

"The images of God are many, [Joseph Campbell said], calling them 'the masks of eternity' that both cover and reveal 'the Face of Glory.'... All our names and images for God are masks, he said, signifying the ultimate reality that by definition transcends language and art. A myth is a mask of God too—a metaphor for what lies behind the visible world."

Bill Moyers in the Introduction to *The Power of Myth*, 1988.

"All visible objects, man, are but as pasteboard masks. But in each event—in the living act, the undoubted deed—there, some unknown but still reasoning thing puts forth the mouldings of its features from behind the unreasoning mask. If man will strike, strike through the mask! How can the prisoner reach outside except by thrusting through the wall? To me, the white whale is that wall, shoved near to me."

Spoken by Ahab in Herman Melville's
novel *Moby Dick,* 1851.

"'Why do you tremble at me alone?' cried he, turning his veiled face round the circle of pale spectators. 'Tremble also at each other! Have men avoided me, and women shown no pity, and children screamed and fled, only for my black veil? What, but the mystery which it obscurely typifies, has made this piece of crape so awful? When the friend shows his inmost heart to his friend; the lover to his best beloved; when man does not vainly shrink from the eye of his Creator, loathsomely treasuring up the secret of his sin; then deem me a monster, for the symbol beneath which I have lived, and die! I look around me, and, lo! on every visage a Black Veil!'"

Spoken by Father Hooper in Nathaniel Hawthorne's story,
"The Minister's Black Veil," 1836.

"On this mountain he will remove the veil of grief covering all people and the mask covering all nations. He will swallow up death forever. The Almighty Lord will wipe away tears from every face…"

The Book of Isaiah 25:7-8 (God's Word Translation).

Mirrors, Windows, Doors

"But we all, with unveiled face, beholding as in a mirror the glory of the Lord, are being transformed into the same image from glory to glory, just as from the Lord, the Spirit."

Saint Paul's 2nd Letter to the Corinthians 3:18;
(New American Standard Bible, 1995).

"On the other hand, by going down into the depths of his own nature, a man may become conscious that he is all in all; that, in fact, he is the only real being; and that, in addition, this real being perceives itself again in others, who present themselves from without, as though they formed a mirror of himself... For the thing-in-itself, the will to live, exists whole and undivided in every being, even in the smallest, as completely as in the sum-total of all things that ever were or are or will be. This is why every being, even the smallest, says to itself, so long as I am safe, let the world perish—*dum ego salvus sim, pereat mundus*."

Arthur Schopenhauer, in his essay *On Human Nature*.

"Better keep yourself clean and bright; you are the window through which you must see the world."

George Bernard Shaw (1856-1950).

"But we never knows wot's hidden in each other's hearts; and if we had glass winders there, we'd need keep the shetters up, some on us, I do assure you!'

Spoken by Mrs. Gamp in Charles Dickens' novel *Martin Chuzzlewit*, 1844.

"The face is a threshold where a world looks out and a world looks in on itself."

Anam Cara: A Book of Celtic Wisdom, by John O'Donohue.

"For the mind of man is far from the nature of a clear and equal glass, wherein the beams of things should reflect according to their true incidence, nay, it is rather like an enchanted glass, full of superstition and imposture, if it be not delivered and reduced."

Francis Bacon.

"For now we see through a glass, darkly; but then face to face: now I know in part; but then shall I know even as also I am known."

Saint Paul's 1st Letter to the Corinthians 13:12 (King James Bible).

"If the doors of perception were cleansed every thing would appear to man as it is, infinite. For man has closed himself up, till he sees all things through the narrow chinks of his cavern."

William Blake, *The Marriage of Heaven and Hell,* 1793.

"The house of fiction has in short not one window, but a million... These apertures, of dissimilar shape and size, hang so, all together, over the human scene... They are but windows at the best... they are not hinged doors opening straight upon life. But they have this mark of their own that at each of them stands a figure with a pair of eyes, or at least with a field-glass, which forms, again and again, for observation, a unique instrument, insuring to the person making use of it an impression distinct from every other. He and his neighbours are watching the same show, but one seeing more where the other sees less, one seeing black where the other sees white, one seeing big where the other sees small, one seeing coarse where the other sees fine..."

Henry James, in the preface to volume 3
of *The New York Edition*, 1908.

Deception and Secrecy

"An example of huge-scale maskirovka in the Soviet Union was false maps, with distorted locations of settlements, road forks, river shapes, etc. ... All this was supposed to confuse a potential invader."

Wikipedia article on Military deception.

"The belief in the magic virtue of names was shared by the Romans. When they sat down before a city, the priests addressed the guardian deity of the place in a set form of prayer or incantation, inviting him to abandon the beleaguered city and come over to the Romans, who would treat him as well as or better than he had ever been treated in his old home. Hence the name of the guardian deity of Rome was kept a profound secret, lest the enemies of the republic might lure him away, even as the Romans themselves had induced many gods to desert, like rats, the falling fortunes of cities that had sheltered them in happier days. Nay the real name, not merely of the deity, but of the city itself, was wrapt in mystery and might never be uttered, not even in sacred rites."

Sir James George Frazer, *The Golden Bough*, 1950.

"Truth telling is not compatible with the defence of the realm."

George Bernard Shaw, *Heartbreak House*, 1919.

"In time of war, when truth is so precious, it must be attended by a bodyguard of lies."

Winston Churchill.

"Falsehood is invariably the child of fear in one form or another."

Aleister Crowley.

"Nothing is easier than self-deceit. For what each man wishes, that he also believes to be true."

Demosthenes.

"The nature of self-love and of this human 'I' is to love self only, and consider self only. But what can it do? It cannot prevent the object it loves from being full of faults and miseries; man would fain be great and sees that he is little; would fain be happy, and sees that he is miserable; would fain be perfect, and sees that he is full of imperfections; would fain be the object of the love and esteem of men, and sees that his faults merit only their aversion and contempt. The embarrassment wherein he finds himself produces in him the most unjust and criminal passion imaginable. For he conceives a mortal hatred against that truth which blames him and convinces him of his faults. Desiring to annihilate it, yet unable to destroy it in its essence, he destroys it as much as he can in his own knowledge, and in that of others; that is to say, he devotes all his care to the concealment of his faults, both from others and from himself, and he can neither bear that others should show them to him, nor that they should see them."

Blaise Pascal, in his Pensee
On the prevalence of self-love, 1662.

Self-knowledge

"Being entirely honest with oneself is a good exercise."

Sigmund Freud.

"The unexamined life is not worth living."

Socrates.

"A man is but what he knows."
Francis Bacon.

"The total picture of life is almost too painful for contemplation; life depends on our not knowing it too well."
Arthur Schopenhauer.

"For in much wisdom is much grief: and he that increaseth knowledge increaseth sorrow."
The Book of Ecclesiastes 1:18 (King James Bible).

Free Will, Reason, Thought

"Men think themselves free because they are conscious of their volitions and desire, but are ignorant of the causes by which they are led to wish and desire."
Baruch de Spinoza.

"There is in the mind no absolute of free will; but the mind is determined in willing this or that by a cause which is determined in its turn by another cause and this by another, and so on to infinity."
Baruch de Spinoza.

"A man always has two reasons for the things he does—a good one and the real one."
John Pierpont Morgan.

"The heart has reasons which reason cannot understand."
Blaise Pascal.

"As an archer makes his arrow straight, so a wise man makes straight his trembling and unsteady thought, which is difficult to guard and difficult to hold back. As a fish taken from his watery home and thrown on the dry ground, our thought trembles all over in order to escape the dominion of Mara. It is good to tame the mind, which is difficult to hold in and flighty, rushing wherever it wishes; a tamed mind brings happiness. Let the wise man guard his thoughts, for they are difficult to perceive, very artful, and they rush wherever they wish: thoughts well guarded bring happiness."

Buddha, in *The Dhammapada.*

Memory

"Memory! What do they mean by memory, anyway? That passage I read you by what's-his-name, remember? about the araucarias. You look at the araucarias, all the intricacies of their leaves and branches are impressed on your retina, you *see* them with absolute authority, but the next day a slight blurring is noticeable, in a week you remember the trees but without that intensity of exactness, and in a year? Ten years? And that's true of all memory. So what is memory after all but an act of forgetting, of omission."

Steven Millhauser, *Enchanted Night*, 1999.

"Memory is the thing you forget with."

Alexander Chase, American journalist.

"Mem'ries may be beautiful, and yet,
What's too painful to remember,
We simply choose to forget..."

From the song *The Way We Were*, by Alan Bergman,
Marilyn Bergman, and Marvin Hamlisch, 1973.

"A man's memory may almost become the art of continually varying and misrepresenting his past, according to his interests in the present."

George Santayana, *Reasons and Places*.

"The Memory represents to us not what we choose but what it pleases."

Michel de Montaigne.

"Forget your troubles and just get happy."

Ted Koehler's song *Get Happy*, 1930.

"If we remembered everything, we should on most occasions be as ill off as if we remembered nothing. It would take us as long to recall a space of time as it took the original time to elapse, and we should never get ahead with our thinking. All recollected times undergo, accordingly, what M. Ribot calls foreshortening; and this foreshortening is due to the omission of an enormous number of facts which filled them."

William James, *Psychology: The Briefer Course*, 1891.

"Individuals with hyperthymesia can recall almost every day of their lives in near perfect detail, as well as public events that hold some personal significance to them… On December 19, 2010, actress Marilu Henner was featured on the US television program *60 Minutes* for her superior autobiographical memory ability. Henner claimed she could remember almost every day of her life since she was 11 years old."

Wikipedia article on hyperthymesia.

"Life is all memory, except for the one present moment that goes by you so quickly you hardly catch it going."

Tennessee Williams.

"There's rosemary, that's for remembrance; pray, love, remember: and there is pansies, that's for thoughts."

Spoken by Ophelia in William Shakespeare's *Hamlet,* 1601, act IV, scene v.

"You shouldn't confide your defects to friends, or even to yourself, were that possible; but since this is impossible, make use here of that other great rule of life, which is: learn to forget."

Baltasar Gracian, *The Art of Worldly Wisdom*, 1647.

God and Religion

"Religion is a defense against the experience of God."

Carl Gustav Jung.

"Wanting to hide in the crowd, to be a little fraction of the group instead of being an individual, is the most corrupt of all escapes… God in heaven does not talk to us as an assembly; he speaks to each individually. This is why the most ruinous evasion of all is to be hidden away in a herd in an attempt to escape God's personal address."

Søren Aabye Kierkegaard.

"Truly you are a God who hides himself, O God and Savior of Israel."

The Book of Isaiah 45:15 (New International Version, 1984).

"Religious ideas have sprung from the same need as all the other achievements of culture: from the necessity for defending itself against the crushing supremacy of nature."

Sigmund Freud, *The Future of an Illusion*, 1927.

"...For many people, perhaps most people, there is a deep, ineradicable desire not to cease to exist. Perhaps this desire, this fear of falling into what Lord Dunsany once called the 'unreverberate blackness of the abyss,' is no more than an expression of genetic mechanisms for avoiding death. Or is it more? It is easy to understand why any person would think death final—everything in our experience indicates it—but I share with Unamuno a vast incredulity when I meet individuals, seeming well adjusted and happy, who solemnly assure me they have absolutely no desire to live again. Do they really mean it? Or are they wearing a mask which they suppose fashionable while deep inside their hearts, in the middle of the night and in moments of agony, they secretly hope to be surprised someday by the existence and mercy of God?"

Martin Gardner in his essay *Why I am not an atheist.*

"Faith in a holy cause is to a considerable extent a substitute for the lost faith in ourselves. The less justified a man is in claiming excellence for his own self, the more ready is he to claim all excellence for his nation, his religion, his race or his holy cause... All forms of dedication, devotion, loyalty and self-surrender are in essence a desperate clinging to something which might give worth and meaning to our futile, spoiled lives."

Eric Hoffer, in his book *The True believer,* 1951.

"There is no fortress that is any defense from the power of God... The unseen, unthought of ways and means of persons going suddenly out of the world are innumerable and inconceivable. Unconverted men walk over the pit of hell on a rotten covering, and there are innumerable places in this covering so weak that they won't bear their weight, and these places are not seen... Almost every natural man that hears of hell, flatters himself that he shall escape it..."

Jonathan Edwards, in his sermon
Sinners in the Hands of an Angry God, 1739.

"Think of a man standing at night inside his house, with all the doors closed; and then suppose that he opens a window just at that moment when there is a sudden flash of lightning. Unable to bear its brightness, at once he protects himself by closing his eyes and drawing back from the window. So it is with the soul that is enclosed in the realm of the senses; if ever she peeps out through the window of the intellect, she is overwhelmed by the brightness, like lightning, of the pledge of the Holy Spirit that is within her. Unable to bear the splendor of unveiled light, at once she is bewildered in her intellect, and she draws back entirely upon herself, taking refuge, as in a house, among sensory and human things."

St. Simeon the New Theologian.

"Imagine a sheer, steep crag with a projecting edge at the top. Now imagine what a person would probably feel if he put his foot on the edge of this precipice and, looking down in the chasm below, saw no solid footing nor anything to hold on to. This is what I think the soul experiences when it goes beyond its footing in material things, in its quest for that which has no dimension and which exists from all eternity. For here there is nothing it can take hold of, neither place, nor time, neither measure nor anything else; our minds cannot approach it. And thus the soul, slipping at every point from what cannot be grasped, becomes dizzy and perplexed and returns once again to what is connatural with it, content now to know merely this about the Transcendent, that it is completely different from the nature of the things that the soul knows."

St. Gregory of Nyssa.

"O proud Christians, wretched weary ones, who, diseased in vision of the mind, have confidence in backward steps, are ye not aware that we are worms born to form the angelic butterfly which flies unto judgment without defense?"

Dante, in his *Purgatory*, 1321.

"Prayer is the best armor we have; it opens the heart of God"

Padre Pio.

"And the peace of God, which surpasses all understanding, will guard your hearts and your minds in Christ Jesus."

Saint Paul's Letter to the Philippians 4:7.
(New English Translation Bible).

"He only is my rock and my salvation: he is my defense; I shall not be moved."

The Book of Psalms 62:6 (King James Version).

"Put your trust in God; but mind to keep your powder dry."
Oliver Cromwell, advising his troops
who were about to cross a river.

"Our lives are in the hands of the Great Spirit. He gave to our ancestors the lands which we possess. We are determined to defend them, and if it is His will, our bones shall whiten on them, but we will never give them up."
Tecumseh in his *Speech to Major General Henry Procter, British commander, Fort Malden*, September, 1813.

"The Lord is my strength and my shield..."
The Book of Psalms 28:7 (King James Version).

War

"I tan i epi tas"
(Either with it or on it)
In ancient Sparta, spoken by mothers to their sons before they went off to war: come back with your shield, victorious, or on it, dead.

"When the men of the Yuki tribe in California were away fighting, the women at home did not sleep; they danced continually in a circle, chanting and waving leafy wands. For they said that if they danced all the time, their husbands would not grow tired."
Sir James George Frazer, *The Golden Bough*, 1950.

"On seeing two pregnant women in the Warsaw ghetto, an unknown diarist noted: 'If in today's dark and pitiless times a Jewish woman can gather enough courage to bring a new Jewish being into the world and rear him, this is great heroism and daring... At least symbolically these nameless Jewish heroines do not allow the total extinction of the Jews and Jewry.'"
Lucy S. Dawidowicz, in her book,
The War against the Jews 1933-1945.

"Dead and wounded women and children and little babies were scattered all along there where they had been trying to run away. The soldiers had followed them along the gulch, as they ran, and murdered them in there. In one of the gulches, two little boys who had found guns were lying in ambush, and they had been killing soldiers all by themselves."

Black Elk, recalling the massacre at Wounded Knee.

"All real Americans love the sting and clash of battle. You are here today for three reasons. First, because you are here to defend your homes and your loved ones. Second, you are here for your own self-respect, because you would not want to be anywhere else. Third, you are here because you are real men and all real men like to fight..."

From General George S. Patton's
Speech to the Third Army, June 5th, 1944.

"Strength lies not in defense but in attack."

Adolf Hitler, *Mein Kampf (My Battle)*, 1933.

"Defense is the stronger form of waging war."

Carl von Clausewitz, *On War*, 1832.

"I don't want to get any messages saying, 'I am holding my position.' We are not holding a Goddamned thing. Let the Germans do that. We are advancing constantly and we are not interested in holding onto anything, except the enemy's balls. We are going to twist his balls and kick the living shit out of him all of the time. Our basic plan of operation is to advance and to keep on advancing regardless of whether we have to go over, under, or through the enemy. We are going to go through him like crap through a goose; like shit through a tin horn!.."

From General George S. Patton's
Speech to the Third Army, June 5th, 1944.

"Hence that general is skillful in attack whose opponent does not know what to defend; and he is skillful in defense whose opponent does not know what to attack."

Sun Tzu, *The Art of War*, c. 490 B.C.

"Long, I pray, may foreign nations persist, if not in loving us, at least in hating one another; for destiny is driving our empire upon its appointed path, and fortune can bestow upon us no better gift than discord among our foes."

From *Germania,* written by Publius Cornelius Tacitus around 98 A.D. Contained in *The Complete Works of Tacitus,* translated by Alfred John Church and William Jackson Brodribb, 1942.

"...we shall defend our island, whatever the cost may be, we shall fight on the beaches, we shall fight on the landing grounds, we shall fight in the fields and in the streets, we shall fight in the hills; we shall never surrender."

Winston Churchill in his *Speech on Dunkirk*,
House of Commons, June 4, 1940.

"War is a bloody, killing business. You've got to spill their blood, or they will spill yours. Rip them up the belly. Shoot them in the guts. When shells are hitting all around you and you wipe the dirt off your face and realize that instead of dirt it's the blood and guts of what once was your best friend beside you, you'll know what to do!"

From General George S. Patton's
Speech to the Third Army, June 5th, 1944.

"We shall defend every village, every town and every city. The vast mass of London itself, fought street by street, could easily devour an entire hostile army; and we would rather see London laid in ruins and ashes than that it should be tamely and abjectly enslaved."

Winston Churchill in a *Radio broadcast*, July 14, 1940.

"It is not a field of a few acres of ground, but a cause, that we are defending..."

Thomas Paine in *The American Crisis*,
no. 4, September 12, 1777.

"God grants liberty only to those who love it, and are always ready to guard and defend it."

Daniel Webster in his *Speech in the Senate*, June 3, 1834.

"The bitter lesson that may be drawn from this tragedy [the Moslem conquest of India] is that eternal vigilance is the price of civilization."
Will Durant in *Our Oriental Heritage*, 1935.

"The problem in defense is how far you can go without destroying from within what you are trying to defend from without."
Dwight David Eisenhower.

"There is no way in which a country can satisfy the craving for absolute security, but it can bankrupt itself morally and economically in attempting to reach that illusory goal through arms alone."
Dwight David Eisenhower.

"Let every nation know, whether it wishes us well or ill, that we shall pay any price, bear any burden, meet any hardship, support any friend, oppose any foe, in order to assure the survival and the success of liberty."
John F. Kennedy in his *Inaugural Address*, January 20, 1961.

"We recognize that the application of recent scientific discoveries to the methods and practice of war has placed at the disposal of mankind means of destruction hitherto unknown, against which there can be no adequate military defense..."
Harry S. Truman, Clement R. Attlee, and W. L. Mackenzie King, *Declaration on Atomic Energy,* November 15, 1945.

"If I knew they were going to do this, I would have become a shoemaker!"
Albert Einstein, commenting on the atomic bombing of Hiroshima. In 1939, he had co-written a letter to President Roosevelt suggesting that the US build an atomic bomb.

"War is cruelty, and you cannot refine it."
General William Tecumseh Sherman, *Letter to Atlanta*, 1864.

"The Indians addressed all of life as a *thou*—the trees, the stones, everything. You can address anything as a *thou*, and if you do it, you can feel the change in your own psychology. The ego that sees a *thou* is not the same ego that sees an *it*. And when you go to war with people, the problem of the newspapers is to turn these people into *its*."

Joseph Campbell in *The Power of Myth*, 1988.

"We tried to run but they [the soldiers] shot us like we were buffalo."

Louise Weasel Bear, recalling the massacre at Wounded Knee.

"Kanika continued, 'If thy son, friend, brother, father, or even the spiritual preceptor, anyone becometh thy foe, thou shouldst, if desirous of prosperity, slay him without scruples.'"

From the *Mahabharata*, Book I, Adi Parva, Section CXLII.

"We have met the enemy, and he is us."

Pogo.

"Angels and ministers of grace defend us!"

Spoken by Hamlet in William Shakespeare's *Hamlet*, 1601, act I, scene. iv.

Destiny

"You will hear of wars and rumors of wars, but see to it that you are not alarmed. Such things must happen, but the end is still to come. Nation will rise against nation, and kingdom against kingdom."

The Gospel of Matthew 24:6-7; (New International Version).

"Because a laugh's the wisest, easiest answer to all that's queer; and come what will, one comfort's always left—that unfailing comfort is, it's all predestinated."

Spoken by Stubb in Herman Melville's *Moby Dick*, 1851.

"A man, as he dies, should make one last throw with his spear. It is a high thing, a bright honor, for a man to do battle with the enemy for the sake of his children, and for his land and his true wife; and death is a thing that will come when the spinning Destinies make it come. So a man should go straight on forward, spear held high, and under his shield the fighting strength coiled ready to strike in the first shock of the charge. When it is ordained that a man shall die, there is no escaping death, not even for one descended from deathless gods. Often a man who has fled from the fight and the clash of the thrown spears goes his way, and death befalls him in his own house..."

From the poem *A Call To Arms*, by Callinus,
7th century BC, translated by Richmond Lattimore.

"That was what you did. You died. You did not know what it was about. You never had time to learn. They threw you in and told you the rules and the first time they caught you off base they killed you. Or they killed you gratuitously like Aymo. Or gave you the syphilis like Rinaldi. But they killed you in the end. You could count on that. Stay around and they would kill you."

From Ernest Hemingway's novel *A Farewell To Arms*, 1929.

"A cowardly man thinks he will ever live, if warfare he avoids; but old age will give him no peace, though spears may spare him."

From *The Elder Eddas of Saemund Sigfusson,* 1906,
translated by Benjamin Thorpe.

"You can't run away from trouble. There ain't no place that far."

Uncle Remus in the movie *Song of the South*, 1946.

"God, give us grace to accept with serenity the things that cannot be changed, courage to change the things that should be changed, and the wisdom to distinguish the one from the other."

Reinhold Niebuhr, *Serenity Prayer*, 1944.

"What ought one to say then as each hardship comes? I was practicing for this, I was training for this."

Greek philosopher Epictetus (55-135 AD).

"At that time there shall arise Michael, the great prince, guardian of your people; It shall be a time unsurpassed in distress since nations began until that time. At that time your people shall escape, everyone who is found written in the book."

The Book of Daniel 12:1-3 (New American Bible).

"Saint Michael the Archangel,
defend us in battle;
be our protection against the wickedness and snares of the devil.
May God rebuke him, we humbly pray:
and do thou, O Prince of the heavenly host,
by the power of God,
cast into hell Satan and all evil spirits
who wander through the world seeking the ruin of souls.
Amen."

Prayer to St. Michael.

"He shall cover thee with his feathers, and under his wings shalt thou trust: his truth shall be thy shield and buckler. Thou shalt not be afraid for the terror by night; nor for the arrow that flieth by day; nor for the pestilence that walketh in darkness; nor for the destruction that wasteth at noonday. A thousand shall fall at thy side, and ten thousand at thy right hand; but it shall not come nigh thee."

The Book of Psalms 91:4-7 (King James Version).

"Finally, my brethren, be strong in the Lord, and in the power of his might. Put on the whole armour of God, that ye may be able to stand against the wiles of the devil. For we wrestle not against flesh and blood, but against principalities, against powers, against the rulers of the darkness of this world, against spiritual wickedness in high places. Wherefore take unto you the whole armour of God, that ye may be able to withstand in the evil day, and having done all, to stand. Stand therefore, having your loins girt about with truth, and having on the breastplate of righteousness; and your feet shod with the preparation of the gospel of peace; above all, taking the shield of faith, wherewith ye shall be able to quench all the fiery darts of the wicked. And take the helmet of salvation, and the sword of the Spirit, which is the word of God."

Saint Paul's Letter to the Ephesians 6:10-17
(King James Version).

Endurance

"I believe that man will not merely endure: he will prevail. He is immortal, not because he alone among creatures has an inexhaustible voice, but because he has a soul, a spirit capable of compassion and sacrifice and endurance. The poet's, the writer's, duty is to write about these things."

William Faulkner in his *Speech after receiving the Nobel Prize for Literature*, December 10, 1950.

"I have fought the good fight, I have finished the race, I have kept the faith."

Saint Paul's 2nd Letter to Timothy, 4:7
(New International Version, 1984)

"No mas, no mas." (no more, no more).

Boxer Roberto Duran, November 25, 1980.

***

Psychological Defense Mechanisms - Catalogued by a Sub-Sub-Librarian

I am not a mental health professional—I've been a teacher and a librarian for most of my life. However, I have read about psychological defense mechanisms as part of the research for my novel, and I thought that some readers might be interested in a short summary of what (I think) they are about.

In Freudian psychoanalytic theory, **defense mechanisms are unconscious psychological strategies** used by the mind to cope with the harsh realities of life and with the dangerous impulses flaring up from deep inside of us. Sometimes these defense mechanisms protect us from anxiety or social sanctions; sometimes they provide refuge from situations with which we cannot currently cope.

They are often called **ego** defense mechanisms because they protect the ego or the self from three things: one, the strong, unruly impulses of the **id**, two, situations where id impulses conflict with **superego** values and beliefs, and three, external threats.

What are the id, the ego and the superego? Sigmund Freud proposed that each person's mind is divided into three structures: the id, the ego and the superego. I don't know if Freud or anyone else ever proved that this "trinity" exists, but it seems to make sense.

The **id** (or the "it") is the selfish, primitive, childish, pleasure-oriented part of the personality; it is all instinct and impulse, with no ability to delay gratification; it is the source of unconscious drives like love and lust, aggression and hatred and fear.

The **superego** (or the "over-I") is the conscience, where society's standards and our parents' teachings tell us what is right and what is wrong, what is good and what is bad. It helps us fit into society by getting us to act in socially acceptable ways. When we don't act in an acceptable manner, the superego makes us feel guilty, or anxious, or inferior. The superego is often in conflict with the id. Much of the action of the superego is unconscious.

The **ego** (or the "I") is the seat of conscious awareness, though some of its actions are unconscious. It is the moderator between the id, the superego and external reality; it seeks to make compromises between the raw impulses of the id, the internalized standards of the superego, and the hard facts of the real world. Some people think of it as the **self**.

When there is a strong conflict among the id, the superego and external reality, the ego employs **defense mechanisms** to help it deal with feelings of guilt, anxiety or inferiority. These mechanisms either block the impulses coming out of the id, or distort them into acceptable forms.

Most defense mechanisms are used without our conscious knowledge. Anna Freud, Sigmund's daughter, wrote that, "All the defensive measures of the ego against the id are carried out silently and invisibly."

Some of these defenses are used by healthy people every day. Others are used by those unfortunate people who have severe problems coping with life.

In 1977, American psychiatrist George Eman Vaillant arranged the various defense mechanisms into four categories. I'd like to list them in reverse order:

IV. Mature Defense Mechanisms. These are commonly found among healthy adults—like you and me. They have been adapted by individuals through the years in order to optimize success in life and relationships. They help us integrate conflicting emotions and thoughts while still remaining effective. Their use enhances pleasure and feelings of control.

They include:

A. Altruism: You deal with feelings of anxiety or guilt by developing a great concern for others. You put much of your energy into constructive service to others, and that brings you pleasure and satisfaction.

B. Anticipation: You engage in realistic planning to deal with future discomfort, and thereby reduce some of your current stress.

C. Humor: You deal with unpleasant ideas and feelings by making jokes about them.

D. Identification: This is the unconscious modelling of one's self on another person's character and behavior. It can include identification with either positive or negative role models. For example, an individual might derive strength by identifying with a team, a club, a nation, or a religion. On the negative side, a boy might become an aggressor or a bully so he won't have to fear an aggressor or a bully.

E. Introjection: You identify with some idea or object so deeply that it becomes a part of yourself. This seems similar to Identification.

F. Sublimation: This is the process of transforming libido (sex drive) into creative or socially useful achievements such as art, science, or sports. It can transform instincts or negative emotions into positive actions, behavior, or emotions.

G. Thought suppression: You deliberately push thoughts out of your conscious mind. "I'll deal with that problem later—I have enough to do now."

III. Neurotic Defense Mechanisms. These are fairly common in adults. They offer short-term advantages in coping, but can often cause long-term problems in relationships, in work and in enjoying life.

They include:

A. Displacement: This is the shifting of sexual or aggressive impulses to a more acceptable or less threatening target; redirecting emotion to a safer outlet. For example: a mother may yell at her child because she is angry with her husband.

B. Dissociation: This is the temporary modification of one's personality or character to avoid emotional distress. It allows the mind to distance itself from experiences that are too much for the psyche to process at that time. In its most common form, mild dissociation includes day dreaming, or "zoning out." More serious traumas can bring on amnesia.

C. Hypochondria: Hypochondriacs are convinced that they have a serious illness, or are about to have a serious illness, even if the medical evidence shows otherwise.

D. Isolation: This is the separation of feelings and emotions from ideas and events. For example: describing a murder with graphic details while showing no emotional response.

E. Intellectualization: This is a form of isolation. You concentrate on the intellectual components of a situation so as to distance yourself from the anxiety-provoking emotions. You think it but you don't feel it.

F. Rationalization (making excuses): You convince yourself of something through faulty reasoning. For example, you think: "It's not wrong to steal from a big corporation since they can afford it." Or you tell yourself: "The grapes I could not reach were probably sour anyway."

G. Reaction Formation: This is converting unconscious wishes or impulses that are perceived to be dangerous into their opposites. The result is behavior that is completely the opposite of what one really wants or feels. For example: a very aggressive man becomes a pacifist. Or: a person who secretly likes pornography joins an organization that fights it. Or: two people who are really fond of each other fight all the time to suppress their desire of love for each other.

H. Regression: This involves a temporary reversion of the ego to an earlier stage of development rather than handling unacceptable impulses in a more adult way. An adolescent who feels overwhelmed by new challenges in life might revert to sucking his thumb or wetting the bed. Or, an individual fixated at the oral stage might begin eating or smoking excessively, or might become very verbally aggressive. A fixation at the anal stage might result in excessive tidiness or messiness.

I. Repression: This involves burying an unpleasant idea in the unconscious mind. One result might be: seemingly unexplainable memory lapses or lack of awareness of one's situation. Another might be: failure to acknowledge input from a sense organ.

J. Undoing: A person tries to undo an unhealthy, destructive or threatening thought by engaging in contrary behavior. For example, after thinking about being violent with someone, one would then be overly nice or accommodating to them. Another example: Lady Macbeth washes her hands over and over again to clean up her guilt.

K. Withdrawal: You remove yourself from events and interactions that could remind you of painful thoughts and feelings.

II. Immature Defense Mechanisms. People who use these too often are seen as immature, hard to deal with, or out of touch with reality. Their occasional use by adolescents is considered normal. These defenses are often present in adults with severe depression and personality disorders.

They include:

A. Acting out: A person expresses an unconscious wish or impulse in action. An example would be a temper tantrum in a young child. In adolescent years, acting out in the form of rebellious behaviors such as smoking, shoplifting and drug use can be understood as "a cry for help."

B. Fantasy: A troubled person retreats into fantasy in order to resolve inner and outer conflicts.

C. Idealization: You unconsciously perceive another individual as having more positive qualities than he or she may actually have.

D. Passive aggression: You don't like someone, and you deal with them indirectly or passively by using such tactics as procrastination and obstructionism. You sulk or speak to them in ambiguous language to frustrate them.

E. Projection: This is when you have unacceptable or unwanted thoughts or emotions, and you project them onto another person or group. Some examples: 1. when you blame another person for your own failures, 2. a man wants to cheat on his wife, and feels guilty about it; he projects that his wife has thoughts of infidelity and may be having an affair. 3. a person who really doesn't like blacks projects his own prejudice onto another group of people, and says that *they* don't like blacks.

F. Projective identification: This is when one's behavior towards the object of projection invokes in that person precisely the thoughts, feelings or behaviors projected. For example: A delusional person, Dan, believes he is being persecuted by police; so, when he is near police officers, he acts strangely; this raises the suspicions of the police officers and makes them "persecute" Dan. It is, in a sense, a self-fulfilling prophecy. How does it help Dan? Dan felt that he had done something wrong. He projected that anxiety onto the police officers; now, he can feel that they have done something wrong, not him.

G. Somatization. You transform negative feelings about others into negative feelings toward yourself, into anxiety, or into pain or illness. Sigmund Freud's famous case study of "Anna O." featured a woman who suffered from numerous physical symptoms, which Freud believed were the result of repressed grief over her father's illness. This seems similar to Hypochondria.

I. Pathological Defense Mechanisms. These defenses permit one to rearrange external experiences to eliminate the need to cope with reality. The users of these defenses frequently appear irrational or insane to others. In "normal" people, these defenses are found in dreams and throughout early childhood, but when used by adults in their waking hours, they are considered "psychotic" defenses.

They include:

A. Delusional projection: This involves gross delusions about external reality, usually of a persecutory nature. The person views others as the cause of his difficulties in order to preserve a positive self-view. Examples: 1. a person mistakenly believes that he is under constant police surveillance; 2. a person believes that aliens have removed his brain; 3. a person falsely believes that someone else is controlling his thoughts, feelings, or behavior.

B. Denial: You refuse to accept external reality because it is too painful or threatening. For example, you say: "I don't really have a drinking problem; I can stop any time I want." Or, you think: "My husband isn't cheating on me—it's just that his job requires him to work a lot of late hours."

C. Distortion: This is a gross reshaping of external reality to meet internal needs. Examples might include: 1. taking isolated cases and using them to make wide generalizations; 2. focusing almost exclusively on negative or upsetting aspects of an event while ignoring other positive aspects; 3. drawing conclusions from little (if any) evidence; 4. magnifying an incident beyond its reasonable significance, or minimizing a truly important incident.

D. Splitting: This is when negative and positive impulses are split off and unintegrated. For example: a person sees other individuals as either all good or all evil, rather than as whole continuous beings.

E. Extreme projection: You deny a moral or psychological deficiency in yourself, and you perceive the same deficiency in another individual or group.

F. Multiple personality disorder: Some call this Dissociative Identity Disorder. It involves the splitting of the personality as the result of severe trauma during early childhood—usually extreme, repetitive physical, sexual, and/or emotional abuse. Each distinct personality (or alter ego) has its own pattern of perceiving and interacting with the environment, its own unique set of memories, behaviors, thoughts and emotions. Vaillant did not put this disorder on his list, but others do consider it "a defense mechanism out of control". A famous example from literature would be: *The Strange Case of Dr. Jekyll and Mr. Hyde.*

***

FOR MORE EXCITING BOOKS, E-BOOKS, AUDIOBOOKS AND MORE
J.R. ROBERTS
Bleeders
Bill Pronzini
THOM DEESE
TAC
MAAN MEYERS
ROBERT J. RANDISI
IDIOTS
WHITE MALE INFANT
BARBARA D'AMATO
SEALS
BOOBY TRAP
BILL PRONZINI
DON BENDELL
HARD EVIDENCE
SURVIVALIST
ALASKA
BENEATH THE ASHES
SUE HENRY
GHOST
MAX ALLAN COLLINS
COLORLAND
ANNETTE MEYERS
GROANING BOARD
THE SLEEPING
L SYDNEY ABEL
DEMONS
BILL PRONZINI
visit us at
www.speakingvolumes.us

www.ingramcontent.com/pod-product-compliance
Lightning Source LLC
Chambersburg PA
CBHW050555260626
47157CB00002B/567

* 9 7 8 1 6 2 8 1 5 9 7 0 7 *